COUCH

D1040653

a novel

BENJAMIN PARZYBOK

Small Beer Press
Easthampton, MA

This is a work of fiction. All characters and events portrayed
in this book are either fictitious or used fictitiously.

Copyright © 2008 by Benjamin Parzybok. All rights reserved.
www.ideacog.net

Small Beer Press
150 Pleasant Street #306
Easthampton, MA 01027
www.smallbeerpress.com
info@smallbeerpress.com

Distributed to the trade by Consortium.

Library of Congress Cataloging-in-Publication Data

Parzybok, Benjamin.
  Couch : a novel / Benjamin Parzybok. -- 1st ed.
    p. cm.
  ISBN-13: 978-1-931520-54-6 (pbk. : alk. paper)
  ISBN-10: 1-931520-54-2 (pbk. : alk. paper)
  1. Roomates--Oregon--Portland--Fiction. 2. Sofas--Fiction. 3. Voyages and travels--Fiction. 4.
Self-actualization (Psychology)--Fiction. I. Title.
  PS3616.A788C68 2008
  813'.6--dc22
                                        2008030700

       2 3 4 5 6 7 8 9

Printed on 50# Natures Natural 30% PCR recycled paper by Thomson-Shore of Dexter, MI.
Text set in Minion 11.5.

Cover art ©Andi Watson (andiwatson.biz).

I. The Couch

From above, from a thousand feet up, an eagle's-eye view, it's a strange spectacle still. A six-legged insect, stiff and ungainly, too long on the grape vine gone to vinegar.

From five hundred feet one sees a mutant, an insect with three heads, each imbued with its own purpose. Each with a desire to carry its midsection somewhere else. First moving one way, and then the next, drifting here and there like three hands on a Ouija board.

From one hundred feet up, the height of a mere eight-story building, it becomes obvious that each pair of insect legs is joined at a human torso, with human heads, and between them, the three, they share a burden. A piece of furniture, seemingly.

From ten feet, a guardian angel's view, the view this tale will take, three men carry a couch. An orange, knit couch of considerable size.

Thom moved his meager possessions into Tree's apartment. It was a high-ceilinged, early twentieth-century affair that had obviously been reworked in the seventies, destroying much of its charm. He put his books in the living room in an attempt to add some sort of decorating touch, and they sat there like moldering sea chests.

Thom moved his chairless desk around his room, trying to figure out how to fill in the emptiness that a lack of dresser, bed, and every other item that a person usually owned caused. He occasionally glanced toward the window across the corridor between the buildings to see if he was being spied on, at once trying to hide his actions and trying to make them presentable and interesting on the off chance there was a single woman across the way who might be interested in a fairly intelligent, bumbling ogre of a man with a slightly below-average self-esteem.

Slightly? Thom's brain said.

"Yes, slightly," Thom replied firmly. Brain was the entity of indeterminable size that sat somewhere above Thom's right eye, one inch in. The origin of headaches. That Muppet cynic gallery that studied his every move from some disappointed forefather's eyes. Part logician and part patriarch, brain intruded on Thom's consciousness primarily as a backseat driver.

He uncased his laptop, tracked down a wireless signal, and got on his knees in front of his desk to check his email. "As if to pray," brain said. "I know, I know," Thom replied.

Erik burst through his door, knocking after the fact as he had done the other three times Thom had encountered his new, somewhat excitable roommate. Erik was in his mid-twenties and would be considered handsome but for an utterly uncombable head of dark hair.

"Donuts!" he said like a herald, like the king had arrived. He lowered a giant box of donuts to Thom's eye level.

"Ah," Thom said. "I can't eat them. They look good though."

"Can't eat them?"

"I can't eat wheat," he intoned for probably the millionth time in his life, knowing it always led to confusion. "I have sort of a strict, ah, strict eating habits."

"Good Lord, man. This is a celebration. We'll go running in the morning. There's a park around here. I've seen it on the map, and I'm going to find it. We can get up at dawn, get our one-twos in."

Thom repressed a shudder. "It's not a diet diet—it's a stomach sort of thing. Gluten intolerance, among other things. I can't eat wheat."

"Gluten, huh?" Erik raised his eyebrows. "*Glutentag*," he said brightly. "Okay, man, they'll be in the kitchen if you change your mind. Nice room you got here. Like the desk placement. What kind of games you got on that thing?"

"Nothing much, really."

Erik nodded vigorously. "Alright, man, see you around. I'll be in the living room if you need anything."

Thom shook his head. He was fairly sure he wasn't living with any of the chosen people.

```
To: thom@sanchopanchez.net
From: richardd@shopstock.com
Subject: bad news
Hi Thom,
I've got bad news for you. ShopStock has decided
once and for all that in this economic climate, hav-
ing a strong web presence for a local grocery store
is just not practical. Ahem. As we've known all
along. So they've decided, effective immediately, to
cut the web development team.
I'm sorry about this. I know you could use the money.
Email seems like a bad way to break it, but know-
ing you I thought it'd be better. I'll keep on the
lookout for other jobs for you. How's the apartment
hunting coming? Let's have a beer soon and talk more
about where spammers fit into Dante's Inferno.
Richard
```

Thom put his head in his hands. The last three months had been a spiral in which life seemed bent on unhinging him from every stable situation he'd had a feeble grasp on. At least he had an apartment. His stomach churned. He opened up his website and thought about how to phrase his newly found freedom in a way that wouldn't read "laid off." "Now available for freelance work! ;-)" he wrote, and then deleted the idiotic smiley. Then deleted the entry altogether.

He fretted about how to write his self-descriptive summary at one of the many job-networking sites he belonged to. "I am professional (still have all my teeth!)," he wrote as filler text to keep his fingers busy while he thought, "stable (no longer living out of a hotel!), competent (kung-fu coder still can't code his ex-girlfriend back), and motivated (as big as an ogre and twice as bright)." Then a migraine took over and he closed his laptop without saving.

"Thom!" said Erik. "Have a seat, big guy."

Thom sat on the couch between Tree and Erik. The couch was miraculously large and held the three of them without testing his personal-space requirements. It was comfortable too. It sucked you in and gave you the impression of continually sinking. *The Simpsons* was on, and there was silence among them until a commercial. You did not talk during *The Simpsons*.

Tree tucked a long strand of hair behind his ear and picked up a spool of baling wire from the floor. He drew a length and cut it with a pair of needle-nose pliers and began to twist. His thin hands moved with great agility, making quick definitive bends to the wire, working its straightness to a ball of something. And then, to Thom's astonishment, Tree opened his palm to reveal a perfectly shaped three-inch horse with a long horn on the front of its head. A unicorn. Thom studied the couch to make sure Tree hadn't discarded the wire and plucked the unicorn from somewhere. Thom beamed his approval, but Tree seemed unconscious of him.

Tree fashioned a tornado from the same spool and twisted the bottom of it into the green shag-rug carpet so that it stayed upright. A tornado on shag-rug plains. He planted the unicorn in the rug so that its horn just pierced the midsection of the tornado. A battle in miniature.

"Just like jousting windmills," Thom blurted loud enough to make Tree jump.

Erik stared at it. "Well," Erik said. "Here we all are." He rubbed his forefinger vigorously across his mustache.

"Yes," Tree said.

"There you have it then," Erik said.

Thom counted his teeth with his tongue—twenty-seven? Could he really have an odd number?—as a defense against whatever words his brain might try to dislodge into the quiet air like a donkey's bray.

"I lost my job." Thom pulled at a string on his pants. "Just got an email."

"Alright, buddy!" Erik gave an irksome punch to Thom's arm. "Join the club. How about you and me drive down to Labor Ready in the morning after our jog? Guaranteed payment daily, can't beat that. They'd love the likes of you."

"I'm not sure about the jogging part."

"Just jumping jacks then, no problem."

"I'm not sure about the Labor Ready part either."

"I don't really like to work," Tree said. He hugged his knees up against his slim frame.

Erik and Thom stared at Tree.

"Except lawn care."

"It's the middle of winter, amigo. You won't be doing lawn care for another five months."

Tree looked thoughtful. "Maybe something will come up."

"Get a rich girlfriend. That's the ticket," Erik said.

Hearing the word "girlfriend" made Thom's stomach ache, a compost pile too long in the sun, methane fuming from the bottom of the heap. "My girlfriend broke up with me," he blurted out, belched.

There was a long pause in which nobody was sure what to say.

"I've never had a girlfriend," Tree said.

"What a bunch of freaking sad sacks!" Erik said.

Thom started to chuckle. The chuckle gained momentum into a giggle, and then he was holding his gut and belching and giggling and the others were caught by surprise by the cacophony until they joined in laughing, laughing the laugh that only the bottom rung laughs, crying laugh tears.

If one were to graph the traffic through the front door of the apartment, a downward-sloping curve would begin to emerge, so that by the end of the week it would be apparent the door was being used half as frequently as at the beginning.

The apartment's gravity drew them in like some amassing black hole. Each outward foray grew more difficult and less successful.

As their comfort level with each other increased, and with no great purpose outside, the path of least resistance lay in the hallways of their apartment.

Monday morning found Thom in his shiny clothes on the streets of Portland, wielding a résumé laden with tech acronyms and buzz-words: Ruby, Python, Perl, XML, PHP, SQL, C++. He paced through the downtown corridors, traveling the route from Internet startup to established technology company, finding them either closed for good, moved to the suburbs, or "weathering the storm." And even those he suspected had room to grow were looking for sharp shoot-ers, sharp talkers, sharp lookers from other failed tech companies, not veterans of ShopStock who wore overly baggy clothes, couldn't find the right words at the right time, and towered over them. More than once a startled remark was made: "It says here you have a Mas-ter's in English Literature—oh, that's too bad, we're really looking for someone with an MS in *Computer Science*." Never mind that most colleges still weren't teaching the skills that the companies needed, skills that Thom possessed from being a part of the actual move-ments that had created the software. Thom was not one to point this out. He failed to mention, too, certain legal troubles he'd had concerning a certain slightly less than legal thing he'd done which would certainly, beyond a doubt, prove his computer expertise.

Possibly to address the question *Why are we here?* or to toy with creationism versus evolution, Tree created a lineup of wire figures from fish to monkey to hominid on Monday, planting them into the back of the couch in order. He admired them from a distance and several angles and then, not yet satisfied, added a larger man-like creature at the beginning of the line that sculpted wire fish out of a bundle of its own wire. In his bedroom, he picked up his shrinkwrapped Bible and then put it down again without unwrap-ping it. Then from under his futon he pulled a spiral notebook full of pages wildly scrawled in pencil. As always, he studied the hand-writing, marveling that it was his and so different from his daytime script. He read and reread the last five dreams. In the hundred or so dreams before this, not one of them took place within the last several thousand years, and now these. He closed the book and passed an hour he wouldn't recall later staring at a fixed point. He folded some clothes, then arranged some wire sculptures, setting scenarios and adding roommates. He washed dishes and then made a large batch of split-pea soup and waited for Thom and Erik to come home. The phone rang three times, and each time the caller hung up when Tree answered.

Erik spent the first hour of the first day of the week trying to unplug the toilet using improvised instruments—a spatula, vinegar (did vinegar even work?), a soy-sauce bottle—still wondering how what had come out of him could really have come out of him.

Then he prepared. He shaved his mustache, did fifty push-ups and all the Tai Chi he could remember, put a baseball cap over his unruly plug of hair, donned a silk shirt and headed out along trendy Twenty-third Avenue to see what turned up. At Twenty-third and Flanders a possibly stranded young woman stood on a street corner, and Erik took it as an opportunity to introduce himself and offer his navigational services. Not long after, he was having coffee with the young Wisconsinite and talking about airline safety in Third World countries, with an emphasis on Latin America. By four o'clock Erik had a lipstick stain on his chin and fifty-eight dollars in his pocket that she had given him to buy tickets to a "three-day dinner-theater performance" he'd mentioned that they absolutely must go see together.

Alone, he headed up to Forest Park and ran through bushes for a half hour to punish himself for being such a snake, hollering, stumbling on the wet ground. Rotting leaves clung to his shoes and pants. With his face sufficiently bush whipped, he dropped by the grocery store, picked up a case of cheap beer, and went back to the apartment to celebrate his earnings with his roommates.

Night found them embedded in the couch, drinking Erik's beer, eating Tree's popcorn, watching TV, while the fishing line of their collective fates intertwined, became inseparably tangled. The

7

couch cast the late-night spell that couches cast on their occupants the world over. And they became comfortable with each other—if by no other way than by the proximity of their bodies.

On Wednesday Thom completely reworked his résumé to accentuate his Master's in English Literature degree while muttering curses at various employers at high-tech companies he wished would get trapped in Porta-Potties. He printed fifty copies and spent the first half of the day farming out his statistics to law firms looking for research assistants, newspapers looking for junior editors, businesses looking for copy editors and, frankly, anyone else who'd listen. He carried his massive form dutifully from office to office, crowding doorways, looming over desks, frightening secretaries. He wished for some shred of success he could use to ground in truth his increasingly fictional emails to his mother. By two in the afternoon he'd had all the human contact he could take and headed home.

He found Tree in the kitchen baking a pie. A young, hippy, wire-working Martha Stewart, delicately smoothing out their home life, Thom thought.

Tree was bent on his purpose, one-tracked but with an absent-minded carelessness, leaving plates barely balanced on counter edges, so that Thom would lurch forward and scoot the plates into the safety of the counter behind Tree's back.

"Wheat-free," Tree said after five minutes of silence.

"Wow. Thanks, Tree, but you don't have to do that for me."

"I like to cook. Any luck?"

"Not that I can tell. I shook about twenty hands, handed out all résumés. Fifty copies. I figure that's got to be some kind of record. I felt like a political pamphleteer. And that's not including the résumés I sent by email the last few days. I'm bound to scare someone into hiring me sooner or later."

"Seems like someone with as many skills as you wouldn't have a problem."

"Yesss. One would think. I'm afraid there's a bit more to getting a job than having the skills."

Tree nodded. "Maybe you should take the next few days off."

"That'd be nice, though I suspect you'd rather have a rent payer living here." Thom smiled. He found a spot out of Tree's way in the small kitchen.

"It's not so important."

Thom stared at Tree, watched him wipe cutting boards of flour, wash measuring cups, sweep the floor. Sometimes Tree looked like an elf: petite and only half-human. Thom never felt sure if they were having the same conversation. "Surely it's important," he said. "The rent will become due."

"I had a dream it would work out."

Thom repressed a chuckle. "Excellent. I can always use a sub-conscious advocate. Your dream mention my salary?"

"Well, you don't have to get a job. That's why I said you should take a couple of days off."

The phone rang, and Thom picked it up. He heard a click on the other end.

"Hang up?" Tree said.

"I guess so."

"Somebody's keeping tabs on us."

"Oh?" Thom experienced a quick wave of full-body itchiness, and he jerked to scratch several places at once. What the hell was the kid talking about? His brain couldn't seem to come up with any reasonable response, and he began to long for some kind of computer project, something logical and solitary and problem-solving intensive, something that worked, something he could create, his own digital Garden of Eden to craft. Something without the strange unpredictability of human interaction. Surely God was a programmer, fleeing his own creation after he'd introduced code that spawned its own bugs: humans.

"I saw those sculptures on the back of the couch," he said, hoping to change the subject. "Really something. You should try to do something with that."

"I have pretty clear dreams, and sometimes they sort of come true," Tree said.

Thom wasn't sure what to say, so he pushed on. "You could take those down to Saturday Market. I'm sure you could sell them. Get a little stand." That's what God needed, Thom realized suddenly. He should have created himself a quality-assurance department first thing. There were a lot of programmatical errors in human nature that could have been worked out.

"I dreamed you wouldn't have to worry about getting a job, so I'd hate for you to have to waste a lot more time looking for one, you know?"

"What did you dream?" Thom sighed.

"Oh, I don't really like to talk about them."

Thom blinked. "Pie smells great," he said finally. "I'm going to do some work for a while. How's Erik's job search coming, by the way? Any word from him?"

"He doesn't need to find a job either, actually."

Thom nodded. Of course, he thought.

Somehow the smell of the pie baking was stronger in Thom's room than in the kitchen, as if the smell had intensified into a presence, looming over him. His mouth watering, he opened his laptop. There were two emails from prospective employers that weren't hiring. He weighed the threat of human interaction against eating a piece of pie and went back to the kitchen.

"Smells really good."

"It's done. Want me to cut you a piece?"

"Sure, sure, yes." Thom considered his reaction to Tree's dreams. So he had dreams he thought came true, or he had dreams that came true and he doesn't like to talk about them. That's okay. Thom's ex-girlfriend had been an amateur *I Ching* diviner, and when Thom had done something contrary to what her reading had recommended she'd get irritated with him. Sure it was possible to dream about the future, Thom tried to make himself believe momentarily, and then felt himself losing the effort.

Tree set a gorgeous, steaming plate of pie in front of him.

"Beautiful," Thom said. "Where did you learn to cook?"

"I grew up on a commune. We all had to take turns at the chores. There were a few people with strict eating habits."

Thom nodded. Suddenly anxious not to hear anything else

about the commune, but he nevertheless felt compelled to ask, "What type of commune?"

"The usual sort." Tree turned away.

Thom saw the back of Tree's neck redden. He felt certain the kid preferred that he not pursue the subject, and he wondered if it'd been some sort of cult.

"So what else can you tell me about this dream?"

Tree turned and beamed at him, his voice the tone of happy announcements. "I think we're going on a journey together."

This wasn't speculation. This was conviction. "Really?" Thom's stomach bubbled up hotly from the center of the Earth, and he excused himself to the bathroom. On the way there, Erik burst through the front door. Thom noticed that he had a full mustache again.

"Hide me, you've got to hide me. I'm not here. I am not here."

"You're not here?" Thom burping the last half of the question.

"You don't even know me. You've never even seen me."

"I've never even seen you," Thom repeated gratefully and continued to the bathroom. With the door closed safely behind him, Thom looked in the mirror, raised his eyebrows at the racket that was continuing outside the bathroom, and proceeded to create some gaseous racket inside the bathroom. How did the guy grow hair so quickly? Thom barely shaved more than once a week, and Erik had grown a full mustache in two days.

There was a fierce shout, and a noise Thom felt could safely qualify as a yelp. He searched his face for something to pinch and stared into his pupils as the sound rose outside. He thought he should see what was happening.

Erik was backed up against a wall in the living room by a gentleman holding a pocket knife to his throat. The man was in his forties, wore a tightly fitted outdoor-style shirt, and seemed to have the upper hand. In the doorway a young woman vacillated between outrage and infatuation for Erik. Thom took a stride across the living room and grabbed the man's hand until the knife fell to the floor and the man cried out.

Erik picked up the knife, leapt back, and yelled, "We take them!"

"We're not taking anybody," Thom said. He held his arm out so Erik would stay back. The man eyed Thom and backed toward the doorway. "What's going on here, Erik?"

"Don't listen to him," said the woman in the doorway.

The man rubbed his wrist. "Let's just forget the whole thing, Sherry," he said.

Thom turned to Erik, who shrugged.

"Sounds like we're forgetting the whole thing," Erik said. "I'm willing to do that. Let bygones be bygones. Let them who is without sin throw the first stone." Erik kept the knife raised.

"Cast the first stone. It's cast the first stone. Somehow I doubt this is about martyrdom." Thom looked back toward Sherry and tried to appear upstanding, which took the form of a smile and better posture.

Sherry closed her eyes for a moment. When she opened them, they were rimmed with the beginning of tears.

"On Monday I met him on the street and he seemed nice and we had coffee and talked for a long time and then he, well, we made some plans and I thought he was nice and I didn't know the city so it was nice to meet somebody nice." Sherry inhaled just shy of a sob and looked up at the older man. "Like maybe we would go see this theater performance that he'd heard about and we made plans for where to meet and I gave him money for the tickets because what else am I going to do while I'm here and he never showed up," Sherry said in a hurried exhale. "Then we saw him on the street and I'd already told Dad about it and when we saw him he ran and we followed him and then Dad and he got in a fight and . . . then you got here."

"Ah." Thom wished he was back in the bathroom.

Tree appeared, looking sleepy. For a minute Thom feared that Tree was going to wave at him, like a mother waves at her child onstage in his first play.

Thom sighed. "Erik?"

"I meant to go buy the tickets, but I got . . . I meant to go buy the tickets."

"I'd still like to see the theater thing," offered Sherry hesitantly. She leaned against the door frame, one foot toe first to the floor.

She smiled at Erik, and Erik waved back. She was probably no more than seventeen, maybe an honors student, Thom thought. She'd tried to do something with her makeup, under the influence of the city, that her clothes and hair couldn't keep up with.

"Not with him you won't," said her father.

"Alright, how about giving the knife back, Erik," said Thom. He swallowed twice. "With the money."

"I don't have the money," Erik said, not moving.

"I have some money," said Tree. Everyone stared at Tree as he went to his room and returned a minute later with a small stack of bills. Tree took the knife from Erik's hand and handed the knife to Sherry's father and the money to Sherry.

"Thank you. We won't trouble you any further," Sherry's father said and shot a dark look at Erik.

After the door closed, the three roommates held their places for a moment. A frame frozen in time, the transition between outside conflict and inside conflict. Actors repositioning, new arguments and explanations boiling up. Tree and Thom turned to Erik.

"I meant to buy the tickets."

"I believe you," Tree said.

Erik studied Tree for a moment and then continued with confidence. "And they were sold out. But when I went to look for her, I couldn't find her."

Tree nodded, and Thom didn't say anything.

"Is the mustache supposed to be a disguise?" Thom finally asked.

"What?" Erik rubbed his forefinger like a jigsaw across the fur on his upper lip.

"That's a real mustache then?"

"It grows kind of fast."

Thom nodded again, turned to Tree. "And how much money did you give her."

"Fifty-eight dollars."

"How did you know how much?"

Tree looked startled. "I don't know, I just did." He blushed brightly.

"Were you involved in this, Tree?"

"Yeah! How did you know? What's up with that?" Erik stepped forward, taking the opportunity to turn the focus. "I'm not the paranoid type, but I'm pretty sure, no no no, I'm positive I didn't mention it."

"I, I think I dreamed it."

Thom let out a great roaring rumble of gas and both roommates turned toward him, polite, startled smiles on their faces. Had he said something? they seemed to be asking.

"Oh man, was that real!"

"I have a stomach—"

"You just came in and grabbed the knife from that sucker, just like that. You were amazing. You had them so handled!"

Thom felt so immediately grateful that Erik wasn't talking about his flatulence that he allowed himself to laugh in relief.

"And then you grabbed the knife from me," Erik said. "I didn't know who was going to stab who!"

"And I knew how much money to give her," Tree said, trying out a laugh.

Erik frowned. "I still think that's spooky. But I do appreciate the loan. You know I'm good for it, right?"

Tree nodded.

"Alright then, let's go have some pie and beer," Thom said.

"We should team up," Erik said excitedly. "All three of us. We should make some kind of a team."

"I think you mean gang," Thom said.

"Hey, I'm not talking about illegal stuff." He turned, trapping Thom just outside of the kitchen. "I'm talking about some kind of enterprise."

"That's a spaceship, right?" Thom joked to no apparent effect.

"I'm talking about a business venture. With your brawn—and brains—and my, you know—seriously! Think about it."

"Tree wants to join." Thom finally pushed through the bottleneck of Erik into the kitchen. "He's got a plan."

"Oh . . . ," Tree said and stared at the floor.

༄

If you were to squint from the roof of the apartment building midway up the West Hills, with Portland proper below, you could almost, with practice and a shifting of scale, morph the scattered buildings into the teepees of the people who'd inhabited the riverside some five hundred years ago, at the same time an explorer from Spain was rediscovering Cuba, the land their forefathers had discovered eighty thousand years prior. Or at least that was the legend. Men had been absentmindedly discovering land they'd already traversed, built civilizations upon, fucked and cried on for as long as there had been men.

Among the teepees below, a society pulsed, children were fed, art was made. There was a hierarchy, and at the bottom of it were the unchosen who huddled together and wondered what purpose they were intended for.

By Friday, it was fairly clear to Thom that going out into the world was negative. He preferred to traverse and re-traverse the small follies he already knew his way around—the loose shower knob, the stubborn toilet, the web of lies that kept his mother proud of him, the other two unchosen. A certain emotional neutrality was reached in the apartment. Occasionally that neutrality passed into positive ground—laughing about knife encounters, eating popcorn in front of the TV, drinking beer in the kitchen. And sometimes it passed into the negative—knife encounters, for example. But a makeshift brotherhood emerged. Thom spent the day doing as Tree had recommended: not looking for work. He spent the day on the couch.

Erik decided he certainly wasn't going out into the world. This was his second trick in one week that had gone awry and now he feared simply stepping through the front door. Outside he was a wanted man; inside he was comfortable enough. Bored, but comfortable.

There were many little mysteries in the apartment that worried Tree: the drapes across from his room that always closed when he glanced over, the phone without a caller, the older man who stationed himself on the front stoop, watching them come and go, and the large couch that lulled him to sleep.

The couch wasn't free until late afternoon, after Thom had moved to his room and Erik had sated himself on bad television. Tree removed all his wirework and pulled off the cushions. Something about this couch, he thought. There was a nagging in his mind, a leftover fleck of dream or a mishandled scrap of intuition, nothing more than a reminder that the couch was an item that required some kind of attention. He tucked his hands down into the crevasses, squeezed the cushions, put his ear to it. He tentatively touched his tongue to the armrest and recoiled from the smell of Erik's BO. He tipped the couch onto its back. The underside revealed little. The uneven and haphazard stitching led him to guess it was handmade, or at least had once been repaired. However he tried, he couldn't pry the backing off, and the thread used for the stitching was incredibly strong, resisting even a knife. Finally he loosened a seam and opened up a gap so that he could see into the intestines of the couch.

The couch sighed—there was no other way to describe it. A faint smell spilled out: spines of old books, flowers past prime, the smell of things so long dead that only a nasal whisper remained. Tree realized he'd fallen back. Had he fainted? He leaned forward, but the gap had closed and the couch again smelled like a couch ought to smell.

The disaster came late on Sunday night. Erik was asleep on the couch and Thom and Tree were in their rooms, but the apartment above thumped with activity. An inebriated romantic encounter between a gymnast and a horse jockey had gotten a bit too creative. A table next to a waterbed was upturned. A lit candle from the table rolled next to the bed, catching a small pile of newspapers, dirty laundry, and a book of matches on fire. The fire licked at the underside of the waterbed, burning a hole that drowned the small fire. Fate lent a push, however, and several powerful pneumatic jostlings by the pair atop the waterbed opened the hole wider and pushed the water out with great throbbing force until the couple noticed they were sinking. By the time they had their wits about them, half the bed had leaked onto the floor. They ran for towels—which were useless against the massive flood of water—then gathered a meager collection of pots and pans that could not hold the gallons still flowing from the bed in biblical proportions.

Erik woke startled and flailing from a dream in which a horse had been pissing on him. He leapt from the couch and flipped on the light switch to see their apartment turned into a waterfall. Frantic pounding footsteps sounded from the apartment above. Water bowed the sheetrock in the center of the ceiling and had broken through the plaster. The green shag rug had taken on the appearance of a swamp.

"Tree! Thom! Ho-lee shit!"

He ran down the hallway, pounded his fists on his roommates' doors and yelled, "Wake the hell up, goddamnit!" He gathered all the towels out of the bathroom. In the living room, he let the towels drop as he realized he didn't have the faintest idea what he was going to do with them. Thom appeared in the hallway, his eyes wide as searchlights, and Tree appeared a moment later.

"What, what did you do?" Thom said, staring over Erik's shoulder at the wreckage of the living room.

"I didn't do anything!"

"Wow," Tree said, "this is really . . . really." He tapped his temple with his forefinger repeatedly.

A rapid, angry banging came from the door. Erik sloshed across to open it and found that the swollen rug had sealed the door shut. He put his foot against the wall, his hands firmly around the doorknob, and pulled with all his might. His hands slipped and he landed on his back in the swamp water. He got up and managed to yank the door open a crack, letting water into the hallway. A very stout, enraged woman shook her fists and yelled at him to *Turn his goddamn water off, he was sinking them back to the fucking Stone Age!*

"It's upstairs, upstairs!" he said breathlessly and pointed at the ruined ceiling. She pounded off, presumably toward the upstairs.

"Power cords!" Thom yelled.

Tree jumped in the air like a stung fish, curving and turning, and landed on his back on the edge of the television, hurling it to the floor and pulling its power cord from out of the socket, stopping the electricity from surging through the water.

"Holy shit!" Erik waded toward Tree to help him up.

"I'm looking for more power cords," Thom yelled and rushed around the apartment, a great spray of water leaping up from each footfall. He unplugged two more and saw that the downpour was beginning to slow.

Tree was laid out on his back on the couch, slow drips landing on his knees, lip, and sternum. Erik was angrily sloshing around.

"How you doing, Tree?" asked Thom.

"Nothing is broken, I think. I don't feel great though."

"You'll be sore. That was a hellish fall. But shit, you saved us, I bet."

"Not the TV though," Tree said. The three looked at the TV, upside down in a corner, surrounded by water, like a shipwreck stuck in the surf.

"Probably not," Thom said. "Doesn't look good for the TV. Or the apartment."

"What in the fuck?" Thom raised palms toward the upstairs, or the sky. Or God.

"Waterbed upstairs," Erik said. "Some kind of fire underneath it. That lady came back. She's so mad." Erik smiled. "I mean, she's mad. The whole waterbed let loose. I'm mad too, I guess. All the water in here is soaking the apartment below us, the poor suckers."

"This is really screwed," Thom said. "Let's get out of here. I'm treating everyone to breakfast. Does your car still work, Erik?"

"If it doesn't, at least it's dry."

Outside, rain was streaming from a black sky. "Celestial waterbed," Thom joked and was ignored. The three piled into Erik's car and headed for an all-night diner across town, black smoke curling up behind them, an ocean of rain in front. Every once in a while Erik would bang on the steering wheel and curse.

❧

The restaurant was full of the regular assembly of stylish, alternative Portland nightlife—people none of them felt at home with. Velvet Elvises mixed with local artists and black lights on the walls.

Erik ordered two pieces of pie, Tree a grilled-cheese sandwich, and Thom complicated things with eggs without cheese, no toast, and Italian sausage that he felt guilty ordering in front of the vegetarian-looking waitress. Beers were had all around.

"So, dreamboy, what are you going to do now?" Erik said. "Dream this one too?"

"I did have . . . I've had a lot of dreams with water lately. Sort of thought it was one of those."

"Oh, you did, did you? Next time let's have a little more warning. I woke up from dreaming that I was getting pissed on by a horse."

Thom chuckled and noticed the bar was playing his ex-girl-friend's favorite band, Neutral Milk Hotel. *Oh comely, I will be with you when you lose your breath.* A tingle went up his spine.

Erik lurched up and over to a group on their last drinks of the night. He came back with a lit cigarette.

"Yep," he said, "yep yep yep." Exhaling smoke. "It was pretty funny though. You've all got to admit that it was pretty funny. Tree's swan dive. The whole thing like a SeaWorld exhibition."

"Yeah," said Thom, "it'd be funnier if I wasn't so entirely screwed. Maybe I'll go live with my mom."

"Hey, at least you can," Erik said. "My folks are probably lost in a jungle somewhere. Home-home has been gone for decades."

"Yeah," Tree said.

"Yeah what?" said Erik, covering Tree in smoke, waving it away.

"Mine too. Not a . . . err, not a jungle, but same sort of thing."

Erik exhaled another cloud of smoke in a sine wave, nodding vigorously. "We could always get arrested." His white teeth picked up the glow of a black light somewhere. "It's better than the rain."

"I think we . . ." Tree started and then looked down at the table, fingered the saltshaker. He grabbed the pepper and made the two spices do a self-conscious jig.

Erik and Thom exchanged looks.

"Not more of that dream shit. That's freaky shit," Erik said.

"It's not so freaky," Thom said. "The mind is an interesting entity. The dreams may be subconscious wishes, snatches of extrapolated information that seem like premonition. Jung even talked about tapping into a collective mind—so he may have lifted the fifty-eight from your mind, or it may have been a lucky guess. But the important thing I think is not to get too carried away."

Tree nodded vigorously, Erik jabbed the cigarette into the ashtray with repetitive violence, and their food arrived.

"Well, I'd like to hear it, dammit," Erik said.

"I wasn't saying I didn't want to hear," Thom said.

"No, you said you weren't going to believe it."

"I didn't," Thom protested.

"Well what the hell do you think you said? And shit, if he can pick a number out of my mind while I'm sleeping—how about that guy over there?" Erik pointed to an older man nursing his coffee, a ski cap tight around his ears. "What's that guy thinking?"

"I can't," said Tree, and his face reddened. "It doesn't . . . I don't . . ."

"He's thinking he'd like to get the waitress naked," Thom said with too much on his fork, trying to pare down the load. "Just like the rest of us who are too afraid to admit it."

"That's the spirit!" Erik took a swig of his beer. "That's exactly right. He's thinking he'd like a pair. See those greedy eyes? That one sitting up there"—he gestured with the bottle to a woman dressed as a goth, black tights on slender legs, beautiful lips with dark lipstick—"*and* the waitress."

Thom and Tree shyly studied the goth.

"Heh heh," Thom said, an ache in his throat. Thom's brain repeated his mantra: *She is pretty; I am homely.*

They looked at their plates, pushing around food they were too exhausted to eat.

Thom grabbed a handful of his hair and squeezed, felt several of the strands pop from their roots. "What in the hell are we going to do? How can so many things possibly fail at once?" He tried to put a humorous tone on his words but knew he couldn't keep it up.

He was this far away from real depression, the state that puts you in bed for a couple of weeks, too weak to move.

"Hey, big guy, none of that. No despair at this table. Tree's got it all worked out." Erik nudged Tree.

"Uh!" Tree rubbed his side where Erik had elbowed him. "I don't, really, I just think that . . . maybe something else might come up. Maybe we'll eat some foreign food."

"What in the Jesus hell are you talking about? What kind of a plan is that? We're trying to cheer Thom up. Come on now, foreign food—we're heading to a Thai restaurant next? Listen, this is how you do it. I've got an uncle that lives in one of those fancy houses in the hills, great place, there's a hot tub, it'll be warm and dry, big improvement right there. He's away in Europe for three months, and I know where the spare key is. Fantastic kitchen, view of the city, we'll get girlfriends and have them over, it's a hell of a place. Just to get back on our feet. You'll get your job, Thom, and then whatever happens, happens."

"Really?" Thom smiled dreamily. "We could do that?"

Erik rolled his eyes. "No, man, come on, think I'd have been staying in that apartment if I had a place like that? I was just showing Tree how to cheer somebody up."

"You sonofabitch."

"Sorry, sorry about that—this is what's going to happen. The water will have made the apartment pretty much unlivable. The landlord will tell us to get our shit and get out, because it's got a lot of repair time and they've got to check electrical and structural and all hell, and while they're at it, why not just renovate the damn thing so it gets more rent?"

Thom put his face in his hands and stared between fingers at his Italian sausage.

"We're going on a trip," Tree said.

"You dreamed this?" Thom said.

"Hey, man"—Erik pointing at Thom—"don't knock dreamboy, I told you he had a plan."

"But I'm not sure. Sometimes they don't . . ." Tree stared at his plate.

"Quit saying that! So your dreams don't always come true. Mine don't come true. Yours come true, Thom?"

"Not a one."

Erik brought his beer bottle down to the table with a heavy thud, "That settles it then. We leave tomorrow."

"You have got to be out of your mind. Where to, what money, why?" Thom said.

"Come on, you big worrywart, what have you got going here?" Erik said.

Thom looked hopelessly at Tree.

"I don't have anything going," Tree volunteered. "But we could find another apartment."

Erik spread his hands wide in mock indignation. "Just a minute ago you were talking about a trip. Besides. Who is going to rent to three unemployed types?"

"I have some money from my grandfather," Tree said.

Erik nodded several times. "How much?"

"Erik," Thom growled.

"Hey, it's cool, man. Don't tell me. I was just asking."

"Fifteen hundred."

Erik calculated on the ceiling for a moment and then mashed the remains of his second piece of pie into a liquidy hash with his fork. "Well, that's an extremely short apartment rental or a long trip."

"I'm going to live with my mom," Thom said.

"Where's that?"

"Central Washington."

"The hell are you going to do there? I say we just get in my car and head south, seek our futures in less rainy climes. Go to Mexico. Think about fifteen hundred bucks in Mexico. *Viva México!*" he yelled, fork in the air. Heads at several tables turned toward Erik then back again.

Tree shifted uneasily in his seat.

"Let's get out of here," Thom said. "I want to look at the apartment again."

When they hit fresh air, Thom decided all at once he wanted the trip. He wanted to get out of town, do something different, see somewhere different. He needed to move, to ramble, to let road dust and sky patch tight the various holes in his life. "I'll do the trip," he said.

"Yes!" said Erik. "We've got a plan. You're in, right Tree?"

"Okay," Tree nodded and smiled.

"Okay!" Erik started the car, revved it, and, with a whoosh of smoke and a bang, it gave out and would not start again.

Thom clapped his hands in glee. "I'm cursed. Let's all of us just coast this thing into the Willamette River. Us in it."

Erik pounded on the steering wheel.

"Tell me about your uncle again," Tree said.

With nowhere else to go and no other way to get there—the buses wouldn't start for several hours—they walked. Down Clinton Street to Twelfth, two miles, down Twelfth to Burnside, three miles. On Burnside a car brimming with party revelers pummeled them with fast-food remains. A milkshake struck Thom square in the chest, exploding onto Tree and Erik in a chocolatey mess. Erik turned and ran after the car, holding his middle finger up and shouting incomprehensibly. He made it a full two blocks before he ran out of steam. Thom and Tree waited, scooping off globs of milkshake.

Burnside to the river, over the bridge and the frigid glare of the Willamette River, the Superfund ecodisaster. Thom imagined the slick, rubbery bodies of suicides floating coldly under the bridge, merging into the Columbia and then finally out to sea.

They continued up through downtown and then up to Twenty-Third, three miles.

By the time they got home, they were exhausted. A note from the building manager was taped to their door. *Hi Tree, heard about the leak. Will have a look in the morn.—Bob.* As if they'd had a small issue with a leaky toilet and he'd be around to fix it when he got the chance.

Erik checked the couch and was amazed to find it dry. "Feel it! It's dry. Think all the water soaked in?" Both roommates dutifully felt the couch.

"There's something about this couch," Tree said.

Thom sighed. "I'm going to bed wherever I can."

"What's about this couch is it's where I'm going to sleep, that's what's about this couch," Erik said. The others curled into dry corners of the apartment wherever they could find them, with clothes and scavenged dry blankets piled over them for warmth. The sound of dripping echoed through the apartment like a cave lullaby.

The apartment manager was at their door first thing in the morning with an older, well-dressed gentleman in tow.

The knocking came to Erik like announcements in foreign countries. Like undersea drums, leagues away. He couldn't seem to separate the sound from his dreams, and even on his feet he was unsure which part of the wrecked room the noise was coming from. He found the door, forced it open enough to look out, and the two men on the other side took a half step back. A smell of must and rot bustled past them and filled the hallway.

"*Fue una noche terrible, bien mojada,*" Erik said, and felt his voice didn't sound right. His hair stood out at angles like the sweeping end of an abused broom.

"What?" said the gentleman.

The manager glanced at the other man, swallowed and said, "*Qué pasó?*"

"I speak English," Erik said, confused and irritated.

"What happened?" the manager said.

"You were speaking Spanish," Erik said, ready to close the door.

"In the night, what happened in the night?"

"Oh. Waterbed upstairs."

"But how about with your apartment?"

"Ever seen *Titanic*?" Erik asked.

They both nodded, and Erik stared at them until he realized they wanted to come in. He wrenched at the door, then went to take a piss. When he got back, all that was left of the men was a scattering of fading shoeprints in the wet rug. One set of shoes had spent a fair amount of time at the couch, he noticed, and then Erik folded himself back into it and back to sleep.

Tree woke to the smell. It smelled like a house on the commune when a cat had died in the basement and lay undiscovered for a week. He ran to the bathroom and lost the remnants of the grilled cheese sandwich from the night before.

He found Thom and Erik in the kitchen, drinking coffee from paper cups. Thom handed him a cup.

"Electricity is off," Thom said. "They're worried about fire danger and other problems. It's all old knob-and-tube wiring through here. So we went out and got coffee."

"Thanks," said Tree. He took a sip and let it wash down the terrible taste in his mouth. "I threw up," he said. "That smell is terrible."

Thom nodded. "Erik says he can't smell it."

Erik shrugged.

They drank their coffee and watched the rain through the kitchen window. The apartment was cold and uncomfortable, and Thom filed through his life looking for bright spots.

"Boy, that was a fun night." Thom raised his cup in a mock toast.

Tree got a pair of needle-nose pliers from a kitchen drawer and began to dismantle the small wire house that he'd made and set on the kitchen table in a spirit of home.

"I think we're going on a trip," Thom said.

"Not you too," Erik said. "Why aren't I having these dreams?"

"No dream," Thom said. "I just think we should get out of here."

"I have eighteen dollars to my name," Erik said in what both roommates felt was an uncharacteristic moment of truth. "And you know where my fucking car is."

"You're a realist today," Thom said. "It doesn't really become you."

"Well, I don't think you can even take the Greyhound anywhere for eighteen bucks. Maybe Salem or something, but I'm talking about getting out of here."

"I've got a couple of hundred," Thom said.

"You guys know how much I have." Tree's disassembled house quickly morphed into a bus shape under his pliers. "I'm in." He paused and looked up at them. "I can front you."

But why? Thom wondered. We don't even really know each other. A faint paranoia coursed through him. There was a knock, and Tree went to get the door.

It was the building manager, his hair tied up in a ponytail. He wore a Grateful Dead shirt, slacks, and work boots, and took a step back when the smell hit him.

"Hey, Tree," he said fondly. He worried his lip with his teeth, raised his eyebrows. "That's quite a smell."

"The rug, I guess."

"Ah, it'll have to go." He exhaled dramatically and put his hands on his hips. "So I've got bad news for you guys."

"We've got to move out?" Erik said.

"Everything has got to go. We're going to overhaul the three apartments entirely." They nodded and stared at the floor. "I'm sorry about that, guys. Here's your deposit back, Tree." He handed Tree an envelope.

"The couch was here when I moved in," said Tree.

The manager studied the couch through the opening in the doorway, "I know," he said. "It's funny. This morning the owner said to make sure you take the couch with you. Not sure why he would say that. I can have the workmen chuck it for you, though, if you don't want it. Or better yet, you guys could just haul it over to the Goodwill. It's only two blocks away. That might be easier, if you don't mind—I'd probably have to charge you otherwise."

"It is a nice couch," said Thom, thinking of the extent of his furniture. "The owner came by this morning?"

"Yeah, we spoke with . . ." Pointing at Erik. "Sorry, I don't know your names, just Tree since he's on the lease. I'm Bob."

Erik and Thom introduced themselves.

"This morning?" said Thom.

"Yeah, we knocked at about eight a.m."

Tree and Thom stared at Erik, who wore his eyebrow-raised, open-eyed look.

"Okay," said Tree.

"I'm really sorry," Bob said. "There's just nothing really to be done about it."

Thom nodded.

"You could let us take a couple of swings at the people upstairs," Erik said.

"You've got to wait in line for that, my friend."

They busied themselves with undoing what they'd done just a week before. Packing clothes, this time divvying up what could be taken on a trip and setting the rest aside to be donated, thrown away, and forgotten.

There was not much to pack. Tree had his wire and pliers, the Bible he'd never opened, some slightly damp dream journals, a change of clothes. Fetching a knife from the kitchen, he opened the Bible and cut carefully along its spine, separating the Old Testament from the New. He packed the Old. With a deep sigh, he threw his entire sculpture collection in a box, and the box in the dumpster.

The fact that every several years or so Erik lost everything he owned kept his possessions to a minimum. He had extensive personal hygiene equipment, a few shirts, and several hats, one of which was straw. He took off his shirt and put his straw hat on and did some maneuvers in front of a mirror. He had a fake beard, which he'd never used but always liked the idea of using. He threw it all in a pillowcase and busied himself with eating whatever was left in the refrigerator and cupboards, which included a Jell-O mix that he ate by the spoonful. The sickness that followed he tried to chase away by eating half a block of cheese.

Thom spent the first thirty minutes inventorying his computer gadgetry, packing it, taking it out, and putting it in the Goodwill pile, feeling heartbroken, and then packing it again. It was a nice laptop, if a bit old, he admitted, going over its curves. All of his projects were uploaded to a server, so he could access them from anywhere. But still, the laptop was a connection to a whole people, to a different people, his people. Most of his friends he'd never met in the flesh, though he would never admit this publicly, especially not to Erik or Tree. His virtual, fleshless relationships were the domain of the ultranerdy, the hopelessly introverted and socially maladjusted, especially in the absence of real relationships. If his mother knew the level to which he had sunk, she would weep. A Brazilian expert on TCP/IP protocols, a German and an Israeli working on PHP stuff, a Taiwanese and Chinese guy who were working on rival open-source databases, a Japanese Objective-C guy, a girl in Vermont who specialized in information design, several South American Apache-server people, a scattering of Americans and Canadians. They weren't *friend* friends. He knew little to nothing about their lives. But they were friends, and he loved them deeply. They didn't talk about much but their area of specialty, and they all seemed to utilize a wry banter that acknowledged that they knew where they stood in their own societies, which team they were on. A few of them had become filthy rich, but mostly they were people with unmatchable attention spans, people who could spend fifteen hours a day for weeks in front of a computer working on a murky, obscure problem that would most likely never be appreciated except by a tiny handful of people in their world. Most of them had shitty jobs working for companies that didn't understand them. They were close to the machine. They thought with steadfast logical minds and occasional explosive bouts of creativity that, at times, would reengineer the way machines interacted with humans or the way machines interacted with other machines.

The phone rang, and Thom heard Erik say: "Stop calling. We're leaving, you molester-bastard-pervert-cocksucker."

"Don't tell them we're leaving," Tree said belatedly from down the hall.

Thom shut his door. He decided to take the laptop. With it he threw in his cheap digital camera, a radio modem, and a couple of changes of clothes that he carefully folded and packed around the equipment in a backpack. He decided to send his pots and pans, desk, and whatever else to the Goodwill. He thought his life was changing; it must be changing. Fate had certainly cleared out any holds he'd had on life here.

Then in the living room he ran into his books. With an ache in his throat, Thom went through his entire sodden collection, water still an inch deep at the bottom of the box. Bloated and falling apart, their glues melted, covers warped. He pulled out a reprint of *Independent People* by Halldór Laxness, and the sheep on the cover came off, stuck to his thumb. The pages of Haruki Murakami's *Dance Dance Dance* were oatmeal, indistinguishable from each other. And a book apiece by Rick Moody, E. Annie Proulx, and Richard Powers respectively had become like Siamese triplets, the whole inseparable without fatally damaging each of its parts. All of them doomed to the Dumpster.

The couch was surprisingly light. Erik and Thom each carried an end and Tree ran around opening doors, making sure they angled it down the stairs properly. Thom wished he had a place to store it. He briefly thought of his ex-girlfriend's basement and then wished he hadn't.

Both Erik and Thom were aware of being out in daylight, in public view for the first time in a while. Here they were, announcing they were leaving. They were taking the symbol of sedentary life and getting rid of it. They were off. They felt exultant.

They carried the couch the two blocks down Burnside and realized they were something to look at. Three men and a couch at a stoplight. Several people waved and they smiled in return.

They came to the Goodwill parking lot and carried the couch to the garage-style entrance, the weight of it beginning to pull on them.

The man in charge of donations was in his late sixties and dressed in blue jeans and a blue sweatshirt. His face was lined and grim, and his nose projected from his face like a geometry problem gone awry. He came and stood over the couch, fingered the back of it for a while.

"I can't take this," he said. He tapped it with his shoe and inspected the stitching, picked up one end and measured the heft. "No, sir, I can't take it." He adjusted his baseball cap, revealing well-groomed gray and black hair.

"Can't take it?" Thom looked over at the wall of donations and saw a mound of couches in far rattier condition than theirs.

"Can't take it."

"Why on earth not?" Thom said.

"It's not a brand-name couch."

"It's a handmade couch," Thom said. "Don't they sell?"

"Yes, but this one won't."

Tree nodded. "There's something about this couch."

The older man nodded with him. "Yes, there is," he said.

"What are you guys talking about? It's a perfectly nice couch." Thom waved one arm up and down and tried to tamp down the confusion. "If we weren't leaving, I'd keep it. What's wrong with it?"

"Do I know you from somewhere?" Erik said.

The man squinted his eyes at Erik and then shook his head decisively.

"Hmm," Erik said. He rubbed his middle finger over the scrub of a newly shaved mustache. "Okay, okay." He looked at Thom and Tree. "Well, this is no setback, guys. We'll just dump it in your dumpster there." He pointed to a giant Dumpster on the edge of the parking lot.

"I can't let you do that."

"What? Come on. The hell are we going to do with it?"

"You could try William Temple. It's another secondhand store down Twenty-third, on Glisan, about six, seven blocks from here."

"Seven blocks from here." Erik's voice climbed an octave. "We've brought the damn thing far enough."

"Sorry, can't help you," the man said and walked away.

Erik hauled back and kicked the base of the couch.

"Come on," said Thom. "It's our last Portland task. It's the last trial."

"What's he going to do if we just leave it," Erik mouthed and jerked his thumb at the old man.

"Come on," said Thom.

"I've got it." Tree stood at Erik's end, placed his hands under the couch, and squatted, waiting for Thom.

Thom picked up his end, and they backed out of the loading bay. Erik followed.

"What if they don't take it at this Willard place?" Erik said. "There are buses leaving right now!"

"William," Thom said. "I suspect they'll take it. That guy was nutty. There's nothing wrong with this couch." With Thom walking backward holding the front end of the couch, they returned to Burnside and Twenty-third.

Twenty-third was the most fashionable and ritziest of Portland's streets. Full of posh, expensive shops and fancy restaurants. Only Erik had felt at home on the street, but now he continually looked over his shoulder, making sure none of his past marks were about. It was the kind of street that made Thom feel larger, more stooped, fleshier, more clumsy. Beautiful women were everywhere.

At the first block, a woman in her forties pulled up in a Mercedes.

"Looking good, boys. After this, I've got a couple at my house you can move around."

"You'll have to wait in line, ma'am. We're wanted from coast to coast for this work," Erik said, finding his voice.

"I can imagine, I can imagine. What's your job then?" She winked at Erik.

"I'm in charge of precision." He raised his eyebrows suggestively.

"Oh my." She winked again and drove off.

"This isn't so bad," Erik mused. He rolled his shoulders, cased the street.

Halfway to Davis Street, a group of four young women parted to let them through, smiling and waving them on. A small, lithe brunette with a frightening number of freckles smiled directly at Thom. Thom couldn't remember the last time a woman had smiled at him. He chuckled to himself, a pleasant tickle along his spine. *I'm fine. How are you?* His brain carried on conversations with her for the next block. We don't look like workmen, he thought. We just look like some guys carrying a couch. We're just a couple of guys carrying a couch on the poshest street in Portland. The couch felt light and comfortable in his hands.

"How about letting me ride on the couch?" Erik said. "We might as well give these people a nice show."

Thom rolled his neck. "We've got a trip. I don't think your riding on the couch is going to help our progress much. Let's just get it there."

At Everett they set the couch down on the corner and waited for the light to change. Tree instinctively sat on it to rest, and the two roommates followed, which brought a drove of honking, waving, and laughter from cars driving by.

"This is really the oddest experience," said Erik. "If I'd known about this phenomenon earlier, I'd have been out here every day with this couch."

Thom nodded. It suddenly felt like he was part of something. They were somehow making headway in the world. They'd received a social upgrade, just for carrying a couch.

A car pulled up to the curb, and a man leaned out the window. "Performance art?"

Thom chuckled. "No—"

"Yes, sir," said Erik. "What do you think?"

"I love it, I love it." He reached his arm out the window toward Erik. "Where's your hat? Here's a fiver."

Erik's jaw could be heard snapping open. He leapt up, shook the man's hand, and took the fiver. "Well, I'll be dipped in shit," he said when the man had driven off.

"So will I," said Thom.

Erik did a jig and sunk the fiver deep in a pocket. "Let's stay here. We're artists!"

Thom shook his head. "Ah geez. We're going on a trip. Let's keep moving."

The light turned green, and Erik took up Tree's end of the couch. A group of people from the opposite corner called out and waved, and they smiled. Thom tried to gauge if these reactions were condescending or the type of reaction a crowd had to a freak-circus act and reassured himself they weren't. They turned right at Glisan, following the directions, and Thom thought he felt something shift within the couch.

"I've got to rest for a second." Erik dropped his end of the couch about twenty steps down the street, and Thom lurched to a stop and swore.

"I don't think this is the right turn," Tree said.

Erik sat on the couch. They were down the street slightly and shaded by trees, out of sight of traffic and pedestrians.

Thom stepped out in the street and looked for the William Temple sign. "It's right there," said Thom. Tree nodded, but to Thom he looked bafflingly unconvinced. "It's right there," he said again. "Half a block away. Let's do this."

They picked up the couch again, this time with a great effort.

"What in the hell?" Erik's face was turning red.

"We've come a pretty good distance." Thom backed down the street. He felt tired, and his arms ached. They made it to the loading door of William Temple and rang the bell.

"Finally," Thom said.

"I agree, gets damn heavy after a while. But that was fun." Erik shook his arms out. "Going to have to remember that." He pulled the five dollar bill from his pocket and waved it at them, and then wiped the sweat off his forehead with his sleeve. It began to rain lightly.

The door of the loading bay slowly rolled up, revealing a small dingy area crammed with what appeared to be rejected donations stacked in great disarray. A man in tan overalls with a prominent nose stepped into the doorway, and they all gawked.

"You work at the Goodwill!" Thom said.

"Vhat?" said the man with a faint Eastern European accent. He raised his eyebrows.

Erik glanced uncomfortably at his roommates. "Listen, we know you work at the Goodwill. Don't jerk us around."

"I do no such think." The man backed up a step.

"We just saw you, buddy," Erik said. Thom nodded his head, and Tree stared at the ground.

"I do not tolerate rudeness," the man said calmly. "Thees is not part of my job." He shrugged his shoulders and pressed a button, and the loading-bay door started to roll down.

"Wait!" Thom threw his arms up. "Our mistake, our mistake!" He leaned down to appeal to the man and caught him with an amused smile. "Listen, we're sorry, we've just got this couch, great couch."

Erik jumped forward and reached his arms under the door to stop it. The man delivered two quick whacks with a cane, and Erik jumped back again. When the door was at the man's ankles, Erik gave it a swift kick and then held his toe.

"I never, ever thought it would be so hard to get rid of a couch," Thom said.

"What an asshole!"

"Maybe the couch doesn't want us to get rid of it," Tree said.

Erik lunged for Tree, got him by his collar, and shook. "Shut up, shut up, shut up!"

Thom grabbed Erik and pulled him off of Tree. "You alright, Tree?" Tree nodded and smiled.

Erik pranced around energetically on the curb. "Maybe the couch doesn't want us to get rid of it," he mimicked in falsetto.

"Erik, stop it!" Thom said.

"Sorry, dude, I'm really sorry, but ARRRGH!" He balled his fists. "How hard can this fucking be?! Let's leave it here. That old bastard."

"Leave it here, I wilt call cops." The old man's voice came from a speaker next to the loading bay.

Erik jabbed the Talk button on the speaker. "You bastard!"

"Ha ha ha," said the speaker.

Erik grabbed the speaker and tried to yank it off the wall.

"Erik! That's enough." Thom grabbed Erik's arm and pulled him back.

Erik was frothing mad and wheeled around in several directions until he came back to the couch, which he flailed at until he had exhausted himself. "Alright," he whispered angrily. "We'll take it to the corner and leave it. They'll never be able to find us."

Thom looked skeptical.

Erik gestured at Tree with his chin. "Your turn."

Tree nodded and handily picked up his end of the couch.

"That is the same guy though, right?" Erik pulled on his upper lip.

Thom wasn't good with faces, but the two did seem similar, even identical. Then he realized it made absolutely no sense. "No," he said at last. "They have to be different people."

Thom took his end and noticed that the rest had relieved the ache. They walked about thirty steps toward Twenty-third when the man leaned out of another door. "Don't leave it at zee corner," he shouted after them.

Erik turned and ran back, but the door quickly shut.

"Thom?" Tree said, the quality of squint on his face that of a child before he asks why whales don't have fingers.

"Yes?"

"I want to try an experiment."

"Okay," Thom looked back to make sure Erik was coming. He felt mildly alarmed at being alone with Tree.

"Walk the other way."

"Back toward William Temple?"

"Yes."

"Why?"

"I just want to see what happens."

"Okay . . . ," Thom repressed a sigh. The boy was odd, but it was a harmless request. He looked over his shoulder and backed toward William Temple, keeping his eye on where the old man might come out.

"What are you doing!?" Erik's voice had notched to a higher pitch.

Thom's muscles burned with tiredness. What in the hell were they doing?

"See?" said Tree.

Thom turned back to Tree, who wore a smile of wonderment.

"See what?"

"It's heavier."

"What?"

"It's heavier this way. Watch. Walk back toward Twenty-third."

They changed directions, and Thom noticed he didn't feel as tired, like someone had taken over a share of his burden.

"See?"

"I don't know, Tree."

"Walk back the other way again."

"Stop it! Stop it! Are you idiots!?"

But Thom was curious now, and indeed the couch took on a whole new weight.

Thom looked up at Tree, his eyes wide with surprise. "It's not possible."

Tree nodded. "Heavier." He pushed toward William Temple and then pulled Thom back the other way. "Lighter!"

"You guys!" Erik hopped twice in frustration.

"You try." Thom offered Erik his side.

"I don't want to carry it. I want to get on a bus."

"I'll carry it, I'll carry it. Just pick it up for a second."

"I don't want to, Thom."

"Do it," Thom growled.

Erik gave Thom a hurt look and reluctantly took his end of the couch.

Tree backed Erik toward William Temple and after six feet stopped and changed direction. They took two steps, and Erik shrieked and dropped his end of the couch. Tree fell heavily on the armrest.

"I felt something get off!" Erik yelled.

Thom chuckled. Erik's face was pale, and his eyes showed more white than seemed possible. "There's got to be some kind of explanation," he said.

Tree shrugged.

The old man appeared again. "I call zee cops!"

"We're going, we're going," Thom yelled.

"Run!" Erik hissed.

"Oh, come on, Erik." Thom said. He and Tree picked up the couch and headed toward Twenty-third. "I can't think of what might do that to a couch. Do you have any ideas?" Thom asked, fearing what Tree might say.

"I don't think the couch wants us to get rid of it," Tree said. "At least not here."

Thom shook his head. "That's not the kind of explanation I was looking for." He punctuated five footsteps in a row with a rear-facing, gaseous exhale.

At the corner, Thom felt eyes on them everywhere. There was no way they could leave the couch here.

Thom saw a burrito joint down half a block. "Let's go get a burrito, talk this over." A good deal of the morning had passed, wasted by the couch. Buses were escaping to promised lands. The rain had stopped, and the clouds were beginning to thin out. They put the couch down just to the left of the burrito shack, ordered, and sat eating quietly.

"It's not wet," Tree said.

"Hmm." Erik said.

"It's been raining."

"I know it's been raining," Erik snapped.

"This has been a very unusual twenty-four hours," Thom said.

A kid of about eighteen with a burrito sat down next to Erik, bringing the couch to capacity. "I love that they put a couch out here for us," he said, taking an enormous bite of his burrito. "How do they keep it dry?"

Erik nodded enthusiastically. "Amazing, isn't it? What a smart thing for a restaurant to do." Erik eyed the burrito shack to make sure no one could see them.

Thom smiled. Erik and he seemed to have come to a decision. It was obviously the burrito shack's couch, not theirs. The teenager finished his burrito in about three more bites, waved good-bye and headed on. "Okay," said Thom, and they stood up.

A cop car came to a slow halt in front of them. The cop in the passenger seat rolled down his window and stared at them.

"Officer." Erik gave a quick half-salute.

"We got some kind of call about disturbing the peace, apparently"—he drew the word out and sucked in, looked back at his partner to register the joke—"some kind of issue involving a *couch*."

Erik raised his eyebrows.

"You wouldn't happen to know anything about that?" The policeman let his gaze come to rest on the couch.

"Well, sir." Erik rolled out a hand in explanation, straightened his posture, deepened his voice. "We were trying to donate this couch, seeing as how it's a nice couch, and we're moving just now and not needing it. We were down there at William Temple"—Erik pointed—"and this crazy old codger gets irate, I suspect because my friend Dave here"—Erik gestured to Tree—"didn't think the doorbell was working, and he might have pushed it a time or two too many for that old man's patience." Erik gave a know-what-I-mean look and licked his lips. "We were there just to donate this couch, and before we knew it that man had pulled a gun on us. I'm not one to know when a gun is legal or not, but certainly we knew we weren't wanted there, and so we decided to just go ahead and carry our couch to our new apartment"—Erik gestured down the street—"to see if we couldn't just go ahead and use it after all."

The officer nodded. He looked at his partner and then back at Erik. "Well, see to it that that couch makes it to your apartment without any more doorbell ringing or yelling."

"I sure will, sir." Erik nodded a series of quick, courteous nods.

The police car slowly pulled up the street and turned toward William Temple.

Erik gave his mustache a couple of quick rubs and turned to his roommates. "We've got to see that this gets to our new apartment."

"Good job, Erik." Thom shook his head. "I never thought this would be so complicated."

"They'll be back around, they always are."

"Let's bring it down to the industrial area at the end of Twenty-third and lose it down there. Or we could hit one of these side streets, but they seem sort of crammed with people," Thom said.

"This is ridiculous."

Tree smiled. "Maybe this is it," he said cheerfully. "Our trip. Maybe we were meant to carry this couch."

Thom and Erik ignored Tree, picked up the couch, and headed

down Twenty-third. They had tired of the hassle, and the occasional cheers of pedestrians didn't lift them as much. *What does he mean meant,* Thom thought crossly. *Meant to be* stumbles into faith and belief and destiny. These are not terms to describe furniture-moving.

"Hey," said Erik, "what about Forest Park? We could haul it up there."

"That's kind of littering." Thom looked in the general direction of Forest Park and measured his annoyance at carrying the couch. "But I'm willing to try it."

"Let's take our next left then."

At Irving they turned left, and only twenty feet up the street the couch became unliftable. Erik dropped his end first.

"Couch doesn't want to go that way," Tree said.

"I don't give a rat's ass which way the fucking couch wants to go! I've never had a couch order me around before, and I'm not about to start now."

Thom gave the couch a kick to emphasize Erik's point, which he found he had no problem agreeing with. "This," he said, "is a very strange experience."

"Should we just keep carrying it to the end of Twenty-third then, like you said?"

"Sure, sure." Thom picked up his end of the couch again, and Tree picked up Erik's end. Erik was in the bushes taking a leak. Thom wondered if perhaps the couch was their trip after all. Just like with programming, puzzles were irresistible to him. *Counter weights,* brain volunteered, *magnets, gyroscopes.* The whole feel of the couch was different for him now. This was something special, something unpredictable in his hands, something with a will, or at least an impressive mystery; and it was a bit creepy.

Twenty-third was crossed by alphabetical streets, beginning at Burnside and ending at Thurman. *Eleven blocks to go,* Thom's brain calculated. *A lot of distance.*

A woman leaned out of a lingerie storefront. "Where you taking that thing?"

Erik had caught up with them. He took a half-bow, smiled.

"Why, this is the Couch Across America campaign." The woman laughed heartily.

"We could do that," Erik said after they'd passed.

"Carry it across America?"

"Sure." They crossed another intersection.

"You have a short attention span, my friend," Thom said. "A minute ago we were trying to dump it in Forest Park. Do you know how many miles that is?"

"Sure, sure, it's a lot of miles, lots of miles. I know. This is the Couch Across America campaign. We're carrying this couch across America to fight hunger," Erik announced to a passerby, who looked awed, confused, and suspicious all at once.

"Good luck, hell, good luck!" the man said when he'd determined Erik was being serious and walked away shaking his head like there was water trapped in his ear.

A woman in her thirties with curly, shoulder-length hair sat on a nearby bench. "Did I just hear you say you were carrying that across America?" she asked.

"That's right!" Erik said proudly. Thom rolled his eyes.

"How do you feel about press?" The woman stood and began to walk beside them. She had a bookish air, Thom noticed. As if at any moment she might quote Howard Zinn or Mary Shelley. He swallowed a small lump of fear.

"Like news people?" Erik screwed his face up, thinking about it.

"Like news people." She smiled. "If you're really carrying this across America, you'll want some coverage." She raised her eyebrows to see if she could gather a level of seriousness from the three roommates. Tree remained passive. Thom tried his best for a wry smile. *I might be with him, or I might not.* She winked playfully. Did she really wink?

"Definitely." Erik nodded vigorously. "Of course that makes sense. Definitely. We believe in touching people personally, and that's why we haven't sought coverage before now."

"Ah," she said, "of course." Thom couldn't tell if Erik was playing her or she was playing Erik. Tree and he kept the couch moving. They crossed another intersection together.

"So what news are you from?" Thom could see Erik was in over his head.

"I'm a radio journalist. Public radio."

"I like radio," Erik said and patted a couch cushion, raising a small cloud of dust.

"Great. So I can do a story on you?"

"You bet," Erik said. "Shoot."

"What's your route? I'll have to catch up in a day or two."

Erik turned and looked at Thom, a nervous pleading in his eyes. There didn't seem to be any question as to whether Erik would carry a couch for two days to be on the radio. Thom could tell Erik had as much knowledge of which roads went out of town as he did of radio journalism or the distance across America. Tree had the expression of his namesake. Thom sighed. Should he mislead the obviously interested, apparently intelligent, and quite nice-looking radio journalist by telling her that, yes, the three socially inept nerds were indeed carrying a ratty couch across the United States for no particular purpose that they yet knew of other than they were depressed and unwanted here and sex freaks had broken a waterbed over their apartment? He decided he wasn't morally capable of it. He'd call Erik's bluff, they'd ditch the couch, and catch a bus destined for some special haven for people like them.

"We're taking I-84." His stomach rumbled with surprise at his own words. "We're taking Middle America, I-84 through the Oregon desert, to Boise, Idaho, and on through there. We're not fast. In a couple days' time you should be able to catch us up in no more than an hour, hour and a half maximum. We'd love to do an interview. Awareness brings justice," he added, just to put the cherry on top.

She smiled at him, a whole new level of seriousness in her demeanor. "Perfect. Awareness is what I can bring. In two days I'll head out I-84 and keep my eye on the road. Not much out there," she went on. "That's bleak territory." They crossed another intersection. "You'll need provisions."

Erik nodded fiercely. "Not going to be an easy trip. We know, ma'am."

"I'm Thom." Thom smiled. "Your name is?"

"Jean Sidklowski." She waved. "I guess you don't probably want to shake."

"Erik." He pumped her arm vigorously. "And this is Tree at the front of the couch."

Jean smiled at them. "Thom, Tree, and Erik. I'll see you in a couple of days. Good luck!"

Thom watched Jean walk away. Maybe he could follow her and check up on the roommates in a couple of days. Knowing he wouldn't. Knowing that following would never get him anywhere except sad in some cafe. They carried the couch silently for several blocks.

"So what'd you have in mind here, Erik?"

Erik shrugged. "I've never been on the radio before."

"You are a slut," Thom said. "An attention slut."

Erik shrugged again. "It'd be kind of cool being on the radio. I mean carrying this across America isn't such a bad idea."

"It's insane, pointless, ridiculous, absurd. It's incompletable. It's over three thousand miles, that's walking, over three thousand miles of walking, carrying a large piece of disagreeable furniture. Do you know how far three thousand miles is?"

"She was nice. Let's walk for a day and see how it goes, you know?"

The cop car slowly rolled by, the patrolmen turning their heads like lizards in the sun, their eyes blinking in slow motion. Erik waved.

"What do you think, Tree?" Thom said.

"I don't know yet. The desert doesn't feel right to me. I feel like . . . we're headed west."

"Well, technically we're headed north right now, Tree. We are currently considering taking the couch east, and the fabled bus ride out of here that this whole fiasco was supposedly about would be in the direction south. Does that clear anything up?"

"I still think west," Tree said.

Thom nodded. He realized that if a contest were held now, for the first time in his life, he would be the chosen of the three.

"It's doing something," Erik said. "It's like we're a movement."

"And what do you think the political significance of carrying a couch across America would be?"

"Other people have marches. Or, you know, hunger strikes."

"Yes . . . but they have a cause."

Erik fielded a couple of waves, smiling. Like a politician, Thom thought.

"So all we have to do is come up with a cause. That shouldn't be hard. Don't you have one?"

Thom smiled. This isn't how it was supposed to work—first you felt the injustice, then you came up with the vehicle. But yes, he had causes, plenty of causes: environmentalism, cultural imperialism, rampant consumerism, an overstimulated, superficial culture obsessed with sensation, excessive privatization of ideas, and excessive individual privacy loss. He had causes. Some he even got on soap boxes about when they weren't buried under the shame and heartbreak and struggle of living.

They made it to Thurman Street. It was a busy intersection, with an on-ramp to the I-5 freeway, which led quickly to I-84. Five hundred cars passed here per hour. All of them with purpose, smog tails tracing their paths, making their mark, Thom thought, carving out their own lives, networking, connecting, all part of the interconnected system called society of which they were not. Doing what humans were born to do: to glom and herd. He should be in an office somewhere working on some company's ecommerce engine, making loads of money. That's what his peers were doing. An easy life, of sorts. A forgettable life. A comfortable life with habits, favorite restaurants, potlucks, and girlfriends.

"That way is I-84." He pointed to the right for his roommates. "Just a couple of blocks that way"—he pointed in the opposite direction—"is the Food Front co-op. If we are really going to carry a couch several days east, we're going to need provisions." His roommates nodded, and they began carrying the couch toward the co-op.

"The couch wants to go this way," said Tree.

"It's light this way, but that doesn't mean it doesn't want to go the other way too," Erik said.

Thom rolled his eyes. "Maybe it's just hungry."

At the co-op they left the couch at the front door and bought dry goods, water, snacks, and whatever else they thought they could carry and eat on the road.

"We shouldn't be getting such heavy stuff," said Thom, hoarding his supply, including a sizable hunk of organic, free range, college-educated salami he hoped to conceal from his roommates.

"We'll put it on the couch, maestro." Erik popped a handful of salted almonds in his mouth from the bulk bin. "The couch will carry it."

Thom shook his head. He could go live with his mom. He could get a huge cash advance on his credit card and try to get an apartment here.

The newspaper at the cash register spelled out doom for the computer and internet industries. There was always a war going on, a budget crisis, an environmental disaster. Thom imagined headlines. *Couch Carriers Save World.*

They regrouped at the couch and put the sacks of food on it.

"I'll take a turn, Tree," said Erik.

"How come I'm always carrying the couch and you guys are taking turns?" said Thom.

"You're the big guy," said Erik.

"But the couch isn't heavy."

"That's because you're the big guy," Erik said with a tone reserved for patient explanations.

Erik and Thom lifted the couch and headed back toward I-84. Within a step, Thom felt the weight again. Not a sudden weight, but an increasing downward pull, as if a giant gravity knob were being cranked up.

"Erik, either I'm no longer the big guy or this couch is getting heavier."

"Probably just the food," Erik said, not looking convinced.

Tree nodded. "I thought so."

They took several more steps, and the couch became very heavy.

Erik dropped his end, and Thom lurched to a halt. "Tell me

when you're going to put it down, nimrod. I've had enough of your dropping the couch."

"Shit shit shit!" Erik did his flailing, kicking dance. "I was going to be on the radio!"

"Maybe it just wants to start from the coast," Tree said.

"Okay," Thom said. "Let's think for a minute, let's be sane, let's theorize. Let's just for a minute take it for granted that this is a magical couch—or technology advanced to a state that we think of as magic. First of all, we'd have to admit the presence of magic in a world that is generally devoid of it."

"When it's going west," Tree added.

"Right. Thank you, Tree. And if it is magic, and it is getting us to carry it in a certain direction, can we not also assume that it has a will? Unless we're talking about some kind of magnetic polarization that acts on a horizontal as well as vertical basis. Horizontal movement triggers a vertical effect, which changes willy-nilly— because a minute ago we were carrying it the same direction as we tried to carry it when we headed toward Forest Park, and it was very light that time."

"Uh-huh," Erik said. "Light that time."

"On the other hand, let's not forget to take in the psychological effect. We've had very little sleep in the past twenty-four hours and a lot of shock. In the past four weeks we—at least you and me, Erik—have had very bad luck with job situations. I've lost my girlfriend; we lost our apartment. It could be simply how moving one direction makes *us* feel. We were having a good time on Twenty-third, and our brains wanted us to stay there. That's why it was hard to pull off of that street. We were emotionally disinclined. Plus, truthfully, it's the first activity I've done in a long time in which I wasn't the only entity involved, if you don't count CVS code repositories. We were a team, and that was fun. People's reactions and your mouth made it funner."

Erik smiled at the compliment. Tree waited patiently.

"So what I suggest is that we think positively about going out on I-84. Which might be hard. I'm finding it sort of hard myself. It's a freeway, and we've got a hundred miles to go before the interview.

You're obviously not overcome, Erik. How about you, Tree?"

"I feel like the couch wants to go the other way. West."

"But which direction do you want to go?"

"I guess I want to go the direction the couch wants to go."

Thom closed his eyes. "Okay, but let's assume that the couch, as an inanimate object, as most couches are, doesn't really have a sense of direction much less a predilection for one. In which case, would you like to carry this hunk of wood and fabric out on I-84 to meet up with the journalist?"

"But. . . . Okay."

"Okay, okay," Thom exhaled and shook his fingers out. "I'm going to pretend that the journalist thought we were interesting people and wants to have another talk with us and not that she was humoring us or making fun of one of the most absurd things she's ever heard of, and for that reason it would be interesting to talk to her again, because she's interested in us, and therefore I'm going to will myself to want to go toward I-84." *And toward her*, brain whispered.

"Okay, Professor," said Erik.

"Okay, Mouth. Here I go! I'm excited about going east!" Thom awkwardly hopped up and down. "Let's pick it up again, this time feeling happy. We are feeling happy about going toward I-84. Happy!"

"I've always been happy to go that way," Erik said.

"Just pick up the couch," Thom growled, aware that cars were whizzing by, aware of hopping, of arguing about which way to carry a couch.

They bent down to pick it up, and it lifted easily.

"Great, there we go, that was it," Thom said, relieved he'd figured it out.

They took several steps toward I-84, and the couch was too heavy to carry. They set it down again.

"Honestly, this is going to make me cry," Thom said.

"Think the military would be interested in this?" Erik said.

"Yeah, Erik. The military. Jesus Christ."

"Let's just see where the couch wants to go," Tree said.

"I'm with Tree," Thom said. "I want to find out what's going on here."

"I wish I'd gotten her phone number," Erik said. "We could have had her meet up with us the other way." They picked up the couch and walked west up Thurman Street.

"Yeah, she was pretty. And a journalist," Thom said, wishing, too, a phone number were involved.

"I don't know, she was too . . . I don't know, too librarian to be pretty."

"What? Too librarian?"

"I could go as far as cute," Erik said.

"Then I get the rights to flirt if we meet her again."

"Why?"

"Because I'm more attracted to her than you," Thom said.

"I think she's pretty."

"Well, we won't ever see her again. Which is good, because it doesn't mean we're roped into carrying this thing across America."

Erik shrugged. "I thought it'd be fun."

They walked in silence for a while, passing commercial and residential areas and getting deep into the Northwest Industrial area of Portland. The road turned into Highway 30, which curved to the north along the Columbia River and then west to Astoria, at the mouth of the Columbia, and finally into Highway 101 along the Pacific Ocean. They would pass Thom's ex-girlfriend's house on Sauvie Island. A belt of anxiety tightened around his middle.

"When we come to a resting spot, I want to have a good look at this thing. There may be some kind of strange gyroscopic mechanism inside. By the way, we seriously need to consider a sleeping place. It's the middle of winter. We should have brought blankets. It'll probably rain all night."

"I brought a blanket," said Tree.

"So did I," said Erik.

"Hell," said Thom.

A car passed and honked, two young kids in the back stared.

The streets were deserted. They passed lots full of discarded iron parts, tin buildings with the discordant rumble of machinery inside. They sweated in their jackets.

Thom began to dread the onset of darkness with its threat of rain and cold and nowhere to sleep. He marveled again at where he'd been twenty-four hours ago. Watching TV, his life full of anxiety and no purpose. The only difference now, he realized, was that he wasn't watching TV. They'd reached the end of the industrial area when Thom made the decision that had been itching at the underside of his brain.

"Hold up a second, Erik. Let's put it down. I've got to find us a place to sleep tonight." Erik and Tree looked wonderingly around the edge of the Northwest Industrial district, saw nothing but abandoned, unwelcoming areas, a small workmen's cafe, and no shelter.

They lowered the couch, and Thom went into the cafe, borrowed the phone, dialed an all-too-familiar number.

Sheilene answered. "Hello?"

"Hi, Shei. This is Thom."

"Thom. Where are you? I haven't heard from you in a while."

"I know. It's been a funny couple of weeks."

"It's been a month. How are you?"

"I'm not sure. I found an apartment and lost it, lost my job, and now I'm involved in the strangest thing of my life."

There was silence. "I wish you'd keep in touch."

"I know." Thom paused. "I wasn't feeling that great about things. I thought I'd call when things got better. You know, start off with good news." He tried to chuckle, failed.

"I see. So are things better now?"

Thom thought about it. He'd never been so absolutely without plans in his life. But five minutes ago, yes, he'd felt . . . not quite happy, but intrigued at the very least. "I think maybe," he said.

"Hmm. So where are you now. What's this thing?"

"I'm actually calling to see if I can spend the night at your house."

"Ah. That might be kind of awkward, Thom."

"Well, I've got two friends with me, and we're on foot coming from northwest Portland, and we're carrying a magic couch, and I think we're carrying it to the ocean." Thom smiled, knowing Sheilene would approve of Thom's display of whimsy, that for once he'd be surprising her.

She cackled. "Sure then." Warmth stole into her voice. "I can't wait to hear the story. Skunk misses you."

Skunk was Sheilene's black lab.

"It'll be a while. We won't be there until after dark."

"Watch for cars."

"I think you'll like my friends," he added. One of their problems had been Thom's lack of, and lack of interest in, friends.

"Great. I'll make dinner."

"See you soon," he said and put the receiver in its cradle. He stared at the phone, two pieces, receiver and cradle, paired, one coming to rest on the other. They were matched, they were permanent, they fit.

Erik and Tree had apparently decided to give Thom a rest. They picked up the couch as he came out. Thom jogged toward them and mimed jumping on the couch, and they flinched. He felt happy, and he measured his happiness. Getting back together with Shei was not an option, he knew. He could not be what she wanted, and she knew it too. But staying out on the Sauvie Island farm, wrestling with Skunk, eating Shei's cooking, laughing with Shei as friends, this seemed suddenly all he could desire of life. Shei's house had more feeling of home in it than he ever imagined encountering again. They came to Highway 30 and crossed to the opposite side. Trees loomed over the road. To their right was a hill covered with the wreckage of old shipping equipment, and then the slow Willamette River carrying city sludge to sea.

Their feet and arms hurt, and their hunger grew. They felt the loneliness of the road. Darkness came and with it a light rain. Each of them fell into the black hole of his own thoughts, the dread and misery of what they were doing occupying their consciousnesses, the lack of reasonable alternatives pushing them on. The burden they carried began to feel demanding, no longer a piece of furniture they wished to abandon but an entity that drove them on. Cars lurched past, headlights carving out the dark and leaving them blind. They became a momentary spectacle, worthy of thirty seconds of conversation in cars headed home to warm houses, food, family, the security of success.

They came to their last out: St. John's Bridge, a giant gothic beauty connecting Highway 30 with the northernmost part of Portland. They could walk across and be in a warm bar, stay in a hotel, be a part of the city.

"Only about four or five miles now and we'll be at Sauvie," said Thom.

The last miles were beyond effort. They were a blurred memory of rain and pain and cars, their bodies numb, their throats choking on exhaust.

And then, like a lighthouse beam, a car illuminated the sign for the Sauvie Island Bridge.

They turned onto the bridge, away from the cars on Highway 30, and entered into a thick Sauvie Island fog. "Only a mile more," Thom said, and just saying this made his body ache. Each mile seemed longer than the last, so that this last one, lost in a deep fog in the dark, soaked through from rain, he could only imagine as the unending mile, where his body would finally come to rest, the Sisyphus mile, stuck in a freezing Hades. And then Skunk was barking and wagging his tail and the house glowed and Sheilene was on the porch joking around about the furniture-moving company, her muscular farmer's frame garbed in overalls taking over Tree's end of the couch, remarking on how light it was, what was all the complaining about?

With the couch under cover of the front porch, she gave Thom a giant, tight hug and then to be fair embraced a speechless Erik and an unusually present Tree.

Dinner was yams and salads and the richest of home-baked, wheat-free breads. Peas and red sauce and polenta and wine. Cheese and pie and ice cream and then a bottle of whisky and the easy laughter that comes from exhaustion. Sheilene wanted to know everything, loving the story, Thom knew, whether it was true or not. She had no problems believing anything if told by someone who believed they were telling the truth. If they'd told her the couch could fly, she'd laugh heartily and toast to flying couches and would only become bothered when someone would not believe. She was not a friend of skeptics.

Thom and Sheilene put Erik and Tree to bed like children and stayed up late talking amiably about things not related to them. They talked about the couch, Thom letting himself, at last, be carried away into the fantasy of it, what it was, where it'd come from, what might happen.

"I think it's an old man," Sheilene said, "with hollow bones and a sad heart. A sailor. You're probably carrying him to his fishing vessel."

They talked about the farm, the weather, Erik and Tree. And when it was past midnight, she put her calloused hand around Thom's wrist and led him to her bedroom. They both knew that they were going to have the good-bye they should have had, the good-bye that two lovers who still cared for each other have when they realize their futures are parting indefinitely.

Afterward, Sheilene said, "I heard something the other day that I thought might apply to you. It was by Eduardo Galeano. Know him?"

Thom nodded.

"It was something like—I'm sure I'm murdering it here—Your purpose in life is to find out what your purpose in life is, and then not to let it kill you once you've found it."

"Cheery."

"Yeah. But you know what I'm getting at, right?"

Thom went through the catalogue of complaints she'd registered with him over the course of their relationship. That he was stuck, that he sat at his computer all the time; that he wanted to do good things in the world but didn't, and the weight of it was burying him; that he was dreary, a skeptic, a cynic; that he believed in nothing, that he avoided all human contact; that he was gaining weight; that he was avoiding the important political, emotional, complex human world in favor of the clean, logical, functional world of computer code, that he was becoming a drone; that he was becoming a machine.

"Yeah," Thom said, hoping she wouldn't repeat any of them, knowing they were all true and that hearing them again would make them all sting. Or at least that they had been true before even that world had dropped out from beneath him.

"Then maybe carrying a couch with those two to the end of the earth is exactly what you should do right now. For you, Thom."

Thom woke up several hours before dawn. He watched Sheilene sleep for a while and then quietly dressed and went to walk the property with Skunk, passing the couch on the way out, giving it a few experimental prods. Sheilene's farm was half organic vegetables and half u-pick berries. The winter was down-time, however, and so the workload was relatively small. He cleaned up some brush and branches that she'd pruned, realizing he was sore from the day before. He checked the oil in the truck and the tractor, knowing as he checked that they'd be fine. She was more mechanically inclined than he. He walked across the neighbor's property, and their yellow lab joined him and Skunk to the edge of the island. He watched the confluence of the Columbia and Willamette rivers and stared across at Washington, the state he'd been born in. He picked up a rock and went over its edges with his thumb. The dogs horsed around in the river as the sun came up, biting and splashing, and he looked on the view for the last time and threw rocks as far out into the river as he could until he wept.

Back at the house, he wandered around the downstairs. It was an early twentieth-century farmhouse, with wood floors and Sheilene's dried-flower, rock-pile, bird-feather, pottery-bowl decorating touches everywhere. There was a beautiful old piano neither Sheilene nor he had known how to play and ancient wallpaper mismatched with newer experimental paint jobs. He went through his old office, which had turned into a makeshift library for Sheilene's voracious reading habit. Books were piled in precarious stacks around the room. Where his desk had been, there was a large potted plant. Mysteriously, on the wall were numerous newspaper articles about Thom that he didn't remember being there. Clippings from several years ago when Thom had had his brief moment of fame, when he'd last felt really alive.

Thom snagged the digital camera from his bag, went to the front porch and snapped a photo of the couch. Back in his ex-office, Thom powered up his laptop and plugged into his other reality. He uploaded the photo of the couch to his website with a simple line of text: "Handmade couch of unknown origin, exhibits odd weightless tendencies while moving certain directions. Have data?" Not many people visited sanchopanchez.net. Only friends, open source geeks, and the occasional fan. But those that did usually liked a riddle and would go to absurd means to solve it.

In the kitchen he brewed some coffee and fired up a batch of waffles and waited for the smells to rouse others. Sheilene brought her *I Ching* to the kitchen table, mischievously looking at Thom. Tree and Erik joined them not long after.

"So what's the deal with this couch?"

"We're carrying it across America," Erik said, his fork raised in front of him like a saber.

"America is the other way," said Sheilene, jerking her thumb eastward. "The way you're going is ninety miles of depressed, forgotten places soaked through with rain and alcoholism, and then the ocean."

"Oh," said Erik. Thom noticed his mustache was well on its way and his hair looked dangerous to touch.

"The couch is taking us somewhere," said Tree.

Sheilene nodded. "Where?"

"I don't know, but I think it's far away."

"Astoria is a long way by foot," Thom said.

"The couch let us come here," said Erik. He grinned. "Maybe this is where it wanted to go."

"This has always been a favorite stopping-off place for couches." Sheilene smiled, and Thom glanced at her to see if there was anything to be read in the remark.

"Maybe it wants us to stay here." Erik crammed a huge forkful of waffles in his mouth.

"I don't think so," Tree said.

"Oh, come on, Tree." Erik said. "You're just using that couch to get someplace. Where do you want to go?"

Tree shrugged. "I'm not, really."

"Are either of you familiar with the *I Ching*?" Sheilene asked.

"I am," said Erik. "Ancient Chinese riddle book."

"Yes, it's sort of like that," Sheilene said. She set out three coins with square holes in their centers. "Throw them twice each."

She clucked or whistled with each of their throws, raised eyebrows at Thom, and, when they were done, read from the book.

Inner Truth. Pigs and fishes.
It furthers one to cross the great water.
Perseverance furthers.
Wind over the lake: the image of inner truth.
Dense clouds, no rain from our western region.

The movement of heaven is full of power.
Thus the superior man makes himself strong and untiring.
It furthers one to undertake something.
The lake rises up to heaven.

When she finished, no one spoke for a full minute.

"What in the hell does all that mean?" asked Erik with obvious exasperation. "Pigs and fishes?"

Thom giggled.

"Well, you'll each need to derive whatever meaning you can from it," Sheilene said, focusing on Thom.

"We're going to cross the great water," Tree said.

"Most likely that's a metaphor," Thom said.

Sheilene shrugged.

She helped outfit them. She had a wealth of camping equipment in various states of disrepair in her basement. She fitted them with matches, pocketknives, tarps, a map of Northwest Oregon, eating utensils, a first-aid kit, and spices. To Thom she loaned a sleeping bag, a camp stove and some pots and pans. She gave Tree a hand knit hat and Erik a compass. She gave them jars of jam and dried fruit, bread and cans of beans, soup mixes and water.

Tree in return sculpted from a single long wire three men—big, medium, and small—carrying a couch. "So you'll remember us," he said.

She looked at Thom. "I don't think that'll be too hard."

Highway 30 was loud and unwelcoming, with cars blazing past, all exhaust and noise. Looking down from the Sauvie Island Bridge, they saw railroad tracks that followed alongside the road. The tracks seemed far more peaceful than the highway for couch-carrying, and a movement was made to do the trek on those. The couch felt light and easy, and Thom almost convinced himself that the weight issues of the previous day were imagined.

They pushed the couch down the weedy slope to the railroad tracks, and the three studied them, trying to determine how often trains passed. Erik laid his ear on the rail and declared, "Not a train in a hundred miles!"

The tracks were rusted, but a streak of polished metal gleamed through, tracing a silvery line into the distance.

Thom and Erik carried the couch, stumbling over the ties. Their ankles twisted and blisters that had started the day before began to bloom. Tree walked trying to balance on the rail or guide the couch. They spoke little, issuing only grunts and couch directions. Thom was lost in thought over the Sauvie Island house. Unresolved issues bubbled up in a stew of emotions.

After only an hour or two of walking on the uneven surface they were exhausted. They stopped to apply moleskin to their feet and to take lunch, setting the couch crosswise on the tracks and pulling out various items from their gear, spreading everything out in a disorganized radius.

"Well, this is fun," Erik said after the eating had slowed. Tree crammed more bread and jam into his mouth. All of them had been sweating through their winter clothes, and now the cold set in. The cloud cover was thick, with dark welts threatening at the edges. They rubbed their hands together to keep warm. Thom fought off sleep, comfortable on the couch. Ahead was a black-berry-bush corridor, a hallway of thorns with the rails down the center. It was an inviting green passageway, just large enough for a couch and those who might carry it, but an restricted one, the thorns dense and bristling on either side. Erik pulled out a ciga-rette and smoked slowly.

"Where'd you get that?" Thom said.

"Emergency gear." Erik held it at arm's length and studied it. "Gives you the impression you're warm even if you're not."

"You know, I think I'd like one."

Erik pulled a cigarette out, lit it from his own, and gave it to Thom.

"Yes sir," Thom exhaled. "Three boys lost in the Arctic."

"I wonder how many days it will take to get to Astoria," Tree said. He'd found a second small jar of blackberry jam and was spreading it thickly across a hunk of bread.

"Not more than another month or two," Thom tested to deter-mine his roommates' knowledge of distance and endurance.

"Wow," Erik said, confirming Thom's suspicions.

"I'm joking. It probably won't be more than a week. It'll be hell-ish, though, if we walk on these damn tracks the whole way. We should build some kind of wheeled gizmo for the bottom of the couch."

"Yeah," Tree said, "let's do."

"This vacation is cheaper than I thought it was going to be." Erik pulled a wad of bills from his back pocket. "I've still got, like, fourteen dollars left."

"You're loaded," said Thom.

"I didn't have any dreams last night. It's the first night in a long time that I haven't had dreams."

"That's because a winter day at Sheilene's place is very much like a dream." Thom blew smoke. "I could go to sleep right now."

"How'd that go for you? I've been meaning to ask. I mean, first of all, why'd you leave her? She's, you know, she's a catch and all. Muscular." Erik raised his eyebrows suggestively.

"It was nice there," Tree said. "I wish we could have stayed longer."

"First of all, I didn't leave her. She kicked me out."

"She doesn't seem like that kind of person at all," Tree said.

Erik nodded. "What'd you do? Must have been something bad."

"Well, she didn't kick me out. More like she suggested I leave. I don't know, we just weren't getting along. We had different interests. I went in to work at a job I hated all day, didn't really have any interests other than computer stuff, and she . . . I don't know. She wants a groovier guy, you know? She wants someone a little less of a nerd, someone less logical that can, I don't know, fill up the house more. She admires what I do and all, it's just that, I don't . . . I'm half machine."

"Six Million Dollar Man," said Erik.

"Except not that much."

"The Thirty-Four Dollar and Ninety-Five Cents Man."

"Listen!" Tree yelled.

"To what?" Erik heard a bird chirp, the distant din of the highway.

"Shhh!"

"I don't . . . Train!" Thom tried to yell, but his voice went suddenly hoarse. He leapt off the couch, stumbled to his knees on the uneven tracks, and lurched back to his feet. His giant body became a blur of motion. He started throwing everything they had left on the tracks to the side: bags and shoes and first aid kits and packs and tarps and food. Erik and Tree lifted the couch and each tried to push it the other way. Tree slipped and fell under the couch and then the train rounded the bend behind them.

"Get away!" Thom yelled. "Get away!" his voice came back.

The train let out a whistle that made his molars ache.

Tree stood up, disoriented, and Erik gave the couch a mighty shove that knocked Tree off his feet again and into the blackberry bushes and set the couch on the tracks at an angle. Thom realized there was no way to save the couch short of throwing it up onto the bank. Erik and Thom lay in the ditch. Thom looked up briefly to see the impact with the couch, and then it was gone. A blur of orange, a wooden concussion.

The train passed for what felt like hours. The wheels were just feet from their heads, flinging small rocks violently off into the ditch. When it passed, a ringing silence followed, a sound that was the absence of sound. The couch was nowhere in sight.

Thom and Erik stood up. It looked like their belongings had been air-dropped from five hundred feet. They helped Tree extract himself from the blackberry bushes.

"It's gone," Tree said.

"Well, that's that," Erik said, dusting his hands.

"There's got to be traces of it. It can't have just disappeared," Thom said. His body trembled from fear and vibration.

"It definitely disappeared." Erik gestured to where the couch wasn't. "There ain't nothing left. Think if one of us had been hit. We'd have been exploded into a million bits."

Thom brushed gravel from his face. "I don't think it was atomized. Either it was thrown into the blackberries or it's stuck to the front of the train."

They paused and considered the image of the couch snagged on the front of the train, fastened haphazardly by an armrest, one end dragging on the ground, being torn to shreds as it sped away from them.

"Nahhh," Tree said, clearly shaken. "Couldn't be."

"It could. It's highly possible. Else where is it?"

"Spread out!" Tree yelled. He took four or five steps up the slope into the blackberry bushes to try to get a better vantage point and became immediately ensnared.

Thom watched Tree jerk one way and then the next, as if he were a marionette whose master had discovered a spider in his ear. Then he slipped on the mud and disappeared into the blackberries with a cry.

"Help?" A thrashing came from where Tree had disappeared into the bushes. "Help!"

Thom could feel himself on the verge of giggles. Did he want this? Mothering these two miscreants? He missed the cleanliness, the anonymity, the dullness of computer work, multitasking, keeping his own projects hidden behind the work windows, solid puzzles to chew on, keeping the mind occupied, distracted, insulated from life by function calls, arrays, variables, SQL statements, SELECT * FROM the_brain WHERE memory LIKE "%Tree falling in blackberry bushes%."

Erik ran back from where he'd been searching, and they scrambled after Tree, pushing blackberry branches to the ground with each step. Tree was lying on his side, long blackberry thorns piercing his clothes. With each move, he became further enmeshed. They removed him thorn by thorn and finally managed to pull him to a standing position. He was bleeding from four or five small punctures on his face. Thom picked him up like a child and carried him back to the tracks.

"Lucky you're wearing a lot of clothes. Now all you need is a crown of those, you silly fool." Thom set him down. "That thing could bleed you to death." He gestured loosely toward everything around them.

There were only two ways out: back the way they'd come or onward.

"We lost the couch." Tree wiped a dot of blood from his forehead.

"It'll turn up," Thom said, doubting it would. They were only an hour from Shei's house, he thought.

"It's around here," Erik said. "It's got to be. If not, I think we should go find another."

"Another couch?" Thom said in disbelief.

"Another couch. We'll need another couch." Erik thought of radio journalists, fame. He was having fun.

"You've really become committed."

"We've got to see this through!"

"What is it exactly we're seeing through again?" Thom said.

"This! Carrying the couch!"

Thom looked at Tree, and Tree shrugged. "I don't think another couch would be the same," said Tree.

They trudged on down the tracks. Tree's despair wavered. He was unsure of what was lost with the disappearance of the couch. They walked for a half hour, doubly burdened with their gear. Another sound came from the direction they'd come.

"Train!" yelled Tree, and then Thom heard it too.

They ran to the ditches and lay facedown. The train was coming very slowly. And something was wrong with the engine. It was high-pitched and slow. Then around the corner from behind them came the smallest train Thom had ever seen. It wasn't a train, it was a small platform with wheels. On top of the platform was a great white dog, its head up and its hair blowing back. It looked like the arrival of a king, stoic and regal upon his litter. Thom stood up in disbelief and saw that two men were sitting in low chairs at the back of the platform. One of them killed the motor, and the platform coasted slowly past the three roommates and on up another twenty feet or so.

"Well, what have we got here?" the smaller man said. He was dressed in a bathrobe, wore a hunting cap, had giant glasses on, and several weeks' worth of beard. In one hand was a bottle of beer that he used to gesture. "What have we got here, Edward?" He looked around at the roommates' scattered possessions and stepped off the platform. "Camping?" the man said incredulously.

"Hi," Erik said. "We thought you were a train."

"That we are, that we are," the man said. "We're a train of thought. Peace train. Training wheels. The Train 2000. Has anyone got a cigarette?"

"Yeah." Erik fished one out of his pocket and handed it to him. "Light?"

Erik took out his lighter and lit the man's cigarette.

"Okay, then, what are we all doing here?"

"We lost our couch," Tree said, and Erik and Thom gave him disapproving looks.

"I see." The man took a deep draw off the cigarette. He tipped his head and blew the smoke straight up. "Lost your couch then."

"It was hit by the train"—Tree motioned to the tracks—"and we don't know where it went."

"Trains do that. They hit things, especially if you leave them on the tracks. It's the darnedest thing. Did you leave it on the tracks?" Tree nodded.

"Well, that's your problem right there." The man coughed harshly and finished it off with a few sneezes. "They left their couch on the tracks, Edward," the man hollered over his shoulder. There was no reaction from the cart.

"We think it might have gotten knocked into the bushes."

"Uh-huh. I doubt it, I doubt it." He looked back at the cart, "Want to have a look?"

The large man on the cart stood up, a towering figure. He shaded his eyes and turned in a circle, looking into the blackberries, shook his head, and sat down.

"Uh-huh." The smaller man took a long drink off his beer, a drag on his cigarette, and then exhaled toward the sky again. "Well, hop on then. You're hours from anywhere on foot." The man turned and wove a half circle back toward his platform. None of the roommates moved. "Let's go! Move it!" The man yelled and clapped his hands, and the roommates jumped to action, getting their packs together and scrambling onto the cart.

"Introductions," the man said and waited for them to begin.

Erik pointed first at himself. "I'm Erik." Then the others. "Thom and Tree."

"All right. You're a big man, Thom. I'll need you at the opposite end from Randall." He patted the larger man on the shoulder. "Randall is the fabricator of this great vessel." Thom nodded at Randall, thinking that the man had called him Edward several moments ago. He noticed that Randall was at least as large as he was, a behemoth of a human, with giant features and a great bald head partially covered with a ski cap. Randall returned Thom's nod.

"I'm Theo, Theo the navigator. Theo is short for a longer name that also begins with Theo but which is not necessarily important for you to know, and that's Edward." Theo pointed toward the white dog at the front of the cart. The white dog looked briefly back in apparent distaste. Thom, Erik, and Tree sat cross-legged on the cart and tried to make themselves as small as possible.

It was cramped. Five men, a dog, backpacks, and an electric motor with two car batteries to power it on a piece of wood the size of a king-size bed. Theo started up the motor. It whined and complained, and the cart didn't move. He hopped nimbly off, swayed, and with one hand guarding his beer bottle pushed with the other. When they had a little momentum, he did a dance over the railroad ties until he'd managed to dance himself back onboard. The cart picked up speed until they were moving along at about twenty-five precarious miles per hour.

Thom smiled inwardly and with some embarrassment at the novelty of it, rolling along on this wooden stage as they were. Unsure still if they'd fallen in with bad company—but to be off his feet felt worth it for the moment.

Theo had a case of beer at his foot. He replaced his empty beer, pulled out another, knocked the top off with a swift tap on the side of the cart, and took a long swig. He reached back and grabbed what looked like a tiller, though there was obviously no steering mechanism. They raced round a bend, and everyone leaned to the left to keep the cart from tipping over.

"Now this is moving," said Erik. "This is the way to do it!" Erik felt someone staring at him and looked over to see Edward sizing him up, grimly inspecting, disapproving. "Hey boy, good dog." He held out his hand. Edward stared at the hand and then turned his head back to the front, peering into the distance like a figurehead. Erik hugged his knees.

"Never drive drunk," Theo hollered and toasted everyone with his beer. "Welcome to the Railmobile 1-4-7! So what's all this about a couch?"

Thom realized he didn't have the faintest idea what to say. He looked at Erik, who seemed nervously preoccupied with the dog.

"We're on a quest," Tree said. "We're carrying the couch across America."

"America is that way." Theo jerked the thumb of his tiller hand over his shoulder, mimicking Sheilene's gesture. "And you've got no couch, I feel it my duty to point out. Cigarette."

Erik pulled another cigarette out and handed it and his lighter to Theo.

"Why is it the 1-4-7?" Erik said.

"Isn't that a great number? God, I just love that number." He lit his cigarette. "So what does one go carrying couches across America for?"

Thom managed not to say "We're with the Society of Useless Acts."

"Actually," Tree said, "the couch wanted to go this way. Or at least, it was too heavy to carry the other way." Thom put his head in his hands.

Theo nodded thoughtfully. "So whose quest does that make it, yours or the couch's?"

"Ours," said Tree. "And maybe the couch's too. I'm not sure yet." The corridor of blackberries opened up, and the tracks ran parallel to the highway. Cars full of passengers gawked at the odd half-dozen people on the tiny platform. Theo waved his beer at them, half hello, half go to hell.

Thom realized that he'd found himself among more of the unchosen. But they were of another sect, the superchosen, perhaps, brain adding the new category, people who didn't understand that there are chosen and unchosen people and wouldn't give a damn if they did.

They came to a mild incline that twisted away from the traffic, and Thom could feel the motor lagging. They were a lot of weight for a small electric motor going uphill. He leaned forward, urging the motor on. *I think I can, I think I can*, his brain volunteered.

"Jettison!" Theo hollered and stood up on the edge of the platform, unzipped his fly, and commenced pissing over the side, weaving precariously back and forth. On one deep sway half a dozen hands went up to steady him. A magnificent view of the Columbia River with a freighter in its middle came into view, then disappeared.

"Hey!" Theo pointed with his beer bottle toward the boat. Then he finished, zipped up, and sat heavily down in his chair like a sack of potatoes thrown from the back of a truck. Simultaneously the motor went silent with a clunk and a puff of smoke. Their ascent came to a stop, and their descent commenced.

"Piece of blistering crap!" Theo broke into an awful fit of coughing. Randall reached over and activated a brake, and they stopped in front of the view again.

The dog, facing toward the tracks in front, started barking.

"I know, Edward, I know. But what can you do?" Theo said.

Edward turned toward Randall and barked twice more.

"Too much weight, Eddie," Randall said, and rose up to a towering stand on the platform.

Theo jammed his empty beer bottle back into the case, pulled out a fresh one, and counted how many remained. Edward whined and lay down.

"Shoot," Thom said. "We're really sorry. I . . . obviously we'll walk. I didn't think we'd . . ." *The little engine that couldn't,* brain thought.

"We'll all be shit walking now!" Theo waved his hands in the air. "Afternoon train!" He let out a gust of air, his eyes opening to the size of golf balls. "Cigarette."

Erik dutifully got out a cigarette and handed it to Theo.

"Light."

"You've, uh, got that already."

Theo gave him a skeptical look and went through his many pockets, finally finding the lighter with a measure of delight. "So I have, so I have."

Randall pulled the outer casing from the motor.

Tree stood next to him, and Thom was struck by the drastic differences in size. They seemed two different species entirely. And then Tree began speaking the language of electric motors, first with Randall and then with the motor itself, his and Randall's hands slipping into the casing.

Thom went to stand with Erik and Theo, who were smoking in front of the view. He saw that Erik had managed to wrest a beer from Theo's stash and was working the bottle into his gestures. In deference, Thom supposed.

"So you boys are on a quest. That's good, real good. You've got to have quests. The world has too few quests these days. We could all get off our asses and quest about some more." He nodded vigorously. "But do you know what the quest is for?"

"We might be on the radio."

"Well, that's dandy, but what are you going to tell the radio? That you used to carry a couch, that you're three guys in search of a couch, some kind of Holy Couch of Grails?" He made a sweeping motion with his beer bottle. The freighter slipped slowly from view. "You look a little lost without your couch, not that I saw you with it. You may all just generally have lost looks. Now most likely we'll come across this couch of yours, provided we manage to get rescued from this shipwreck. It might be a bit shredded then, might be a bit destroyed. Might be a mile from here, a hundred miles. But that doesn't give you a reason to do what you're doing. You need some grandness of purpose. If you have the chance, always risk the great failure over the small success. Look at me! Ha ha ha." He gestured wildly with the beer bottle in one hand and the cigarette in the other, and Thom and Erik, on either side, leaned away so as not to be hit by the implements. "You need something big, really big! I mean not something like you're out to find out what the meaning of life is. We all know what that is." Theo winked at Erik, who nodded. "But something like that."

Thom watched Theo take a pull off of his cigarette. He held it too far up, Thom noticed, cradled deep between his first and second fingers with his fingers straight out. *We all know what what is?*

From behind them came raucous laughter, and they turned to see Randall and Tree gripping the sides of the cart and laughing.

"What the hell is so funny?" Theo hollered.

Tree and Randall shrugged simultaneously, like something out of synchronized swimming.

"How about you, big fellow?" Theo turned to Thom.

Thom felt clumsy. For an instant he stifled the impulse to run, imagined himself like an overly fat bear ambling off on two legs, trying to climb over logs and failing, falling on his back like an upside down turtle, like a turtle on two feet, with a bear's head, duck's feet. "Truthfully," he said, and not quite sure what the truth was or what to do with his hands while he thought up the truth, he jammed them into his pockets. "Truthfully," he said, "I'm scientifically intrigued. The couch is . . . heavy and not heavy."

"So you believe that too, do you?" Theo looked back at Tree to make sure he was out of earshot. "I was beginning to think your friend was a little ding-dong." He clocked his head back and forth like a bell.

"He is," Erik said.

"Hey," Theo said severely, frowning. "You've got to have solidarity now. Solidarity!" He raised his beer bottle into the air in salute. "Got to have it if you're on a quest. I suspect you're all a little"—Theo clocked his head again—"and we'll just have to see about this couch thing. But I do like the idea of couch movement. Couches and movement are antithetical by nature, and that's good, that's real good. You've got antithetical working for you. So you're uprooting the sedentary, restationing the stationary, mobilizing the immobile. There's something to that, but you'll need to develop it more. Want a beer, big fellow?"

"Okay," Thom said.

Theo reached into a pocket on the inside of his bathrobe and pulled out a beer bottle, clinking it against several others stashed there. Thom couldn't figure out how to open it. It wasn't a twist off, and the beer was labelless. He realized it was probably home brew. He put on a quick show of pulling at the top feeling stupider by the moment. Erik grabbed the bottle, placed the cap against the neck of his, and gave it a swift whack with his palm. The cap popped off, and he handed the foaming bottle back to Thom—who felt absurdly grateful.

"Good man." Theo nodded. "Solidarity, that's what it's all about. You've got to have your skills, that's important." He patted Erik on the back. "Specialize. Except when you shouldn't, of course. Get over here and stop moping, Edward." Edward reluctantly got up and walked with composure to the edge of the view and sat at a distance of ten feet. Theo nodded. "He's a proud sonofabitch," he whispered to Thom. He looked back toward the cart and hollered,

"You geniuses think you're going to make that thing run again?"

Tree pulled his wire and needle-nose pliers from a coat pocket, began to twist and work the wire, pulling bits out of the motor and putting bits back in. Randall watched over his shoulder with his hand on his chin, nodded once or twice, added a word of caution or advice, nodded.

"Let me tell you gentlemen a story." Theo dropped his cigarette to the ground and crushed it thoroughly under his heel. He stared down at the river and lapsed into a sudden sobriety. "Round about a thousand years ago, there was a young, fiery lad with flaming red hair by the name of Leif Ericson. Leif came from a long line of criminals, not the least of which was his father, Eric the Red, who was kicked out of Norway, and then out of Iceland, both times for murder. Eric headed west and found Greenland, a not-altogether-hospitable place with a heart of solid ice, and started the first European colony there. He tussled with the locals, the Tuniit, and likely gave them a pretty hard time, as they aren't around anymore, as Europeans are often wont to do to the brown-skinned type. Somewhere along the way, Eric the Red had himself a couple of kids with an equally mercurial lass, among which was a boy named Leif. Leif had his father's temperament—a combustible temper and a belief that there was more out there to be found. When Leif saw geese flying overhead to winter on continents his kind had not yet discovered, he yearned to follow, death be damned. Many a time his father's men had dragged him off makeshift rafts he'd cobbled together to sail the Atlantic on—and this when he was only a yearling. He carried with him a constant itching for the unknown. Downright horrible fellow to be around, I imagine. At the age of twenty-four he up and sailed west in search of what he wasn't entirely certain, where he ran smack dab into a little wooded island that later came to be known as North America. You might remember another fellow who ended up there claiming the discovery five hundred years later." Theo nodded repeatedly to himself as if he were discovering this history in a new light. "What is most interesting about Leif is that he sensed what others could not. He paid attention to the signs, even if they were self-made, and was brave enough to bring these to their conclusion. I don't mean to imply that you've created your own story here, but I have no doubt that if Leif were here, he too would notice an oddity with the couch and would carry it westward, against all logic, to where he believed it wanted to go. Or where he wanted to go. Was it an object he followed or did he invent the justification for his own questing? It's often difficult to distinguish among the things that motivate us. Even as we attribute them to external factors, they may be our own."

The motor whirred to life. Everyone turned toward the mechanics, on the verge of applause, until smoke started twisting up from the motor again and they switched it off.

Edward whined, and Theo gestured palm outward toward the dog. "Hey, none of that. Optimism! Look here, Randall and the kid will get it running in nothing flat." He turned back to Thom and Erik. "So that's my story about quests and their purpose."

"Hmm," said Erik. He shuffled his feet in the gravel. "Cool. Didn't Columbus . . ."

"Five hundred years later."

"Wow, so what happened to them?"

"Most were killed by the Native Americans," Thom said, who knew the story.

"Oh." Erik took a sip from his beer and sighed. "So . . . what are you guys up to?" he said to Theo.

"Hate cars." He adjusted his glasses from one skewed angle to another. "Hate 'em."

Erik nodded, not sure whether to pursue it further or not.

"Cigarette," Theo said. And Erik went through the ritual. Theo still had the lighter but Erik had to tell him which pocket it was in. "But I like movement. Randall and I make a bunch of different things that move but that don't use combustion engines. I think them up, Randall thinks up how to build them. Edward does what Edward does. I'm Theo, Doctor Theo," he announced loudly, and then shook Erik's and Thom's hands again. "What do you gentlemen call yourselves?"

"Erik," Erik said.

"Full name, please."

"Erik Glakowsky.

"Polish boy, always like to meet a Polish boy. I'm a quarter Polish myself. Been there?"

"No, sir."

"Better get over there. What's your name, big fellow?"

"Thom Bakker."

"Doctor?"

"What? No, no."

"Why does that name sound familiar? Were you on some kind of cooking show? Wait a second, you're that one guy, aren't you?"

"I don't think so," Thom said.

"Sure you are. You're that guy who, come on now, refresh my memory. The computer-computer guy, right?"

"Oh."

"The monkeys guy?"

Thom smiled shyly. "Yes, I guess I am that guy."

Theo let off something between a cough and a hurrah and socked Thom on the back. "We're practically related," he yelled. "We're kinsman!"

"Heh heh." Thom feeling just slightly less like the nine-hundred-pound bear.

"What about your mechanic, Pine or whatever."

"Tree," said Thom.

"Could use a kid like that."

"Yeah," Erik said. "He's not so bad."

They watched Tree and Randall toil in silence. Thom, despite himself, felt a new courage for being recognized by Theo. That was something that he'd done—he hadn't always been such a wreck. Once he'd been a whipsmart and devious computer hacker before he'd spiraled down to becoming a computer hack at a grocery store.

The motor burst to life. They held their breaths, and then Edward leapt onto the cart with a joyous round of barking.

"Onward!"

"Probably we shouldn't put much weight on it," Tree said.

Randall nodded. "You three walk to the top of the hill."

Theo looked crushed and gave the enterprising dog a withering glare. He handed fresh beers to Thom and Erik and gave Randall a quick salute.

Tree climbed on board, Edward took up position and the brake was released.

They watched the cart go up and out of sight around a curve.

Theo sighed. "Don't care much for walking either," he said, and to emphasize his point stumbled across a couple of railroad ties, started into a fall, and with his body pitched forward he ran tripping and stumbling over more ties, his arms out and ass in the air, things tumbling from his pockets, beer bottles clanking together while he tried to keep his legs under him, then came to a stop off the tracks and up the side of a bank thirty feet down the way, holding his now mostly empty beer up triumphantly.

They continued their slog up the tracks, and Thom began to worry about sleeping situations again. Nightfall wasn't more than a couple hours away.

"So where are you and Randall going?"

"Longview, Washington. We can take you as far as that. After that, you're on your own."

At the top of the hill they saw the couch. Randall and Tree had loaded it onto the Railmobile and sat atop it sharing the comfortable, companionable silence of two people who rarely felt the need to speak. Thom saw that there was indeed something different about it. Like a three-dimensional object on a flat surface, or color in a black-and-white picture, it stood out, seemed larger than it ought to, held your eye.

The couch hung over the sides of the cart, and Edward sat in the small space in front of the couch, staring intently down the tracks.

"Now I'm not saying that I didn't believe you boys," Theo marveled, "but look at that. That's a hell of a nice couch. Nice to see the old hummer in person."

"Just found it here," Tree said, and Randall nodded.

Thom shook his head, not sure how to feel about having the

couch back. He ran his hands over the armrest, looking for damage and finding none. It seemed to be weathering the trip better than he was.

The Railmobile was exceedingly full now, backpacks and gear crammed into the space at the front of the couch with Edward. The three roommates sat on the couch, shaking each other to stay awake. Were they so tired already? Randall and Theo sat in their chairs.

They made good progress, whipping through several towns, citizens gripping their children and pointing at the living room passing by on railroad tracks. They looked like a group of men situated in front of the television for Sunday football, their dog at their feet, hoisting bottles of beer, the man in back smoking like a chimney. Thom felt sure Theo and Erik and Edward loved every minute of it. He grinned shyly and mostly wished he were hiding at the bottom of a well.

Behind them was the active volcano Mount St. Helens and the dormant Mount Hood. To their right the Columbia meandered along, all that remained of the great flood that had shaped the region thousands of years prior. When they wound away from the highway, the territory felt prehistoric to Thom and as if they were the sole occupants for many hundreds of miles. About an hour before nightfall they arrived at the small industrial area across the river from Longview, Washington. The roommates pulled their couch sadly off of the Railmobile 1-4-7. Randall stood and smiled and Theo gave a round of hugs, weaving between them like a drugged tap dancer.

"Careful," Theo said. "Afternoon train will come anytime now. Don't be leaving this precious couch on the tracks, ding-ding."

The couch carriers nodded dutifully. Edward gave a last bark and Randall headed the contraption across the rail bridge connecting one state to another.

"Well, that feels sad," said Tree.

Erik nodded. "That's one hell of a fun life. I hate cars too," he volunteered, and thought guiltily of his broken car parked in front of the diner.

The tracks wound between companies and residential areas for a short way and, with the threat of dogs and security guards, they felt exposed. Erik and Thom picked up the couch and tried to make good time. They quickly remembered the toil of carrying the couch, their blisters resurfacing, ankles sore and twisting on the ties. Then the tracks led into the forest again, following along the bank of the Columbia, the river just twenty feet down a sharp bank. Giant ships loomed over them. Ships with Arabic, Chinese, and Japanese names. English ships and American ships. The engines of commerce importing electronics, exporting grain. Massive holds full of the stuff people never tired of. The highway followed the crest of a hill to their left, far above them.

"We've got to find a place to sleep."

"I wish we could sleep at Sheilene's again." Tree adjusted the knit cap she'd given him.

Erik checked his new compass reflexively.

They came to a wooded area and decided to camp. Exhausted, they ate only a little and spent the twilight and the first hour of dark sitting on the couch watching the river go by. Tree fell asleep immediately. The freighters were lit like carnival rides, gliding by in the darkness, their giant waves crashing onto the banks followed by silence when they'd passed. A drizzle started.

"At least we can discount the *I Ching* reading about the no-rain part," Erik said.

Thom grimaced.

Erik slept on the couch, Tree on the ground at its front, rolled in blankets, and Thom at the back in his sleeping bag. Over the top of them they unfurled a tarp, which was only partially effective in protecting them from the night-long rain.

The rain filtered into Tree's dreams. He saw them surrounded by water, spinning in some kind of current, a hazy threat behind them.

Thom and Tree woke up miserable. The rain had been intense and they'd spent the night thrashing around to avoid the rivulets of water that soaked their bedding.

Thom felt more estranged from the world than ever. Lost in

a no-place with two nobodies on an unidentifiable quest that no one would notice. At least Don Quixote had an author to write up his journey. He got up at first light and paced along the river, trying to warm himself. Tree joined him after a while, looking like an elephant had rolled over him in his sleep. They split one of Erik's cigarettes filched along with matches from a coat pocket, just for the warmth of the fire on the end of it, and watched the water go by. A forested, uninhabited island divided the river, and there wasn't a boat or house or road in sight, only railroad tracks that seemed to stretch for a hundred miles in either direction.

Thom imagined diving into the water, letting it take him, letting it carry his body like a dead seal out to the ocean. The peace of surrendering the struggle was calming.

"I dreamt we would be on water," Tree said. "We would go by water."

"Go where?"

"I don't know. They were strange dreams. I think . . . I think someone is trying to steal the couch. Someone wants it."

Thom couldn't help but laugh. "More power to them," he said. "Right now that'd be fine with me."

"I don't know. I think that this . . . might be important."

They waited another hour for Erik, Thom quietly bitter, until finally they decided to wake him.

Erik was nearly comatose. Thom had to resort to shaking him until Erik finally cracked his eyes, a frightened-animal look in them.

"Get up, Erik. We've been up for hours."

Erik tried to focus. He saw two human forms in front of him and trees beyond. That much he was sure of. He couldn't remember where he was. I've been in a fight, he thought. I've been knocked out. He waited for his body to register pain, but nothing came. I've been drugged then. But the two phantoms in front of him finally crystallized into Thom and Tree, and his memory began to come back. He could barely move his limbs and glanced down in a moment of suspicion to make sure they hadn't tied him up. Had they drugged him? He couldn't remember eating, couldn't remember food at all. He managed to swing a leg over the side of the couch to stand, and then he was facedown on wet earth, where he stayed.

Thom picked up Erik, who had rather suddenly launched himself at the ground. Erik's head rolled back, and his eyes went up into his head. "Tree! Help!"

Tree helped steady Erik while Thom righted his head and opened his eyelids with his thumbs.

"Erik! Wake up!"

Erik could hear the sound but couldn't make sense of it. And then, like surfacing from deep, icy water, he burst into consciousness, hyperventilating, awake and frightened.

"Shhh, it's okay, Erik. You were just asleep."

Erik realized he was yelling and closed his mouth over the sound, opened his mouth again to gasp. "I . . ."

"You were really out. Do you always sleep like that?"

"I . . . no."

"There was a moment when I thought you were dead."

"I'm a light sleeper."

"No, you're not. Trust me."

Thom set Erik back on the couch, but he leapt up and stumbled to a tree.

"What in the hell is wrong with you?"

"I don't know. I just know I don't want to sit on that couch."

Thom sighed. "I'm going to make some coffee." He fished for coffee and the small camp stove in his pack while Tree and Erik talked. He lit the stove, stifling thoughts of escape, and put the coffee on. He realized they were running low on water.

A freighter passed slowly, swamping the shore with waves. He served up coffee to Tree and Erik, who sat on the bank smoking a cigarette. "How you feeling?"

"Not so good," Erik said. "Did you ever put a thing about the couch up on your website like you said?"

"Yesterday morning. It seems like months ago. I forgot all about it."

"Can we check to see if somebody replied?"

"I don't know how far out the radio modem works, but I could try," Thom said.

He fetched his laptop. He had about seventy minutes of charge left on his batteries. The modem connected. He checked email and received five rejections from jobs he'd applied to. He cursed and called up the couch bulletin board. There were three responses already. His roommates read over his shoulder.

12:28 / ip 123.91.2.01 / verified

Thom, you're a loony. Is this a real question or are you toying with us? Here's my go. I did a search (using my s. engine, sam-o-search, thank you, thank you very much) and came up with some interest using search terms like: gravity+couch, supernatural+couch, magic+couch, flying+couch, weird+shit+couch, etc.

Here's this from a conspiracies page: During the cold war with USSR and at the beginning of the Vietnam war, the pentagon had a huge budget for experimental weapons. It was currently the theory that propaganda and mental conditioning were winning wars faster than military efforts. During this time a lot of radio stations were launched—we broadcast American propaganda and anti-communist messages into Cuba, Russia, China and numerous other communist countries. This is all public knowledge. What isn't public knowledge is the testing the pentagon was doing on the American public in mind control. A lot of which consisted of trace additives in food—Aldous Huxley's soma, more or less. They tried everything from subliminal messaging in radio and television broadcasts to [here's where you come in] lacing the fabric of couches with substances that induced apathy. They were fighting just as much of an ideological war at home as they were fighting abroad, but they found, of course, using force in their own country usually worked against them.

Apparently only a couple of couches were made, perhaps each with a different substance and different effect, frankly it was just too expensive to get these couches properly into the distribution channels and the pentagon has never been known for making stylish furniture, and food additives were very successful (eat organic!). No one knows what happened to them.

There you go amigo, maybe you've got the apathy couch, I'd chuck it asap. Never know what other shit they put in there. -Sammy

---

16:04 / ip 212.171.12.1 / verified

Interesting bunch of bullshit that Sammy came up with. He's always been a conspiracy nut. Not that I ever doubt rumors spawned about the pentagon, as I'm sure there's just as much that we've never thought to even spawn rumors about. I didn't do my research here as Sam did, (nor do I have a Maggie-O-Search that I'm desperately trying to promote, wink wink), I just idly mentioned it to a friend because I thought it was a funny sort of joke (knowing your humor) that you'd put up on your site. My friend went to art school at RISD and she said there was a guy in the industrial design department that started experimenting with witchcraft on his designs. Witchcraft is what she said, I don't think she knows a whole lot about witchcraft, but let's assume that he was experimenting with some kind of quote unquote black magic stuff. Apparently at one point he claimed to have given a couch a soul. I thought this was interesting—I don't know if he thought he'd created a soul, or "gotten" one from somewhere else. But at any rate, the story turns spooky as it was said the couch exerted a not altogether positive influence on those that sat on it. I asked her what she meant but she'd heard it third-hand and couldn't elaborate. But the clincher is, the art student later died in a furniture moving accident in which he fell down a flight of stairs and a couch landed on top of him. FREAKY, no? I'm assuming it was THE couch he was moving, but who knows.

What do you need a couch for anyway? Couches are for watching telly. Roller chairs are for computers. Couches: passive, roller chairs: interactive. Speaking of which, how come it's been so long since you've updated the php image libraries? You're not watching a lot of telly? are yOU?

-Mags

00:47 / ip xx.xx.xx.xx / unverified

Hi Thom, I'm a fan of your work. It just so happens that I've been looking for a couch exactly like that. It's a beaut. Would match everything I own. Would you be willing to sell? Name your price. Email me at demx741@mailhaven.com

Thom typed mailhaven.com into a browser and came up with a web-based email service. No hints there. There was nothing unusual about the message, he thought, except that the person had managed to obscure the IP address, and as far as Thom could tell there was no reason to do so based on the message. It set off an internal alarm. He typed a quick reply to demx741@mailhaven. com explaining he was rather attached to the couch and wouldn't part with it for less than ten thousand. Thom set the price impossibly high. If he/she were still interested, then either the individual had plenty of money, someone was just fucking with them, or the roommates had a hold of something very valuable.

He powered down his laptop and tuned into the heated debate going on between Erik and Tree.

"That's why I was so freaked out when I woke up." Erik's eyes were wide. "Probably that soul did something to me in my sleep!"

Tree looked over at the couch and then looked back at Erik. "Do you think you can really put a soul in a couch? Where do you even get a soul?"

"How the hell do I know?"

"I don't think the couch has a soul, Erik," Tree said.

"Then I was drugged!" Erik's voice bumped up an octave.

For once, Thom saw Tree was playing the skeptic, and he joined in. "There's definitely something unusual about the couch. Maybe it's even drugged and has got a soul. But believe me, Erik, you can get any kind of thing off of the Internet. Before the day is out I bet there'll be several more bizarre rumors for you to choose from. Some of them will be my friends trying to out-best each other's stories. It's normal. Especially for my site, which isn't usually the epitome of sincerity."

Erik looked unconvinced. "Listen, I know when something weird happens to me. I'm not sleeping on that couch again."

"That's okay with me," Thom said. "I slept miserably."

"At your own risk, man."

Thom changed the subject. "Someone wants to buy the couch, and we can name a price. I told them ten thousand."

"Ten thousand!" Erik yelled. "Hell yes! Yes yes yes!" He hopped up and down, trying to click his heels together.

"I'm not selling," Tree said.

"What!?"

"I'm not selling. I have first claim to the couch."

"Okay, listen, I'm not either," Thom said. "Let's not get into this. I just put it out there as bait to see if they were really serious."

"What in the hell is the matter with you people?" Erik rubbed his mustache furiously. "This is a couch! Ten thousand is ten thousand dollars!"

"If the first person who comes along is willing to pay ten thousand dollars, then we have something very valuable. If they really offer that—and I'm trying to express extreme doubt here—then let's talk about it."

Tree nodded.

"Okay, okay," Erik said. "I see. Good idea. Then we could say twenty thousand. That would be better."

Thom stretched his neck and tamped down a smile. Point number one why Erik isn't a salesman, he thought. "I think it was a hoax, so don't get your hopes up."

They packed up. Their gear was wet, and a steady breeze made their fingers go numb. Erik, who still had a drugged look in his eyes, refused to carry the couch.

"Erik, you're going to have to chip in at some time," Thom said.

"I don't want to carry it."

Tree stared at Erik for a long time without saying anything, then said, "You have to carry the couch, Erik. It's your quest now too."

Like a firework whose fuse had run out, Erik sprang at Tree, grabbed him by the collar, and began to shake him. Thom watched Tree's head flop back and forth on his neck, and then he was there restraining Erik.

"What in the hell has gotten into you?" Thom held Erik by his collar.

"That couch is fucked! It wants to fuck with us. And we're letting it! Look at us carrying it. What in the fuck are we doing? Like a bunch of manslaves. I believe everything now—that couch was trying to kill me, and I don't want to get within a million feet of it. We should sell it! We need money!"

Thom's brain automatically calculated the mileage of a million feet, a machine, feed in a number, answer is? "That's just under two hundred miles," Thom said. "Let's carry it for two hundred miles outside of Portland, and then we can go home. Besides, I'm carrying it because I want to."

Erik shook his head no. "I'm through."

"Erik, would you please just be reasonable for a minute?" Thom said. "We had a tarp over us, it was extremely dark, the sound of rain hypnotizes, the tarp probably made it so you were breathing a higher carbon-dioxide content than usual, it was a strenuous day yesterday, you were just really asleep. Don't be so damn reactive. You were always this asleep at the apartment too."

"I slept on the couch then too! Why can't you believe me for a minute?"

Thom sighed and appealed to Tree, who said nothing.

"Fuck you, you patronizing, fat sonofabitch," Erik added.

Thom clenched his fists and then shrugged. They were all packed up. Thom picked up his end of the couch and waited for Tree. Why was he arguing, he wondered. It was just a couch. And he'd only known the guy a couple of weeks or so. With the couch in his arms he felt the ache of his feet and ankles. Tree and Thom started out again, leaving Erik smoking angrily on the bank.

He realized he was quite a bit more excited now that he'd read the bulletin board. Someone wanted the couch. It didn't make sense. You don't buy couches over the Internet. Or maybe you do, but not used couches with no antique value. Or was it an antique? Most likely the interested party had no idea where he lived. He could be in Seattle or New Orleans. Shipping on a couch couldn't be cheap. And shipping would probably depend on how much the couch weighed, he thought with amusement.

They rounded a bend and lost sight of Erik.

"Do you think he's really not coming?" Tree said.

"He's coming," said Thom. "He just had to make his point, and now what's even tougher is he's got to find a way to join up with us again without feeling like a fool. His mind is fixated on the possibility of money. I played this trick through my whole youth, the stomp-off. He'll be around."

Tree nodded.

"What's strange about Erik is he's a conman, so he makes his living by enticing others into a pseudo-reality. But he also believes the stories of others easily. You'd think he'd be a little more cautious." Thom readjusted his grip. "Okay, let's talk about the couch. I want to hear everything you think, no reticence."

"It's hard to know what to believe, Thom, like you said, or if any of those couches are related to this one."

"True, true, but the last one about someone wanting the couch, that is very bizarre. Unless it's a joke or something."

"I knew someone wanted it, maybe a lot of people."

"I don't feel I should believe it, but I do. That's why I want to keep carrying it, I guess. Isn't this what everybody wants, for something different to happen to them? We figured out the secret, you just have to be so desperate and broke and lonely that something happens. Voilà!"

"Voilà," Tree repeated.

"So come on, tell me about someone wanting it and the water thing."

"I don't really know. I just . . . it's just a feeling. Sometimes my dreams are more vivid, and I could tell you details, but . . . Well, I'll tell you this, I got an image of us sitting on the couch, and it was floating in water."

"Ha ha," said Thom. "There's no way this could float. Right?"

"I also think . . . I think there's some people who want us to have the couch."

Thom nodded, stuck in the limbo between humoring Tree and trusting him. It was a familiar sensation for Thom as of late—stuck on the fringe of belief. He worked back through the details he knew. Someone wanted the couch, someone wanted them to keep the couch, the couch had some weight issues, it had some sleep issues. Maybe it was the CIA's, or maybe it used to be owned by a dead design student. Maybe it was just an old orange knit couch they'd inherited from the apartment. They were on a quest. Were they on the couch's quest or their own? What would he quest for if he did quest? *How many quests could a woodchuck chuck,* brain said.

They'd started early, and it would still be some time before

Thom felt like they could justify stopping for lunch. Thom was in front and he'd turned around, carrying the couch against his back, partially so he wouldn't have to look Tree in the face for hours on end. There was still no sign of Erik, and he began to wonder if they really had seen the last of him. Such a bad parting, Thom thought. It wouldn't be fun with just two.

After another mile or so, the tracks veered away from the river, near houses and through several intersections. A dirt road pockmarked with puddles ran alongside the tracks. At the third intersection, Jean, the journalist they'd intended to meet going east, leaned against a car. Her curly hair was wrapped up in a kerchief. She wore glasses, a thick canvas jacket, leather boots, and men's slacks low on her waist. Thom did what he always did when he approached a woman he was attracted to; he tried to find the quickest way out. His mind worked through a thorn-infested escape toward the river, and then it was too late.

"You're a bit lost, aren't you?"

"Yeah. About that . . ." said Thom. "I-84 is up here somewhere, right?" They set the couch down a safe distance to the side of the tracks. Thom glanced at his watch, wondering if the trains ran on a schedule. "How'd you find us?"

"Well, that's a funny thing. You know I drove for several hours out on I-84 yesterday, and what do you know, there was no sign of you. I got home and just happened to ring up my father, and he said he gave a lift to some funny gentlemen carrying a couch."

"A lift?" Thom traced the day before and couldn't remember being in a car, and then remembered. "Your father is Theo?"

Jean smiled. "I know, I know all about him. You don't have to give me that look."

"He was great," Tree said.

"Thanks. The comments I get about him are generally all over the place."

"So you talked to him and—"

"He told me where he left you. We decided you'd probably camped right away, and I figured if I got an early start I could be up here in time. I'm pretty familiar with these tracks, as you can imagine."

"I can imagine," Thom said.

"So how's the big journey coming, besides the, you know, compass issues. Where's your friend?"

"Erik is having sort of a hard time with us, as well as the couch, right now." Thom studied her and wondered if they were really doing something that merited being followed by a journalist. He wanted privacy to figure out what was happening here for himself before anyone else was involved—but then he wanted her validation . . . *And let's be frank*, brain said. *You want her to admire you.*

"Yo!" Erik jogged toward them.

"Ah, looks like he's recovered," Thom said. "There have been some issues around the couch."

"Issues?" Jean said and saw Thom and Tree exchange glances. "What sort of issues?"

"Truthfully, I don't even know where to start."

Erik jogged up. "Hey, guys, how's it going? Jean," he said and stuck out his hand, "good to see you."

"Hi, Erik. I heard you had some issues with the couch."

Erik glanced at Thom and Tree. "Nah," he said. "I was just taking the morning off."

She raised her eyebrows.

"Well, I had one or two tiny issues with it." He smiled and looked apologetically at Tree. "Tiny little ones. And maybe I . . . expressed my issues dramatically. And maybe I thought the couch was trying to kill me, us, for just a tiny, little moment, ha ha. But I'm over that. I'm shipshape now." Erik did a couple of quick half-squats, balled his fists and waved them in the air like a cheer.

"That doesn't sound *entirely* sane, but I'm sure it is," Jean said. She gave Thom a mock worried look.

"It's not a normal couch," Tree said.

"We have had a little bit of couch gossip. We've done some speculating," Thom said. A pressure began to build on his lower intestine.

"I'm not getting the story here," Jean said.

"Well," said Thom, feeling his face redden. "This is pretty hard to explain, and it's not going to be very believable. The reason we didn't go out I-84 was because the couch was too heavy to carry that way."

Jean squinted.

"What I'm saying is, we've noticed times that the couch is heavier going one way than the other. And we've tested it. I'm positive it's not an attitudinal thing."

Jean shook her head. "I guess I'm having trouble believing you."

"I understand," Thom said.

"The other thing," said Erik, "is the couch tries to kill you when you sleep in it." Erik did his best to say this like a joke.

"Ha ha," said Jean. She took her keys from her pocket and fondled the ignition key.

"Erik feels that the couch has put him in a deep sleep every time he's slept on it." Thom eyed the keys in her hand. "The best I can do is assure you that we're not going crazy and that we're approaching the couch in a scientific manner." His stomach gurgled. A scientific manner, he thought. What the hell was he talking about?

"Jean," Tree said. "Try it." Tree picked up one end of the couch and waited for her.

"No. I probably shouldn't." She turned toward her car and then changed her mind. "Oh, what the hell," she said. She walked to the couch. "Is there some kind of method?"

"Just pick it up. I'll show you about the weight," Tree said.

Thom tensed. Maybe they were all delusional. He willed the couch to be strange.

She picked up the couch, and Tree took her through the back-and-forth routine. The expression of skepticism turned to surprise and then wonder on the next back and forth. "Okay," said Jean. "That is very, very odd. Did you tell my father about this?" She ran her hands over the couch, inspecting it.

"No. Theo is Jean's father," Thom said to Erik.

"Wow, I love that guy!" Erik reached out and shook her hand again, and she smiled. "You believe us now, right?"

"I have to believe you about the weight." She shook her head. "Really that is just very strange. I can't imagine what kind of mechanism could do that."

"Only a gyroscope," said Thom. "That I know of. But you've got to spin it, and nobody has spun this one. The bottom is impossible to get open—you can't cut into it with a knife. Unless, unless it's some kind of perpetual-motion gyroscoping . . ." Thom's voice trailed off.

Jean nodded. "You must understand, for one, I'm a journalist, and objectivity and truth are hypothetically sort of high on my list, so you shouldn't take it personally when I doubt you."

Thom nodded. "I know."

"And secondly, if I go writing stories about a couch that's a different weight when you carry it a different direction, I might not have a job after a while."

"I know. I put up a bulletin board on my site for people to talk about the couch. Mostly it's weird, but interesting nevertheless. I'm a programmer, and this sort of stuff doesn't work into my belief system very well either." Thom borrowed her pen and wrote down the address for his website.

"Sanchopanchez.net? That's your site?"

"Yes."

"You're Thom Bakker?"

"Geez. Your father recognized my name too. I've never met so many people who knew who I was. It's really, really rare," he said more to Erik and Tree than to Jean.

"Don't take this wrong, but you're a hero of mine."

"Hero." Thom belched and put his giant hands over his face, feeling like a polar bear. "Just a moment," he said, and then added, "I think I'm taking it wrong."

"What's all this about?" Erik said. "Some kind of computer thing?"

Jean nodded. "You guys don't know?"

Tree and Erik shook their heads.

"You're traveling with a famous criminal," she said, and Thom blushed again.

"Wow," said, Erik looking impressed. "What'd he do? What'd you do, Thom?"

She eyed Thom and then after a minute said, "I'll let him tell you."

"I'll tell you later," Thom mumbled, feeling like a fool with his hands over his face. Just be normal, he counseled himself, take the compliment, say thank you, change the subject, say that's a nice jacket. He breathed deeply, removed his hands. "That's a nice jacket," he said.

Jean looked down at her jacket. "But anyway," she said, "that is interesting. It adds a whole new angle to the possibility of a story, though then again, I'm not sure if I've got a story here."

"Why not? It's more of a story now, right?" Erik said.

"Well, when I left you last it was a human-interest-type story. You were carrying this couch across America to fight hunger or something."

Erik smiled. "That's right! That is what we're doing." He nodded twice sharply, then worked a couple of expressions with waning confidence. "Actually, no, you're right, that's not what we're doing." He looked at Thom for help.

"We don't know what we're doing."

"Thom!" said Erik.

"Right," Jean said. "There's no story yet, partially because the couch is . . . whatever the couch is, and that makes it a lot more complicated for me. That doesn't mean I don't believe you have something going though. You do. You've just got to figure it out."

"I think we're going somewhere far away," Tree said.

"Okay." She smiled. "Here's my card so that you can get a hold of me." She handed them each a card. "That still doesn't help me much. Have you got any ideas on what you're doing?"

"Sure, sure," Thom smiled. "We're an absurd quests movement."

"Yeah, that's how I feel coming out here to interview you. But really, that I could write an article on. But I don't think you can be doing that with a couch like this."

"I know," Thom said. "I've been thinking about what Theo said, that this could be more of a symbolic protest against modern American culture. We're taking the symbol of sedentary life, and we're making it an action."

"Hmm, an anti-apathy protest?"

"Yes, something like that."

"I like it. That would be fine, except, again, the couch issue. If it were a normal couch, yes. Go get yourselves a normal couch and I'm set and the article is written."

A large Ford truck drove up and came to a stop next to Jean's car. A man leaned out with sunglasses and well-groomed hair. "Is that an abandoned couch there?"

"No, sir," Erik said. "It's ours."

The man slowly removed his sunglasses. "I see. How much do you want for it?"

"It's not for sale." Tree put his hands on his hips.

"It's a nice couch. Are you sure you wouldn't consider an offer?"

Tree repeated that it wasn't for sale. Erik asked the man what his offer was.

"Seems to be a little dissent among the crew." The man smiled. "I'll give you two hundred bucks. Good price for an old couch."

Erik pointed at Tree. "He's right. It's not for sale."

"Five hundred then."

"Sorry," Thom said.

"A thousand."

"It's just an old couch," Jean said. "Is it really worth a thousand dollars to you?"

"Sure. I've been looking for a couch just like that. It would please the missus to no end. I think a thousand dollars to please a lady is a reasonable amount."

"Is the couch for sale, boys?" Jean said.

Thom shook his head. "I hate to disappoint your wife, but I think we're going to hold on to the couch."

The man drew his lips tight over his teeth. "What if I were to offer you two thousand?"

"It's not for sale!" yelled Tree, his voice wandering across octaves. "Go away!"

"No sense in being rude about it. Have it your way." He did a slow U-turn and drove off in the direction he'd come.

"Uh, two. Thousand. Dollars, Tree! I think we need to huddle here pretty soon and talk about some things. Two thousand dollars!" Erik yelled. "Idiots!"

Thom nodded. "We sure do. I wish I'd thought to ask him what his email address was."

"Well, that was extraordinary," Jean said. She pulled a pad from her back pocket and thumped it against her thigh. "This is definitely a story. I just don't know what the hell it is."

"You alright, Tree?" Thom said. Tree stood with his hands clenched. "Tree?" Tree looked at them blankly for a moment and then relaxed.

"Hi," Jean said. "Remember us?"

"Sorry," Tree said. "I'm just nervous. Other people want the couch."

"Nervous! You're more than that." Erik threw up his hands. "You're insane. It's an effking couch!"

"He would have offered more than that," Jean said. "He was doubling the price without much hesitation. That man wanted your couch. Anyway, that reminds me, I brought you things. You seem a lot more prepared than the last time I ran into you, but I brought food and water. You probably won't be needing the map of I-84."

They rifled through the things Jean had brought them.

"Even a bottle of wine," said Jean and smiled, pulling a two-liter bottle of red wine out of a paper bag.

"You're a goddess," Erik said and grabbed the bottle.

Jean smiled at Thom. "Don't be telling anybody. I don't want to be seen bribing my story. I'm supposed to be the neutral observer, not the . . . ah . . . goddess."

Thom risked a friendly wink. Perhaps he could mean it as the neutral observer, semi-neutral.

Erik uncorked the wine. "Why don't you come with us?" He took several gulps off the bottle, and they passed it around.

"I don't think so," she said, "though I'm not going to say you don't make carrying a couch look fun."

She'd brought picnic fare: bread, cheese, olives, grapes, and the wine, and they feasted on the hood of her car, the couch just to the side of the tracks.

A train roared by, and they collectively cheered in relief and then had to tell Jean about the mishap of the day before.

They left Jean waving good-bye and promising to meet them in Astoria in two days. They carried the couch around a bend in the tracks, and the journey took on the feel of an occupation. The forest loomed on one side, the river coursed deep on the other, and they traversed the thin trail between, where they felt the loneliness of a journey with an unknown destination, the melancholy of a quarter of a two-liter bottle of wine each, the anxiety of leaving civilization.

They trudged on. Erik took turns again on the carrying. The tracks twisted close to the river, putting them in view of the freighters and fishermen, and then away again, through industrial areas. They went under grain silos and passed concrete and gravel plants. They had a run-in with a dog—Erik threw rocks and growled back while Thom and Tree hurried the couch by.

They walked through a town, looking like some medieval band on a supernatural crusade, a grand parcel in tow, bruised and dirtied and limping. A young farmhand driving a battered pickup pulled up and offered a ride, and Tree declined.

"We don't always have to carry it," Erik grumbled. "I don't know what the difference is. Back of a truck sounds pretty nice."

"We won't know which way it wants to go if we don't carry it," Tree said.

Erik looked at Thom, who shrugged, and they left it at that. Thom traded Erik positions on the couch, and Erik ran up to a gas station and brought them back candy bars, cigarettes, and sunflower seeds.

"Oral fixations!" he announced, arriving back at the couch caravan. He passed out the candy bars, and Thom realized he was having fun. You don't know how depressed you are, he thought, until you utterly change your situation. He remembered how he'd been spending his time, sitting at his computer sending out résumés, being beaten over the head by a wet umbrella. They were on an adventure. They set the couch down next to the tracks across from the town's main street, sat on it, and ate their candy bars. Cars honked or people stared. Erik looked uncomfortable sitting on the couch for the first thirty seconds, and then relaxed back.

"I hope we're saving the world," Thom said.

"That'd be cool," Erik said. "We could be stars, meet girls."

Thom tried to think of someone who had saved the world and felt suddenly the world was short on world-saving heroes. Perhaps saving the world was impossible unless you were the fellow who refused to push the big red button when the time came. There were millions of heroes, each saving a very small part of the world. When Thoreau had been jailed for civil disobedience, Emerson had come to visit him in jail and asked, "What are you doing in here?" And Thoreau had answered, "What are you doing out there?"

Jean had called him a hero of hers, but could he really be a hero for such a silly thing? She had aroused in him a desire to do good, or a desire to do something, to make something matter, to be a real hero. Rosa Parks and Akira Kurosawa. Ansel Adams and Denise Levertov. Did they get all the sex they wanted?

"Okay, so this is what I did."

"Oh, Mr. Hero is going to educate us finally," Erik said.

"It's not really a big deal. I got into a little bit of computer trouble a couple of years ago. Mostly it's made it hard to find a job, for one, and mostly it was because I was immature and a bit proud." Thom faded off, wondered if perhaps that was all he needed to tell them.

"Annnnd?"

"Alright. I had a bet going with some friends. You know that saying about a thousand monkeys with a thousand typewriters could write all the literary works if they had eternity to work in? I said it was impossible, and friends were telling me it was statistically possible. I won't go into the argument, but anyway, I knew where I could get a thousand monkeys and a thousand typewriters; I just needed to come up with eternity." Thom noticed he was getting baffled looks from his audience. He forged on. "What I did was write a program that installed itself on computers, a virus, more or less, and that virus then downloaded and installed another program. The second program was a lot more substantial. Its job was to link computers together to work on a particular problem, or in this case to output random characters. To make a long story short, I took a bunch of computers and made it one big computer. And I set that big computer to writing all the world's literary works. I never did resolve that bet. . . ." Thom looked off into the sky.

"That doesn't sound bad," Tree said.

"Well, I did it to a rather well-known company in Redmond, Washington, and basically used the processing power of about sixteen hundred of their computers to try to do it. Had them going for a full five and a half hours . . . each of those computers typing letters at random, with a dictionary filter to flag pronounceable words, some grammatical filters in there too. All of those 'monkeys' were generating a massive amount of random keystroke data. There were other little details, like I weighted the space bar; because of its size, a monkey would likely hit it more often. That's a hell of a lot of processing time, and a hell of a lot of data leaving through the pipeline. Just over a year of processing power in a little over five hours. If you think about it in terms of monkeys, those computers each could churn out thousands of characters per second. I estimated a monkey churns out one to two characters per second, and we're taking it for granted these monkeys are on some kind of hyperstimulant and thus never need to sleep for all eternity. So if you do the math . . ."

Erik and Tree watched Thom move his lips and stare at the sky for a bit.

"It was more like having 2,666,667 monkeys typing for five hours. Or, if you flipped the monkeys and time, that'd be fourteen hundred and sixty-seven days of a thousand monkeys with their thousand typewriters pounding out one to two characters per second around the clock—or the equivalent of ten novels per hour. I racked up just over four years of monkeys and amassed three hundred and fifty-two thousand novel-length works. Somewhat shy of eternity, but it was really cool. I got caught, and they claimed I'd cost them a fortune. . . . Sixteen hundred people unable to work for a day, plus their network was shut down and the time it took them to fix the computers and undo any supposed damages. A million in damages." Thom grinned.

"So what happened?" said Erik. "Did you go to jail?"

"No. Almost. The computer world is a funny place. In the settlement, I had to give them the rights to the source code for the program, and I was on probation. They sell pieces of it now, and believe me have more than made up for the money that they said I cost them."

"Holy shit, you mean you could have sold it in the first place?"

"I suppose so."

"You're crazy, man."

"Yeah, I guess. I wouldn't be here with you ducks if I'd sold it."

"Did it write any books?" Tree said.

"Good question. Possibly. There are some grave problems with the original question. Is the monkey required to write a complete novel, sans nonsense? Or could they contribute only a single line? All we need to do is read back through a hundred and ninety billion characters for some plot structure. As soon as we can make computers that recognize plot . . . Well, we'll be making us, we'll be making humans, we'll be God. Which was my original point anyway."

"How did they let you do that? Don't they have something that'd catch viruses?"

"Well, a lot less than you think but . . . ah . . . I was working there at the time. The message was generated internally from the human-resources department—I sent them a Christmas card in the form of a script. People trusted it. And when they double clicked on it, they got a real Christmas card. It was a silent virus. They didn't even know they were infected until a month later when I ran the monkeys." Thom shrugged. "I think someone could do it from the outside as well. And even though a lot of people were outraged, some key people thought what I'd done was very funny, interesting, I hope, and I suspect they let me off a bit easy. I was fired, of course."

"That's cool," said Erik and patted him on the shoulder. "You're a nerd, it's obvious, but that's a cool thing to do if you're a nerd."

"Thanks, Erik. I'm glad I have your approval."

They used Sheilene's map to try to spot a good campsite. They found a secluded, deeply treed area along the bank of the Columbia. It was a dark campsite, enshrouded in shadows, but after a day of wary looks from townspeople, the privacy appealed. The tracks wandered inland away from them, and they weren't eager to begin the inland trek away from the river in the morning.

They set the couch up on the side of the campsite closest to the river and cleared areas to sleep. Tree made a fire, and after numerous tries with wet wood finally got the flame to stick. With an hour of light left in the day, Tree boiled water on a rickety setup over the fire and began making a potato and onion soup, expertly cutting an onion with no surface to cut on. Thom set up a makeshift shelter using the back of the couch as one end, and Erik busied himself with finding an obscene amount of firewood until, bored of that, Thom saw, he did some sort of silly looking martial-arts thing facing the river.

Thom wrapped his laptop in layers of plastic, fearing another rain, and stayed as packed as possible. Erik had done his best to spread his meager possessions evenly over the campsite, as if he were planting seeds for a later harvest of better gear.

With the soup cooking, they took up perches on the bank, dangling their legs over the three-foot ledge, the river running fast below them. Erik handed out sunflower seeds. The sun pierced through a cloud-covered sky at the very edge of the horizon. They spit shells into the river, watched the water take them, Lilliputian craft spinning helplessly in the current, then talked idly and quietly. There were bird sounds and the unsettlingly lonely hoot of an owl. The deep throat of a giant diesel engine as a ship passed. Night fell, and the fire emphasized the darkness, the rest of the world a painting that had been blotted by a sea of ink.

Thom fought a paranoia that something was just beyond the feeble arm of firelight, something watching them. They transferred the sunflower seed shell-spitting into the fire and waited for the soup to finish. The shells twisted and cracked in the heat.

"People used to be able to just go places," Erik said. "We're along railroad tracks, and that's why we can more or less walk in a straight line. But all this is owned by people. Fences everywhere. You can't walk anywhere anymore."

"Been that way for quite a while."

"A couple hundred years ago you could get on your horse and see the country," said Erik. "The Indians had such a more intelligent idea of ownership."

"Well, the people settling were farmers," Thom said. "They had reason for fences."

"Some had, others were just greedy. *I* think."

"Yeah, I suppose so. It's true that the world is colonized—there's nothing left to make you feel free, like you could head off into the unknown."

"Exactly, exactly! That's what I'm talking about. What if you don't want to earn money. Be stuck in this. There's no way out. If you try to do something different, then you're unpatriotic. I'd love to be a hunter-gatherer."

"That soup smells so good I can't believe it." Thom's stomach ached hollowly. "When's it going to be ready?"

"Another ten minutes."

"You've got these people that get off the grid," Erik spit a slough of shells into the fire.

"Watch the soup," Tree said.

"Sorry. And that takes a lot of money. I mean I guess you could live in a cabin in the woods without electricity and water and whatnot."

"Some communes emulate tribal systems," Tree said.

"Yeah," said Erik. "I guess what I'm saying is I would have loved to live sometime in the past when the struggle for survival had something to do with how you were able to find food, firewood, build a place, ride a horse, fend off the wild . . . and not how well you could bag groceries at Safeway or," he gestured toward Tree, "make sure somebody's lawn had the right level of grass"—he nodded at Thom—"or type numbers into a screen."

"What I do . . . It's, uh, a little more complicated than that."

"Yeah, but we're just slaves in somebody else's system. There's no place left anymore to make your own system or live differently. If you don't pay taxes, you're an outlaw."

Thom nodded. "Could you really give it all up though? I think we're addicted to our own adrenaline. The hypercapitalist world is a dreary struggle, but it's also fraught with danger and excitement and crime and stimuli, and we're addicted to its rush."

"If I could be anyone, I'd be Robin Hood, robbing rich fuckers and then giving to the people. That'd be plenty of rush."

"I didn't know you had such a thing for the people."

Erik shrugged, and Thom thought he heard him mumble something about his parents.

Tree turned sharply, looking out into the blackness. "Something's out there."

"Eh?" said Thom.

Erik leapt to his feet. "Who's there?"

There was silence outside their haven of light, the crackling of the fire the only sound, and Thom smiled at the paranoia of his roommates. He felt something on his neck, and he reached his hand back to brush it off and connected with metal. He turned and saw a man holding a gun on him, and his gut dropped out from under him. Another man was aiming a shotgun at Erik. They were dressed in long overcoats, one with a cowboy hat, the other a ski hat, and for a moment Thom thought he'd conjured them out of the past with their conversation. He'd never had a gun held on him before and thought it possible—his teeth starting to chatter—that he was one of those who gets on his knees and begs.

"Hi," Erik said. "You gentlemen are just in time for supper."

"We're here for the couch."

"You can't have it," said Tree.

"I don't see you have much of a choice."

"He's definitely got a point there, Tree." Erik calmly fed the fire another stick. "But of course, if you guys think holding guns on people is the best way to outfit your living room, that's your own choice. To me it seems downright silly. But hurry on up, take your furniture and get out of here."

"Pick it up," said cowboy hat and gestured to Erik with his chin.

"Ah, you want furniture movers too. Now that's another story. I don't move furniture for no one. I guess you'll have to kill me."

Cowboy hat looked at his partner, then nodded toward Tree and Thom. "You pick it up."

Thom scrambled to his feet and stationed himself at one end of the couch. Tree and he picked it up. Thom was grateful that the weight seemed unchanged. He didn't want to have to explain that under the barrel of a shotgun.

"Throw it in the river, boys," yelled Erik. "Let them fetch it from there."

"You bring it over here," said cowboy hat.

Thom started to walk to where the man had gestured and realized Tree was pulling the other way with a surprising strength. Tree's eyes were wild, and firelight flickered across his face.

"In the river," Tree said through his teeth.

"Tree," Thom appealed, nodding his head toward the men with guns. Thom had a slippery foothold on mud, and Tree managed to pull him a step toward the bank.

"Sorry, fellers," said Erik, "we've got this all worked out. It's going in the river." Tree pulled Thom another step toward the river, and then he managed a foothold on a rock.

Both men with shotguns took a step toward the couch, and Erik stood up, his fist straight-armed, and caught cowboy hat in the throat.

The man in the cowboy hat dropped the gun and held his throat, unable to breathe.

"Sorry about that, mate," Erik said. He picked up the shotgun as ski hat turned on him. He walked slowly toward him, both of them pointing at each other. "Ever been in a standoff?" Erik asked the man. The man held the rifle to his shoulder and began to sweat.

"I'll shoot you right now," said ski-hat. "I'll kill you right now."

"You're not holding your gun right. You've never killed anybody, have you? First time you've held a gun, I bet. You're not going to do it like that. Look, you don't need to aim. You need to concentrate on me. Aiming isn't going to get you anywhere. I'm right in front of you. You're not going to miss. We're no longer at the gun-skills part of the evening."

"You're full of shit," ski hat said, and if Thom could have found his voice he would have backed him up. "This wasn't my idea anyway. We were just paid to pick up a couch."

"I've killed for furniture before." Erik shrugged. "It's not such a big deal. I used to work for Castro." Erik took the shotgun in one hand and pushed it against the man's crotch. "Now that would suck, wouldn't it?" He smiled. "I knew a man who had his crotch blown out once. Terrible thing, just terrible."

Ski hat pushed the gun against Erik's chest. "That's enough. I'm going to kill you, you sonofabitch."

"Sure, sure, sure you are, it's your job, and then you've got to do that to my two friends too. Imagine trying to do that with your crotch blown out." Erik laughed heartily. "That would not be fun."

Thom came to his senses finally, realized he was still stupidly holding the couch, set it down, grabbed the big rock under his foot, and knocked it over the man's head. The man fell to the ground unconscious.

"Jesus Christ, what the hell is wrong with you! I thought you were good at this sort of thing," Erik yelled at Thom. "I almost shit my pants."

"Sorry, I . . . you sounded like you knew what you were doing."

"I did! I was waiting for you to knock him out, goddamnit!"

There was a giant splash behind them, and Thom turned around to find that the couch and Tree were gone.

"Holy crap, Tree!" Thom yelled.

"In the water," said Tree. "Come on, hurry, I can't hold against the current much longer."

Thom and Erik ran to the bank and held their hands out into the blackness. They couldn't see Tree. The vicinity of the fire created a veil of darkness on its edge. "Can you see us?" said Thom.

"Yes, I can see you. I don't want back up; I want you to come down. I've got a hold of a branch, and it's breaking."

"The hell are you talking about," said Erik. "There's no way in hell I'm getting in there."

"Yes, you are," Tree said. "Don't worry, the couch floats."

Erik looked at Thom to see if it was just him, or had Tree gone mad. Thom reassured him that Tree had gone mad.

"He dreamed this," Thom said. The boom of a shotgun blast sounded behind them, and Thom looked at Erik to make sure he was still alive and then without thinking dove into the icy Columbia water, surfaced shivering, his teeth clattering from shock. A hand reached out of the darkness and grabbed him, guided him shaking onto the couch, which miraculously continued not to sink. A moment later another hand reached up and they pulled Erik onboard, and the couch still did not sink. The branch broke and they spun off into the current, watching flashlight beams strobe around the water behind them.

"I am no longer speaking to you," Erik whispered.

Tree nodded solemnly. "Okay."

"We were doing just fine. There's no freaking reason to have thrown the f-f-f-f-f-f—agh!—fucking couch in the water," Erik said as a convulsive shiver ran through him. They could just barely see each other in the dim light. Erik wiped his hand over his head, and water poured from his hair. "We're going to die out here. And it's your effking fault, Tree."

"Hypothermia," Thom said. "You're right."

Tree handed him a hard shape that emanated heat. "Soup," he said.

"How in the hell did you manage to get the soup down here?" Erik said.

"My laptop!" Thom said. "Shit!"

"I got it," Tree said and handed Thom a spoon.

Tree handed Erik a bowl and spoon. "I didn't get much of your stuff. It was sort of spread out."

"Hey, listen, asshole, I'm not talking to you," Erik said.

"Here's a towel," Tree said.

"Where did you get a towel?"

"Sheilene gave it to me."

Erik shook his head in wonder, then wrapped it about himself. "My fake beard," he said.

"What?"

"And my straw hat. What if I need a disguise?"

The couch spun on. What they could see of the shore moved, changed. They were in the gyroscope of the river, movement, wetness, the force of the current on every side.

"Don't worry, I dreamed this."

"Listen," said Thom, "your dreaming it doesn't mean it's going to happen. Your doing it because you dreamed it does. Don't you think you might not be dreaming about what we should do, but what stupid things you are going to do?"

Tree didn't answer.

"That's right. You're the asshole that threw us into the water, not your dreams."

"I never thought of it that way."

Erik huffed and scratched fiercely at his face. He was growing hair at an alarming rate. "Arrrrghh!" he yelled into the night, and the yell echoed across the water.

"Well, it's easier on the feet," Thom said.

"Yeah," Tree said, "easier on the feet."

"*You* shut up," Erik said. Erik attempted to take his shoes off without touching the water, rocking the couch, elbowing roommates. "Someone tried to steal the couch, for fuck sake. What is this madness? They had shotguns!"

"Nice job back there. I take that back about your losing fights all the time," Thom said.

"See?"

"But—" Thom watched the moon appear and disappear again, wondered at these strange creatures he traveled with—"you didn't really work for Castro, right?"

"No, but I met him. Nice guy, loves to eat."

"How in the hell did you meet Fidel Castro?"

"Friend of my dad's. Forget about it."

Thom saw the giant form of a freighter behind them and then realized they didn't have any way to steer. "Ship," he said. "A ship is coming."

They sat cross-legged to keep their feet out of the water, but the couch floated surprisingly high with the three of them sitting on it. The water was black and roiled about the couch burbling and murmuring to itself, and the couch did constant slow circles. Thom saw the ship gaining on them, heard it pushing a wall of water in front of it. Giant engines churned the water. Clouds covered the moon so that the shore was invisible. Black water melted into black shoreline, into black trees and a black sky. It was only them, a black dot on a blanket of black, and the looming, illuminated ship, now only a hundred yards away. Thom, Erik, and Tree had their hands in the water trying to paddle to one side, pawing frantically. At thirty yards away they could see the crew on the edge of the ship, oblivious of the tiny couch far below them. They yelled and screamed but could scarcely hear themselves over the roar of the ship. A wall of metal rose before them. Thom imagined himself again the character in movies who gets on his knees and pleads. What about the life-flash-before-my-eyes thing? His mind calculated the probabilities of death. Multitasking. Hello? How about a little help here, brain. *Dive!* brain said, *Dive off!* Of course. Thom eyed the tar-water at his feet and chose the couch-death probability scenario. The ship a mere couch-length or two away, pushing them up, sucking them in.

And then the river made a decision. A tiny thread of current twisted them slightly to one side while the ship turned to the other and within seconds they were on one side of an island and the ship on the other. They could see the faintest glow and hear the sound of the metal monstrosity through the trees. They were in a slow, thin channel, the shore just an outline of blackness a short distance away.

"Holy shit, that was close!" Erik exhaled great lungfuls of air. "Let's go to shore. This isn't a good idea, dreams or no." He looked at his roommates, dark forms in the darkness. There was no reply, only a soft burbling of water and the even softer exhales of sleepers.

"Hello?" Erik grabbed the form closest to him and shook. "Tree! Wake up!" The couch rocked back and forth in the water, and Erik could feel the drowsiness seeping into him. He let the limp form go, and Tree's body fell back into the couch. Erik balled up his fists and pounded on Tree's legs and then his own, trying to fight sleep. He dug among the gear spread around the couch and found some mostly dry blankets and put them over his wet roommates. They passed the island, and he saw the freighter had pulled ahead of them. Its wake came at the couch and rocked it, and Erik put his arm across his unconscious roommates like a seat belt as the couch bucked. He kept his eye on the black haze of water, searching for sticks, garbage, anything he could use as a paddle. He caught a branch the size of a baseball bat and fruitlessly stabbed at the water with it, trying to move the couch to shore, trying to fight his body for consciousness. The darkness of his surroundings made it difficult to know if his eyes were open or closed. He held his fists to his eyes until he saw red, but it quickly faded back to black. He beat the stick against Thom's chest. "Wake up! Goddamnit!"

He began to hallucinate, or dream, half in one world, half in the other, the couch's strange spell slowly wedging him into its limbo world. Horses out on the water, standing in the middle of the river, grazing. His parents waving from the recently passed freighter. A brilliantly lit carnival on one bank, or was that real? A girl laughing, a kid with cotton candy. He worked at his eyes, stabbed at the water. Saw the white, colonial church of Zacotecas, Mexico, an island, a haven in the river. He stabbed toward that, and the river faded away, bright cobblestone streets, traffic everywhere, a taco stand, *tienditas* selling cola and cigarillos. He dodged a cab and pitched into the water, surfaced gasping, the couch a disruption in the blackness. He lunged for it, grabbed an armrest, and hoisted himself dripping wet on board, nearly rocking his roommates off. His teeth chattering and body shivering uncontrollably, he pulled a corner of Tree's blanket over his head and curled deep into the couch.

Thom woke to a clear blue sky and water in every direction. No sign of birds, no sign of anything. Tree was on his knees peering off toward the sunrise, toward the direction land must be. There was a pile of wire sculptures next to him, and he gripped his needle-nose pliers in his right hand. As far as Thom could tell, Erik was the compressed, wretched-looking ball at the opposite end of the couch. Thom's legs were curled crosswise underneath him, and he found he could scarcely move them. They seemed like append-ages someone had added on as an afterthought, forgetting to con-nect the nerve tissue. With the help of his arms, he stretched them straight out and had pins and needles like hammers and nails, blood entering into the cramped feet like a dam burst. SELECT * FROM reality_life WHERE EXISTS "couch in pacific." His brain automatically sorted through any memories that would assist in explanation.

"Look," Tree said, "I did these wires in my sleep." He picked up a human figure from the tangle, turned it in his hands. "I've never done that before." The figure seemed grotesque somehow, wire curves hinting at the disfigurement and limbs akimbo of accidents or death.

Thom raised his eyebrows, feeling too asleep for a conversation like this. "Wow," he said. And then, "Where are we?" Realizing the question was absurd, he added, "We're not in Kansas anymore?"

Tree nodded. "The river must have been really fast. I don't even know which way land might be."

Thom pointed east. "Land that way. Unless we jumped an ocean or something. We are moderately fucked, I'd say. How in the hell did we get here? How much water do we have?"

Thom and Tree looked through the things that Tree had man-aged to throw on the couch at the last minute and found a gallon jug with a pint's worth of water left. They moved like a movie reel slowed down, their bodies rediscovering sinew and tendon and muscle at each bend.

"Okay, I'm going to upgrade us to very fucked." The couch rolled gently in the ocean, and he saw nothing but horizon lines, so much air, so much water. The world was split into two uninhabit-able spheres. "Maybe you ought to try and wake Erik up, and we'll, ah, have a little conference. Or maybe you ought to let the guy sleep, I don't know. I'd prefer doom dealt out to me in my sleep, I guess." Leadership seemed futile, team-rallying long past its usefulness. Thom felt control slipping, panic rising. How long would the couch float? how long could they live? how far could he swim? His brain replaying every lost-at-sea story he'd ever heard. Forty-one days in a rowboat, lost in the Atlantic. A speck in the largest wilderness on the surface of the planet.

Tree shook Erik and called his name. Erik, on a far faster reel, leapt to life, his legs and arms springing in opposite directions, climbing up the armrest and poised on the verge of tumbling into the sea when Tree caught the back of his shirt and pulled him back.

"Holy shit! We're in the ocean!"

Tree and Thom nodded solemnly.

"You bastards fell asleep last night. I tried to shake you awake but you fell asleep."

Thom nodded again, "I . . . know. It's hard to believe. I was shot at. You might be right. . . . The couch might be a little weird with the sleeping. Wasn't there a big ship?"

"What'd I tell you? I told you so. What'd I tell you? Who believes Erik? Yes, there was a big ship! What in the hell are we going to do now?" Erik's hair jutted away from his head in unlikely positions, and Thom noticed he had a full mustache again, though hardly any other facial hair.

"Well, we're going to hope a ship comes by."

"Paddles! We need paddles!"

"If you find paddles, I don't know how far you'll be able to get this ship anyway. We could be ten miles from shore or a hundred."

"I think it's going to be okay," Tree said. Thom and Erik stared at him. Tree's face was pale, and there was sweat on his forehead.

"You alright, Tree?"

"Ugh. Seasick I think," he said. He turned around and leaned over the back of the couch and groaned. "It's going to be alright," he said again, his voice muffled.

"That's nice for you." Erik angrily chafed at his mustache.

Tree threw up into the water, and when he finished he blew his nose into his hand and washed it in a swell and then took a swallow of saltwater.

Thom sighed. "Why do you think it's going to be okay? You better think so, I should add, since we got on this damn couch in the water in the first place because of you. Erik and I had the shotgun situation handled without your diving into the water. Hey," he tapped Tree on the back. "Don't drink sea water. It'll just make you thirstier, and sicker."

"I dreamed we'd be picked up by a ship today."

Thom nodded, realizing he had little choice but to hope that Tree's dream was true. He closed his eyes and tried to force his breath to slow to regular intervals, his heart to slow, his mind back to a state of reason. "Okay," he said, "Okay. We got held up last night for our couch. With *guns*."

Tree and Erik nodded.

"And then, because of Tree, we jumped on the couch that mysteriously floats . . . couches shouldn't float, you know. I mean, maybe a little, but not like this."

"I know!" Erik said.

"We weren't even to Astoria. How far can you float in, say, nine hours?" Thom calculated a worse-case scenario, ten miles per hour. It was forty miles from their previous camp to Astoria. "We could be as far as fifty miles out at sea," he said, an adrenalin-fed desperation making his voice rise at the end of the sentence.

Erik stared in weary disbelief at the water lapping against the base of the couch.

"I've got these." Tree held up the wire sculptures. "That's something else."

"Nobody is ever going to believe this," Thom said.

"Nobody is ever going to have the chance," Erik said morosely and then jerked his head up level with the horizon. "What's that!?"

They looked and saw a dot on the water far off in the distance.

"I bet it's a boat," Tree said. "It's just like my dream."

"Paddle!" shouted Thom. The three roommates began to paddle. Erik leaned over an armrest in the bow, his arms up to his elbows.

Thom and Tree gripped the back of the couch with one hand and paddled frantically with the other.

Thom watched the sun ease up the sky as his arm turned to numb exhaustion, his hand shriveling into complex topographies. They appointed Tree the official waver and he spent the day waving a handkerchief toward the speck, trying to make a visual commotion. The speck seemed to get closer. It was now twice the speck it once was. Thom tamped down the rational brain that noted that a ship would have disappeared hours ago, that the optical illusion of the vastness might be showing them a freighter or a floating can. More hours went by, their arms aching from the effort, doling out teaspoons of water at a time from the pint, the saltwater numbing their hands and the effort making them sweat. Thom estimated they'd had three quarters of the sun's path now. Time passed rapidly at times and unbearably slowly at others.

"How come we're not asleep?" Thom asked. "We're still on the couch."

Erik shrugged. "Maybe it's got a time limit?"

They both looked at Tree.

"I don't know," said Tree.

"What about your computer," Erik said. "Can't you write for help?"

Thom stared at him. Of course, his computer. He fetched it from the bag and was amazed to find it was still dry even though they'd spent the better part of the day pelting themselves and the couch with saltwater. He opened it up, happy to see that he had quite a charge left, and tried to connect. Nothing. He tried again. Nothing. They must be miles and miles away, out of range. He closed the laptop and shook his head in defeat and then rapidly reopened it again and stared at the date in the upper right-hand corner. "What day is it?" Thom said.

Erik counted on his fingers. "It's the twenty-sixth of February," he said. "Tuesday."

Thom shook his head. "My computer says it's the twenty-seventh."

Erik nodded. "Okay, then it's the twenty-seventh. So what?"

"So it should be the twenty-sixth."

"Like I said," said Erik. "It's the twenty-sixth, then."

"But my computer says it's the twenty-seventh."

"You said that! So what? So we're wrong or it's wrong."

"It's not wrong," said Thom. "It doesn't just go changing dates."

"We've been on the couch two days," said Tree.

Erik gaped at him. "No way. There's no way we've been out here for two days."

"We slept all day yesterday," said Tree.

"I didn't," said Erik. "We talked to Jean, we carried the couch. I didn't sleep. Maybe you were asleep, dreamboy."

Thom nodded. "He's right. We slept for about thirty-four hours. By the way, you're sunburned." His mind automatically added up the possible distance out at sea, three hundred miles. Hope dropped like an elevator.

Erik stood up, and the couch rocked precariously. "Fucking couch," he yelled. He tried to leap up to be parted from it and came down kicking the back of the couch while balancing on the cushions, and then he was overboard, surfacing and gasping and calling for help.

Thom and Tree pulled him aboard, and they sat silent for a while.

"We're going to die, aren't we?" Erik said through shivers.

"Looks that way."

"A ship is going to pick us up," Tree said.

"You better be right," Erik said. "Hey, as I was falling I saw that speck again. It's not very far. It's not a ship. It's something in the water, garbage. Maybe we can use it for a paddle."

The three reached in and paddled with a renewed frenzy. An hour later they had in their hands a large white cooler containing a case and a half of Olympia beer.

"This is what we've been working all day for?" Thom looked in disgust at the contents. "I guess it's better than spending the day thinking."

"Hey," Erik said, opening a beer, "dying isn't so bad after all." He raised it to his lips. "The universe provides!" He took a terrifically long drink until the beer was finished. He crushed it and threw it in the water.

"Erik, don't litter," Thom said.

"What do you think we are? Want me to save it on the couch till we all go down?"

Thom shrugged. "We shouldn't drink beer," he said. "We'll get dehydrated even faster."

"Buddy, you don't have much of a grip on reality here, do you?"

Tree shrugged, grabbed a beer, and Erik took another. Thom stared at them for a minute, then took one too. It was the best-tasting beer he'd ever had in his life. From now on, he made a pact with himself, he would be devoted to that brand. He didn't have much choice, seeing as how the only source of beer for the rest of his life was the Oly at their feet.

They drank, and drank some more, floating the cooler in front of them and resting their feet on it. "That's what we've needed this whole time," Erik said gleefully. He was already four beers in on an empty stomach. "An ottoman! This makes all the difference! Do you think that that's what this couch has been looking for? An ottoman? It's been lonely! Poor, poor couch." Erik broke up into hysterical laughter, and his roommates laughed and then quieted and watched when Erik wouldn't stop.

At eight or ten beers and dusk, Thom began to drunkenly holler out his will and well-wishings to friends. "May Megan find the dreamboat she's always looked for, Izaac learn to eat better and drink less, may my mom find a husband." Tree was unconscious at his elbow. Erik, several beers ahead of Thom, had lost control of his limbs and had already fallen in several times trying to piss over the edge, crying occasionally, or was it laughing, and bursting into twisted phrases of Spanish songs, saltwater and beer and tears mixing into one. The space was too small for his jerkiness, and Erik always verged on being overboard. Thom held out his arm to Erik in the water without interrupting the hollering of his will, latched strong fingers over Erik's floundering arms, and yanked him back on ship. A soft drizzle began to cover them and wash away some of the salt. Thom kept his mouth wide, catching enough water to coat his tongue, chasing it with beer. The beer was giving Thom terrible gas, and with one great outburst Erik broke back into hysterics and went over the side again. "Ha ha," Thom said, held out his arm into the darkness waiting for Erik's wet fumbling, but it never came. "Erik," he yelled, impatient, his arm getting heavy, his head beginning to nod. "Erik!"

No sound came. Only the slightest white noise of the drizzle hitting the ocean. There'd been chaotic splashing, or was that last time? How long had he waited with his arm outstretched? Usually there was the rattle and splash of Erik. With effort, he raised his head up and tried to focus, made sure that Erik wasn't sleeping in a corner of the couch. He looked over the back of the couch: darkness, his head swimming with the effort, no sign of him. They'd lost control of the cooler, and he caught a white glint of it about twenty yards out, floating its own course. "Erik, Erik has gone down, Davey Jones' locker." What did that mean? "Erik!" he hollered. "Errrrrrrrik!"

He'd tucked a number of beers in next to him on the couch, and he opened one now. "Here's to you, Erik!" he wiped at his face. "One down, two to go!" he yelled. He poured the beer into the water next to him, imagining it finding its way to the drowned Erik. He pictured Erik with his arms spread, his mouth caught in a bit of Spanish song, bubbles rising up, Erik floating down into the deep, his stubborn hair stuck at whatever angle. The beer he poured into the water like an isolated golden stream falling through the water into his open mouth. He opened another and also poured it into the ocean, thinking this time of him and Tree, their similar fates, the inevitability of falling off the couch, their bodies filling with saltwater, his body becoming more bloated, drifting down to a bottom a million miles of water pressure away. It had to be a prank, Erik just out of arm's reach, giggling at the folly. "Erikkk!" he yelled again. "Stop fooling, you dumb bastard." A swell tilted him back, then forward. His panic level rose and fell with each sway. He considered pushing Tree off the couch into the water, holding him under, keeping him from the fate of waking up on the couch hungover, his body water-starved, saving him from the more terrible death of thirst, of boredom, of fear, exposure. Give him death now. He gave the sleeping form a half-hearted push. Everything came down to water; everything returned to water. He opened another beer, held it up, and yelled "Errrrrik!" and downed it in several long gulps. He gave the small body next to him another hard push with his right hand, throwing himself off balance. Thom flailed, one leg and arm in the water, pulled himself back onto the couch and swore. He grabbed another beer, this time yelled "*Fuck you, Erik!*" and then his head lolled back and the moon came out from behind a cloud to spotlight the lost.

II. Undertow

When Thom was young, and before he'd become a giant, he'd been the victim of torturing in school. A gang of four boys delighted in making him miserable, and he always managed to say something odd or backward or strange to elicit their violence. Once, the cruelest time, they threw him down, one of them sitting on his head, smashing his ear into the ground, his head feeling like it would collapse from the weight, another holding his legs, the other two throwing him punches in the gut until he puked.

Thom woke with these same four boys, his cheek pressed against his own puke, his head set to burst from pressure. Every part of him hurt. But there were no boys, just a bare lightbulb, wool blankets, a tiny room that spun and bucked, a terrible smell emanating from him. He looked up, saw the boards of a top bunk above him.

Twisting his way out of the bunk without dragging himself through his own puke he managed to get his legs out onto the floor. He waited for the spinning to slow, holding back whatever else his stomach wanted to shove out of him.

He stabilized himself, trying to find the strength in his legs, then launched himself up and outward. He slammed his head against the top bunk and landed on the floor on his knees, gripping his head. He was alive, he thought. This must be alive, only being alive hurt this much.

He stayed where he was; no movement was the best movement. The room rocked enough for both of them. He needn't add his own reckless motion. He was saved . . . was he saved? He thought of Erik's last vault off of the couch. Had he held his arm up to be saved? They were dead. They had thought they were dead, and now he was alive. Erik—the memory of the drowning brought on a series of dry heaves. When it passed, he rocked back onto his feet, gripping the floor, one hand in the mess there, and then the bottom bunk. With his hand clutching the top bunk he brought himself to a standing position. An amusement ride: Tea Cups, the Hammer, the Octopus. He was naked, and there was nothing in the room that would clothe a body. The top bunk was empty, with no sign of anyone having slept there. A hollow uncertainty in his chest, a dread. Had he been the only one who made it? A distant memory of a push. He was alive, his body convulsed with shivers. Thank God it hadn't been him, his brain said and Thom silenced it. Erik was at the bottom of the sea and he was alive, and he felt sick and stupid and like he'd won the lottery. He was a survivor.

The room was white, and the walls were made of metal—maybe it was the afterlife after all. He gripped the bolted-on iron frame of the bunk bed and let the room's movement take him. The room really was rocking, he realized with immense relief. He was at sea, not just the sea of his hangover. The couch. The valuable, troublesome couch. Why hadn't they sold the damn thing? He stayed there with his fists fastened around the frame for an eternity, eyes on the closed doorway, unsure of what a next move might be, and with little will to move at all.

The door opened and an older man Thom vaguely recognized entered, a giant, angular beak of a nose on him. The man was on a TV show maybe, an advertisement, he'd been selling pain medicine or vitamins for the elderly. The man smiled, carefully stepped around the watery mess on the floor, and set a small stack of folded clothes on the top bunk. He wore an old baseball cap at an angle that made him look sloppy despite his handsomeness, a white line cook's jacket, and a destroyed pair of tennis shoes. Half-a-dozen days' growth of silver beard covered his jaw. Outside a man in overalls walked by the entrance and glanced in. Thom felt exposed, but the best he could do was to grip the bed frame more tightly.

"Good to see you up. We've been a little worried. They call

me Shin. I'm the ship's cook." The man didn't hold out his hand. "You're Thom?"

Thom nodded, said nothing. The movement of his head was painful. He was sure some bastard had pushed his eyes back in their sockets six inches while he was sleeping.

"Take your time. If you want to shower, there's one across the hall, and second door on the right will take you down to the dining room. Come down when you're ready. You'll need to get rehydrated." He handed over the water bottle he carried, then reached into his pocket. "Here's a pill that will help with seasickness." He reached into another pocket and fished out several more pills. "These will help with the hangover."

Thom tried to nod again but only managed a prolonged blink. He held out his hand to take the pills. Fought a temptation to run out and hurl himself overboard.

Shin smiled kindly, touched his brow good-bye and left.

Thom stood and tried to make up his mind. A hot shower seemed like the best chance for a resurrection. He wondered if he could manage to get dressed before heading across the hall and thought not.

Thom clutched the stack of clothes to his chest and opened the door to his cabin. The light seared his eyes, and he lurched out and caught his toe on the tall threshold. Off-balance with the movement of the ship and his own internal mechanism, he plowed head first into the door across the hall, which opened with the force his head dealt it. He brought himself to a halt against a toilet stall and yelled out, the folded clothes falling to the floor.

Thom felt better clean, hot water bringing back circulation and washing away saltwater and sweat. He hadn't showered since Sheilene's house, which felt like another lifetime. How would he tell Sheilene that Tree and Erik had drowned? He put his head against the shower stall with the hot water beating on his back and let himself moan without caring who heard, let the sound fill up the tile bathroom with echo.

∽

Dressed, he stood at the edge of the ship. A giant red shell in the water, a freighter. He was in a rear tower that rose out of a long cargo bay, giant doors opening into who knows what. They were heading south. Thom thought about the movement that would take him over the edge, left hand on the metal rim, a quick gymnastic jump to launch his body into the largest of graves, a great watery hole. He wavered on the edge, thought about the immediate physical relief it would bring, traced the motions in his mind, the gulping of water into the lungs.

Turning away, he saw it propped against a white wall, a shallow pool of water around it. Orange threadwork and a high back. It was still with him, his curse.

After he'd mentally buried him, seeing Tree alive and drinking coffee across from Shin in the ship's dining room caused an involuntary squeak to issue from Thom's throat. Tree stood up and shook his hand. Thom pulled him into a fierce hug and tried to get his language back.

"Tree! I thought . . ."

Tree nodded. He had deep rings under red eyes, a bruised, starved look about him.

"We made it." Tree smiled. "I knew a ship would pick us up."

"Erik?" he looked about. Perhaps he could not be trusted; he'd already killed off Tree. He was willing to forfeit his take on reality in the hope that another was more optimistic. "Erik?" he repeated.

Tree stared at him blankly, and for the briefest of moments Thom wondered if Erik were someone he'd dreamed up.

"Erik's not here," said Tree. "They only found you and me and the couch. He must have fallen off. I . . . I thought maybe you knew."

Thom nodded and sat down, aware of Shin, trying to act reasonable. Trying to act like he knew how to deal with situations like these. He was at a table in the kitchen. People sit at tables. It was a cramped affair, everything fastened down, pans with Velcro straps across them to keep from banging about in bad weather. His stomach fired off several internal geysers so that he felt the pressure against his belt cruelly. He looked down at his gut. How did it find cause to agitate? he wondered. There's nothing in there. Conspiring stomach.

"Erik drowned," he said finally. "I held out my arm . . . it was dark . . . and he never took it. We had been drinking."

Shin nodded. "I'm sorry."

Thom put his hands over his eyes, the memory too fresh. The line between Erik being there just last night and now, simply, just not being—it was unclear, too sudden, too strange. One of the first laws of physics was that matter cannot be destroyed, only changed. But, the complete nonexistence of Erik defied this law. His shell of a body bumped along the sand at the bottom of the sea, but where was the rest of him, the voice, the action?

Shin cleared his throat. "The captain wants to talk to you. I'm afraid it looks like you both are going to South America as we don't have time to stop." Shin waited while Thom digested the news. "Can I fix you something to eat?"

Thom nodded. Anywhere was fine with him. Take me to the end of the earth, he thought. He resigned himself to this dark undertow that had taken over his life, no matter which direction he struggled in, a greater malevolent force seemed to be pulling him deeper into its own ocean, literally and figuratively.

Shin served them scrambled eggs and toast, and Thom ate the wheat toast to punish himself, tore into it ravenously, anticipating the havoc it would cause in his stomach later. He didn't want to feel well. How much of his own subconscious was involved in the creation of that undertow? he wondered. After years of stagnancy and inaction, was he responsible for this upheaval? He felt slightly better after eating, and for the first time focused on Shin.

And then he saw, a puzzle piece fit into place, his brain, the solver, exultant, the fear of conspiracy blooming. "You're . . . you're the Goodwill guy!"

Shin chuckled. "Yes, I am the Goodwill guy. Also your apartment-building owner, among other things."

"What the hell are you doing here? You"—he jabbed his finger at Tree—"goddamn well knew it was the Goodwill guy."

"Well, I've been up for hours," said Tree. "We've been talking."

"It's your fault, you bastard." Thom stood up, towering close to the low ship ceiling. "If you'd taken the damn couch in the first place, none of this would have happened." Thom reached out and grabbed Shin's shirt and pulled him toward him.

"Well, looks like we're feeling better." A hardened voice with the resonance of command came from the doorway. A handsome man in his fifties dressed in blue jeans and a sweater walked toward them, thick gray hair needing a cut wind-whipped about his head.

"I'm Robert." He held out his hand toward Thom. "I'd recommend unhanding my cook."

"This man is a fraud," Thom said. "He works at the Goodwill in Portland, and he's responsible for all of this." He loosened his grip on Shin.

The captain laughed heartily. "I'd like to hear this! Seems to me you were the bloke adrift at sea with your living room. Truly, that was one of the oddest things I've ever seen. I even called in to see if there'd been floods. I imagined people getting swept from out of their living rooms by torrents of water!" The captain fetched himself a cup of coffee and sat at the table.

"He . . ." Thom had no idea where to begin. His position didn't look very strong. "We tried to bring our couch to the Goodwill," he said, already resigned to not being believed, "and he wouldn't take it. And he was at another place, and that was weird, and he wouldn't take it there either, and so we were just trying to get rid of it, and that's how . . . it all started." Thom felt vaguely like Erik, wondered if he'd inherited part of Erik as the last one to see him.

Robert nodded, running his fingers through his hair. "I see." Trying not to smile. "Shin," he said, "when's the last time you left the ship?"

"Japan," Shin said. "About three months ago."

Thom looked at Tree for backup, but Tree had his pliers and wire out, twisting a ship into shape. That'll be the first thing I throw overboard, Thom thought, those damn wire and pliers, right before Tree, and then Shin, and then myself.

"It's okay," Shin looked at the captain, "I don't mind. . . . There were originally three of them."

"Ah," said the captain, his face going grave. "I didn't know. I'm sorry to hear that. Losing someone at sea is the hardest loss."

Thom nodded and stared at his feet.

"Of course, a couch isn't the most seaworthy vessel. It's very lucky both of you are alive. I didn't even know couches floated."

Thom practiced more nodding, ashamed, his head still a coconut, the water beating painfully about his brain.

"I wasn't even going to take the couch on board, but Shin convinced me that the crew might enjoy a couch. At any rate, I'd like to hear the whole story sometime. We'll have plenty of time in the weeks ahead. Perhaps Shin has mentioned to you that I can't spare the time to take you to shore? Sorry about that, just the way it is, I'm late already and didn't expect to be picking up living rooms. South America wants televisions, and the company wanted me there two weeks ago."

Thom looked up at the captain, knowing he owed him something. "Thanks for picking us up," he said. "I don't mean to seem ungrateful."

"Not a problem," Robert said.

"You didn't happen to see a laptop on the couch, did you?"

The captain laughed. "Yes. It reeked of beer. I gave it to our computer guy to air out. We've got a computer room upstairs in the meantime if you want. Probably you ought to write your families and let them know not to send the coast guard in search of you. And of course, it's your job to notify the other fellow's family."

Tree finished the twisting and sculpting of his ship and handed it to the captain.

"Isn't she a beauty." The captain admired it from all sides. Tree had fashioned an eight-inch-long intricate skeleton of the ship. "I'll take it as fare for passage."

The captain left, promising to have dinner with them, and Thom glared at Shin.

"Sometimes things make less sense when they're explained," Shin said. "But a lack of understanding does not take away from their importance."

"What's that supposed to mean?"

"It means that my destiny is as tied to that couch as yours."

Thom gawked at him. "What!?"

"Just that it's my duty to see the couch gets to where you're taking it."

"How did you fool the captain into thinking you hadn't left the ship?"

"I haven't left the ship. I haven't been off since Japan."

"But you just fucking told me you were the Goodwill guy!"

"I was. I was him too. Sometimes things make less sense when they're explained."

Thom turned in exasperation to Tree, who shrugged. "Aren't you going to say anything? Doesn't this seem weird to you?"

"I don't really think about it much."

"He doesn't really think about it much," said Thom. He grabbed a handful of hair on his head and squeezed. "He doesn't really think about it."

"I realize that this all seems a bit out of the normal, but the truth is that there is an aquifer of abnormal just beneath the surface of the normal. Usually it doesn't come to the surface. You just happen to be a crossover. So am I. And you've been given a duty."

Thom felt cornered in nonsense. He could have counted on Erik for backup, at least a reasonably startled expression. His intestines contracted, sharp pains echoed through his lower gut, the air filled with gas. He remembered hearing that the most important skill for a person in the information-heavy age was the synthesis of information. He was used to looking at hundreds of websites a day and knowing within seconds the validity or importance of the information, simply by the tone or construction. But this? He couldn't even get a foothold on what he was hearing. Shin's eyes were watering, possibly from the gas. Thom needed to escape, escape into something nonhuman for an hour or two. Tree had gotten up and seemed to be inspecting pans in the corner of the room farthest from Thom. He'd go to the computer lab, barricade the damn door. He'd find his computer. Shin seemed to be waiting for some comment. More gas welled up about him, and Thom realized he had to find a bathroom. "How glorious," he said to

Shin and sprinted toward the stairs. "I'm a furniture mover. Of the third kind!"

After some time in the bathroom, Thom found his way to the computer lab, passing various crewmates among whom he held a certain amount of fame. They either wisecracked about floating sofas or looked at him with obvious regard for attempting such a foolhardy act. Those who had heard about Erik gave condolences, shared their own stories.

The "computer guy" was in the lab with Thom's laptop, and after the initial formalities, Thom realized he was one of the straight-laced, clean-cut, socially awkward computer guys with fixations on order. He handed over the laptop and vacated the lab, and Thom felt grateful that the computer industry was speckled with those types. The laptop smelled vaguely of beer. It made him queasy, but it worked fine.

He plugged the laptop into the ship's network and spent a frustrating hour working on a five-line email to Sheilene.

> Sheilene,
> There's little other way to say this. We somehow ended up at sea on top of the couch, got lost . . . Erik drowned. We're now picked up on a ship and heading for South America. Tree is okay. We're all stunned and mourning the loss of Erik. Sorry to break the news to you like this. I have no idea how to get a hold of his parents, I'm trying.
> Love, Thom

He did a couple of feeble searches for Erik's parents on the web, dreading he'd find something. There was an email from Jean: she was waiting in Astoria, and where the hell were they? He worked up another email of roughly the same content, adding a line to let her know that Tree believed the quest was more on than ever. He was tempted to ask her if she wanted to meet them in South America. Or wherever the hell they were going. Jean. The mind spun her around, knowing he should be graver, knowing he should eschew the possibility of romance. He wrote his mom, letting her know that he'd found an apartment and was busy working in Portland, how were the cats? He wrote his ex-boss to say that he was hard at work on a project and wouldn't be able to go out for a beer for at least a couple of weeks. He wrote himself one.

```
Dear Thom,
Please be involved in something worthwhile.
Learn to control the undertow.
Stop eating wheat!
Yours, Thom
```

His inbox consisted of another half-dozen job rejections and a message from the person on the bulletin board who'd offered to buy the couch.

```
Thom,
Ten thousand dollars for a couch is a bit on the high
side. I was sort of surprised at the price, perhaps
you said that as a joke? However, it turns out that I
rather want the couch and can't stop thinking about
how nice it'd look in my house. Where do I send the
money? Let's take care of this asap.
-dem
```

Thom couldn't believe the email and read it several times. It defied any sense. Was it all a ploy to make fun of him? His brain roughed out the logistical problems of organizing this many people for the sole purpose of Thom's befuddlement. What was the extent of Thom's sanity? It was against his nature to trust without knowledge, to believe without proof. Deduction and logic were two essential skills in the arts of programming, but the number of oddities were adding up to an inductive proof. Circumstantial evidence. He wasn't getting anywhere with denying everything. Better to play out the odd hand to find out where it went. He wrote back and said the price of the couch was now one hundred thousand dollars. Why the hell not? He pulled up his couch bulletin board and saw a message from an ex-girlfriend who was now a married reference librarian in New York City. The message was a giant stream of nonsense characters. He recognized the code at the top of the nonsense as an old key that they had used to encrypt messages between friends a few years ago. She was paranoid.

16:04 / ip 212.55.1.8 / verified

So Thomas. You're always involved in the weirdest shit. But I've got some scum for you. What else am I going to do, you can only get so many requests for the book "7 habits of highly effective people" before you start wrenching your fingers into sprains to avoid the sarcasm that spills over your lips like so much bile.

So I dodged around for a day looking for this stuff for you. Then I came back to the bulletin board armed with what I'd learned and found that someone was offering to purchase the couch (!). I hope after you read this you decide not to sell. Yes, I got paranoid, yes I know that you'll think I'm too paranoid, no I don't care. If you're reading this you've obviously remembered how to decrypt the message.

I know we're occasionally at odds about various things because I shamelessly believe everything, and you shamefully believe in almost nothing. Though you seem to have a habit for falling for chicks that believe too much. Some kind of hidden desire in you, perhaps? Or the opposites attract thing. So what I've got for you is a bunch of things you're not going to believe. Some of them dating back thousands of years. Truthfully, you shouldn't believe most of them, I don't even believe all of them. But one thing is for sure, among the histories of various couches, whether famous or used for occult purposes or that have some kind of rumor of magic about them, not a single one apparently is benevolent. Perhaps it's that humans generally have a malevolent history as a whole, and there's been very little room in the writings of the present or past for benevolence. It's remarkable how little of history actually contains truly good or heroic deeds, perhaps that's why the smallest heroics make it into songs. Or perhaps I'm a bit at odds with this silly species, is it too late to be from another?

1) Speaking of Aliens, here's a nice little rumor from the UFO files. As you know, UFO people are divided between the people who think aliens are bad and are out to try to control the minds of the human race, or simply destroy them, and the ET types who think that aliens are cuddly. What I've got for you is of the first camp. Apparently a couch was planted on Earth by aliens (they thought they'd plant something recognizable to humans as harmless, I guess) and it's a giant antenna. It's debatable what this antenna does. Some argument has it that it actually has some power over airwaves and controls or puts messages into TV programming. More apathy stuff like that other guy said, perhaps. Is it Aliens who want us to buy useless crap from corporate America? What a relief. Another argument is that it's an antenna into the unknown, into the paranormal, basically into another world where laws of physics and logic are reversed. The word antenna is interesting . . . bugs have them to sense what is around them. Cars have them to pick up radio signals. Radio stations have them to broadcast those signals. So antennae have many functions. If you have communication going both ways, receiving

and broadcasting, then an antenna may, in this case, be compared to a doorway, a portal.

2) This is a sick little one in my book. There lived a barbarian wizard king (how's that for a title?) who was apparently largely responsible for the collapse of the Roman Empire (you've got to give him credit there) by using blitzkrieg style raids on their monetary supplies. Though it's argued in some books that rarely see the light of day that that wasn't what brought about the destruction of the Romans. He was a busy fellow. Apparently he fucked a lot of women (Roman women, it seems) on an enchanted couch. When they had orgasms (apparently he was quite the stud) they immediately died and their souls were sucked into the couch. Another couch/ soul story. At any rate, this couch was given as a present to Romans. A sort of bewitched Trojan horse. The Romans, of course, liked soft things. When they raided the English, or what were the English before they were the English, they laughed at them because the Romans brought pillows with them that they'd place under their soft bottoms before sitting. The English thought they were a bunch of sissies. At any rate, the couch was said to wreak havoc among the political circles, but not much was elaborated on here. What does a couch full of souls do to one who sits on it? Needless to say, it's known that there was much de-moralization, and amoralization within Rome.

3) Found a note that suggested that Pandora's box was concealed in a seat of some kind. No more information on that one. Intriguing, though.

4) This one is interesting. A well-respected historian I quite like also writes books a little less believable under a pen name . . . I only know this because he's a library regular. In one book, he

claims to have found some information that was omitted from the Old Testament. It basically claims that God was so angry that Adam and Eve had stolen the apple of knowledge that even after he kicked them out, he pretended to make a sort of peace with them by giving them a gift. You guessed it. It was a couch, or what passed for a couch in those days—who knows, some kind of pine-bough sitting apparatus? This historian claims that the single greatest flaw in human nature to this day is the inability for vision, we don't have vision that spans generations in either way, we don't think as a species, we think as individuals, and for that reason we're bound to commit the same mistakes, reenact the same wars, century after century. I don't think I need to delve into his argument very much other than to mention the environment, global warming, continuing religious wars, species extinction, etc. Blah blah blah, the examples are endless. The apple itself was never evil, knowledge by itself is not evil. It's the inability to perceive the effects of knowledge misused that's evil. God apparently gave Adam and Eve a sort of vision-blocker in the form of this couch. As long as Adam and Eve or their descendants sat on this couch, its power held. It was his revenge. With their visions blocked, they'd never be at peace as a species.

In those days, of course, God was a lot tougher candidate before he got remade into the softer more Santa Claus-like character from the new testament. He was a god that was not above giving an eternity's worth of revenge.

5) This stuff isn't as fun for me, but we've got at least a half-dozen books in our arsenal written by sociologists, anthropologists, etc., about the couch as a symbol of civilization at its worst. Basically

that a society makes and uses couches when they've given up on bettering themselves. The couch is the symbol of a lifestyle in coast. It's the symbol of a civilization gone to apathy, laziness, obesity, basically we're talking about some fancy words for what we all know as the Couch Potato. They've even talked about the way a couch orientates you. It prohibits interaction, because it faces people in a single direction. It's a seat that encourages passivity.

That's it for your librarian. So what are you doing with this couch? Let me know your plans, I'd be curious. And be paranoid! When are you going to bring your giant handsomeness out here for an adulterous visit? Bring that couch and we'll see if I lose my soul in it (just joking . . . that just gave me the shivers. I mean, just joking about the couch part, not the rest . . . that is to say, I've got a nice couch out here already, there's a bed too . . . when Jim's at work...)

love, clare

Thom smiled. Clare was a constant flirt. She had a rare but appealing combination of gullibility and paranoia. He drummed on the desk and realized that he'd started to let himself sincerely believe things. He was going to believe Shin and Tree and Clare, and this admission allowed the weight of the possibilities to seep into his consciousness. His head began to reel with the information. He lurched up and found his way out onto the deck. Rain was drenching everything, and the air smelled impossibly good. He spent a moment watching the rain fall into the ocean, tiny drops into the well, cycling up and down, piece by piece by piece. Erik was out there; Erik's body was out there. Somewhere at the bottom. Osmosis balancing out the specific gravity difference between him and the saltwater.

He found Tree with a scattering of books in front of him in the ship's library. The ship had a library! What would Melville say?

He debriefed Tree on what he'd learned from Clare.

"That's exciting," Tree said.

"Is it? When did Adam and Eve happen, how many years ago was that supposed to be, eight thousand? That's an old couch we've got." He experienced a tingling of fear and excitement, the realization that they possibly had in their possession one of the most valuable things on the planet. *Get as far away as possible*, brain warned.

"Very old." Tree flipped through the pages of a Bible. "We need other texts," he said.

"Yes," Thom said. "If it's this old, it will have spanned many cultural shifts. There were many centuries of polytheism after Eden. Seems like we've either got a choice between very old—Adam and Eve, the Romans, Pandora—or very foreign, not forgetting the alien option. There are just too many questions. This was easier when I didn't believe it, but believing opens up a bottomless crevasse of mystery."

With a small jolt the ship's engine changed from the constant hum they had gotten used to. Thom raised eyebrows in question to Tree. *Was a stop planned?*

"I miss Erik," Tree said, ignoring the ship's movements.

"Yeah." Thom felt relieved that Tree felt anything and that there was no implicit blame in the statement. He'd been perturbed by Tree's mysterious aloofness. It was hard to measure mourning. Was an amount required? Erik had flashed in and out of his consciousness all day. He'd lose an hour with the memory of his own lazy, drunken outstretched arm over the water and the silence from where Erik was supposed to have been. It wasn't just his fault. Erik's arm was supposed to have been there, the drunk shit, it was his fault too. How could he have given up hope so easily? He'd considered drowning Tree; the guilt charged through his slumbering synapses with an alarm-clock ring. Death was so dead. Only in *Star Wars* do the dead come back to have reassuring conversations in the form of holograms. He'd never see Erik's mustache again.

"I've always dreamed there would be three." Tree had an innocent, absent look to his eyes.

The ship's engine idled, and Thom went to have a look. The couch was outside but sheltered from the rain, and one of the crew was asleep on it. Thom shook the man, and then shook him again with full force.

The crewman did a dance similar to Erik's. He fell to the ground, looking suspiciously at Thom, squeezing his eyelids together in exaggerated blinks, his eyes still a thousand miles from consciousness.

Then the captain was there and the crewman seemed suddenly very awake. He managed to look busy doing nothing, and then wandered off, weaving slightly.

"Well," the captain said, "you'll never guess what else we dragged out of the sea. This is like a fishing trip. We just picked up a Mexican kid, half drowned and hypothermic. Looked like a drowned monkey. I'm starting to feel like a real hero here."

"A Mexican kid?" Thom said.

"Doesn't speak a lick of English. He's sick as a dog. The medic is going to look at him now. I've got a couple of Mexicans on board who are going to try to speak with him, but for now we'd best let him rest. My man who talked to him said the kid has lost it, completely delirious."

"Can I see him?"

"You speak Spanish?"

"No."

"Sorry, he's in quarantine. I know you'd probably like to relate to him, but it's not going to do you any good right now. Give it a couple of days. We've got plenty of time here. When he's better, I'll send a translator in with you, and you can chat to your heart's content."

Thom,

I hope you're doing ok even though you don't ever call me anymore. Should I get the cell phone and would you call me on that?

Carter died the other day and I know that will make

you sad. I thought maybe you'd like to come home so
we could bury him. Right now he's in the garden shed
but it's so cold out—we have two feet of snow on the
ground!—I think he'll be OK until you can make it
home. I'll wait for you. But hurry because I don't
like to go out there now.

I tried to call your work but they put me on hold for
ten minutes! Could you please look into the phone
service there? I also tried to call Sheilene but I
only got an answering machine message.

I hope you're well, honey.
Love,
Mom

Shin was in the kitchen cleaning up after lunch, and just entering
the room Thom felt the hunger coil up in him.

"Hi, Shin." Thom fashioned his voice in what he hoped was a
conciliatory tone.

"Thom." A smile and nod. "Glad to see you. Have some time to
think?"

"Yes, yes, I did. Is that lasagna?"

Shin deftly served up a plate of lasagna, salad, and sour dough
bread and handed it to Thom.

Thom ate, pushing the bread to the side of the plate for later
consideration, throwing caution to the wind on the noodles. He
stalled until he figured out what he was going to say to Shin. The
man was appointed? To watch the couch, or what? What did he
know about any of the rumors on the bulletin board? Now that
the believing switch was on, and he knew that people were trying
to get the couch, how could Thom know Shin didn't want to take
it too? Nearly any of those rumors on the bulletin board made the
couch priceless.

"So, Shin, I'm waiting for you to explain everything. I'm believing everything now, as a rule, so go ahead and tell me all the weird

fantasy shit about couches. You've got my complete attention. And by the way, we've got to move that couch or risk sending various crewmen into comas."

"Pardon?" said Shin.

"When you sit on the couch, you fall asleep, and it's almost impossible for anyone to wake you up."

"Really. Is that how you got so far out at sea?"

Thom shrugged.

"Interesting." He rubbed down the stove top with steel wool. "I'll tell you what I know, though you'll probably be disappointed."

"I'm listening."

"I'm not the only one. I belong to a council, but I'm not allowed to know the other members. I know only the woman who brought me into the council, and she knows two—me and the one who brought her into the council. We learn certain skills and we're given things to watch over. I have no idea how many of us there are. A lot of what we do is watch over objects from different . . . ah, different ages. Our belief is that humanity as a whole has not evolved to the point of being able to care for itself properly, and in many cases has devolved. And so the council tries to keep the species from destroying itself."

"Sounds real noble," Thom said. He loaded up his fork again.

"There are certain objects that have come down through time that are more than what they appear to be. But there are collectors who want them for themselves, who want to use them for their own benefit."

"I'm believing everything," Thom said cheerfully through a mouthful of food. He picked up the sourdough and eyed it. "Throw it at me, whatever. I'm not making any promises on comprehension though."

"A lot of things are unclear, and truthfully I don't know if anyone has the answers. I don't know if you three were carefully chosen and brought together to perform the quest, or if the quest was created because the three of you came together. I only know that a situation that had been waiting for a long time suddenly matured. Presto!" Shin said, like toast popping up.

Thom paused, slightly open mouth full of half-chewed sour-dough bread. He realized that the hardest thing to believe was that he'd be involved in anything important. That someone outside of his small circle of geeks would have anything to do with him. Chosen. When had he ever been chosen in his life? On the rare times he'd hit the ball, it had always flown heroically from the field as if shot from a cannon. But even then he was still never chosen, not even Little League, not even softball. What did ability matter—not that he had excessive sports ability by any means—when your cool ratio was a negative number? And now this? He was Thom. He was an unchosen. It had taken several decades, but he'd resigned himself to the role.

Shin was waiting for a response.

"Okay, you're right, I don't have the faintest idea what you're talking about. Tell me about the couch."

"I know almost nothing about it. It's probably not going to hurt you knowing nothing about it. Instinct and intuition might serve more than knowledge. It's a bad thing, as you've probably gathered. At least its nature affects things badly."

"Where are we taking it?"

"To a safe place, the only safe place."

"Come on, man! Help me out here."

"I don't know where you're taking it. Ask Tree. He might have a better idea. He wouldn't have any names, but he might have seen it. Each of you has a specialty, and that's Tree's."

"Okay, okay," Thom said, thinking of Erik's pet name for Tree, dreamboy. "Does the couch want us to take it a certain way? It gets lighter if we go in a certain direction."

"Or it gets less potent. In one direction its power accumulates. In the other it disseminates."

"What?"

"Just a theory. But it was certainly useful in getting you started."

"Just a theory," repeated Thom. "So what's your job?"

"I make sure that the job gets finished. I ward off interference and make sure you keep on. I try to keep the collectors from knowing about you, and now I accompany you to the end. There may be more than one council member assigned to the couch. I'm prohibited from knowing."

"What, so one day your teacher-lady just said three guys are going to come walking by with a couch?"

"Something like that."

Thom finished up the plate of food, feeling tremendously better, and then realized he'd eaten wheat bread and wheat noodles and that in a very little time his stomach would be a witch's cauldron and the air about him an airborne toxic event.

"Interference like those guys with shotguns?" Thom said. "We didn't get much help there."

"Sorry about that. I underestimated a little. Believe me, it'll be far worse when you get to South America."

"Far worse?"

"Speaking of which, be careful what goes up on your website."

"You know about that?"

"Of course I do. The collectors know too. And encryption is certainly not going to stop them."

The hairs on the back of Thom's neck stood up.

"No one knows what it is, but everyone has ideas and the power of it is clear," Shin said. "There are many objects with power associated with them, an artifact from an Egyptian tomb or an old piece of artwork that collects power as it is viewed thousands of times. We are an uninformed age, an ignorant age, and we have few objects of power that aren't a creation of science. This is the material age, the scientific age, and much of the rest of human possibility is ignored. The couch . . . the couch is The Object. If there are things more potent, then they haven't surfaced. I don't think we're supposed to know what it is, where it came from. But right now Portland is changing in the absence of the couch, and that change is spreading across North America."

"How is it changing?" Thom tried to quell exclamations of disbelief, to stifle a sardonic smile.

"It's too early to tell, but it's changing positively."

Thom shook his head. He realized that the empty cup he'd reluctantly allowed his mind to become had just begun to overflow with unbelievable things. "Okay, I think I've heard enough to get me started. I'm going to have to finish up on this another time." He let the first cloud free with a drum roll. "Sorry," Thom said. He frowned and stared at the tabletop, used to the embarrassment. "Gluten intolerant. I can't eat wheat."

"You should have said something. Why did you eat that?"

Yes, why? he wondered. "I don't know," Thom said. "Sorry." He reddened. "Maybe we should go move the couch?"

The couch was gone. Shin raced off surprisingly quickly for someone his age, counting lifeboats on each side of the ship. Thom held his stomach and wondered what his specialty was.

Shin came back breathless. "All the lifeboats are here. I bet it's in the sick bay."

"In the sick bay?"

"Someone is trying to kill Erik," he said and strode off down a hallway.

"Erik is dead!" Thom heard his own voice bursting out with exasperation, and his stomach rumbled over, filling the hallways behind them.

Shin looked over his shoulder and snapped his fingers, barely veiling a look of disgust, either for the fumes they were leaving behind or Thom's lack of knowledge. "We just rescued Erik."

Thom remembered reading books about people, upon hearing good news, whose hearts sung. He wondered if there were any remaining organs that weren't working on some soliloquy.

Erik was the wrong color, and the darkness under his eyes seemed to go too far down his cheeks. He had a full, bristling mustache and seemed surprisingly thin and frail for only several days at sea, as if his body had begun to eat itself. Someone had moved him off the sick bed and onto the couch. He was as still as snow.

Shin grabbed under his arms, Thom grabbed his feet, and they moved him back to the bed. Shin took his pulse, felt his forehead, listened to his heart.

"He's still alive. I thought the depression you said the couch causes might push the life out of him. It doesn't put you into a coma. It takes away your will to wake. The person who moved the couch here probably knew this."

Thom admired Erik's mustache. Alive. The guilt seeped out of him.

Shin pointed to a beer cooler in the corner. "They spent a good while prying his hands away from that thing. He wouldn't let go."

"So that's how he stayed afloat. I was trying to picture him swimming." Thom eyed the cooler as he eyed everything now. Perhaps it was magic too? An ancient beer cooler from aliens or gods. Some Mesopotamian artifact, a casket, a trove, an ark. *An ice chest,* said brain.

"Move the couch to your room, keep an eye on it at all times. Someone else is here. This was a chess move, a smart one. Without Erik, the errand cannot be completed. I'm grateful they didn't abandon ship with it, but then they would have been easy to catch. They want the couch, but ensuring you fail is their first priority."

Thom nodded, temporarily tamping down the fear. *Someone else.* He sat on the bed and put his hand over Erik's heart and left it there. He could feel the muted, slow thump. The Mouth was back.

Tree came in and sat on the bed and smiled. "I knew there was supposed to be three. We can go on now."

Erik opened his eyes and recoiled when he saw Shin.

"*Hijo de puta, qué haces, no me toques.*"

Thom stared at Erik and wondered for a moment if it weren't Erik after all but a Hispanic kid they'd picked up.

"Shh, you should rest."

"*Pinche pendejo, vas a llevar el sofá o no?*"

"The sofa? Over there."

"*Te voy a matar, cabrón, sin no me dejes, voy a matarte.*"

Shin sighed. "Well, his Spanish will come in handy in South America. I don't have the faintest idea what he's saying."

Thom looked nervously at Tree. "Is he okay?"

Tree shrugged.

"Erik," Thom said, "can you speak English?"

Erik's eyes did a focusing dance, skittering between Tree and

Thom. He raised his head, and then his eyes gave up, rolled back under the lids, and he passed out.

"Ah," Thom said. "I guess not. Is there something we can do for him?"

"I'm going to go chat with the medic to see if he knows anything about the couch. Other than that just let him rest. Talk to him when he's awake. See if you can bring him back."

A week passed on the ship. Thom's waistline kept on diminishing as he relied on Shin's simple resources for wheat-free diets, and from carrying the couch before that. The roommates were together again. Even though Erik mysteriously hadn't found his English tongue despite the ship doctor's fastidious attention, Thom and Tree used Carlos, a Panamanian crewmate, to translate. Thom took it as an opportunity to learn some Spanish, finding that he could ask Erik in English and he'd reply in Spanish.

"Teach me some good phrases, Erik."

Erik was still confined to bed by ship's orders. He'd passed from hypothermia into a fever and was only now beginning to resemble his old self, minus his native tongue.

"*Lo que sea mejor por el país.*"

"What does that mean?" Thom asked Carlos.

"He means, what is there that is better for the country."

"Whatever is best for the country," Thom said and repeated the Spanish phrase. He wrote it into a little notebook he'd taken to carrying around. He wrote everything he had trouble believing into the notebook. "I guess that's useful, Erik. I was thinking of stuff more like, Where's the bathroom? How much does this cost?"

Erik smiled. "*Mis labios estan cerrados.*"

"*Mis labios estan cerrados,*" said Thom slowly, laying a thick, deep-throated, syllable-slurring accent across the phrase. "What does that mean?" He turned to Carlos.

"My lips are closed." Carlos shrugged.

"Erik? How's this going to help me?"

Erik bit his lip, and his eyes twinkled mischievously. "*Son muy buenas, muy importantes, estas oraciones.*" Erik spoke toward Carlos.

"*Es cierto, él no tiene la oportunidad de aprender español que podría usar antes de que llegemos. Entonces, le enseño unas cosas que pueda decir. Es mejor que parezca misterioso que tonto.*"

Carlos smiled nervously toward Thom.

"*Aquí es la mas importante,*" Erik said. "*Puedes usarla en cualquier situacion: Pero mi perro no tiene dientes.*"

Thom looked at Carlos, a pained expression on his face in expectation of what Erik had said.

"He said this one is most important." Carlos bit down on a smile. "My dog has no teeth."

"Erik! That's the most important?"

Erik nodded vigorously.

Thom practiced his three new Spanish phrases until he'd mastered them, mouthing them to himself as he wandered around the ship's metal hallways, staring off to sea, thinking of his mother, Clare, Sheilene. Thinking of the city of Portland receding into the distance like some passed comet.

His mind fixated on Jean, their forsaken journalist. There had been energy there in the way she seemed to speak only to him.

Come to S. America, Thom wrote her, *Erik is alive! This is a story, join us.* He sweated in the computer chair, tapped on the desk, wrote: *I'll need a salsa partner.*

Thom rarely saw Tree that week. Whenever he went looking for him, he was either sleeping or having hushed conversations with Shin. And so he spent the week feeling the weather warm as they traversed ever farther south. The itch of paranoia always at his back, he expected their mysterious pursuers to loom like a police car in the rearview mirror. He obsessively checked on Erik. He sized up crew members to find out if one of them was a "them," as Shin had said. The one who'd moved the couch.

```
to: thom@sanchopanchez.net
from: demx741@mailhaven.com
Thom,
Obviously you are playing with me. But if you will
```

sell the couch, I will pay the 100k. Yes, it's an absurd amount of money, and shame on you for being so greedy. But I want it, and I don't want to play any more games. I'll transfer the money this moment, give me the word.

-dem

———————-

to: thom@sanchopanchez.net
from: itbelongstous@yahoo.com
You have no idea what you're doing or what you're playing with. A ship is coming to meet yours, hand over the couch or face the consequences.

———————-

to: thom@sanchopanchez.net
from: clare@nyc_library.ny.state.gov
subject: Double Header
Hey boyo, remember that historian I mentioned, I told him about your couch deal, and he's become extremely interested and went weak in the knees. He's doing some further research but I showed him the letter I wrote to you and he thinks that per-haps several of those were the same couch! That is, maybe the wizard barbarian king guy had a hold of Adam and Eve's couch, etc. Who knows, who knows, but thought I'd pass it along. If you've really got that couch, you seem to be tapped into a real mystery. He's going to try to get me something more substantial and mentioned wanting to meet you. But truthfully he's a little bit of an oddball and I got concerned over his level of interest . . . I told you him were going to S. America thinking that would discourage him. Loved the photos you sent, how did you get on a boat again? Your friends sound nice. So you've got a possible interest? Tell me all about her. Yes, I've heard of a language being jarred out of somebody's memory by an incident, so

I'm going to guess he's not just playing with you.
Just count yourself lucky that it's a language he
knows and not one he's making up. In no way does
being on a freighter in the Pacific seem to be heading this way.
love, clare

---

to: thom@sanchopanchez.net
from: jean@sidklowski.net
subject: Re: false alarms and drowned monkeys
Hola Thom! You're going to S. America then . . .
that's a bit out of my range, normally. I've been
talking to my editor, though, and it looks like
there's a chance I might just make it. We've talked
about the possibility of 4 articles with vague S.
American leanings, plus yours, plus adding in some
vacation time. Why am I doing this? I don't know, I
honestly don't. You really think you have a story?
What have you got for me? Or? If you think you can
actually keep one of your promises, though, let's
meet up somewhere. How about we meet in Guayaquil at
the Museum Nahim Isaías Barquet around noon. Their
website says you can see genuine shrunken heads.
What do you think? I get there the day before you.
Erik lives!
-Jean
(she-who-would-learn-salsa)

---

to: jean@sidklowski.net
from: thom@sanchopanchez.net
subject: south american rendezvous
I've got a whole three Spanish phrases now, so I'm
ready to tackle the southern continent. Yes, you
should come. Yes, we have a story. Yes we'll stumble
over each others' toes to a latin beat. There's all
kinds of excitement here. We've got death threats!

Resurrections! It now seems that I can promise you
the fast-lane of journalism. I'm trying to pretend
that I'd like you to come down and meet up with us
solely because "it's such an interesting story."
I'm failing. But I understand if your motivation is
solely journalistic.
Meeting place sounds superb—my brain has outgrown
its britches and some shrinkage would do me some
good. Onward, to Guayaquil!
-Thom

Thom stood at the ship's rail, watched the constant undulating sine wave of the water. A hundred thousand dollars for the couch, a death threat, a couch causing trouble throughout the ages, and *Jean*, not the usual assortment of email. Breathe in Jean, exhale fear-dread-lust.

Thom, Tree, and Shin sat around the kitchen table snacking on carrot sticks and talking about plunging a lifeboat in the Pacific with the couch aboard and setting off separately.

"What about your council thing, can't they do anything?" Thom said.

"We're not exactly organized for speed. We've been around for a long, long time, and to just go send a rescue boat out in the middle of the ocean before the bad guys arrive is not exactly our specialty. I have to tell my teacher, she tells hers, and so on, the main council might not even hear about it for weeks. We're, ah, trying to do some reorganization, but in the meantime we're a bit on the Luddite side, sorry."

Thom exhaled in disgust. "When you guys want to come into the present, let me know and I'll set up an email server for you. For crying out loud."

"We could just put the couch back in the water and float off on that, see where we end up," Tree said. He opened and closed his pliers—they looked like a fish trying to breathe on land. He had run out of wire, and his hands suffered for it.

"The last thing I want to do is fall asleep on that couch in the ocean again," Thom said. "That'd be it for us." Thom's stomach had given him a week of peace, with Shin's wheat-free cooking, and very little stress until now.

"Hey hey! I'm alive!" Erik bellowed from the top of the stairs. It was the first time they'd heard Erik speak English in almost two weeks. His upper lip glowed waxily with newly shaven nakedness.

"Erik!" Thom yelled. He got up and wrapped him up in a hug without thinking, and Erik cringed.

"Good to see you too, big guy."

"*Mi perro no tiene dientes!*" Thom hollered proudly. "I thought you forgot English. I thought I was going to have to learn another damn language just to talk to you."

"Yeah, funny that. It felt like I was speaking the right language."

"How come you know Spanish?" Tree said.

"Oh . . . I'll tell you all about it sometime, dreamboy. Alrighty! What's going on here? Why's everybody looking so glum? Missed me, I reckon. Shin, I've heard all about you now. No hard feelings even if I don't trust you farther than I could throw you." Erik reached out his hand.

"Thanks, Erik." Shin shook Erik's hand. "I'm flattered."

"Death threats," Thom said.

"What about them?"

"We've got them."

"Oh boy, we're really in a movie now. But what are they going to do, send missiles out?"

"They're sending a ship." Shin adjusted his baseball cap, and a shock of silver hair stuck out at an angle. "We have no idea when they'll get here or how strong they'll be, and I can't really tell the captain. We're not supposed to talk about the couch at all to people who don't know about it, for one, and secondly, to him you all are stowaways. He's got his job to think about and would hand you over in a minute if the boat seemed authoritative."

"Well, handing over the couch sounds right nice to me." Erik put one leg over the bench seat on the table and sat, "I've already had a whole load of fun. Looking for a stand-up job in Portland sounds just fine." He pared several carrot sticks down to nothing like a chipmunk.

Thom let out a deep sigh and went through the various possibilities for what the couch might be, watching Shin to see if he would reveal belief in one theory over another. Thom realized he was in the quest until the end. He neglected to tell Erik that someone had offered a hundred thousand dollars for the couch.

"Well, geez," said Erik. "That's quite a story. What do I believe?"

"This is something I can tell you," Shin said. "Since you've left with the couch, people in Portland are sitting on their own couches less."

Erik spent the next four minutes guffawing. "You're delusional, old man. What, you think we're carrying King Couch or something?"

"Yes."

Erik guffawed some more. "Why aren't you guys laughing? Can't I have some solidarity here?" He looked at Thom. "Come on, you're Mr. Science Guy."

"Well it's kind of different for me now. There are too many little things that add up. And I just got a death threat, Erik. It tends to make you believe that something rather serious is going on."

"Doesn't mean you can't laugh about it a little. People in Portland are sitting on their couches less? How do you survey that? Isn't that one of the funniest things you've ever heard?"

"I guess so," Thom said.

Shin smoothed the front of his white chef jacket and smiled. "But what that means is that for perhaps the first time in their lives, people are noticing what's going on around them. They're being released from a spell, they're leaving their TVs, they're leaving their houses, they're paying attention. They're taking a look, really, at what humanity has fallen to."

"I'm convinced," Thom said, a chill traveling up the back of his neck. He noticed Erik staring at him with disbelief. If only Erik had been there a week before, they could have stood up to the weirdness together, but with a week to himself Thom had refashioned himself into a hero. "We need a plan," he said. "We need to get off the ship as soon as possible. How far are we from Ecuador?"

"We're close, maybe a day's journey."

"That means we're off the coast of Colombia somewhere," Erik said. "My dad lives there. I'm almost home."

"Lives there?"

"Yeah." Erik raised both hands in quote marks and said with drama. "He's a terr-or-ist."

"A guerilla?"

Erik nodded. "Not the group who does the kidnappings. They're just plain, old-fashioned, unsuccessful peace-and-justice fighters. Socialists. That old shit. You know."

"That's why you speak Spanish."

"We moved there when I was eight. I'm not sure where my mom is. She wasn't all gung-ho about the guerilla life. She might be in Ecuador. I heard from her several years ago when she lived in Quito."

"I take it you don't get along with them too well," said Thom.

"Not so much. I rather wanted a nice North American childhood. I ran away when I was sixteen and made it back to the States. Had to go wetback with a coyote across the Mexican-U.S. border, just like everybody else, because my parents burned all our U.S. identification. They hate the States."

"Damn," Thom said. "I guess my childhood was cinchy."

Shin slapped the tabletop. "Talk about it later. We need a plan now."

In the moment of silence afterward they heard the engine's note change, and a panic rose in all of them. Shin spoke with furious speed. "Go grab the couch and make sure you're on the opposite side of the ship from wherever the oncoming ship is. I'll try to talk them out of it, but you may have to jump overboard and stay out of sight. They'll probably spot you anyway."

"This is fun." Erik grabbed another fistful of carrots. "I just learned how to speak English again, and now I'm getting back in the drink on the couch."

Shin snapped his fingers at Erik, and he shut up. The four raced upstairs. From the deck they saw a smaller, armed ship approaching. "Colombian coast guard," Shin yelled. "Go!"

The couch was incredibly light. They pulled it around to the side of the ship opposite the coast guard and considered the prospect of hurling themselves the twenty-five feet down to the water.

"What if it's just, you know, some coast guard guys?" Erik said.

"We should jump now," Tree said. "I know it. This is the time we jump."

"It would suck to jump for nothing," Thom said. "I don't feel like getting wet." The sun beat down on the ship, and the metal of the rail burned to the touch. With the speed cut, the wind was gone, and everything began to sweat and steam. He wondered how these things worked. Did the coast guard get on the ship, or did they just yell from where they were? The water below frothed around the hull. How did they know they wouldn't be churned up and spit out by the propeller? What about sharks?

"Let's listen for a second, Tree." He pushed down on the end of the couch that Tree was trying to maneuver over the railing. Tree gave him the driven, wild-eyed look that seemed to haunt his face more and more, like he'd begun to fade—become a ghost, only inhabiting this world peripherally. He gave Erik a keep-a-watch-over-Tree look and stole over to where he could see the coast guard boat. To his surprise, four well-armed men were already on board. A great fear crept into him. He started to turn back, to say throw it overboard, even though they'd certainly be found, but something in Shin's voice stopped him. Shin and the captain were speaking to the armed men. Shin looked like a lackey in his cook's outfit among the uniformed men. Thom could just barely make out the words.

"We're going to search your ship until we find it," one of the uniformed men said. He was obviously the leader. He spoke English without an accent and had blond cropped hair under a coast guard hat. His pistol was drawn.

"Of course you are," Shin said. "But we're not carrying arms. We're carrying televisions." Thom heard a kindness in Shin's voice he hadn't heard before, like he was speaking to a grandson he was proud of.

"We're looking for a couch," the leader said with annoyance. "I never mentioned anything about arms."

"Of course, you're right, but if you'll come with me you'll see that our cargo is full of televisions. This is a peaceful ship of commerce."

Thom could feel that something was at work, and for a moment he wondered if the ship were carrying arms. He saw the leader's brow knit together. His eyes focused on his pistol and then jerked straight again.

"We're not looking for arms," the man said, but there was a questioning lilt to his voice.

"You wouldn't want them to fall into the hands of the rebels," Shin said. "I understand. Please feel free to have a look at our cargo. You'll find there isn't a gun on board."

The leader nodded, resignation in his posture, as if he'd been caught stealing candy.

"I'm sorry that you have to go. Perhaps when we come back through you can stay for dinner."

The leader nodded again and holstered his pistol. The men climbed over the side and down a ladder out of Thom's sight. A few minutes later, the coast guard ship pulled away from the freighter. Thom saw for the first time that far away in the distance, through a haze, there were juts of land sticking up.

"You sure handled them well," Shin said to the captain. "It's strange they would come looking for arms on a licensed freighter."

"It sure is." The captain jumped to life. "I don't like armed men boarding my ship. I'm going to call this in to the company." The captain turned and left.

Thom approached Shin from behind the wall where he'd been hiding. "They were looking for arms?"

"They were looking for you." Shin had a troubled look.

Thom paused, confused, a memory that couches had been talked about slowly surfacing from some depth.

"I talked them out of it, but the main fellow was difficult. He had training. Not enough, but some. He suspected. We've got about forty-five minutes to an hour. He'll be back, and he'll know what he's dealing with this time."

"You . . . did something with your voice," Thom said, feeling a new awe for Shin.

"Schoolboy's trick. I don't have time to teach it to you now, but it's easy to overcome if you know how and you've practiced. I should have been teaching you some things all week, but I assumed I would be going with you. Now I see I've got to stay. Look, we need to get you out of here. Let's get a lifeboat ready. We'll slip it over the side, and you've got to go like hell."

"Teach me how to avoid the voice thing."

"There's no time."

"But I want to learn." Here was something else, something new, another magic. "It's just like—hey, it's just like—"

"Well where do you think Tolkien got it?"

"No—Obi Wan Kenobi!"

"We don't have time for this."

"But what—" Thom tried to find a starting place for the enormous number of questions he had, "is it some kind of vocal frequency or—"

"It's nothing. Alright, quickly. I'll teach you how to ignore it. I'm going to convince you to lie down. To stop me, focus on something around you, and repeat its name over and over until I stop speaking. Got it?"

Thom nodded and stared at Shin's ugly, cooking-stained tennis shoes and repeated his newly learned Spanish word for "shoe."

"You'd feel so much better lying down, Thom," Shin said. "You should take it easy on yourself."

Zapato zapato zapato zapato zapato, Thom said to himself.

"Your knee would stop hurting if you just rested a little."

A sharp pain coursed through Thom's knee and his teeth felt like he was chewing on aluminum. He repeated furiously, *Zapato zapato zapato zapato zapato.*

"You're so tired, your knee hurts, rest cures all. What a nice place to lie down you've chosen."

Zapato. Thom did feel tired. *Zapato.* All this running about, worrying about couches, and what with his bad knee. He knelt and put his hand behind himself to ease back.

"Thom! I haven't got time for this now."

Panic surged through Thom, and he remembered the coast guard was coming back, and then remembered *zapatos*, and he was lying down. "Holy crap!" Thom said. "How'd you do that?"

"You've got to practice, only focus on one thing. Come on, let's go."

Thom followed Shin in a daze, still fighting the urge to lie down. He'd lost all sense of time and was surprised to see Erik and Tree still struggling with the couch—Tree trying to push it over, Erik holding it back, the two bickering. The image looked like something he'd dreamed about weeks ago though he knew he'd just left the scene for a few moments.

"Tree," Shin said. "Stop." The two stopped as if frozen and put the couch back onto the deck. "Use a lifeboat, for God's sake."

The three of them looked excitedly up at the orange, spaceship-like, covered lifeboat anchored to the side of the ship.

"We can't use that," Shin said. "They'll notice that missing. There's an old ship's boat below. I've got to go buy us twenty minutes with the motor cut. I'll be right back."

They hauled the boat up from below, a six-person aluminum affair that had been used mostly for sport and fooling around. When they ran across crew members, Shin would proclaim, "We're going fishing!" And by the time they reached the railing and were lowering the boat down to the waterline, Erik and Tree were excited about the fishing trip and Thom was repeating *zapato* to himself like a mantra.

They managed, with not a little hassle and jostling, to lower first Erik and then the couch onto the rowboat. They set it crosswise, where it hung precariously over each side. Erik organized the boat while Shin, Tree, and Thom ran around gathering up gear, getting Thom's laptop, and getting ready to set out. At the last minute Shin came up with a motor and a five-gallon tank of gas. Shin worked his voice for interested crew members who came to have a look.

They went away believing they had important business elsewhere, and occasionally Tree would wander off with them, looking for his important business until Shin called him back.

"The voice is a real pain sometimes," Shin said. He lowered a box of hastily packed foodstuffs down to Erik. "It's like herding cats. The mind thing is better, but I can only do one at a time, and I can't be doing other stuff at the same time. What you need to know is any time you feel a seed of suspicion, keep focused. Practice your focus all the time. You'll only get a second where you feel like someone is telling you something very strange, and then the voice will take you over. Sometimes you'll have a physical reaction," he shrugged. "It's different for everyone. My toes hurt when I hear the voice."

Thom nodded, now wary of anything. *Pazato pazato*, he said to himself for good measure. Was that the word for *shoe*? "You can't come with us?"

"I've got to deal with the coast guard when they come back. I'll catch up."

Thom felt a pinch of fear: alone again with nothing but the couch and the water. And then they were all in the boat with Erik in control of the motor, Tree in the very front, and Thom wedged uncomfortably against the couch. Shin waved encouragingly while the anxiety of being in a rowboat in the Pacific Ocean swelled over them. They had no idea where they were going. Only Tree had a vague direction in mind. Before they'd left, Shin had pointed to where he thought they were on a small map of South America. The plan was that Tree would point the way, under the assumption that he had some internal navigator, and that they would work it out as they went.

They were quiet. The small gas motor a tiny bee buzzing them onward. They kept an eye on the distant speck of the coast guard, watched the freighter diminish. Water bounced off the sides of the boat and wet the underside of the couch.

Occasionally Tree would urgently point and Erik would roll his eyes and bring the front of the boat around. Thom busied himself with going through their foodstuffs, passing around potato chips, and then sodas, and then raisins, and then whatever else would help pass the time. In not too long, if they were not killed by the coast guard or swallowed by sharks, if they were not marooned or capsized, if the sky did not fall or the earth come up to swallow them, if the couch did not make them sleeping beauties or decide it wanted to go back home, they would be in a foreign country. The only foreign country Thom had ever been to was Canada, and even there he'd felt culture shock. The money, the walk signs for crosswalks, the strange food, even the pigeons had seemed different. Cooing in some northern dialect. He'd gone around in a paranoid daze, waiting for people to start pointing at him, the giant from the U.S., a representative from the land of big money and movies and warlike politics. But no one had noticed him. He hoped it would be like that in Ecuador.

Shin was gagged and tied—a strip of duct tape forcefully applied over his mouth—before he could speak a word. Ten men boarded with automatic weapons, some of them were Colombian but most of them were American. They searched every corner of the ship.

"Where is it?" the leader asked.

Shin stood where he was, hoped against hope the captain might cover for them.

"I don't see how a couch is your business," the captain said, still baffled and angry at having his cook trussed up. "We found it floating in the middle of the Pacific! I've made a call to the company. If there's something your government would like to bring up with us directly, I suggest you have your superior contact mine. Otherwise I consider this trespassing."

"These are our waters. We know that couch was on this vessel. It carried an illegal substance, and those three that were with it are under arrest. We can dock you for harboring criminals and"—he nodded at Shin—"assisting criminal activity."

The captain sighed, and Shin tensed, knowing the captain was going to tell all.

"Some of my crew spotted them getting into a boat about an hour ago. They headed . . ." The captain closed his eyes, swayed ever-so-slightly. "They headed north."

"Get out!" The leader yelled at Shin. "Get out of his mind!" He handed his gun to one of his men, grabbed Shin by the shirtfront, lifted him mightily in the air, and threw him over the railing to the water.

"Hey!" the captain yelled. "Goddamn you! We're a licensed freighter. Do you know how you'll be penalized for not following international law?"

The leader waved at the captain. "Get him out of here." He watched Shin surface and struggle to stay afloat with only his feet free to tread water.

"Here," the leader said and took back his gun. He rested the barrel of the automatic on the railing. Shin floated about twenty feet from the freighter.

"You understand I'm about to kill you," the leader said. His men gathered along the railing, watching the show.

"You could just"—he turned to a man on his right—"Bill? What could he do, do you suppose, to save his life?"

"Where's the couch?" Bill yelled. "Where are the carriers?"

"Now that is a good idea. You could tell us where they are." He kicked the ship's rail. "What about the voice, though, Bill?"

"He can write it."

"Yes, he could. It's up to you old, man," he yelled down. "Tell us where they are, and you live, agreed?"

Shin kicked with his feet once to keep himself upright. He nodded yes.

"Oh good, what a relief. Bill, go down and get him."

A moment later Bill yelled and the leader looked back and saw Shin swimming away underwater, his body undulating like a fish's.

"He dived!" Bill yelled from the coast guard boat, where he'd been trying to hook Shin with a pole.

"Ah fuck," the leader said. Shin was about ten feet from making it underneath the coast guard boat. The leader shot into the water until blood bubbled up.

"Bring me the captain," he said. "Now let's see what he says."

∾

Just when the drone of the motor had become part of their con-sciousnesses—a natural force, a breath in, a breath out—just when they'd been lulled into the safety of continuity, the splash-ing ups and downs, skidding wave to wave, just when the fear began to dissipate off their bodies in earnest, the motor sputtered out.

"Gee," Erik said. He looked thoughtfully at the gas tank and motor for a moment, hefted the tank, and then went into a spasm of kicking. He foot-pummeled the tank, motor, and sides of the boat until it was necessary to cradle his foot. He closed his eyes for a count of ten, then landed another kick on the tank, wrenched the tubes out of it, and threw it overboard.

"Erik!" Thom said. "Erik, Erik. Calm it, man."

Erik shrugged, tight-lipped with anger. He stared at the bottom of the boat, his face a deep red. "Oh boyyyyy," he said and gripped his hair. "Can't anything be just a little bit fucking easy?"

The shore still seemed impossibly far away, only the barest hint of something rising from the horizon. Tree had been steering them south, not toward shore.

"Oars," said Thom. And they looked around the rowboat.

"I'm going to kill that old man when I see him again," Erik said. "Sending us out to sea like this. Haven't we had enough of this? How do we know they really wanted the couch?"

"They did." Thom stretched his legs out and leaned back against the couch, making himself comfortable for the long haul. "I heard them."

"Well, we should have given it to them," Erik said with obvious disgust.

"Julio will help us," Tree said.

"Julio?" Thom tried to remember meeting a Julio. "Was that the big guy on Theo's railcart thing?"

"I'm not sure who he is. I just know that he helps us. He's short, and Erik thinks he talks funny."

"Is he in the boat?" Erik said.

"No," Tree said after some thought.

"Is he in the water then?" Erik stood up to get a better vantage point to yell at Tree from. "Is he a mermaid? Perhaps he's a dolphin? Dolphins talk funny."

"Erik, don't fall in the water. This gives me bad memories already," Thom said.

"Maybe there's a beer cooler out there somewhere—when you're not moving it's murder hot." Erik wiped sweat off his face. He stood up on a seat and looked out over the water, his hand shading his eyes. "Uh-oh," he said.

"What?"

"There's a boat a'coming."

"How far?"

"Speck-far, at the moment. Should I just go ahead and drown myself again? It seemed to work out pretty well last time."

"You're going to if you keep standing up on that seat. Please be unpredictable and don't fall in."

Tree stood up suddenly. "It's them!" He grabbed an end of the couch, hoisted it up, and tipped it overboard, rocking the boat so much that Erik launched off the other end.

"Tree! You fuckall, asshead!" Erik shook his head, spraying droplets of water in a fan, spitting out a mouthful. The couch bobbed in the water. Erik looked at Thom. "I didn't fall in! Not my fault!"

Tree dove in after the couch, surfaced, and pulled himself up onto it. "Come on!" he yelled. "We've got to separate from the rowboat. They'll follow that."

"Tree." Thom opened his hands in pleading. "Can we work on some consensus building? Please?"

Tree waved them over urgently. "Come on, let's go."

Thom looked at Erik treading water.

"He's the navigator." Erik held his fingers up in quotes around the word.

"Erik, could you pull the boat even with the couch? I'm not going to just jump in with my laptop." Thom patted his black plastic garbage bag-wrapped backpack. "Plus, having some food and water might come in sort of handy this time." Thom stared at the couch, remembered Shin's words: the couch dampens the will for action.

∾

Tree stayed on the couch, and within minutes he was in a coma-like sleep, his mouth open, his face in full exposure to the sun. From his position in the water, Thom gently covered Tree's face with his own shirt. They pushed the rowboat away and kicked toward shore. They chatted, trying to keep a low profile, trying to keep the fear of a boat behind them out of their minds. Erik told South American stories, and Thom listened, happy to have someone fill the space of the ocean with sound.

He wondered what was happening at home. How his mother was doing, what she would think if she knew he was paddling behind a couch in the Pacific Ocean off the coast of South America. Her face would turn red; the worry would boil up into a sort of hysteria. Poor Mom. *Poor Thom*, brain said, and he agreed. But there was that tiny sliver of excitement too. He was no longer the doughy computer geek chunking together functions while the rest of the world slept. He had acquired a touch of the exotic.

After hours of kicking, the shore as far away as ever and their boat permanently lost, they decided to wake Tree up to make him take his turn. Their faces felt the sting of sunburn and saltwater. They shook him and yelled his name until he finally came back from the dead, his face an inhuman mask of incomprehension.

"Your turn, dreamboy. Get in here and do some paddling. I've got to take a rest."

"I had the strangest dreams."

"Get in the water, then you can tell us." Erik climbed up onto the couch, a sodden dog. He shook, and Tree backed into a corner.

"I don't want to." Tree clutched the couch. "I'm afraid of sharks."

"So am I," Erik said. "So is everybody. It's because they have teeth. But you don't see me shirking. If they bite you, bite them back."

Tree took off his clothes, baring his pale, bony frame, and eased himself into the water. With his hands white-knuckled around the edge of a cushion, he began to kick. Snoring came almost immediately from the couch above them.

"We're going to the forest," Tree said. "That's what I dreamed."

"In Ecuador?" Thom said.

"I think so. I don't know which country actually. There was a lot of mud, and we were slipping around, trying to carry it. The trail was too small, and I—and Erik had a machete. It was raining, and the direction was confusing, and then there were so many butterflies, like it was snowing popcorn."

"That sounds like the jungle."

"Yes, maybe the jungle. Somebody there wants the couch."

"A lot of people want the couch, Tree," Thom said, wondering if he wanted the couch. Maybe he could put this furniture-cum-artifact to some use of his own.

"Yes, but I think this is the person we're supposed to bring it to. Like. Like maybe we're taking it home."

"All this time we were just a delivery service. I'd been sort of thinking something a bit grander would happen." Thom checked on the ever-distant shoreline and wondered if they were working against a current. They had two or three hours of light left, Thom remembering the shift in dusk and dawn as they went farther south. Twelve hours of light and twelve of night—had they passed the equator? From his limited vantage point he couldn't see any sign of a ship, except perhaps some dots near the shore, fishing boats. They paddled in silence for a while. Thom tried to keep his head down to keep from getting too sunburned. A seagull flew over, then another, and then a whole flock circled above them.

"Agh! Something bumped my leg!" Tree yelled.

"Are you sure? It could have been my foot. I wasn't paying attention." Thom looked down into the water and saw water.

"Something bumped me," Tree said with a wild look. "Agh! There it is again!" Tree scrambled monkeylike up onto the couch, stepping on Erik and climbing as high as he could onto the back. He looked like some kind of cave animal that only came out in the darkness. Like Gollum, Thom thought, thin and glow white and dressed in only wet underpants, long wet hair on his shoulders. Some kind of underground troll child.

"Tree, sharks don't just eat people. They smell blood or they sense you're wounded. Most of the shark stuff is hype." But Tree wouldn't be convinced. He sat on the back of the couch, nervous and crazy, his eyes jerking about, studying the water. Thom tried to keep himself from thinking about sharks. He wondered if sitting high up on the couch like that would put Tree to sleep too. Then he felt something unmistakably touch his leg. It was a solid bump, and before his brain could calm his body he was sitting next to Tree, as high up on the couch as he could go, trying to balance his weight so the couch wouldn't tip over.

"Something, ah, touched me," he tried to say calmly, and Tree nodded. A minute passed, and they studied the water and gripped the couch, but there was nothing. He'd succumbed to fear. His mind had imagined the bump. Thom checked the position of the sun again; they had to get going. He'd get back in the water. He'd just get in and paddle. On the count of three, he told himself. One. Two.

The couch bucked like they'd hit a speed bump. Tree's teeth were chattering. Thom nudged Erik with his foot, talked through his teeth. "Erik," he said. "*Erik, wake up!*" In the blue depths, Thom saw a large whiteness that moved, a curved shape that was there and then not there. It's okay, he thought. Breathe in, breathe out. It's fish or even a shark, and it's just exploring. It's testing. Then one end of the couch exploded out of the water at a forty-five degree angle. Thom and Tree screamed and clutched the couch, and Erik landed in the water gasping and yelling. Thom grabbed Erik's hair and wrenched him toward the couch. Erik howled. Thom grabbed his arm and pulled him back on.

"The fuck!?" Erik yelled, standing up on the precariously bobbing couch. His hands tenderly cupped his scalp.

"Charks!" Tree's words were chopped off by his chattering teeth. "Chit! Chit down!"

Erik wheeled around, and Tree and Thom seized his arms and forced him to sit.

"What!? What is going on?" Erik said.

"You always fall off the couch." Thom could see the couch's sleep haze clearing from Erik's face, no doubt quickened significantly by the hair pulling.

"I do not. If you're talking about the boat, that was Tree's fault."

"Just shut up. It's like a part of your effing personality. You fall off things."

"Is that our food box?" Tree pointed to what was obviously their food box, listing half-submerged about ten feet away.

"Now how'd that get in the water?" Erik's voice was thick with sarcasm.

"I told you. Sharks."

"Sharks threw it into the water?" Erik worked on a sneer.

"They bumped the couch. That's how you ended up in the water."

"Listen, you guys are supposed to be paddling. If everybody is up here, we're going to fall asleep, and then we'll be screwed. And go get the food box!" Erik started to stand up, and Tree and Thom pushed him back down. "I did my turn. It's your turn!"

Thom realized he'd choose starving to death slowly over getting eaten by a shark any day. "Listen, Erik, there are sharks out there. I'm serious."

There was a great splash and a bone-crunching noise and the food box was gone. All three of them screamed. An apple bobbed up to the surface, followed by a few splinters.

"Well, maybe it's had enough to eat now," Erik said with surprising calmness. Thom had stopped screaming. Tree hadn't. "There were granola bars in there, weren't there? I could sure go for one of those."

Tree was hyperventilating and Thom pushed down on the back of his neck to calm him, then remembered his laptop. He searched the couch for his bag.

"Where's my backpack?"

"Ha ha," Erik said. "That shark is in for a surprise. Could it get shocked?"

"Fuck!" Thom scanned the water. There was no sign of it. "Fuck! Fuck! Fuck!" He pounded the couch back with his fists and put his head in his hands. "That was all the money Shin gave us too."

They stared into the water, each hoping for a plastic-wrapped backpack to surface like a fishing bobber. The journey suddenly seemed very, very long. South America: penniless. If they made it to shore.

Tree patted his shoulder. "Sorry, Thom. At least we're still alive. Maybe the laptop will discourage it. It couldn't have been good to eat."

"Boy, that apple looks good," Erik said. They all looked at the apple floating just out of reach. "I'm going to get it."

"Erik, no."

"Might be the last bit of food we eat."

Erik dove into the water while Tree shrieked. About thirty seconds later they were sharing a warm, salty apple, and it tasted like heaven, even with Erik's boasting.

Another giant whiteness just under the water, like a colossal eye coming in for a close-up. They tensed for the impact and closed their eyes. And then it was gone.

They waited. Each nervously scanned the water from their end of the couch. And they waited some more, too afraid to get back into the water, and made no progress toward shore.

And then Tree was asleep, and then Thom. Erik stared back and forth between the water and the land, did his best at a prayer. Please, please, God, he tried, take us to land. I'll never con again. His fingers propped up his eyelids against the immense sleepiness. He tried to cover his roommates as best he could, but they had very few clothes between them now. Please, please, Julio, whoever you are, and mermaids, and who was the god of the sea? Poseidon, please—or was it Neptune?—just to the shore. He studied a speck landward, and it seemed to be coming toward them, or was that only hopeful delusion? But a great hand of sleep bore down on him. He shook Thom, but his arms were sapped of strength, and at last he gave up, curling into the side of the couch like a cat, keeping his limbs from hanging over.

"*Gringos, gringos, despén, gringos.*"

Erik tried to place what was wrong: had the waterbed upstairs burst again? He felt water thrown over him. He pried his eyes open enough to see a small man standing on two logs tied together. A tall mast jutted up between them from which a ragged sail fluttered.

"*Greeeengohssss,*" the man's singsong voice called.

Erik, senses coming together one by one, managed to attach the voice to this elfin gremlin with the mischievous smile who was throwing water on them.

"Okay! Man, that's enough *con el agua, hijo de puta!*"

The little man giggled with great pleasure. "*Que 'cen p'qui?*" He bared a great smile, showing all three of his teeth, one on the top, two on the bottom. With his fishing-line hand, he adjusted his tattered gym shorts, which, besides a bright yellow baseball cap made up his wardrobe.

"*Qué?*" Erik said and leaned closer. It almost sounded like Spanish.

The line in the man's hand began to pull, and the man held up his other hand, *wait*. He did a magnificent dance, boxer prancing barefoot around the two splintered logs as the line wove around the boat, underneath, back out, and finally, after a great struggle, he pulled a two-and-a-half-foot fish on board. He grabbed it tightly by the belly and whacked its head several times against the bamboo mast, which showed evidence of a long history of fish heads being crushed, and then held it up for Erik, all three teeth showing again. "*Corvina!*"

"*Bravo!*"

The man crammed the fish into a suspiciously familiar beer cooler. The boat began to drift apart from the couch, and the man talked incomprehensibly for a minute before throwing Erik a rope. They pulled themselves back together.

"*'de 'sta la vela?*"

"*La vela? Es una sofá, ni un barco,*" Erik said. "It doesn't have a sail, for Christ's sake. It's a couch."

The man giggled raucously again. "Julio." He pointed at his chest.

"Julio! *Mucho gusto.*" Erik looked down at Tree to see if he'd heard that his dream-savior had arrived. The kid really was some kind of miracle. There was a market opportunity there. Erik repeated the gesture at his own chest. "*Enrique. Como va?*"

"*Bin, bin!*"

"*Donde estamos?*"

"*Playas.*"

"*Playas?*" Erik looked toward the beaches, which were now remarkably closer. "*Si, pero las playas donde? En que país, ciudad, región?*"

"*Playas, s'el pueblito. Ecuador.*"

"Hey, guys." Erik kicked at Tree. "Wake up, your guy Julio is here."

Tree slowly came to, studied the scene for a minute, and then woke Thom.

Erik passed introductions around. "*Enrique, Tomás, y . . . y . . . Arbol.*" What the hell else was he going to call Tree? *Arbol* would have to do.

"*Arbol?*" Julio said and laughed. He pointed at himself, Julio, and then at the two logs he was standing on. "*Arbol y Arbol, jo tengo dos arbole.*"

Erik nodded. Things were going just fine. If only he could understand what the hell the guy was saying.

"*Pero mi perro no tiene dientes!*" Erik heard and looked around for which of them had said such an idiotic thing. It was Thom, smiling idiotically.

Julio widened his eyes in surprise. "*Tampco mio!*"

Thom looked at Erik. Perhaps he'd made a terrible mistake.

"He said his doesn't either. I think. Now neither of your dogs have teeth."

Thom smiled idiotically at Julio again.

"Well, apparently you guys have found something in common," Erik said. "I'm glad you've gotten that established. *Julio, que milagro que te encontramos, puedes ayudarnos ir a la costa? Que has visto, no tenemos una vela.*"

"Tell him I dreamed about him," Tree said.

"Tree." Erik sighed, scratched at his mustache compulsively. "I'm not going to tell him you freaking dreamed about him, you freak."

"Then ask him if he'd help us get to shore."

"I just did," Erik snapped.

"*Nadar.*" Julio mimed swimming.

"He says to swim."

"No! Tell him about the sharks," Tree said.

"Uh, that's going to look kind of pansy. Look at his boat."

The sail had about forty patches in it and the faintest painting of a giant bottle of champagne across the dirty smudge of canvas. The logs were shaped vaguely boatlike at the ends, carved up out of the water, except at the back there was a large chunk missing out of the logs that could have been negligent driving or sharkbite.

"*Lo que sea mejor por el pais,*" Thom beamed. *Whatever is best for the country.*

"Would you. Shut. Up."

Julio chuckled. "*Beno, beno.*" He followed this up with several paragraphs of what seemed to be witty conversation, chuckling every few sentences. He pulled his sail tight, and it began to catch the wind.

Tree and Thom looked at Erik, and Erik shrugged. "Maybe we should just hold the rope and see what happens?"

"I thought you spoke Spanish."

"I do! That guy is hardly speaking Spanish. He . . . speaks, he's chopping all his words up, talks too fast."

The rope went taut, and Julio looked back at them from ten yards in front and gave another wave. They all waved back cheerfully, and Thom restrained himself from saying his third and last Spanish phrase. Better not blow them all at once, he thought.

The couch moved slowly toward shore. On the beach was a line of boats similar to Julio's. Gulls and pelicans hovered nearby, begging for morsels. A row of shacks lined the beach, and Thom recognized the word *restaurante* on each. A town sprawled at the end of the beach and up the hill. A small crowd of fishermen gathered, it seemed Julio had caught something other than *corvina*.

They came to the breakers, and Julio angled his boat and caught the waves like a surfboard, riding handily to shore while feeding out more rope to let them manage on their own.

"Okay," Erik said. "Okay. Hold on!" He prepared to paddle-surf to shore. The couch began to squirrel around and rock severely in the waves. Those on the beach were watching the arrival with interest.

A strong wave launched the three of them, in their underwear and sunburns, off the couch. The couch bucked and turned and didn't get any closer to shore, and only Thom's toes could touch the ground. He heard Tree shrieking and saw him flailing about.

"Tree! What's wrong?"

Tree gave him a wild, panicked look. "Erik!" Thom shouted. "Take Tree to shore. He's shark-freaked. I'll get the couch," he said and wondered just how he was going to do that. He could see at least thirty amused fishermen following their progress. Watch out, the civilized world has arrived, Thom thought, come to colonize for the umpteenth time in their underwear and on their floating couches.

He swam behind the couch and pushed. Bumped headfirst into it with each wave. He struggled toward shore, the couch ground-ing with each lull between waves and then jerking forward with each crest. It was going to take him no less than six months to get the couch to shore this way. He looked toward shore to see if he could get a hand, but everyone seemed focused on Tree and Erik. In about four feet of water, he stood up and picked up one end of the couch to see if he could angle it one corner at a time and was startled by how light it was. What was that about lightness that Shin had mentioned? He lifted the corner high and then angled his back underneath the bottom, getting knocked off balance by a wave. Back on his feet, he squatted weight-lifter style and exhaled. With one quick thrust he picked the entire couch up, balancing it awkwardly on one shoulder, his arm bracing the side. Balance was the tricky thing, but the weight was negligible, not more than forty pounds, Thom thought.

He turned toward shore, focusing on where he stepped. It wasn't until he was in six inches of water that he looked up to see the stunned and gawking crowd. The crowd of brown men and two white boys in their underwear. The fishermen averaged around five feet in height. And then Thom saw what they saw: a giant white whale of a man with a large couch over his shoulder, arriving from the sea, a giant stepping out of a legend, six foot six, his thighs like tree trunks, forearms the circumference of masts, feet the size of life rafts and a head the size of the sun, stumbling from the sea carrying an impossibly large object, carrying a house on his shoulders, approaching like a mirage, blocking out the light. Wishing more than ever he was a skinny little thing—a lithe horse jockey or an acrobat, not the giant of the circus—he considered turning and walking the other way down the beach. Maybe they'd forget about him. But he didn't. He walked right into the center of the motley crowd of short people, the ground shaking with each footfall, put down his couch, and announced, his voice a slow, self-conscious boom, "*Pero mi perro no tiene dientes!*"

There was a stunned silence followed by raucous laughter. Fishermen stepped forward to squeeze his biceps, and someone handed him a beer. They'd made it to Ecuador.

Thom and Erik and Tree shook hands and smiled and introduced themselves, drinking beer, wondering what the hell they were going to do next. The sun was falling from the sky, casting an orange glow over them, and Thom wished that just as darkness would erase differences in skin color and height, it would enable a common language between them. How nice to be a fisherman here on a tiny sailboat, feeding the pelicans and drinking beer and eating fish, escaping the hype and noise of American airwaves forever.

Erik asked Julio about a place to stay, and then the whole crowd was moving toward a parking lot. Thom hoisted with the couch back on his shoulders, trying to act the part they'd mistakenly pegged him with. They arrived at a 1974 Dodge Colt that was more rust and dents than vehicle. Julio popped inside and failed at starting it for several agonizing minutes, the engine choking in whining exhaustion. Julio smiled all the while, nodding at his American friends reassuringly, once tapping vigorously on the passenger-side heating vent, where the secret to internal combustion was apparently housed. And then six fishermen whoopingly pushed the car around the parking lot until Julio managed a push start. They piled the couch on top, and the three otherworldly, underwear-clad gringos got into Julio's car and waved good-bye to a great chorus of shouts and cheers. Thom and Erik reached through the windows and held the couch tight as Julio's car sputtered along.

Julio talked without ceasing to Erik while Thom and Tree watched the town go by: signs in Spanish stuck at every odd angle, dirt sidewalks, street vendors with lurid-smelling smoke emanating from the coals. They passed a soccer field, and Julio slowed, talking rapidly and pointing to the fourteen-year-olds playing. Then to the expanse of sea, startling and ultra-blue between buildings. Everywhere there were people on the street. Girls and boys in smart-looking school uniforms and backpacks, jostling and laughing and teasing. Old men on park benches in slacks and button-down shirts. A limping dog with open wounds and an entourage of birds. Women walking down the street with great bundles of vegetables, long black hair draped down their backs, crowds of men smoking and conspiring. Julio turned the car down a paved side street with an acne of potholes and nearly ran down a goat. He drove with the gas floored in second gear, the engine running at a whine and the car swerving frightfully around corners and obstacles. At every corner, the couch strained to launch itself off the roof.

Erik gleefully pounded the window well and joked with Julio.

Thom and Tree exchanged smiles that failed to hide how overwhelmed they were; through the car window a kaleidoscope of foreignness it would take months to begin to understand.

Tree patted Thom's great leg, looked at him once more, said, "We'll be okay," and managed to make it sound like it wasn't a question.

Thom nodded. "We'll be fine. Just fine." He wiped sweat from his forehead. "Erik speaks Spanish. Which is great but, wow," he lowered his voice, "it means we're a little dependent on Erik."

Tree watched Erik talking to Julio. "Erik will do fine too, Thom," Tree said with that tone of his that signified he had *other* knowledge, that the future was indicated to him in his dreams, that everything and everybody had a unique purpose to fill.

He managed to say it without irony, Thom noticed with amusement, even though his predictions had been spotty and had led them five thousand miles from their home. Five thousand miles, Thom thought, and tried desperately to keep himself from falling apart.

At Julio's house they shuffled in, leaving the couch on the roof of the car. They met his wife and three boys, all of them somewhere between the middle of Thom's chest and his belly button in height. Julio spent the first half hour filling in the details of the odd story of the couch's arrival to what Thom thought were excessive giggles from the family. It was a dark, two-story concrete house with a strange scattering of wealth and poverty. The house lacked an oven and, as Thom found out later, hot water, but it had a large TV (one station: soap operas, soccer, and advertisements for American products) and a computer with, it appeared to Thom, an internet connection. *I have a son in New York*, Julio explained through Erik, pointing at the things of value in the house. The floors were cold and bare of rugs, and the walls were concrete and adorned with grime and images of the Virgin Mary and brutal, bloody pictures of Jesus on the cross. While Julio's family listened to the tale, and Julio's wife prepared some kind of hot alcoholic cinnamon drink, Thom felt himself irresistibly drawn to the computer. Standing there, still in his underwear, helplessly exposed, there was one area of familiarity in the room, one thing he knew. Nobody else seemed to be wearing much more than he in the sweaty dimness of the casa. In a moment when one of Julio's boy's attention seemed to waver from Julio's storytelling, Thom shyly pointed at the computer. The boy, a kid of about sixteen, with just a touch of hair going rebellious and a black AC/DC T-shirt, belted out half a dozen sentences of Spanish. Thom stared at him, feeling like an embarrassed astronaut. The boy, who Thom thought had introduced himself as Carlos or Ricardo or Juan, saw that he didn't understand. He shook his head and drew his finger across his throat. Thom shrank back and looked at the floor. What did that mean? He'd kill anyone who touched it? Thom was way out of his element.

"He says it's broken, silly," said Erik with a glint of amusement at Thom's discomfort.

Erik blended in, Thom saw. Even in his underwear he looked as relaxed as a human could be.

"What's wrong with it?" Thom said.

Julio's dog, bearing a strange toothless smile, walked toward Thom's voice and stared expectantly up at him.

Erik and Carlos or Juan exchanged some more Spanish, and then Erik shrugged. "I don't know any of those words. Driver? Something about disks? Hell if I know. You're the nerd."

"Can I look at it?"

"Sure."

"Maybe you should ask him?"

"He already said you could."

Thom stumbled over himself, eager for that bit of familiarity. He sat down in front of the computer, the toothless dog in tow. His heart racing, he switched on the power supply, powered up the monitor, watched the memory line up, DOS talking to itself—of course it would be a Windows system. He wondered if open-source software had caught on here. The Windows icon showed on the screen, and then the screen blanked out, lines through it. Video-monitor driver needs to be reinstalled. Thom restarted into safe mode and brought up the system, and when it fully booted up it was like someone had socked him in the gut. Everything was in Spanish. But of course it was. They're not going to use an English system. "*Mis labios estan cerrados*," he said, and Juan in his AC/DC shirt stared at him. But then Thom realized the language wasn't important. He'd memorized the positions of the commands, and he could steer himself through the various labyrinths of the operating system oblivious to what went on in the room around him except to smile up at Juan occasionally. By the looks of him, the kid was probably training to be one of those Third World virus writers, a seventeen-year-old genius who brought the Western business world to its knees for twenty-four hours, and for that reason Thom desperately wanted to be friends with him. He felt hands around his waist, and he looked down to see Julio's wife wrapping a tape measure around him.

"She's trying to determine if your body would be big enough to feed the family for a week," said Erik.

The hairs on the back of Thom's neck stood up.

"Come on, man, you've got to relax a little. She's going to make you some clothes, because there's no way in hell we could find clothes big enough for you here."

"Oh." He tried to smile. "Of course." Tree and Erik were already dressed, he saw. Tree looking smart in a button-down shirt and slacks, Erik in the same but slightly more ill-fitting. Tree had backed himself quietly into a corner, and although he'd lost his needle-nose pliers in the sea, he was working a six-inch plug of wire that he'd found in the street. He was thoroughly preoccupied with the strip of wire, shutting everything out the same way that he was, Thom realized. Erik was drinking a beer and speaking at a rapid-fire pace with Julio. One of Julio's boys was strumming what sounded like a Rage Against the Machine song on a guitar. Two bare lightbulbs hung from the ceiling, lighting the room. He was a long ways away from an office, from a swivel chair and desk, from a manager who wanted to see his work.

Thom fixed the video-driver problem, and Juan announced the fact proudly to the room. He got some thumbs-ups, some back patting, a lot of Spanish was spoken, a beer was brought. Time to dial in, the reward. He could be here, what surely must be the middle of nowhere, and still touch the rest of the world. An error popped up in Spanish. Thom checked the modem and saw that there was no phone cord attached.

"Phone?" He pointed.

Juan spoke to Erik, but the meaning was clear. Thom's mood went into freefall.

"They don't have a phone." Erik shrugged.

"But they have a modem!"

"Welcome to Latin America, Professor. Land of irony. It probably takes about a year to get a phone installed here, and probably costs about as much as that computer."

Thom hung his head, so close to home. He was going to miss the rendezvous with Jean in Guayaquil, wherever that was.

"Speaking of Ecuador," Erik said, "there are legends about every damn little thing here. And it turns out there's one about us."

"About us?"

"Yeah, Fernanda remembered it." Erik pointed at Julio's wife, who seemed to be cooking, sewing, and making drinks all at once. The one woman in a house full of boys. She had a giant, electric blue sheet in an old-fashioned sewing machine. Thom shuddered, sure it was destined for him.

"At least it seems like it's about us," Erik said. "It basically says that a long time ago, the seat of power, throne, whatever, was removed from the center of the world. It's an Incan thing, maybe, or Cañar, or one of the others—there were millions of different groups here before the Incas came in and wiped everybody out. Then the Spanish came in and wiped them out. But somehow the legends survive, get mixed up, blended into Catholicism, each other. At any rate, having this seat of power far from where it should be has imbalanced the world and opened it up to all kinds of bad things. And it says that three, ah, lost people I suppose is a good way to translate it, or losers is another, will come from far away to return the seat where it belongs."

"That's amazing. Do you think . . . do you think it's true?"

"Uh . . . no. I don't. Do you? Do you believe in Noah's ark? Even if you did, I seriously doubt there's a legend about us. I wouldn't put a lot of stock in it, but then again there are legends here for everything, like I said, and a lot of things come true here that don't happen in the States. This is South America, man!"

Thom was beckoned to the table, where a beautiful plate of fried fish, rice, beans, onions, and avocado awaited. Erik talked with the family, and Thom smiled whenever someone looked at him.

After a while, Erik said: "Where are we going from here?"

"Tree thinks we're going to see popcorn." Thom tried to say it straight-faced.

Tree looked up from his plate and nodded. "Where there are butterflies like popcorn."

Erik grimaced.

"Where is the center of the world supposed to be? Seems like every culture has a center of the world," Thom said.

Erik spoke with the family and then said, "They think maybe the Andes, just a guess. Though," he smiled, "they also mentioned Washington D.C., and Hollywood."

"Ah, right. That's a lot of backtracking."

"We need to stay off of the roads," Tree said.

"How are we going to get there then?"

Tree shrugged.

A bottle of something called Zhumir was brought out and passed around and Thom began to feel a sweet tipsiness that deepened with each round. His outfit was finished, a giant tent on the floor, the drunkenness bringing out the cavalier in him, allowing him to put it on, tamping down what fashion sense he thought he had. A giant, electric blue bodysuit. Black buttons down to his waist, a limp collar. One giant bright green pocket covered his right buttock. When he put the suit on, there was a chorus of unabashed laughter. Erik grabbed his gut and snorted.

"You look like . . . God, I don't even know."

"Superman!" Juan said.

"Pajama man," Erik said.

"Like a mechanic," Tree said.

Thom blushed, but it was good to be clothed, and the laughter seemed kind. On a whim he took up a Superman pose, one arm outstretched as if to fly, the other a fist against his side, and the laughter doubled. He wouldn't leave the house, that's what. He'd live here the rest of his life, where they liked him. He was a superhero. Can't beat that. He needed a name stitched across the front. Azul is blue, Erik had said. Azulman. Whose secret powers were flatulence and the ability to think like a machine. Secret powers that allowed him to cry about the stories in books but not his own. Azulman! Endowed with a second brain who sat on his shoulder like a dour talking cat.

An hour later, Fernanda had made a pair of shoes for Thom too. Two slabs cut from a car tire, with canvas straps holding the feet in. A makeshift sandal, utilitarian, brilliant.

With the couch now inside and darkening a corner of the room, Thom, Erik, and Tree lay out on the floor with a layer of blankets.

Thom waited until his roommates were asleep and got up to stand at the window. He imagined the earth from space, and his body upon it, so very far from where it belonged. He heard the sound of something that might be crickets, or some other many-legged thing that delivered fatal bites to your neck in your sleep. It took all his willpower to keep his breathing under control, to keep his body from acting out all his frenzied, panicked emotions. His thoughts leapt wildly from the worthiness of their cause, the exotic excitement of being thousands of miles away from home, and the feeling that he was a lost escape pod, jettisoned from the mother-ship and hurtling ever deeper into space. He forced his breathing to become deep and sure, but he felt lonely. He wanted a girlfriend and a job and a nice family and a home and all things that all right people call their own. The things that the chosen people come by naturally, without brushing up against suicide to get them.

But then he knew that if he wanted those things, or if he wanted those things above all things, he could have them, but instead he was here, partially, at least, of his own choosing. If only there was a tincture that confirmed decisions, a vitamin that pointed the nose like an arrow toward one's proper destiny.

He lay back down next to Tree, who was thrashing about, living in two worlds, the dream world testing him, teasing him, coaxing.

Thom stared at the ceiling deep into the night and tried to place himself. Out the door was a chaotic and foreign world, and for once, he began to feel excited. Later the rain came, falling on the tin roof like hammers in the night.

Morning revealed Tree covered in fifty or sixty mosquito bites, from the bottom of his feet to his forehead, a collage of welts.

"Whoa," Erik said, searching himself and not finding a single bite. "Usually they like me, but you must be tasty. That's one of the rea-sons my parents split up. She couldn't handle the jungle mosquitoes anymore. They never hit my pop. *Los indios* think it's a bad sign if the mosquitoes only bite on one person. They say they smell death."

Thom noted that Tree looked genuinely afraid. He caught Erik's gaze and mouthed for him to shut up.

"Sorry, Tree," Thom said. "Bummer." He didn't have a single bite either. He marveled at Tree's new complexion, a rash of itching spawned in a night. "I heard you scratching, and I thought you were dreaming."

Tree scratched the tops off his bites until they bled. Fernanda, with a motherly look gave him a bottle of insect repellent, and then a bottle of sunblock for the fiery red he'd developed. He'd need something to do with his hands.

They spent a day of rest at Julio's house, who was thrilled to have them. He brought neighbors by and regaled them with the story of how the foreigners had arrived by sea, and Thom, Tree, and Erik accommodated. They felt at the end of the world and utterly unfindable. A fishing village perched lonely on the edge of the Pacific. Thom learned a half dozen more Spanish words. *Cerveza*—beer; *chuchaki*—hangover; *mar*—sea; *viaje*—journey; *disculpeme*—excuse me. Where was Shin, he wondered. Just when would he be showing up to lead and protect them?

They ate ceviche and drank more, and Juan and Thom came to certain computer understandings. It was the way he knew how to talk, his language. He introduced Juan to the tenets of programming and system scripting, hoping it would ignite a passion in him. Since programming languages were mostly in English, or rather they were their own languages but with English phrasing, Thom could steer himself around effortlessly.

After substantial arguments on the nature of financing their voyage, Tree dug up his ATM card from a crack in the couch and Tree, Erik, and Julio went to town to find a bank. They returned with needle-nose pliers and spools of wire, straw hats, and ice cream. Tree handed out money like Christmas, each roommate getting a hundred and fifty dollars.

"They use U.S. dollars here." Erik sounded upset. "I guess they killed the sucre in '99. Sad. That's got to piss off my parents."

Thom was unfamiliar with currencies. "The sucre?" Relieved at another item on the small list of familiars.

Tree twisted and turned wire replicas of the family, meager gifts.

In the morning they pored over a tiny map of Ecuador, eking out a rough plan. Or as much of a plan as one can make without a clear idea of where one is going. Erik pointed to giant areas like they were amusement rides he wanted to make sure they hit. "The Amazon! We better go there. The equator! We should try the toilets. Ingapirca—Temple of the Sun, I've been to a rally there!"

Thom studied the hundreds of miles of land to traverse and tried to imagine what travel was like beyond their village. With his fingers he traced rugged stretches of the Andes, thousands of miles of jungle, all of it impossible territory for carrying couches.

Tree, constantly twitching and scratching himself, repeated *We've got to stay off the roads* until it became background noise. All of them fanning the fronts of their shirts, trying to keep cool.

Erik and Thom begged Tree to give them an inkling of their direction. After much pressure, Tree let his finger glide along the map. He wasn't sure what he was looking for other than the visual imagery that played in his mind—cobblestone streets, a mountain trail, a type of wagon, endless fog. How could he reconcile this with a two-dimensional map? His finger halted at a stretch of mountains to the south. There was a bump in the map, a bit of Braille there just for him perhaps.

"There's a bump here," Tree said and lifted his finger to show the others.

"It's sand under the map, smart guy, not the map."

"We're going here." Tree stabbed his finger down over the bump, a mountainous stretch to the south and east of them.

"It's sand," Erik repeated. "Dude! That's the middle of nowhere. It was just a sand bump. Thom, help me out?"

Thom studied the spot. "Technically, yes, it is indeed sand under the map. That's good enough for me."

Julio generously offered to drive them south to Posorja, where the end of the Guayas River issued monstrous and brown from the city of Guayaquil. There he knew a man, Carlos, who could boat them around Isla Puná, deeper into the mainland, banana country, where presumably they'd pick up their couch and walk into the unknown in the direction of Tree's sand bump. Thom's belly was a furnace of unpredictability. Anxiety sweated off of him. Erik checked doubtfully with Tree. "Are you sure you dreamed that? Are you sure this is the way?"

But it felt good to be in the car, with the couch tied to the roof this time. The wind whipped through Thom's thin blue suit, cooling him. Julio drove like a madman, passing on the left, playing chicken, passing on the right, driving through mud, vegetation, rocks, road, the car weaving like a drunken horse running full-bore down a mountainside. Gas fumes filled up the back of the car so that Thom and Tree kept their faces in the wind, panting for breath. They passed dilapidated buildings, the sky full of wires, signs at precarious angles, mud brick houses and buildings with thatch or rusted tin roofs whose walls were painted over with the faces of politicians, animals in the street, dogs as thin as postcards, chickens, goats, pigs. Julio talking through it all, jerking the wheel this way and that, his tongue clicking against his three teeth to punctuate sentences. Thom held on for dear life to anything he could grab a hold of.

Then Julio would see someone he knew. He'd skid to a stop and tell the *gringo* story from the beginning. Thom and Tree were familiar with the gestures of the story by now. They pointed to the couch on the roof, *gringos* out in the water on it, ha ha ha. And then they'd go again, Julio grinding the engine into a heap of oily filings.

It was market day in Posorja. The streets were full of carts and stands of vegetables and spices and meat and goods. A sea of black hair that came up to Thom's chest, stacks of fish on tables, a tangled web of crabs tied over the shoulder of a man who yelled *Cangrejo! Cangrejo!* A table with a pile of yellowed pig's heads, a fork jutting from a snout, a baseball-sized rock jammed into the mouth of another, sides of beef dangling from hooks, blood pooling in the dust, butchers throwing stones at dogs, a woman in a bowler hat with a lamb over her shoulder chatting with an old man with one hundred and fifty years of wrinkles astride a mule. Women sat on blankets on the ground with heaps of leafy vegetables around them, sat against walls, sat everywhere, surrounded by pyramids of tomatoes, cabbage, shucking corn, mounds of green bananas the size of fallen elephants. A man tap-tapping a human skeleton with a rod, yelling his cure through a megaphone. A woman with a handful of chicken legs in her fist, connected to live chickens, their heads dangling, eyeing the world from upside down. An escaped hollering sow charged through the stalls with a man just taller than a bar stool in hot pursuit. Everything was in chaos, streets disappearing under the bustle.

With the car finally parked, Thom exited Julio's spacecraft and gave Posorja its first-ever alien encounter. *Azulman!* Everywhere eyes followed this blue behemoth ducking and grabbing his head with each impact against vendor stall or ceiling or doorway. His face a balloon red, mumbling what he knew, *gracias, hola, mis labios están cerrados.*

Tree refused to leave the couch, and Julio led the others through the market. Thom acquired a small following of children. When he turned, they scattered into hiding. He cursed his outfit. His sandals sank into the mud streets, the canvas taking on a blackened hue. Julio ducked into the nicest building on the street, two stories of aquamarine-painted cinder blocks with a ceramic tile roof. *If you can't beat them, join them,* brain offered. He turned at the doorway to wave at his crowd of followers, breaking them into a storm of giggles, a few waving back reflexively, scattering. Some ran for their lives. Others smiled and stationed themselves like bodyguards at the entrance of the building while their giant sat uncomfortably inside.

Carlos had a boat, and they needed a ride. It was a big trip, across the great delta, some thirty miles of ocean, and they began the obligatory haggling for the fare. He had a gold ring on each hand, a man who had and liked wealth. They sat around on stools while he sat kingly in his recliner throne, aimed squarely at a TV in the corner. The market scene blared through the open door. A radio upstairs charged the air with salsa. Soap-opera dialogue spilled through the brassy speakers of the TV. There wasn't a sole atom within a mile that wasn't vibrating with sound energy for all it was worth.

Perhaps it was a restaurant, Thom realized. It was a sweaty cave of a place. A picture of the food groups hung on one wall. An Argentinean soap opera flashed on the screen, and Erik knew the characters by name. Julio and Erik and Carlos talked, and Thom hunkered on the periphery, unsure if things were going well, unsure of where they were going and why. He stood and stationed himself at the doorway, where his child disciples waited and asked him questions in squeaky Speedy Gonzalez voices. He mussed a boy's hair who wore a U.S. flag shirt, redneck style. Where was the center of the world? Couldn't it be here? He felt more comfortable with the stares. There was no malevolence, he thought, or hoped, only curiosity and, yes, laughter. *But look at what you wear*, brain said. *You would laugh, too*. A boy of three or four or five?—they were all so small—grabbed his pant leg and shook, looking up at him, *Why? Why?* clearly on his face. Yes, why? Sharks ate my clothes. I'm on an important mission involving furniture. I couldn't find a job in my own country. My girlfriend broke up with me. I'm trying to impress a journalist. That's why. Thom mimed a Superman flying gesture. A creature in an electric blue Superman suit, poised to launch from the earth, leave gravity behind. Their reactions divided by age. An excited murmur rose from the five-and-under contingent; shy skepticism and smiles permeated the six and aboves. Eleven and above scowled skeptically but stuck around just in case. Some ran off to notify parents. He could settle down, get a casa, marry the tallest Ecuadoriana in town, teach the tykes programming, learn the accordion, sell something at the market—websites? American literature? Did he have any skills that applied here? He could be the freak show, charge admission for a peek. His mother would never approve.

Or maybe he'd leave computers behind completely. Emerge once again into a tangible world, try to have relationships with people whose eyes he could see, who moved their lips to communicate.

Negotiations were finished and Erik came to stand in the doorway. Julio was stuck to the TV, unable to leave before the climax of the soap. Carlos had disappeared upstairs.

"You seem like you're getting on fine. *Mande?*" Erik said to a tiny fellow piping up with a question, then laughed. "He wants to know when you're going to fly."

Thom chuckled. "It's the outfit."

Erik winked at the boy. "*Muy pronto. Muy, muy pronto.*" Erik jerked his thumb back toward where the negotiations had happened. "Well, we're getting a ride, but if this guy doesn't chuck us overboard I'll be surprised. And I promised him seventy dollars—quite a huge amount of money here—for the ride, to be paid at arrival."

Erik borrowed a cigarette from a man leaning against the building, and a bevy of questions followed, handshakes, motions to Thom.

"Everybody asks if there's work in the States. Everybody wants to go there." Erik exhaled toward the market. "Thom, I'm really still unclear on where we're going, what we're doing. Is it okay to have doubt? You can't say anything in front of Tree. And I can't even figure out who I'm supposed to be suspicious of. Sure, sometimes we run across someone we can obviously trust, like Julio. The guy wouldn't even know how to double-cross. But this guy Carlos, or Shin, or even Jean—have you thought about that much? Why is Jean meeting us here? That's a long way to come for some dudes she met on the street in Portland, strange couch or no."

Thom took a drag from Erik's cigarette and was immediately offered another by the man who'd loaned Erik one, exaggerated gestures compensating for lack of a shared language. "Yeah, I know."

"I know you think you've got a possible interest there," Erik said. "Hell, maybe she's got the same thing in mind." Erik eyed Thom and bit his bottom lip, raised his eyebrows. "Look—you're the sane, reasonable guy here. I don't exactly have that reputation. But I thought I'd better point that out. Alright?"

Thom nodded, studied his sandals. "Alright," he said. "Point taken."

"I mean. This couch used to be in our living room, thousands of miles away, and now what? We're on a trip. That's fun, I like Ecuador. Maybe I'll even try to find one of my parents. But what the hell, man! We're carrying this couch like some kind of Jesus story."

"Carrying it for other people's sins."

"Exactly."

"Or for ours."

"That too."

"Or worse, really, you see that movie about those guys who were trying to carry a big thing of ice into the jungle to show the natives and it melted before they got it there?"

"Yeah," Thom said. "Doomed quests. What did I tell Jean? Absurd quests movement. But I think we're going somewhere. There have been too many coincidences not to believe something." He gave a smile to his fan base.

"Or it could be a lot of lucky delusion," Erik said and spit into a muddied, oily ditch.

"That's what I'm worried about."

A cartload of watermelons collided with a stand full of fish. An argument erupted. Fish on watermelons, watermelons on fish, the flesh of both exposed, mixing gorily.

"But what about Shin?" Thom said. "The council thing."

Erik shrugged. "He gives me the creeps."

"But what if we are doing something big, what if this is the new war, what if we're removing the world's poison, what if we're changing the planet?" Thom rushed the sentences out of his mouth, all his hopes in one breath of air as his stomach up heaved massively in manic response. He saw one of his disciples plug his nose.

Erik sighed. "Sure, could be. Never seen myself that way, but what the heck. Yes, let's do it. All the way. My parents would be proud. But how do we know? I mean, it's a couch, you know, so don't get your hopes up." He worked at his mustache, blew smoke. "Or what if we're really lost. Listen, man, no offense, but I don't believe in a center of the world. I don't believe Tree's Garden of Eden stuff, if that even has anything to do with this. Yes, I think the couch is strange . . . but . . . pfff, there's just no other way to say it, it's a couch."

Carlos and Julio joined them, and Julio affectionately patted Thom's bicep.

"*Vamanos*," Carlos said.

The boat was an oversized wooden rowboat with deep sides, a steep keel, and a big motor. They loaded the couch in, and Thom noticed Carlos squeezing its armrests, eyeing its frame. He wondered if this was curiosity naturally associated with crazy gringos carrying a couch across the delta or if something more was at play. They piled in, giving Julio a profuse round of thanks. Thom, for lack of the right language of gratitude, broke into a round of "For He's a Jolly Good Fellow." Julio grinned and invited them to hurry back, stay longer.

Julio left and Carlos had stepped off the boat and disappeared. They waited. The water lapped softly against the sides. The boat was tied to a wooden dock protected from the surf by a rock jetty. They waited ten, twenty, thirty minutes, sweating in the sun.

"Are we supposed to drive it?" Tree said, working a mosquito bite.

"No. No." Erik craned his neck about, searching up the dock impatiently. "He said he'd come right back." Erik eyed the motor, began calculating a getaway.

Thom's crowd of children suddenly appeared on the dock, the younger ones demanding he fly before he go. They sat, bare feet dangling in the water. Two blocks away, the chaos of the market buzzed on.

Then Carlos was back, full of cheer and carrying an armload of giant Ecuadorian *cervezas*, Pilsener, popping tops and passing them around. He hopped nimbly into the boat, shirt open to his belly. Like every other vehicle operator in Ecuador, he operated the engine at full speed.

"Beer seems to happen here at any hour, doesn't it?" Tree said, looking at his twenty-two–ounce bottle with mixed emotions.

"Give it here, I'll drink it." Erik reached.

"No, it's cold." Tree held it to his face, the glass dripping wet, sucking condensation from the humid air. Tree's hair stuck to his face, and he incessantly writhed from his insect welts.

Then there was the breeze of acceleration. The keel rose into the waves and bumped heavily. A low outcropping of land lay to their right.

"*Vamos alla?*" Erik pointed at the land.

"*No, es la Isla Puná. Alla les llevo.*" Carlos pointed into a horizon of water between islands: *That's where I'm taking you.* Erik climbed a seat closer to Carlos.

"He says Puná used to be a great island, but hardly anybody lives there now. The people who lived there invented the balsa."

"Balsa?"

"Julio's boat, the balsa-wood trunks with the sails. They sailed them all the way to Central America, farther. Nobody knows how far they went. They were here before the Incans, and when the Incan invaded, they facilitated trade between the Mayas and the Incas."

"What happened to them?"

Erik relayed the question, and Carlos shrugged. "*Desapareci-dos.*" Disappeared.

The water turned murky and then red-brown as they crossed the outflow of a river, a brown sea brimming with city sewage and trash. Just as suddenly it turned blue again.

Carlos passed around more beer, and Tree gave his to Erik, along with what remained of his first one. The beers had warmed in the bottom of the boat.

They passed another great swath of brown and Carlos pointed to the left, the great city of Guayaquil.

Thom stared up the river toward the city where they were to have met up with Jean and sighed. Erik's worries were a moot point after all, he thought. There was just something about her—in only two encounters, he'd managed to manifest a crush. She had a nice mix of looks and smarts and wit but seemed, still, within range for a socially awkward but nonetheless nice fellow with moderate looks, extra-large feet, and a fair bit of intelligence. He swallowed tensely, hoping he wasn't overexaggerating his qualifications. She wasn't off the charts of attainability, anyway. He sensed she could be wooed into considering an unchosen. At least until she found out what I'm really like, he thought, with the antisocial tendencies and confidence lapses like a relief map of the Rockies. And then he wondered if he were really like that anymore or if that was another Thom, heavy and stuck in an office job he hated and arguing pig-headedly with his girlfriend about issues he knew he was on the wrong side of: whether to eat healthily, whether to have friends. He poured the warm beer down his throat and felt a tremendously peaceful buzz come over him. The noise of the engine all but pro-hibited conversation: the beer muted the anxiety of arrival. It was chilling to think of a people on balsas here five hundred, a thou-sand, ten thousand, how many years ago? The sea floor littered with skeletons and history. Had the couch been here before? Was this home? He leaned back against it and closed his eyes.

Tree had made it clear that they were not to be dropped off in a town, that they were to avoid roads, but when Carlos drove the boat up onto a deserted beach with only strange, large-leafed trees and sand in either direction, Thom's anxiety boiled over.

"Tree? What about eating, sleeping, shelter, water?" Tipsiness aided Thom's roll over the side of the boat onto his feet in the shal-low water.

"We'll find stuff," Tree said in a way that inspired no confidence.

Erik paid Carlos. He was weaving, two and a half of Ecuador's twenty-two–ounce beers down and another gripped in his hand, smiling and laughing. He and Thom flipped the couch off the boat and dropped it in the water. They struggled up the beach with it, stubbing toes and stumbling. Erik ran ten steps to the side, opened his fly, and pissed into the sea with numerous exclamations of relief.

Then the three put their weight against Carlos's boat and pushed it back into the water. Carlos waved a cheerful good-bye. "*Suerte! Que les vayan bien!*"

"What'd he say?"

"He said luck. Which I think coming from him means I hope you fall into a hole." Erik peeled off his shirt and slouched against the couch. "Oh yeah, this is the life! I want some ceviche or crab or *langosta* and another beer and half a dozen cigarettes and a woman and a hammock to lie in with her. And a foot massage. That cover the shelter, food, water thing?" He snapped his fingers. "Get that for me, Tree?"

Thom giggled through a series of beer belches and lay down in the hot sand, unbuttoning his jumpsuit to his navel. A forgotten paradise, not a hint of civilization as far as the eye could see. What the hell were they doing?

A somber Tree stood nearby, looking nervously at the tree line that came up to the edge of the beach. "Guys?"

"Don't answer him," Erik whispered to Thom. "I'm not going anywhere."

Thom was content to squeeze sand through his fingers, watch changes in the sole cloud in the sky, listen to the waves crash up on the shore, sweat into his jumpsuit. Maybe in a while he'd take everything off and go for a swim.

"Come on, you guys."

"Tree," Erik whined. "Can't we just chill for a while, work off a buzz on the beach?"

"We shouldn't stay in one place," Tree said.

"Where are we going?" Thom said.

"Into those trees."

Erik swiveled to face Tree. "Those trees up there, know what those are? Giant leaf, stubby little tree, appendages like a thousand penises. Those are banana trees. Know what it's going to be like in there? The ground will be insanely muddy, it's been flooding here like mad, it'll be sweaty as hell, humidity like, like . . . I don't know, like a whole freaking lot of humidity, that's what it'll be like, a lot of humidity, and there will be insects everywhere, and those insects will like you, they desire you, you are insect *almuerzo*, free delivery, get your Tree *almuerzo* delivered straight to your nest, or wherever the hell insects call home."

Tree stood uncomfortably, opening and closing his needle-nose pliers on his forefinger. "Seriously, though, we should go. Thom?"

"*Lo que sea mejor por el país.*"

"The country would be happier if we stayed here," Erik said. "Country? Would you like us to stay on this nice beach for a while?"

"Yes, yes, I would," Erik replied, not bothering to give Ecuador a different voice. "I would like that very much."

Thom laughed, propped himself up on elbows and looked lazily back at the trees. Where the unknown began. A beach was so . . . simple, graspable. Beyond the beach there was a labyrinth of banana fields and forests and jungles, where food was a puzzle, signs a conundrum. "What time is it?" he said, knowing none of them had a watch. His computer at the bottom of the sea or in a shark's belly. His alarm clock . . . where had that gone? The Goodwill. He realized that the blue jumpsuit, the sandals made from car tires, and the one hundred and fifty dollars Tree had given him were the extent of his possessions. *Robinson Crusoe*, brain volunteered. *Gilligan's Island*.

"Maybe we should just take a quick break, Tree," Thom said. "Just for a short while."

In front of him the horizon was empty but for the smudge of the island of the disappeared. Thom leaned back into the sand, closed his eyes.

"I don't have much time," Tree said. He sat in the sand, working his pliers against another bite.

"What's the hurry? It's not like we're going to miss an appointment," Erik said.

"I'm going to get sick."

"Now? For godsake, go into the trees."

"Later."

"Oh. Everybody gets sick, bud. It's a whole part of the exotic foreign experience. You'll sit on the toilet for days. It's great fun."

Nobody said anything. Finally Erik and Thom looked over at Tree. He sat cross-legged, bent over with his head in his hands.

"Hey, Tree, we can go in just a second. I just wanted a minute or two to sit," Erik said. "Can't I freaking have a minute or two?"

Tree nodded imperceptibly.

"What kind of sick?" Thom said.

"I don't know." Tree's voice was muffled. "There's a steep slope, it's cold, there's fog everywhere, you guys are exhausted from carrying the couch, it's hard to breathe, there are lots of rocks, rain, I'm lying on the couch, you're carrying the couch with me lying on it. Or the couch is on something and I'm on that. I'm . . . in a lot of pain. I'm scared. I mean I'm scared now. I can't tell what's going on with me on the couch."

Thom looked at Erik, who mimed a question. *Crazy?*

Thom shook his head, gestured toward the trees, a silent *Let's go.*

Erik came to his feet, stretched. "All right, y'all, what do you say we get this show on the road. Don't worry, dreamboy, we'll keep you safe. Nobody wants to carry you on the couch, so it's in our best interest." He clapped his hands and looked down at Tree, saw him covered head to foot in insect bites, and a fear struck his gut. Yellow fever, dengue fever, malaria, or any number of other things. Maybe the boy really was going to get sick. Then a panic at the thought of this seer. What did he know of Erik? Did he know when they'd die?

"What about me?" he said. "Do you see anything in store for me?"

Tree squinted up at Erik. "I don't answer questions like that, Erik. You know that."

"Well, what the fuck's the use of it then? Come on, I'm getting irritated now. My *ceviche* never arrived. Let's go." He kicked sand toward each of his roommates, and they reluctantly got up. Tree and Thom hoisted the couch.

"Boats," Tree said.

Thom looked up and saw that two boats had slipped into view and were pointed at their beach. "What do we do?"

"Okay, run, hurry, *hurry*." Tree ran his end of the couch up the sand toward the trees, pulling Thom after him. Thom looked behind to see Erik unsteady on his feet but following.

III. Axis Mundi

Being among the banana trees was like stepping into a steamy and heavily oxygenated greenhouse. Tree and Thom could barely keep their footing among the sinkholes, losing their shoes in the muck, slipping and falling, covered in it up to their knees, the couch changing color in the stew. Erik, cursing, led the way, trying to find drier ground, and then fell back to cover their tracks by laying down banana leaves. They pushed on for hours through the endless plantation, their arms aching, the couch light but ungainly, their optimism draining away. Erik took Tree's end of the couch so Tree could slap at insects. Tree's body was a map of red across his arms and neck.

"Aren't you using that insect repellent?" Erik dug his Ecuadorian loafer out of several feet of mud with a *schlock!* sound.

"Shh," Tree said. "Whisper."

"They must really like you."

"Listen." Thom fanned his jumpsuit and took a bite of a mostly ripe banana he'd found on the ground. "There's got to be a service road. Else how do they pick all these bananas?"

"Huh." Erik beat his shoe against a tree, dislodging chunks of mud. "I suppose. This is miserable. What have we come, a half mile?" He looked back in the direction of the sea and saw only endless trees. Was that the way they'd come? "I hope we're not going in circles," he said.

"I hope it's not fifty miles of this until some kind of road," Thom said.

"We have to stay off the road."

"Tree, we also have to be reasonable, practical. There's no fucking way we're going to get anywhere if we just keep going on like this," Erik said.

"I think we're walking parallel to a service road," Thom said. "Just let me scout a bit." Before they could argue, he set off at a right angle, pushing through the giant leaves, watching warily for any lurking swamp animals. There had to be a road. Or did they just plow these trees down when they harvested? He heard a *whop whop whop* in the air, a helicopter. Please let it not be insecticide, he prayed and then wondered if it was looking for them. He pulled a shield of banana leaves in front of him. The helicopter hovered close and loud and then was gone. Plantation owner checking his crop, Thom thought. He hoped Erik and Tree had hidden.

He trudged on and found a skinny dirt road running between the trees. It went one or two hundred yards and curved out of sight.

Thom shouted back to Erik and Tree. Had he gone out of shouting range? He'd lost track. He walked back in the direction he'd come. "Hello?" He heard only condensation dripping from the banana leaves. "*Hello?*" Everything looked the same, trees and mud. Footprints, he thought, but couldn't find any. He'd stepped at the base of the trees to avoid mud and left no prints, or perhaps he'd lost his own trail already. "Hello?" Silence but for the whine of a mosquito. He slapped at his arm and saw he had two bites already with Tree not around to divert traffic. Where were they? Surely I didn't walk this far. He turned and walked at a right angle to his original direction, thinking he'd missed his path, calling. Those bastards, why wouldn't they answer? He scratched at his face, thought he couldn't have gotten this far off the route. He turned around and walked the other way, keeping the memory of the road on his right. Was it on his right? "Fuck!" he yelled and stood still, listening for anything, another mosquito, now four bites on his right arm, two on his left. His neck itched. He rolled his sleeves down and started walking again, picking up his pace, running when he could, slapping leaves out of the way. He flailed his arms around to keep mosquitoes away. And then he saw the ocean. He came to the edge of the trees, furious with himself. Why hadn't they brought water or food? Why did they have to walk through the fucking banana plantation? He tried to calm himself, breathe. They'll wait or go look for me or keep on. All three seemed hopeless. He walked along the tree line, and there was the service road. The same one? He ran down it, hollering as he went. How long had he been away now? A half hour, an hour? The road finally intersected with a larger dirt road. He turned left. What else was he supposed to do? When you're lost in the forest, stay where you are, his meager Boy Scout experience dictated. But who would look for him here?

He followed the road around a bend, and there not fifty yards away were Tree and Erik, loading the couch into the back of a four-door pickup while four men stood around and watched. Thom jogged up, relieved. "Hey. Uh. You got a ride then?" he said, noticing Erik and Tree's absence of expressions.

"Thanks for bringing us the couch, Thom," one of the men said in English. He wore a straw hat and had a friendly round face. He used a nightstick to tip his hat at Thom.

He knows my name, Thom thought. He nodded at the man, feeling relieved the quest was over. They'd brought the couch to these men. He could go home. Turn back toward the sea, forget about adventuring and romance and being brave and quick and strong and everything heroic. He could eat out and watch movies and sleep in for days on end. He'd get a job and make his mom happy.

"You've done a great job. Just follow this road here. You can get a bus in Naranjal. There's a great restaurant on the main street, El Olvidor."

Thom nodded and smiled, his hand to his jaw, where his tooth had begun to hurt. He was hungry, he realized. He saw Erik's shoes were on the ground, muddy and ruined. Tree was still wearing his. *Zapato* went brain, ever-ready to throw up useless information at inopportune times. A ruined *zapato*, and then in a memory of a memory of repetition, Thom repeated it. *Zapato zapato*, a clicking of the consciousness.

They were being robbed.

A volcanic rage rose up in Thom. He jumped toward the truck with a howl and threw the man closing the tailgate deep into the side of the road like a rag doll, howling to shut out the man's voice. He jerked the couch from the back, knocking over Tree in the process. The man with the hat gave a nod and two men came at him, throwing punches. Thom watched his fists go up slowly, like watching a slow-motion nature shot of a bear seeking its nimble prey, a hundred pounds of bone and flesh on the end of each arm, like wrecking balls, he flung them and the men ducked. A pain in his stomach, his face, his kidney, the taste of blood in his mouth. He was blinded and falling and more pain, curling about the pain, his back, his head, every part of him beaten up.

Erik stood over him, the murkiness of dusk about him. Something was wrong with Erik's face; it was distorted like a mask, an eye socket ballooning with red, his nose seeming to angle off to one side.

"I'm going to teach you how to fight, my friend." Erik's hand stretched toward Thom.

Thom attempted to focus. He took hold of the hand and held it for a moment. His entire body felt crushed, and it took a moment to identify the specific wounds.

Erik pulled Thom to his feet. Erik was still without shoes. Thom saw Tree sitting in the middle of the road, his head against his knees.

No couch, no truck, he thought. Darkness a footfall away.

"Ohhhhh, fuck." Thom's head was a compression of pain. He gently felt his body, determining where he hurt most. His lip was an abnormal bulge. There was a giant goose egg on the back of his head. A cracked rib? A series of pains in his lower back, a swollen knee. Lot of good that fucking council does us. Where the hell is Shin?

"Look," Erik said, his arms flailing wide like he was trying to violently hug an overlarge tree. "You can't just throw roundhouses. This is what you looked like." Erik mimed a drunk bear. "They're slow and easy to avoid. Keep your balance." Erik bent his knees, danced to one side, then the other. Thom was amazed Erik could move. Just watching movement was painful.

"This is how you throw a punch. Throw it straight. Quickest path between two points is?"

"A straight line," Thom answered, tamping down resentment.

Erik demonstrated jabs. "Your fists in front to block, see? And listen, think about their body. Pushing someone down is not going to do any damage." Erik approached Thom, fists up. "Throat!" Erik's fist came within an inch of Thom's throat. "Groin! Eyes! Kidneys if his back is to you. This isn't gentlemen's boxing. This is winning."

Thom nodded, noted the pineapple he had to swallow to get the saliva down. He wiped a bead of sweat from the numb, painful area above his eye.

Tree looked up, his face a wash of mud and tears and blood. "Not going to do any good now!"

"Hey, hey!" Erik danced boxer-style, threw jabs into the air. "We'll be ready for them next time. Get up, dreamboy. Let me see you throw a punch."

Tree shook his head.

"Come on, get up." Erik prodded Tree's back with the tip of his toe, danced back. "Come on!" He flipped Tree's hair, jumped out of range, pushed an arm forward, and then Tree had a hold of it like a rabid monkey, his teeth sunk into Erik's forearm. Erik screamed for all he was worth while Thom tried to separate them.

"HolyFuckShit!" Erik said after they'd disentangled. "How come you didn't do that when they were here?" He studied his arm in the growing darkness. "You drew blood!" Erik said appreciatively. "You little fucker!"

Tree curled his head between his knees again, shoulders shaking.

Thom's jumpsuit was torn at the knees and shoulder. His pocket with its small reserve of cash was empty. He swore. "Okay, let's get ourselves together." He limped twenty paces up the road. "Come on, let's get ourselves together," he repeated, hoping this time he'd have an inkling of how to do so. "This way," he said. Thinking it was the direction the man had pointed, Naranwhat?

They limped in silence down the sliver of road, hearing only the sound of each other's tentative footsteps, their labored breathing.

Their homemade clothes were beginning to fall apart.

"Not much farther now," Thom heard himself say—a line straight from his mother. A reassuring lie so utterly far from the truth that it served only to redouble his fear.

From Tree came the low sound of a cornered cat.

"Hey," Thom said. "We'll make it."

The mosquitoes were a hungry feeding frenzy about them, Tree taking the brunt. Hours passed. They stumbled on, their hands outstretched to guard against wandering from the road in the blackness. Erik limped along, his bare feet bruised and bleeding. Tree's shoes failing fast.

And then there was a light on an incline. At first it seemed like a star, unreachable. They hunted along the road for an entrance toward the light, blind to everything else. Rain fell. They neared the point of pain and misery at which the body draws inward, shuts down the nervous system, turns off the brain. Not finding a road, they slipped and crawled through the trees, a struggle toward where the light must be, obscured by rain and vegetation, a lifetime of mud and wet and banana leaves between them.

A rooftop surfaced a ways off. A glow of light on the porch of a large house. A house of stone and concrete, hardwood steps, and a railing up to an elaborately carved door. They pounded on it, three half-humans, not caring if murder waited for them on the other side.

Per leaned on his cane and opened the door to he wasn't sure what. Certainly three apparitions, three corpses recently dug from their graves, three sizes of human in a state of much disrepair. "Come in, come in, good Lord," he said in Swedish-accented English.

The three shuffled in without speaking. They stood in the entranceway dripping while Per summoned his army of helpers. "*Rosa, traiga toallas, dios mio, muchas. Esme, hay mas merrienda? Marita, prepara las camas, tenemos huespedes, extranjeros.*" Per rubbed his hands together. "My God, you look terrible." He smoothed back gray hair, adjusted vest and loosened tie, went to look for his wife while his legion of maids went to work.

Rosa bustled in and wrapped each of the roommates in a towel. They stood frozen, shell-shocked, and while she dried them she chatted idly in Spanish, reassuringly, as a mother would, the towels beginning to drip with mud, blood, rain. She removed shoes from the ones who wore them, went to look for some of Per's clothes for the giant whose mysterious blue outfit was falling off of him, and then decided to dress them all.

They waited in the cool entrance, a huge, modern air conditioner blowing air in, and began to shiver.

Barely cognizant of what was happening, they were towel-dried, hustled into bathrooms, then dressed in dapper outfits. Thom tightly fitted in a 1940s suit belonging to Per, who was a mere half inch shorter than he, but thin as bamboo. The woman named Marita inspected wounds, applied antiseptic or bandages, offered the necessary *pobrecitos*, sympathy words, pulled their socks on. Tree fell asleep in the bathroom, in the bedroom, in the hallway leaning against the wall.

Per returned with a woman just over half his height but with the bearing of a matron. The roommates were assembled like children dressed in Sunday best in a hallway lined with antiques. Per introduced himself again, and they found their tongues. Thom thinking, Per like pear, Tree like tree. Per's wife introduced herself, Alma, which Erik translated later as "soul." Per was tall and gentlemanly, with sun-blotched skin and eyes watering with age. Alma was stout and fast and cheerful. The roommates were each shown to their own rooms. Two of the rooms belonged to Per and Alma's grown sons, photos on the wall of half-Swedish, half-Ecuadorian boys, now being educated in the exclusive corners of the world.

Later they sat at a giant oak table in a stately dining room decorated with china vases, human-figure sculptures, and Expressionist paintings with gilded frames. They were served soup and then traditional Ecuadorian fare, rice and beans, fish, vegetables. Per and Alma hovered and smiled, sipping wine and waiting for conversation to begin. Thom hoped one of his compatriots would step in and make up a story. We're tourists. We got lost. He dreaded the possibility of Tree's voice piping up with stories of magic couches. Here they were at the end of the world, and instead of fire there was hospitality.

But not much was expected of them. Tree fell asleep at the table. Erik drank wine quickly to kill the pain and to dull the coming hangover, bleary-eyed, smiling. Thom did all the polite talking but offered no details, and none were asked. Only, "Where are you from?" "Would you like some more wine? More food?" "Isn't that a heavy rain out tonight?" Thom maneuvered his fork delicately around his giant lip. Erik's face was a mess of swelling and color. Per told stories about late forties New York, early fifties New Orleans, and Ecuador over the last fifty years. A life full of adventures. He smoked cigarettes at the table, switched to cognac, spoke eloquently in English and dropped in words in Spanish in absent-mindedness or for emphasis. He had a smile that crept up wryly at all the years between him and his past. He pointed at the paintings on the wall. "She made them," he said. His wife, Alma, the painter.

Not once did they ask what had happened to the three battered gringos at the table. And Thom knew that were he not so tired and grateful, he'd be suspicious.

The rest of the night was like a mirage. Thom's room was climate controlled and mosquito free. In the most comfortable bed of his life, he listened to the rain and studied the galaxy of glow-in-the-dark stars left behind by Per and Alma's sons.

They passed the next day at Per and Alma's house. It began with pain and exquisite hospitality, and neither diminished much as the day went on. There was exotic fruit and coffee at breakfast, and then Per took them on a tour of the plantation, bananas as far as the eye could see. Workmen flooded in, and Per greeted them by name, asked about families, shook hands, meanwhile giving the Americanos a lecture on working practices in Ecuador, capitalism, socialism, the conversation leading into a giant Italian *almuerzo*. The three roommates showed off impressive bruises, eyes swollen shut. They followed along slowly, moaning when they couldn't help it. Their state did not seem to be slowing Per's enthusiasm at having guests. Thom and Per drank whisky and played chess all afternoon, talked about mathematics and computer science. Plying each other with veiled questions. Erik stuck to Per's TV and his children's video games. Tree went through the fraction of the library that was in English, expressing various anxieties and despairs under his breath to whomever would listen and later posed in Alma's paint studio. His agitation grew with each moment the quest was delayed. At dinner it finally came out.

They were drinking an after-dinner coffee, and the temptation of cognac was on the table—fine drinks were never far from Per's reach.

"I know that legend," Alma said. "There are lots of legends. Sometimes that's all that's left of history. I didn't think it would be a couch though."

Thom glared at Tree for blurting their story out, wondered at how someone could be so cautious and paranoid yet so steadfastly, idiotically careless at the same time.

"Sometimes that is history, what history has forgotten," Per said. He stood with his glass of cognac in one hand, the bottle in the other, a dangerous look in his eye. "Let me show you my collection."

"Per, let them finish their drinks. They're tired," Alma said.

Thom nodded imperceptibly. Yeah, tired, please, he thought. After Shin's talk of collectors, he didn't like the sound of a "collection."

Per waited and they could see there was no getting out of it. Maybe he's got stacks of couches, Thom thought, and we could just take our pick. Maybe that's how he ended up down here in the first place. His couch called him here.

"You've got him started now," Alma said and shook her head.

He led them to two giant rooms filled with locked cases full of ancient tools, pottery, and musical instruments. A string of rough hewn stones the size of boots we re suspended by cords from the ceiling. Per picked up a small wooden mallet and played them like chimes, made notes that vibrated the room.

"There are so many mysteries." Per quieted the last note. "Most of these things we found on the farm. Some I bought from other farmers who think it's all trash. The locals don't give a damn. They all give these things to me. Some comes from the mountains, the Amazon. The history that is written down is a hoax. What you learned in school was made up or rewritten to fit someone's needs. If you ignore the oral legends, which is all that we have left of the people's history, passed on and distorted from one generation to the next, then what you have of the Incas—and because the Incas conquered everyone before them, the whole history of South America—is from the chroniclers. The chroniclers were Spanish conquistadors who were out to ideologically slander the cultures of the New World so that Spain would think them so base that slavery was deserving."

Per cleared his throat, dug in for a lecture.

"When the Incas told the chroniclers stories, the chroniclers distorted them. The Mayas were the first with writing in the Americas. They had an extensive written history, but the Spanish burned all of their books in the fifteen hundreds. What did we lose? The chroniclers focused on cannibalism and human sacrifices. I know half a dozen archaeologists who say there isn't a damn bit of hard evidence there was sacrifice here. Not a bit. What do we really know?

"See these?" Per waved a hand over a collection of carved rock bowls, figurines, and shards. "These date ten to thirteen thousand years before Christ. This is what remains of a culture after fifteen thousand years. Nothing but stone and pottery stands up to time like that. Of course we think them primitive. This continent wasn't even supposed to have been populated until about eight thousand B.C. Some speculate now that people were here as many as eighty thousand years ago. Are you going to tell me they ate boar meat around a fire for seventy-nine thousand five hundred years waiting for civilization to arrive? What if there were another Adam and Eve, a competing race of humans that through disaster and subjugation and intermarriage has been lost? Archaeologists think people came here over the Aleutian Islands, a land link in the north after the last ice age. They don't give these people any credit."

Erik picked up a rock bowl and sniffed it.

"Don't touch that!" Per said, and Erik lowered it with alarm back to where it belonged.

"The Cañaris in the Andes," Per continued. "The Incas, Mayas, all have legends about a great flood, cities disappearing under water never to resurface. Noah's flood was supposed to have happened around 3400 B.C. The Incas built their cities on the summits of mountains, afraid the land was going to sink. North American glaciers were melting from the last ice age. The sea rose. Many of the people believe the forefathers of their cultures came from a people fleeing the great cities that were sinking beneath the ocean. There are one hundred and eighty ancient cities under the waters of the Mediterranean alone. Think of what was lost—just think of it!"

Per swilled cognac in the glass, took a great gulp. "Ever hear of Kuelap? A city lost in the clouds, built at over three thousand meters and not like any other architecture in South America. Twenty-meter-high walls—that's over sixty feet for you Americans. Three times more stone used than they used to build Egypt's great pyramid. Found a bunch of two-meter human skeletons there, tall as you"—he pointed to Thom—"with blond hair. How did they get there, a thousand years before South America was 'discovered'? Nobody knows why they abandoned the city."

Per cursed in what Thom assumed was Swedish. "Archaeologists always say that. 'For some unknown reason, in such and such time, they abandoned the city.' Abandoned the city? Where did they go?" Per shouted thunderously across the room. "Where did they go!?" He brought his voice down to a murmur. "Where did we come from? That's the question.

"The majority of the world's populations were coastal before the great flood. The navigators, the boat builders, left their mark all over the planet. We attempt to explain away that which we do not understand."

Thom looked over at Tree. His hands were frozen around a wire sculpture, eyes as wide as spoons.

"How to explain the Egyptian pyramids, Easter Island, Mayan mathematics and architecture? Detailed books in India by the

Ramas that explain the maintenance and construction of flying machines?

"How do we know what God is? The human brain has such a short perspective on time. If something is over a hundred years old, it's doubted. Five hundred years and it passes into legend, that filmy, elusive word whose meaning lies somewhere between a great historical event and a great story somebody made up to tell his kids. If it happened a thousand years ago, five thousand years ago, then it's myth—that is, except for the fundamentalists, who believe everything is myth except what is written word for word in their Bibles and Korans and whatnot, and they've fought to the death over its veracity for thousands of years."

Per picked up a figurine with metal rays emanating from the head. "Viracocha," he said. "This guy Viracocha"—Per put his fingers up into quote marks—"'The Incan God,' as he was interpreted by the Spanish, is an example. There's evidence now that he was just a good inventor, or that he came from another culture bearing great inventions. What does that mean for Zeus? Perhaps Zeus was from some ancient race in which he played the role of Thomas Edison and was misinterpreted into godliness." Per shrugged. "What is the origin of God? The Titan Prometheus, who gave the Greeks fire—was he a bloke who invented matches five hundred years earlier? Here great men become heroes become legend become myth become gods." Per, waving his cane around, threw himself off balance, stumbled and recovered.

"See this map? See this!?" He downed the rest of his cognac and refilled it from the bottle. "It's a reproduction of a map drawn by a sixteenth century Turkish explorer and pirate named Piri Reis. The map is dated 1513. The fellow himself says he doesn't know where he got some of the maps he used to piece this together. He said some of them may be as old as Alexander the Great, 300 B.C. But these people didn't have the technology to make this map either. He says Columbus had the same map. Columbus discovered America, but you may notice that America is already drawn here! Discovered my ass!—he just followed the map. See this part? That's Antarctica." Per banged on the map with his cane. "Antarctica! Who knows when Antarctica was discovered?"

A stunned silence in the room. The sheepish looks of college kids who haven't done their homework.

"See how it's drawn? Mountains here and river valleys as if the whole damn continent wasn't buried under several miles of ice? Those mountain ranges reflect the mountain ranges we discovered under the ice in just 1959. The mountains on this map are accurate. When was Antarctica discovered? 1820. Not until 1820!"

Per fell into a great fit of coughing. His face had turned red in the excitement. He started again quietly. "Do you have any idea what I'm suggesting? I'm suggesting . . . No, I'm not suggesting, I'm telling you"—Per raised his voice—"educating you. I'm making you understand that Antarctica was mapped accurately before it was covered in ice. This map of Piri Reis is not his map. It is an anonymous gift from the past. Its longitudes are perfect. We didn't know how to determine longitude until the Renaissance. It uses spherical trigonometry—you studied that, Thom?"

Thom nodded.

"Then tell your friends what it means."

"It . . . uh. It's a math . . . they use it to map coordinates on a sphere. They started using it in the seventeen hundreds. Usually used in mapping the globe or calculating the positions of star systems."

"Yet this map says 1513! This isn't too long after Europe's Dark Ages, a time in which much knowledge was lost. What I'm trying to say is that the world had a great civilization in the past, perhaps several of them, and either they made some grave error, completely changed the world's climate, changed it so severely that it all but destroyed them—any of you read the news lately, follow climate trends?—or they murdered each other, or they did any of the countless other things this species does to suicide itself, or perhaps they were simply unlucky. The earth reshaped. I don't know. I don't know."

Per downed and refilled his glass again. He was breathing heavily, and a vein stood out on his forehead. His voice dropped dramatically, low and sinister.

"The remnants of humanity plunged into a dark age, a fear of knowledge, a desperate struggle for survival. *Perhaps* one of the great civilizations was based on the island of Atlan, what you know as the fairy tale of Atlantis. Another history turned legend turned myth. Plato mentions it, says the island, the continent, was destroyed in a day and a night. The few Atlans who did not drown fled, losing more or less everything they'd created. Some integrated with the Mayas. There's new evidence of a great sunken city off of Cuba, very close to the old Mayan territories. Some Atlans went east, others west. I believe there are strains from them still, or from other ancient civilizations, lost and isolated, more cities like Keulap, perhaps, with impossibly precise stonework, and perhaps still advanced, having scavenged bits of technology from the wealth they once had. Just think of what was lost. If you were the last of your civilization, could you make electricity? Paper? Craft a boat? Do you have the faintest idea what goes into making a silicon chip, a radio wave? Do you know how to farm?

"The earth's size is still inconceivable to humans, too small and yet so large. You will never know the street kid's suffering in Myanmar; you will never taste whale meat off of an Icelandic spear. Yet look at the information available to us. We think we know everything. We're misled. We don't deserve what we have, and our arrogance guarantees we'll never really understand it anyway."

Per picked up a handful of solid one-inch glass spheres, turned them around in his hand. "Who knows what these are? Found this one when I dug a well. This one a friend gave me from his place. Pure crystal. I've heard all kinds of theories—decorations, like Christmas-tree ornaments, information-storage devices—know what you can store in crystal? Light refraction. There's been evidence of solar energy use in Atlan. Sure, it sounds unbelievable." Per waved his hand dismissively. "But to make a crystal sphere itself requires very advanced technology—no evidence of metalworking on these either. Something else. Diamond drills? They're perfect spheres. Maybe they were made by the culture that was here before, or maybe their ancestors, or their ancestors' ancestors. Maybe they are gifts from an untraceably distant past."

He waved his cognac hand around, spilling drops among pottery jars. "But that's not the only time we've lost everything. Between the Romans and the Christians, the Library of Alexandria was burned. The early world's greatest repository of information: a million books. They burned it sixteen hundred years ago. Know who the Copts were? Precursors to today's modern policemen. They were the violent monk patrolmen who roamed Alexandria, stamping out anything or anyone even resembling knowledge. And then the world was flung into the most recent dark age—that is, if you don't consider this age a dark age. Knowledge was mistrusted. People believed bathing was evil. The bubonic plague struck, killed thirty million—and even I, I still mistrust knowledge. What can you trust? There are two parts to knowledge. Understanding it, and understanding how to use it and not kill yourself. The Western world, with its nuclear bombs and genetic engineering—you have a great understanding of technology but very little concept or concern for its eventual effects."

"Okay, Per," Alma said. "They've had a long day."

"Mmm," Per said and hobbled around, looking for something among the artifacts. "It took us this many years to relearn what was lost—though we don't even know what we lost! Look at this!" Per held up an intricately carved figure, an iridescent metal. "This is platinum, from the northwest coast of Ecuador, La Tolita. Several thousand years old, I don't know. The technology for melting and forming platinum was discovered in the 1850s—just after the discovery of Antarctica!" Per said sarcastically. "And I use the word 'discovered' the same way I talk about Columbus discovering America. Platinum requires extremely high temperatures to melt. Know how high? About two thousand degrees Celsius; probably about three thousand five hundred degrees Fahrenheit to you. How in the hell did they do that? It's difficult to know what to believe anymore. You can't believe me! An old Swedish conspiracy theorist, I base all my facts in legends, it's true, but they make more damn sense. . . . Since moving here, so many of my beliefs have reversed. I . . . don't even go to the doctor anymore." Per faded off, swallowed the rest of his cognac in a great gulp.

Thom glanced at Erik, wondering what the last bit meant.

"*Curandero*," Alma said. "Witch doctor. Per had cancer. I finally talked him into going."

"It's hard to give up on the belief system you were raised with, and half the shit I hear here is utter bullshit. The old medicines mixed in with cheap showmanship and used for so long that I don't think they even know which is the showmanship and which is the medicine. But after it works, you just give your mind over to it, just say to hell with it, not caring which is which. A guy puts his hands on you, hurts like hell even though his hands are just resting, and then you don't have cancer." He shrugged. "For all I know, it was the witch doctor's secretary who cured me. Your damn country"—pointing at Erik—"exporting its efficiency culture, consumerism, fantasy, sexuality, everything a glossy, irresistible brilliance. I've given in. I have all the newest stuff. Temptation, desire, greed.

"We're losing a culture a day. We're losing our history faster all the time. The Romans stamped out hundreds of cultures to impose their own. Same with the Incas, the Spanish, English, Americans, Japanese, Chinese. And the thousand cultures we've lost repressed the million cultures before them. Ecuador and the oil companies are killing cultures in the Amazon, destroying belief and custom until a great culture that's existed for hundreds, thousands of years knows nothing about itself, a whole race roped into building the pipeline of progress. It's going to take science the next five hundred years to track down the curing properties of the jungle plants that the natives have used for the last five hundred. How many of those cultures think of cancer as petty and curable as a scraped knee? The knowledge is lost because science came in like a blind rhino at a domino tournament.

"So what about the couch? Another magic thing maybe, something hidden in it? Here." Per pointed to a three-foot stone sculpture of a man on his knees, a crescent moon upturned on his back in the form of a seat. "That's an ancient chair, five or six or seven thousand years old, two hundred generations of people, and yet there is no knowledge of the culture that made this. I wouldn't have said so ten years ago, but if you've got something like that and the owner is still around, you better damn well return it. As you can see, I've been a collector. Stolen most of what's here, because humanity is too stupid to reflect, too shortsighted to survive." Per's eyes glazed over, and he leaned heavily against a shelf filled with what looked like stone engine cogs. The room was quiet but for Per's rasping breath.

"Come on, *amor*, let's let our visitors sleep." Alma took Per's arm and led him from the room.

When Per and his wife had hobbled out, the room was eerily silent. The roommates looked at each other in amazement, befuddlement. Thom felt as small as an acorn. An intricately carved cup Erik had picked up suddenly came apart in his hands, cracking, bits of it turning to dust, disintegrating. He yelped, tried to catch the falling pieces.

"Per is smart," Tree said and stared at the space the man had vacated.

The tools and weapons and cookware and instruments felt alive, no longer like dead museum pieces, but belongings their owners were about to come and reclaim. The pieces seemed to hum in anticipation of use. Erik tried to hide the pieces of the cup he'd pulverized.

"How did that happen?" Thom scooped dust into his palm.

"I don't know! It just came apart."

"There goes more history, bud." Thom elbowed Erik playfully.

Tree had one of the crystal spheres in his hand.

"For fuck sake be careful," Erik said with alarm.

"Information storage," Thom said and stared into the sphere Tree held. "Maybe from holograms? That's cool. It could be a million books in there, all the secrets there were. Would the information be on the surface or be inside? With CDs aluminum is burned, I believe, but to burn information on a crystal?" He pulled it from Tree's hands and held it up to the light, a broad rainbow appearing on the opposite wall. "I guess you'd need the right wavelength of light and angle to project what's inside. A lot of angles in a sphere."

"Hey, there's another room." Erik was on his knees. "There's a blue light under here." He tapped the wall, and it sounded hollowly. "It's a secret door!" Erik was hyperventilating with excitement.

"Listen, I don't know if we should . . ." Thom started, then stalled when the door slid into the wall and revealed a room lit by a computer monitor's blue light. "Hey, he's got a computer." Thom strode past Erik, the gravity of silicon electronics pulling him on. He sat at the keyboard, found no password was needed, and was online within the minute. Maybe he had an email from Jean. Erik and Tree were behind him fussing over something in the background. Annoyed, he turned around and saw the walls were covered with sketches of machines, cities, tools, pottery, advanced mechanisms. One that was without a doubt flying, but motionless, a helicopter's pose with no propellers or blades. Is the guy a UFO nut too? A Mayan-like pyramid structure with a giant crystal on top, a rainbow fanning out from it creating what appeared to be holograms on the ground.

"Per knows more than he let on," Erik said. "Or he's off his rocker. Or he's a New Age fanatic. Where'd he get all these?"

Tree pointed to an edge of one of the sketches where there was a tight-scripted notation, a city suspended among trees, obelisks that seemed to float above the forest floor, cocoons. The notation read:

SACALACAS JUNE 1974 0 N 68 W (KXLNNTMTDXERK-KAWS).

"You don't think he's really seen this?" Tree said. Thom studied the notation. "Those are coordinates. I'd bet anything that last bit is encrypted coordinates of better accuracy. Zero north is the equator. Do you think he's been in contact with ancient civilizations that are still existing?"

"Nah," Erik said, "look at these." He pointed to a bookshelf full of fantasy and science-fiction books. Architecture, history, technology, folklore, legends, and survival.

"I don't know. Maybe he's a dreamer, maybe not. Nothing wrong with having a couple of sci-fi books in the house." Thom studied another sketch of a machine that seemed to be doing something with the tides: a giant gear or waterwheel, a pipe back to land. Energy generation? Water desalination? "This one just says rendering from scroll B-28. The hell? So maybe he's found some writings?"

Another wall was covered with photos of real places Thom had seen in TV shows, giant stone ruins, notes taped under the photos, Palenque, Tikal, Macchu Picchu, Uxmal, Easter Island Moai, Egyptian architecture, Olmec heads, Indian temples, Minoan, Mycenaean, Stonehenge. Thom shook his head, feeling swamped in possibility, the earth wasn't flat, the sun didn't spin around them, the universe was infinite.

He turned back to the computer and retrieved his email.

```
to: thom@sanchopanchez.net
from: jean@sidklowski.net
```

```
You bastards can't ever keep a date, can you. So I
moved on to Cuenca, Ecuador, town in the South, to
work on another story. Did you make it here? Are you
in the country? Would still love to meet up if you're
still up to meet.
Funny thing, I was hanging out in a very nice part of
colonial Cuenca, a place where you can get a cappuc-
cino, and I saw what looked exactly like your couch
being moved into somebody's place. You do have the
couch still . . . tell me you have the couch. Made
me miss you. Anyway, you name the time and place this
time. I'll be there. Maybe you will too . . .
-Jean
p.s. I'm staying in a hospedaje named La Casa.
```

"Read this, guys, read this." Thom waved them over toward the computer.

"The couch is in Cuenca," Tree said. "We've got to go. Let's go right now."

"Wow." Erik scratched at his face. "Good old Jean." He raised an eyebrow at Thom. "Pretty damn coincidental though."

Thom ignored Erik's look. "I don't know, Tree, maybe we should leave first thing in the morning. It's, you know, night out? Maybe Per will help us, or maybe it wasn't our couch." Thom skimmed through the rest of his email, disappointed to find nothing else worth reading but a letter from his mother. He steeled himself.

```
to: thom@sanchopanchez.net
from: bmarga379312@aol.com

Do you remember Jim and Ellie Samway? He said he has
some kind of computer job for you.

I'm having them to dinner this weekend. You should
come up and talk to Jim—you'd be welcome to stay
here for a while and catch up. Jim and Ellie look
forward to seeing you.

I love you,
Mom.

to: jean@sidlowski.net
from: thom@sanchopanchez.net

Jean—what a coincidence! The couch was stolen
```

"Dude," Erik said, hovering over Thom's shoulder, "you're not going to tell her we don't have the couch, right?"

"Why not?"

"Think about it. If that's what she's after, and she finds out we don't have it, we'll never hear from her again, and then we definitely won't find the couch."

"Erik—I trust Jean."

"Happy for you, thinks-with-his-dick."

"Shut up, Erik." Thom pushed Erik away and out of reading distance.

Erik threw his hands up, but Thom deleted the line. He put his head in his hands and tried to think of an innocuous message.

```
It just so happens that we're coming to Cuenca. Stay
where you are—We'll stop by your hotel. I look for-
ward to seeing you.
Thom
```

He returned the computer to the state he'd found it. "We should get out of here, gents. It's spooky. For some reason, he's hiding all this information. He could be filthy rich, I'm guessing, with some of this stuff he's found."

Erik nodded, looked around the room for something he could take. Realized he still had a pottery shard, pocketed it.

At breakfast, Per looked as if the effort of the previous night's speech had aged him ten years. Eye avoidance was a high priority. Thom focused on his toast, coffee, the window just above Erik's left shoulder with the steamy view of banana Ecuador.

Alma and Tree were unaffected and chatted idly about portraiture. Tree, finished eating, worked Alma's profile with wire and pliers.

"I would have liked it for my collection." Per stared at a piece of pancake on his fork, dripping syrup.

Thom studied Per's fork, swirled the orange juice around in his glass. He knew Per was talking about the couch. Knew he'd known all along. "I don't think it works like that. If we get it back, we're taking it home, where its . . . whatever . . . won't affect the outside world. You know all this, don't you?"

"I would have liked to have it, to see it at least. If you find it again, if you manage to take it there, if if if, then my life will change here. That's what they say. Look." Per gestured with the loaded fork, waving it in the direction of his house, splashing syrup. "Look at this place, full of expensive things, cooled to a comfortable temperature against the sweltering outside by energy-sucking apparatus. I'm on the line, I don't live like I preached last night. I take advantage. This was the comfortable thing, the easy thing to do. You come all fired up, and then look what happens. You get lazy. You want nice things," he said, a tone of regret and defensiveness in his voice. "As a foreigner, it was too damn easy to get ahead here." He tapped the bite of pancake against the side of his plate. "I've looked for where you're going. Looked and looked. You saw my room last night?"

Thom nodded sheepishly.

"I'm on the line, see. I hope you fail, but I'd like to come with you, see you succeed. I bet it's a marvelous place. I don't know how you'll find it. I don't know if it can be found, or if it even exists. Not in the normal sense anyway. Maybe just the past. Ruins." Per threw his hands up, and the bite of pancake launched from the end of his fork and skittered across the hardwood floor, leaving a trail of stickiness. A cat lunged from under a chair and got its jaws around it.

"Do you know who took it from us?" Erik said. "Was it you?"

Per smiled. "No, of course not. I thought about it though. God, I thought about it. I heard about it after you'd launched it off to sea. Rumors were everywhere. The local shaman came and told me. Wanted me to . . . didn't want me to interfere. No one knows what it is. I'm an old collector, and I know that it's incredibly valuable and it's what you'd call magic in the way that anything inexplicable to the superstitious is magic or otherworldly or alien. You've got a lot of serious collectors after you, but also the council." Per screwed his eyes at Erik, paused. "Very valuable," he repeated.

Erik swallowed and made a sound in his throat.

"But it's more than that. There are corporations that want it, governments, all those entities that have realized the importance of believing in certain myths. You'd be surprised. Though very few people understand, really. Some seek it for its supposed value, not its effect, and vice versa. It's been lost for a long, long time. It's a population-control tool. It affects the way people think, the way people react or do not react. Perhaps its return will change the way the world is ordered." He sighed. "Perhaps not. It doesn't matter to me much. I'm old, and I believe differently than I live. But to a lot of people, it will be a very big deal. If you fail, and I'm trying to be optimistic by not telling you the likelihood of failure, but if you fail"—Per shrugged—"the world will continue as it is. If you believe that's a good thing, then you might as well quit now."

"Can you help us get it back at least?" Thom leaned forward.

Per smiled out of the corner of his mouth. "I'll pay your bus fare to Cuenca."

"So you know it's in Cuenca."

"Sure, I saw them. They got it before I could. They got you. But I know who they are, generally. Collectors don't really get along with one another."

"After the speech we got last night, I expected a bit more. Where are the politics now?"

"This is no longer my fight, Thom. I'm a registered misanthrope. I don't believe the species has a chance. This is yours. I lost the fight with myself a long time ago. Everybody decides where they are going to put their energy. You can either seek out or choose to ignore a collective human vision. I chose the latter. I chose to be comfortable."

"But it's not too late!"

"Yes, it is! Dammit. Yes, it is."

Thom studied Per's face and saw that the discussion was over. He finished his orange juice and tried to avoid his gaze.

Thom considered his face in the mirror, the bruises that marked it, the cuts, the swelling. The crusted blood of the split lip, the skin brown and yellow and black around his eye. He tenderly felt the back of his head where a lump was subsiding. But his face was different in other ways. He admired it, surprised by how different he looked, realized the image of himself that he had in his mind looked nothing like the one in the mirror. His nose was swollen and red and peeling from sunburn, but his face was browned. His skin everywhere seemed tighter. What had been pastry-white cheeks were now stubbled and chapped. There was a series of scratches over his right eyebrow and his eyes were green. "Green eyes," he said out loud to see if it sounded familiar and wondered if he'd always had them or if they'd just gotten a lot greener recently. His chin came out of his face instead of being buried by it, and he had only one. The soft second chin had disappeared. He smiled and liked what he saw, gauged the lights for trickery. Not handsome, no, but not unhandsome either. "Okay," he said, "okay." He took a deep breath, thought of the day ahead and then couldn't keep track of his breathing, his heart pattering along like an Irish drummer.

He balled his fists, echoed the moves Erik had taught him, thinking *zapato*, seeing himself anew as a hero whose trial had just begun, practicing a smile, *mis labios estan cerrados*. Then being driven to the bus in Per's fancy air-conditioned American behemoth of a vehicle, seeing himself again in the rearview mirror. Fear a pressure on his bladder, trying not to pant. Was he having a heart attack? He was the wrong person for this, a coward at heart, a bumbling mound of flesh. How did he get mixed up with this . . . this artifact? Tree stared quietly out the opposite window.

The bus station was loosely centered in a dusty market. Per handed Erik money and pointed. No one was clear whose side he was on. All of them still wore his suits, dressed for an awards banquet, a theater performance, white-collar crime. Their bus was decorated like a jukebox or a race car or a rodeo clown, an abundance of racing stripes, tassels, Christ images, lewd stickers, slogans, *Dios es mi señor* or *Cambiaré una vieja de treinte años por dos chicas de quince.*

They followed the mountain pass up and up accompanied by jaunty music: horns and shouting, hooting, a festive, jangling affair. Their driver kept time to the music with swerves, the engine grinding like a ten-ton dentist's drill. And Thom's fear was like water spilling over the banks of the Mississippi, the Nile flooding, an Amazon of fear, the Colombia's rushing waters, the slow Danube. A pressure in Thom's bowels, against his temples, ears plugged with it, his eyes letting go with a drop of fear now and then. They were going to confront the enemy. He had enemies, real bad people. He was a good guy. Was that what he was? Wasn't everyone always the good guy to themselves? How would the movie be cast? From which perspective? Who would play his part? Where was the screenwriter? Who wrote this joke, dream, illusion, trick? Do I want the world to change, comfortable America, full of stoplights, millions of internet connections, singing fish, dancing teddy bears, corn bread, animal cookies? Tree was asleep next to him. Erik by chance seated next to an Ecuadorian princess, a love goddess, was talking and flirting, and Thom in a hot clench of fear was sweating through his clothes. As they wove up and up and up through the mountains, the temperature dropped. They were on a mud road through an Andean pass, between impossibly steep mountains, garbed in fog. Does Atlas miss his Earth? Is it such a good thing to remove a burden from the world? Wasn't the couch's evil an important and necessary evil? How can you strive if there is no strife?

And then they were over the pass, a long roll down, switchback and switchback to Cuenca, Ecuador. Erik getting off the bus all smiles, a phone number crumpled in his hand, a date for the evening.

In Cuenca they walked through an entirely different Ecuador. Cobblestone streets and cool air and refinement. They walked past two- and three-story buildings. Colonial tile roofs, a clear sky to the south. To the west, the sky rumbled black to the height of the Andes. Cuenca felt like the right place to wear a suit. They barely got a second look. The giantness of Thom only occasionally causing a startled stare. Except for a mad, diesel-spewing bus charging down a street or a suicidal taxi driver, the place seemed orderly. They asked directions and headed to Jean's hotel, hostel, *hosepedaje*. They passed two internet cafes in a row, and Thom gripped Erik's shoulder. "Look."

"Yep, bud. You can whack off all you want. I bet you missed your internet porn."

They were a motley crew, filing in line down the street, Erik absurdly straight, pertly issuing *buenas tardes*, his suit smart if out of fashion, a mustached gentleman from a gentleman's movie. His gaze steadfast on the back of Erik's knees, Tree followed—a silence like coffins, like earthworms, a presence that wasn't there, the ghost of Tree—and lastly the giant, his suit wrinkled and tight and still damp across his back, under his arms, a mountain chill in the air but sweat in his eyebrows, his muscles tensed for flight, walking past two-hundred-year-old cathedrals the size of coliseums, a church on every other block, red tile sidewalks and stone streets, Ecuadorian children on balconies following the progress, *See that one?* Thom imagined them saying. Walking to the south end of town, a hostel called La Casa.

In front and down every street, Thom's dread led to shadowy hallucinations of a friendly faced man with a straw hat and a night-stick, threatening.

Jean came around a corner, nearly knocking Erik over, and there were spontaneous cheers. Hugs. She pressed herself into Thom, and he felt knocked off-kilter by how beautiful she was, desire and fear mixing in the pot, a feeling of losing control. And he couldn't suppress suspicion: how had she found them? How many emotions can you amp at once? He tried for a smile, a look of polite confidence. Was he fooling anyone? Listening with excessive interest to everything she said.

Jean touched Erik's swollen eye, Thom's lip, made the sounds of compassion that make pain so worthwhile. She put her arm around Tree and said, "I can't wait to hear the story."

She led them toward the hostel, and Tree chatted like he hadn't lost his voice for days. Erik got them a room. A dingy three-storied place, with dark, rickety stairs to their room on the roof, a fourth floor, sort of. Plywood walls painted orange with green trim, a bare lightbulb dangling, a queen bed and wooden table at the other end. Thom wondered where they were all going to sleep. Jean with her own room and the three of them in this. *Three here and one in the other room didn't follow the natural law of osmosis*, brain pointed out. Counting desires: first, to die, second, if the first should fail, a hope for an invitation.

They ate at a cafe, told stories, drank. Since Thom's email, Jean had cased the house where she'd seen the couch, and she related the details. All of them pretended to be detectives. Pretended to be action heroes. They worked on a plan. Something that would preferably not get them killed, Erik requested. Thom tried to keep his knees from shaking the table.

After they'd eaten, Erik peeled off to some salsa dance bar for a rendezvous with his Ecuadorian interest.

The streets of Cuenca were dark and quiet. They ambled back to their rooms. Thom imagined trying to share a queen bed with a mosquito-bitten Tree. A sauced, sweaty, smokey Erik piling onto the floor later in the night.

He hesitated in the entranceway. He saw Tree go into his now-familiar getting-ready-for-bed routine: too much toothpaste on his toothbrush, always foam left in the sink afterward, a heavy-lidded walking coma at nine p.m. sharp. He realized how much he didn't want to be in this room.

He wondered what Portland was up to. Tried to imagine returning to any kind of routine there. Can a person go from this back to a life? An apartment and a job?

He looked back at Jean just before going in, just before committing for the night. And she raised her eyebrows. Her head leaning slightly toward her room. Thom raised his eyebrows back. He decided for once not to be timid, stepped out into the hallway, to verify, to try.

"Do you . . . did they give you . . . would . . . would you like to have breakfast in the morning?"

"What?"

"Breakfast. In the morning?"

"We're all going to breakfast. We just talked about that."

"Of course, of course. I meant to say, what's your room like?"

"It's about—"

"I didn't mean that. What I meant was, can I go to bed with you?" Not quite sure he'd said it. He imagined the words in his mouth again to see if they fit. He studied her expression to see if she'd heard what he thought he'd said.

She smiled. "Thom. I . . . it seems so much more real when you say it out loud. Wouldn't you rather have a slow, painful courtship? That's what I usually do."

"Mmm," he said, took a step back. "So. So then I did say that, something about a bed?"

Her face was a mask of seriousness. "I think you did. Or did I?"

"Ah, you may have. I think you said it."

"Ah. Well then. That changes things."

"Does it?" Unsure of what to do next. If death was going to come, now would be a good time.

"Then?" she said.

"After you?"

He kept his eyes on her curly hair, followed her through the labyrinth of the hostel. Toothbrush, he thought, floss, soap, *condom*. Hadn't he only met her a week or two or ten ago? When he was somebody else. A failed computer nerd in the States. Now what was he? Already stripped of his superhero status of Azulman. She went down a stairway, along a passageway, and then up another stairway, her ass at eye level as they climbed, Thom wishing the stairway were just that much longer, the anxiety of arrival, plus the enjoyment of the current perspective. *A bite away*, the brain volunteered, an image of teeth against flesh, then skin against skin.

He was aware while it was happening, while he was following her, that it was he who followed her, he who walked up the stairs, saw every nervous motion of his like an ambivalent second party, a player just above his head, his body being controlled by joystick—ha ha, he thought, wouldn't be the first time—or the up arrow of a keyboard, steering the video game of him lustily up, up, up into the celestial-bound bedroom of Jean, where social disaster could at any time strike, or the bliss of having her, her curvy body that he wanted to squeeze into him like a bear, the brute craving of affection—but she too, looking back once slyly, seductively, seemed to indicate a mutuality of intention.

Then his brain telescoping the image of the videogame player repeatedly above his head, like a house of mirrors, each incarnation of him being joystick controlled by the incarnation above it until in the dimensional distance he could not tell if the joystick controller was he or not. Ssshhhh, he said to his brain, just let me enjoy this, just let me be human.

In her room, she flicked on the lights for a fraction of a second, then off, freezing the room and its obstacles in memory. In the dark their eyes adjusted. A barest hint of moonlight behind a cloud outlined her form across the room. Observing him. Now what. Then he realized she had managed to free herself of her clothes. *Naked*, the brain volunteered. Thank you, I know the word for it. Thom pulled off his shirt, *touché*. There was too much quiet in the room to speak. A voice would sound awkward, excusing, *mis labios estan cerrados*. She edged one way along the wall. A big room with a bed dead center. He edged the other, fumbling a shoe off, recovering. *There's no need to bumble, not now. Does she like me because I did that computer thing. Does she like me? Does she just want sex, want to know what sex is like with an oversized human? Is she using me?* Shut up, brain. His shoes, pants, underwear came off deftly, and he moved like he hoped he'd move, agile, playing this creeping along the wall, this wild animal thing. Or was he supposed to stop now. Was she playing or was he running away? Shut. Up. He stopped, his back to the wall, watched her edge along until their arms touched, the dimness emphasizing curves, everything a shadow within a shadow, both facing outward. She edged farther, over him, her lower back against his hip, her head grazing his arm, touching his collarbone.

She pulled him toward the bed. Thom conscious of the size of him, his size everywhere. She grabbed him there, by that size. Directed him onto his back with it.

Afterward they whispered for hours in the dark. The difficulty of sleeping when you had someone new. There beside you.

They'd pushed the sheet off in the hot night, and Thom lay on his side and watched Jean sleep in the dawn. Strands of her hair twisted in stripes across her lips, lips that were so rounded and lush and perfect that it made his heart ache, lips that shone and sung all the more by being placed between an ordinary chin and a nose with a bump.

His eyes followed the base of her neck into the indentation between the joining of the collarbone, deep enough while she was at rest to hold a capful of mercury, a perfect pool where tea leaves might be cast.

As he watched the slow rise and fall of her chest and listened to the soothing whistle of the gentlest of snores, the breast closest to him goosebumped briefly, the nipple hardening, and he held his hand just above the surface, felt her warmth.

Maybe this is what I've come all the way here for. Maybe this is the most elaborate way to woo a woman ever conceived. He imperceptibly traced the soft skin around her belly button, let his forefinger rest briefly on the concavity there. Her breathing changed, quickened, and she turned toward him in her sleep, scooted in closer, her hand finding the back of his neck and her thigh coming to rest on his hip. She licked her lips, and Thom held his breath until her breathing returned to normal, marveling that sleep allowed this level of familiarity, this level of trust. She trusted him, and he wondered why. His life must seem like a string of chaotic impulses to any recent observer. He lightly grabbed her hip that rose from the bed so alluringly from where her middle thinned, wanted to pull her firmly, violently toward him to squeeze her to him until she cried out. I trust her, he tried out, and found Erik's doubts flooding into the words, drowning them.

How did she know the couch was here? She found them and followed them for thousands of miles. He tried to swallow his fear down. She'd found them, and he'd slept with her so gullibly.

He stared at her closed eyelids. She slept comfortably while his heart rate increased, his paranoia grew.

He was sure of it suddenly. It didn't make any sense otherwise. He, Erik, and Tree were carrying some ancient relic. They were important. They were sought after by everyone, and so of course the collectors had tapped his loneliness, his heartbroken personality, as a potential weakness. To do what?

She was wrapped around him like a spider, clutching her prey. He wouldn't be able to get up without waking her. But he could easily overpower her. Unless there was someone else in the room. He listened for another presence, tried to listen as the sound of blood echoed in his ears like the sea, his breathing like a train. And then he saw that Jean was awake and watching him, her eyes wide but barely visible, large dark shooter marbles, ominous in their unblinking stillness. Then he remembered Tree, who'd gone to bed alone. They wanted Tree. They wanted their dreamer.

He shoved against Jean and yelled, "What have you done to him!" He jumped from bed and ran down the stairs toward Tree's room, a faint, wounded call following him.

He burst into Tree's room and was relieved to see a form there in bed, snoring loudly. Turning the light on he saw the bristling mustache of Erik. "Erik," he shouted. "Erik!" And shook his shoulders violently.

Erik woke bleary-eyed. "Thom! Knock it off, fuckhead."

"Where's Tree?"

"How the hell should I know? I'm asleep, you bastard. Where were you? You're the one who's missing."

"Jean . . ." Thom trailed off. Tree was standing in the doorway, his face the color of desert bone, and Jean stood behind him, hastily dressed. Thom realized he was completely naked, standing in the middle a scene of his own brash creation.

"I . . . I've been in the bathroom a lot tonight," Tree said. He cradled his stomach with his hands.

"Oh sweetie," Jean said and patted Tree on the shoulder.

Thom wasn't exactly sure how to extract himself from the situation he was in, naked and smelling of sex and sweat and full of misplaced accusations.

Erik gave him a sly smile, winked, and rolled toward the wall. "At least one of us got lucky last night," Erik said and pulled the covers over his head. "False alarm, people." Erik's voice came muffled through bedding. "Go back to your love den and let a drunkard get some shut-eye."

Thom walked doggedly behind Jean back to her room. Jean got back into bed with him, but after several dozen apologies Thom still couldn't shake off a seed of distrust.

"Trust me, Thom," Jean said. "I liked you. I was intrigued—by you and the project—and so I followed. I've got a journalist's curiosity, and I don't think I've done anything to earn your distrust."

"Okay," he nodded and smiled. "I'll try—I do," he said, and

believed that he did. To seal the deal and burn off excess doubt, they made love again.

At breakfast they went over the plan and decided that what they'd talked about as a plan was not worth another moment's thought.

Thom's stomach was in a talkative frenzy, but otherwise he felt better than he had in a while. He even cavalierly tried a bit or two of the wheat toast, just to celebrate. *Remember last night?* brain said. *Remember how you were last night? Somebody likes you.* I know, I know. *Yes, but remember the* rest *of last night?* But maybe she does. Maybe she likes me.

He quickly cased his roommates to make sure no one was staring at him and took another bite of toast. "Let's just go down there and knock." Thom smiled and shrugged. "Why not?"

"We'll get ourselves killed? Didn't I already mention that that was a prerequisite, that we not get ourselves killed?" Erik's eyes were rimmed red from alcohol and smoke and dancing and sexual frustration, and he was cross. He took the tines of his fork and raked at his mustache. "Arrgh! When does the freaking vacation part of our vacation start?"

They'd walked by the house where the couch was. The large metal door to the courtyard was halfway down a well-used public stairway, a giant four story house that towered over the river Tomebamba, which Erik had been informed meant Sacrificial Knife Basin. Super. The couch wasn't hidden in an obscure, highly guarded crevasse of Cuenca, but in a house near the social hub.

"You're sure. I mean you are absolutely sure you saw our couch?" Erik grilled Jean for the third time.

"No, Erik, like I said, it seemed like your couch from what I remember of it. It was a couch, and as Thom said one of the men matched your description of who took the couch. However, I don't see you having a lot of other leads."

"Nobody is going to get killed," Thom said cheerfully, not having any evidence to back it up. "Everything will be fine! Besides, Erik, you've already died once this trip. It didn't hurt you any."

"Are you proposing to just knock and ask for it back?"

"Never hurts to ask, that's what my mom always says." Aware that he was being absurd. There seemed ample space for absurdity.

"Yeah, maybe . . ." Tree said.

"Tree, please don't go along with this idiocy," Erik said. "He's being ridiculous. Even you can see that. Something has destroyed his mind." Erik raised an eyebrow at Jean.

"I don't know. My dad used to say that too," Tree said.

Jean giggled. "And if they say no?"

"It's valuable, very valuable," Erik imitated Per.

"Then we'll use Plan B," Thom said

"What's that?"

"Break in. Plan A for ask. B for break-in. C for crush them like flies," Thom said and ground his fist into his palm.

"And D for dying, dumbass," Erik said.

"Sounds good." Tree stood up. "Let's go."

"Tree!" Erik reached across the table and pushed Tree back into his seat. "That is not a plan."

"Really though," Thom said, "let's go up and just talk and see who we're dealing with." He felt he could lift them all up onto his shoulders, carry them parade-style through the city, this lovely group, far enough away from home for none of it to matter.

Erik stared into his coffee, talked with resentment and exhaustion. "Because they'll be on guard, they'll move the couch, they'll be a lot harder to deal with," he said. "But nobody listens to Erik. Erik who's being smart. Hello?"

But the group was on its way already.

Thom stood in front of the metal door in the tall concrete wall and knocked. He was halfway down a wide stone stairway with multiple landings. A stairway Rocky would have used, he thought, and then realized there were Rockys already on it, climbing to the top in their sweaty jogging suits, running down, repeating. The stairway was a major thoroughfare with a doorway in the middle. Jean, Erik and Tree were all at the top of the stairway looking down nervously, ready to fight or run or do whatever their bodies did when fear pushed too hard. Why wasn't he afraid? All that fear yesterday. . . . His brain presented the image of a flushing toilet, *psshhrrrr, flushing backward*, brain reminded, and he knocked.

He knocked a third time—looked at Jean at the top of the stairs, curly haired and nervous for him, her hands clenched together, all of them waving him away, Erik pacing, and he waved back. When no one answered the door, he tried the handle and, voila!, pushed the door open. There was a wide courtyard, a neglected garden in the center, a cement house that was built tall and not deep, scaling the hillside. A set of steps led up to the main entrance. Thom stepped in and swung the door closed, and behind it was the man in the straw hat, his friendly face working through expressions like a slot machine, his nightstick replaced with a sawed-off shotgun. He fumbled through the motions of pointing it at Thom. Thom had imagined this moment a hundred times. He felt practiced, his fists balled, the body tense, ready to pounce, but the brain had neglected to visualize a gun in the scenario, the one that was pushed against his chest.

The friendly face looking friendly again. "How's your head?" it said.

"There's still a lump," Thom admitted, realizing the fear toilet wasn't working. It was backing up.

"You've come for your couch, have you?"

Thom nodded.

"You realize I will have to kill you now," the man said.

Thom nodded again, feeling relieved, a win-win situation. The man was repeating phrases from the movies, which meant at any moment the rest of the good guys would show up. And if not, if the good guys nervously huddled at the top of the stairs talking about plans B and C and D until a shot went off, then the whole adventure would be over for him and he could have a nice restful afterlife buried in Ecuador. What would his mother think? From looking for a job in Portland to dead in Ecuador. *More bugs in the soil here*, brain volunteered, *buried in Incan land*. The man was pushing him across the courtyard. Thom walked backward, his hands up now, the gun being used as a steering device for his body, the brain quickly playing out a couple of action sequences and then dismissing them.

They steered around the upraised center garden, the gun-barrel jabs insistent—*garden needs watering*, brain volunteered; the calmness before death—and then the door opened.

Friendly face glanced towards the door, and then returned his focus to Thom where there was a piston's forward action, Thom's fist at the end of it. "Kerpow!" Thom said, and for a moment the man's straw hat hung in the air without attachment. Drawn permanently at that altitude as the body fell away. And then the hat drifted easily down atop friendly face's chest, where he lay with blood in his teeth.

"Thom!" Erik said. Tree and Jean stood beside him. "Are you okay?"

Get the gun, brain said.

Erik, Tree, and Jean were immobile. The door closed behind them. Thom grabbed the gun, some knowledge coming to him, its use, function. He held it by its barrel in his left hand, comfortable there, his other hand, those hundreds of bones closed in about themselves with a skin wrapper, a knuckle bleeding, his earth crusher. He walked toward the entrance to the house.

"Thom," Jean said. "Wait."

"Let's make a plan." Erik was fixated on the man on the ground. "Nice hit, man!"

"No plans," Thom said and walked up the stairs and to his surprise knocked on the door. *Just open it*, brain said. He twisted the handle; this door was unlocked too. *Not very organized*, brain observed. Inside was plush, leather and paintings and antiques mixed with recent chaos. Broken plates littered the floor, a coffee cup broken among shards of mirror glass, one thrown into the other. A chair at a massive dining room table on its back, the table scattered with paper and books.

From some distant room within, the sound of a TV gone to loud static. A light wind blowing the curtains about where there should have been windows.

Thom moved toward the noise of the TV, brain still running bits from the movies, transparencies over reality, scenarios that always accompany a TV blaring static: a woman on the bed with a knife in her chest; an absurdly thin man with hollowed eyes in an easy chair, a cigarette butt with an inch and a half of ash still in his hand, heroin; a man in a business suit on the floor, his brains making a mural of one wall, gun still in his right hand.

Thom stood in front of the door, listening to the static on the other side, Jean behind him, Tree and Erik somewhere in the house. Thom flushed the fear toilet, breathed, then opened the door.

Inside was a tall Ecuadorian man in his seventies, his hair askew between the straps of dark safety goggles. No TV: in his hand he had a blowtorch making an absurd amount of white noise, and he was applying the torch to the couch. The room had obviously been a den at some point, full of books and ashtrays and a thick rug, but it was piled with tools and broken things and the smell of toxic melting. An armada of destructive tools—a circular saw, drill, axe, hammer, crowbar, all looking as if they'd already failed.

Thom and Jean stood unnoticed in the doorway watching the smoke rise from the couch, a toxic smell, watched the burn hole spread from the flame and the hole close up like new when the flame retreated. After several more attempts, the man turned off the blowtorch, propped the goggles up on his forehead, and let loose with several kicks to it.

"Hey! That's my responsibility." Erik, behind them now, shuffled through.

The man looked up alarmed, fumbled for his lighter to relight the torch, let his hands drop when Erik was there and Thom was pointing the gun and it was too late.

"What were you trying to do? What a mess."

"*Es invencible*," the man said.

Erik shrugged, picked up one end of the couch. "Come on, we got what we came for."

Jean beat Thom to the other end of the couch, and she and Erik hauled it out of the den, down the hallway, and out, with Tree and Thom following. Friendly face was no longer in the courtyard. Thom picked up the straw hat and put it on his head and dropped the gun in its place. "Well," he said. "That wasn't so hard."

"What do we do now?" Erik worked his mustache nervously. He thought about the night before, how he'd like to just take a couple of weeks off for a nice fling.

"I guess take it back to the hotel, right?" Jean said.

"Back to the hotel, Thom?"

"Sure, sure." Thom wondered why everyone was suddenly asking him the questions. Tree trailed behind, forehead sweaty, eyes glazed. *Chop chop chop chop*—a helicopter loomed over them. Thom looked down the stairs as they reached the top and saw a microbus pull up on the other side of the river. A stream of men climbed out, ran toward them. "Guys?" he said. "They look like . . . they look like they're coming after us!" He broke into a directionless run and then circled back to help hurry on the couch.

Erik and Jean were frozen, staring down the stairs and across the bridge at the approaching men. They had guns, and people scattered before them. Thom grabbed the middle of the couch and steered the carriers into action, running down the street past their hotel. Something will come up, something will come up, Thom thought. They went round a corner before the men reached the top of the stairs. Tree stumbled slowly behind.

"Tree, where the hell do we go next?" Thom hollered. What was wrong with Tree?

"Let's just hide it and then figure out where to go," Jean yelled.

They moved as best they could down a cobblestone street. Everyone stopped to watch the strange gringo parade move past.

Tree pointed above buildings toward the Andes, mountains like a Richter scale reading. He dropped his arm without speaking.

The men rounded the corner of the block behind them, running at full speed.

"We're dead, we're dead!" Thom yelled, lunging forward with the couch so as to turn a corner out of view of their pursuers.

"There," Jean said, pointing at a flatbed truck stopped at an intersection. "Erik, you've got to explain to him."

They dashed forward as the truck began to pull out into the intersection. They heaved the couch up, crashed it onto the truck. It slid on and collided with four cases of Inca Kola. The truck skidded to a halt, the driver whipping around to see who the pirates were. Erik ran around the side and got into the passenger side and Thom and Jean hopped onto the back. They watched Erik argue with the driver as the men came round the corner and sprinted toward them.

"Christ, where's Tree?" Thom stood up on the truck. Tree faltered along a few paces in front of the men, his head down, looking like a puppet in the hands of an amateur puppeteer, legs not quite imitating how a human runs. He'll never make it, Thom realized. A man behind him started reaching for Tree, pushing ahead to grab the boy. "Go!" Thom shouted at Jean. "We'll catch up!"

Thom launched off the back of the truck as it lurched forward and ran at full speed toward Tree, his eyes on the six men now only a hairsbreadth behind Tree.

Thom sidestepped Tree and like a linebacker barreled into the man who gotten hold of Tree's shirt. Thom bent his knees and pushed up with his shoulder, catching the man's midsection. The man flew off the ground, whipsawed into a parked car with a sickening sound, and crumpled to the ground. Thom saw Tree still moving, but now he was behind the line of men who were still in pursuit of the truck, which was forcibly stopped by traffic at the next intersection.

"Tree!" he shouted. Tree was barely moving now, less of a run and more of a loose-limbed stumble, his head bobbing with each step, arms muscleless and banging about his sides. Thom turned and ran back toward him, relieved that the other five men were focused on the truck. "Tree," he called. "Tree!" But he was unreachable. Thom caught him, put his arms around him from behind to stop him. There was a brief lifeless struggle, Tree's limbs moving, twitching, and then nothing. Thom turned him around, held him by the shoulders. "What's wrong with you?"

Tree's face was drenched in sweat, and his eyes were slits. Thom glanced up and saw the truck pulling slowly out of the intersection again. Jean stood up in the back, winding up like a baseball pitcher, throwing bottles of yellow Inca Kola at the men who followed. Bottles sailed through the air, and she beaned one of the men square in the head. An alarm went off as another broke over the top of a car. Thom had an immense swelling of pride, followed by the panic of getting left behind.

"Tree!" He gently shook Tree's shoulders.

"I don't feel well."

Thom heard shots and looked up. Two of the men had paused in the street with their guns out. He couldn't see Jean. "Oh God, please."

Thom straightened Tree back onto his feet and put his hand to Tree's sweaty forehead, felt the heat emanating from him. "Shit, do you need to, do you want to go to a doctor?"

"Follow the couch," Tree said weakly.

Thom nodded. "Follow the couch." He looked around for some means of following the couch. How would they follow the couch? The man he'd hit still lay crumpled on the ground. Thom saw a curved wooden thing sticking out from underneath the man's jacket. A gun. *This is just like the movies too,* brain said. *Take the enemy's gun, check it for bullets, spin the cartridge, blow smoke from the barrel.* It doesn't have a cartridge spinny thing, Thom informed brain. And you only blow the smoke after you fire it. He tucked it into the back of his pants like you were supposed to do, and it poked into his spine uncomfortably. Perhaps his pants were too tight. Okay, think, *think!*

"Taxi?"

Tree closed his eyes.

"Taxi!" Thom yelled and waved his arm at an approaching taxi.

He piled Tree into the car, got in, slammed the door, and then realized he had no idea how to explain. Did he even have any money? He pointed in the direction the truck had gone. His back hurt.

The cabbie blinked, stared at his pointing finger. Said a blur of words.

Thom tried again with more urgency, jabbing with the finger.

The cabbie shrugged, gunned down the street. Thom searched his pockets for money, realized the pain in his back was the damn gun. He moved it onto his lap and then stuck it awkwardly in the inside pocket of the suit jacket.

Tree was slouched down in his seat, his eyes closed. Thom searched Tree for money and found a giant wad of bills in his pants pocket. Where'd he gotten all this money? Thom tossed a twenty dollar bill into the passenger seat, and the driver stared at it in puzzlement. Thom tossed another for good measure and thought he felt the car speed up. Out the windshield was a bustle of cars and pedestrians and schoolchildren and no sign of the enemy or the flatbed truck. Please let Jean be okay, please.

"Tree? Help me, where do we go?" Tree slumped as if his bones had left him, his face pale now and the sweat gone, eyes shut. Thom stared. He would be no help. He'd have to figure out where the couch was by himself. He grabbed a chunk of his hair and pulled. They were fucked. Maybe Jean was shot. And then he saw Tree's mouth move.

"What?"

"Left," the mouth whispered.

"Left, left! God, what's the word for left, do you know the word for left?"

Tree didn't answer.

Thom scooted forward and used his finger again to try to point the cabby. The cabby spewed a bunch of words, put on his left turn signal.

"*No . . . no hable español*," Thom said hesitantly.

The cab driver pointed left. "*Izquierda*." Pointed right. "*Derecha*."

"*Izquierda*," Thom repeated with the pointing. "*Derecha*." And then to himself, memorizing, *izquierda, derecha, izquierda, derecha*. Why'd they have to go and make the language so damn complicated? "Tree, you've got to help me here. Stay awake to say directions."

"Mountains." The only animate part of Tree his lips. "Back the way we came."

What was the word for mountains? Thom probed around his memory for some reference. *Mountainos? Esmountains?* He tried both of these on the cab driver with unsatisfactory results. A section of the mountains came into view, and Thom pointed, saying, "*Vamos, vamos!*"

"*Cajas?*"

"What?"

"*Cajas, se van al Cajas, el parque?*"

"Sorry, I . . . uh . . . don't understand," Thom said and farted an anxious rhythm.

The cab driver shook his hand in a frustrated never mind and kept driving.

Thom put a ten dollar bill down next to the twenty dollar bills on the passenger seat. *That's not helping comprehension*, brain observed. I know, I know, but maybe . . . I don't know, listen, I'm doing the best I can here. How much gas does a piece of toast equal? he wondered.

They drove into the mountains. Winding up the road, higher and higher, into the unbreathable elevation, the road like a tangle of wire. Thom felt as if he was leaving them behind. The truck couldn't possibly have gotten up here. Jean, how was Jean, his bottle thrower, his journalist?

They climbed for a half hour, passing ramshackle trout restaurants, men in hats and shawls with burros following, the trees and plant life getting sparser as they climbed in altitude.

And then Tree sprang awake like a mousetrap. "Here! Stop here." His eyes like puddles, tearing and red.

They were in the middle of nowhere.

"Here?"

"Stop him."

Thom went through a variety of gestures, trying to find one that meant stop. The cab driver pulled over, looked at them skeptically.

Tree stumbled out, coming to his knees on the side of the road. He leaned over and put his fists on the ground and vomited violently. Thom tried to gesture to the cab driver that it was Okay, this was their stop. Was it? Christ, what were they doing? Tree seemed to be dying.

The cab driver eyed them as he drove off, shaking his head. Tree stayed on all fours.

"Tree, this is crazy. You should be at a doctor."

Tree spit. "Probably."

"What the hell do we do now?" Thom tried to keep his voice from sounding like a little kid frightened of the basement.

"We take the trail."

"What trail, there is no trail." On the left a rocky slope ascended steeply, and behind every slope and peak was another, each more covered in the mist until there were only dim, jagged shapes, sentries in the distance. On the right there was a subtle downhill until it curved up again into the same terrain. The mist everywhere turned to fog in the distance.

Tree stood, moving one limb at a time. He plodded slowly, carefully, climbed over the railing to the right and started walking.

"Tree! They can't be there, they . . ." Thom's stomach churned like a blender.

Tree continued, on the verge of tipping over. Thom hustled after him, surprised at how fast Tree was moving for how sick he seemed to be. After fifty yards the trail emerged under his feet, like a snake turned belly-up. A thin stripe of trampled earth.

He struggled to keep up with Tree, who seemed pulled by an invisible thread, a magnetic force, feet moving despite the lack of will. Only their pace kept them warm. The air was chill, and a drizzle of rain came and went. Thom's breath came in short gasps. They were above ten thousand feet.

They entered the wilderness of Las Cajas, *the boxes*. Before them hundreds of miles of land too difficult for roads, for human civilization, only the barest, thread-worn pockets of life in the vastness of mountains.

They trudged on for hours. Tree sometimes falling to the ground to vomit uselessly. The mud became intense; their shoes got sucked into it. And then long stretches of ankle-twisting rocks that reached out to graze the skin off their shins. Their clothes dripped from drizzle and mist and trudging through streams. Thom's nose began to run. The trail wove in and around valleys, past lakes, over streams, up mountainsides, and Thom followed Tree, knowing himself to be ever more lost.

Tree finally fell down for good. His lips barely eking out the need to continue, some part of him not connected to his body urging them on. He lay on the ground with his eyes closed, the wet and cold penetrating his clothes. Thom wondered if it were possible to feel more alone.

He replayed the sequence of events over and over. Tree's attacker connecting with the parked car, catching Tree, Jean throwing bottles. When did the shooting begin? There was no sign she'd been hit, was there? She had not fallen in the street. He picked Tree up and continued on. The trail crossed over a pass, and with his burden and the thin air, his breath came ragged and shallow and he rested frequently.

Where were they going? It didn't seem possible that Jean and Erik had come this way, especially with the couch. Tree wouldn't speak. His eyes were shut, and his head lolled back. Thom tripped along in silence. They were too far in to get back to the road before dark, and so Thom continued in a numb faith, shutting out comments from his brain about hypothermia, starvation, dehydration. His thighs began to shake with the exertion. There was sweat under his arms and a frigid coldness in his ears and toes.

He studied the trail for any signs of Incan stonework and wondered how many previous civilizations he was treading over. His eyes hallucinated rock outcroppings into ruined stone walls, old stone walls into rock outcroppings.

From the top of the pass, he saw the trail dipped down into a broad green valley. Soft rolling hills lined the middle of the valley, with sharp rocky peaks rising close on either side. A stream coursed down through the middle. A view of a strange Eden.

Thom saw a flicker of movement on a trail opposite the pass. There were people on it, a lot of them, and . . . could it be them? Yes, they had a couch. He whooped and plunged off his trail, down a steep muddy slope, slipping and falling with Tree jostling about in his arms, a mad relief and glee spurring him on.

He came to the bottom of the slope and headed up the other side toward where he'd seen the couch, hollering as he went. The people came into view over a hill, and, winded, he put Tree on his feet, holding him up with one arm, and waved. "Hello!" Was that

Erik with a gag on his mouth? Ha ha, I've wanted to do that too. There was a loud bang, and Thom squinted to see what might be going on.

They were shooting at him! He grabbed Tree and turned around. He ran down the slope, wove back and forth, slipped and fell heavily onto his back. Now they were both completely covered in mud. There were several more shots, but he didn't have any idea where the bullets were going. He checked to make sure Tree hadn't been hit. Tree was completely unconscious but without holes as far as Thom could tell. *You have a gun,* brain said at last, breaking back into the control tower. He set Tree behind a boulder and pulled the gun out from his coat pocket. Okay, the plan. The plan was . . . the plan was to get Jean back. And also the couch and Erik. He would sneak up and . . . kill them? He began climbing back up the hill. The trail above was obscured from him. He held the gun in his right hand, muddying it in the climbing. To keep from sliding back down, he grabbed the long thin grass he'd seen people working into roofs. Look, his leg had blood on it. He wondered if he'd left Tree dying back behind the boulder. But the blood came from him. He fingered open the rip in his pants where the blood seemed to be coming from and looked at it objectively. Yes, it was him. He appeared to have been shot. There was a ghastly welling of blood and torn skin. Funny there was no pain.

At the top of the rise, the trail and couch caravan came into view again. There was a mini valley between the rise he was on and them. He stood up and yelled what he hoped was a threatening kamikaze yell. Meanwhile brain churned out the code necessary:

```
function attack_method(bad_guys)
{
  if(bad_guys == "armed")
     attack_method = dodge () . roll () . shoot();
  else
     attack_method = chase () . overpower();
  return attack_method;
}
```

```
function use_weapon(weapon)
{
  switch (weapon)
  {
    case: "gun":
      action = "Point, aim, pull trigger";
    case: "knife":
      action = "Move close to opponent, strike blade first";
    case "hand":
      action = "Move close to opponent. Ball fist, strike weak point";
    case "wits":
      action = "Good luck, my friend";
  }
  return action;
}
```

Thom pointed the gun in the direction of what surely were the bad guys and squeezed the trigger. Nothing happened. The trigger was stuck, and they were firing back. He heard a bullet whiz by. Another made a *schlook!* in the mud at his feet. He turned and ran back down the hill, out of sight. He studied the gun, his eyes blurred by panic, fixing on a switch and then losing it, fixing again. The safety, of course, *of course*. He turned off the safety and fired a test shot generally in the direction of the valley. The gun bucked in his hands. Okay, he was in business. He climbed back to the top of the hill and saw that they'd all ducked down. He had them now; they hadn't known he had a gun. Ha ha! The couch was in the trail, and there were several people hidden behind it. He saw Jean now too—Jean!—and a man behind her holding a gun. *That will be a difficult situation*, brain observed.

He squeezed the trigger, the gun jumping all over the place. Was he supposed to be counting bullets? Clint Eastwood would be counting bullets. Were there really bullets coming out? They were all ducking. Someone started screaming. A man jumped up from behind the couch gripping his shoulder. How had he hit a man behind the couch? He felt guilty, he'd hurt someone, but then realized he'd probably won. Game over. Time to get the couch and head home. He put the gun back in his pocket and started walking up the trail, but they were shooting back at him again! He ran and dived behind the hill, but the dive didn't quite work out: more like a belly flop on top of the hill. He rolled the rest of the way out of sight. Okay, think, *think*. He was panicked, he could see that now, or maybe he was overconfident, or in shock. Maybe they were the same thing. They could fire at him any time they liked. There were no rules. For some reason it had made sense that once he'd hit someone, they'd give up. He wished Erik were here—if he concentrated on freeing Erik, maybe Erik would have a plan. Before Thom could register what he was doing, he was back at the top of the hill squeezing the trigger at the caravan, which was now moving out of sight. After fourteen or eighteen or twenty squeezes, he realized that he was making the *bang-bang* noise with his mouth and that the gun had stopped making noise, perhaps some time ago. Fuck, he was bad at this. You're our only hope, Thom Bakker. He needed Han Solo or the Green Lantern or Strider. This wasn't his calling. He didn't like shooting at people. But then the shooting was over if the bullets were gone. What about those council guys? This was their job. Or were they only the librarians of the resistance, recruiting unformed unchosen for their foot soldiers? His leg still didn't hurt, and the thought idly crossed Thom's mind that perhaps he was invincible. That this was his special role in this whole quest thing. Unstoppable Thom. Azulman. He put the gun in his pocket and ran after the couch.

They had disappeared around a bend in the trail. Thom made it up to the level of the trail and sprinted and stumbled along. He rounded the bend, and the caravan came into view. They had stopped, and all the bad guys had their guns pointed at him. He let out a roar, and something spun him around, another bullet! It was in his arm, but there was still no pain. He pulled the gun from his pocket and continued running toward them. He threw the gun with all his might at the fellow in the front and miraculously hit him in the forehead. The man pitched over, and then Thom had a bullet in his stomach, or at least there was a lot of blood coming from there. This one made him go a little slower, sort of like running in the sand. Maybe he was only partially invincible. Wasn't there some film about a guy who healed himself. Maybe he'd take twenty bullets and heal them right up. He reached the unconscious man, the man he'd hit with his gun. He saw Erik, mouth gagged, eyes wide, hands bound, running. Where was he running? Thom picked up the unconscious man by his shirt front and crotch, held him over his head, the strong man, Azulman! He was cut out for this work after all. He threw the man with a tremendous heave and bowled over another of the gunmen. Amazing. He was invincible! But then they must have gotten another bullet in him, because he was on his back, and black spots swarmed like crows in his vision. Must not forget the thin air up here, must be running too much. There was a man standing over him, pointing a gun at his head. Thom kicked up with his leg. I'll get him in the crotch, Chuck Norris-style! But the leg wouldn't go. There was no reaction at all. The movies are great, starring in my own movie, the credits will go up and there will be my name, Thom Bakker, playing himself. The kids will practice karate moves on each other in the parking lot afterward, high on the adrenalin, the superactionhero Thom Bakker. Wait. Actually. He was going to die, his body left to rot in the loneliest place on earth.

Erik was trying to keep from pissing himself. He wasn't having much luck. It wasn't a fear thing; it was that this last part of the adventure was so damn annoying that the annoyance migrated straight to his bladder. A couple of hot, itchy, frantic squirts had already come out. And his mustache itched like mad so that he kept wrinkling his lip up into his nose, which in turn made his nose itch. What the hell was he supposed to do? He'd tried to scratch it on his shoulder, but his hands were tied too tightly behind his back to raise the shoulder to scratching height. At least he wasn't carrying the couch. Follow through, his teachers said; follow through, his father said. And how? They'd put a gag on him after he'd made a suggestion or two too many. The men had caught up, and they were taking them back toward the road. The guy in front of him had grabbed Jean's ass about five times, and Erik was just about to ram his head into the guy's stomach against all survival logic when someone yelled hello from below.

For being such a brain, Thom was the dumbest fuck Erik had ever met. Was he really waving at them? Tree was propped like a mannequin against Thom. If Erik's hands were free, he'd have covered his face in embarrassment. But then Thom had a gun, and bullets were flying all over the place. They'd stopped, and Erik had crowded himself behind the couch because Thom obviously didn't know how to handle a gun. A bullet ricocheted off of a boulder over his head and struck the shoulder of the guy next to him, and Erik made himself smaller. A plan, what was his plan? He could head-butt a couple of them off the trail.

Apparently Thom was finished firing his gun, because they'd started to move again. The men all had their guns out and were looking over their shoulders. What was Thom going to do now? How could he create a distraction? But with the way Thom fired his gun, he didn't have a chance of hitting any of them on purpose, even if they were all tied to the ground. The man behind Erik with the wounded shoulder was cursing and pushing him on roughly now. Then he heard a roar behind him, and Thom was running toward them at full speed. He couldn't believe it, he was the bravest sonofabitch he'd ever met, but he was going to get killed, that much was obvious. Erik started to run around. The least he could do was to bump into the men as they were firing their guns at Thom, see if he could get them off balance. He saw Thom take a bullet in his arm, and he yelled with rage behind his gag. He drove his head into the face of one of the assailants and heard the crunch of the man's jaw, watched him fall to the ground. He saw Jean then, kicking the man in the gut. She was running around yelling—they probably both looked like fools, armless attackers. So this was how it was going to end. And then he saw a man standing over Thom with his gun pointed at his head, Thom on the ground covered in blood. He sprinted toward the man, but he was going to be too late. He could see that there was no way he could make it. But then the man fell, and there were more bullets flying around. Was this ever going to end? Whose side were the new bullets on? The men were running around in a panic. He turned and ran back the other way, and then someone rammed into him like a freight train and knocked him to the ground and he saw it was Jean.

"Stay down!" she said.

"Ight, Ight, 'ucking 'ist al'ighty!"

The gunshots dwindled, and then there was quiet. Erik looked around, but there was no one. Just the body of Thom and the body of his assailant, neither of them moving. His first thought was that he'd be going back to jail, and then he cursed himself for thinking of himself when Thom was on the ground. The guy was covered in mud, and there were far more bullets in him than seemed necessary to kill a man. Thom was dead. He looked for Jean and couldn't see her.

Then he saw a new group of people arrive. Stuck at ground level, he watched a toe nudge one of the fallen bodies. A man stood over him, and Erik tried to place the face.

The man reached down and swiftly cut his gag free with an absurdly large knife and said, "Well?"

Were they here to steal the couch? The man was a great shaggy human, a giant beard and a mustache. In fatigues and a beret that barely fit over a mass of hair. Looking like one of Guevera's generals. One of those guys stuck in the wilderness for twenty years, huge and furry. On second thought, it wasn't human. It was some kind of dirty, rabid bear. Jason Glakowsky.

"Dad?" Erik said, the word going weak and windy at the end like the breath had been knocked out of him. He fished for something else to say, his mouth open.

"Hi, Erik." His dad smiled.

"Dad!"

Jason Glakowsky reached down and pulled Erik to his feet with a singular powerful motion and cut his wrist bonds.

Erik kept his head low. "Are they gone?"

"Yeah. For now. There were too many of us."

Erik looked around for Jean and saw her off the trail, headed away from them, stumbling down the slope and deeper into the Andes. She was still gagged and wrist-tied, and she walked like someone who'd been hypnotized—seeing and yet not seeing. He borrowed his father's knife and sprinted after her. Her eyes were wide, and there were tear marks on her face. When he stepped in front of her, she didn't register him, didn't focus, just sidestepped him.

"Jean! Stop!" He grabbed her shoulders. "Hey, stop. Maybe Thom isn't dead, maybe?" A sear of guilt ran through him for saying it, for giving her false hope, but he couldn't stop himself. He freed her from her gag and bonds. "My dad is here. Maybe he . . . Maybe he'll know what to do." She seemed to at last register his presence, stared at her wrists and then back at him. Her eyes were dull.

"Where's Tree?

"Tree?" Erik had a vague memory of seeing Tree earlier in the day. Why wasn't Tree here? Had Tree been shot and left to die on a hill? He had to keep it together, had to keep everyone together, one at a time. He turned Jean around and faced her in the direction of his father and his father's men, supplied gentle pressure until she began walking that way on her own. It was all him now. It was up to him. The quest could not fail, but how . . . how could it possibly be accomplished? Everyone was dead.

Erik ran in the direction he'd last seen Tree, down one hill and up another, falling and rolling as he ran, back on his feet, tripping and not caring. He finally spotted Tree slumped against a boulder. He had been shot! Erik squatted next to Tree, looked for blood but didn't find anything except a few marks here and there. He shook Tree's shoulder, and his eyes opened.

"Tree," he said. "What's wrong, Tree? Are you okay?" And then a wave of anger rolled over him. "How come you didn't tell us? Wake up, Tree. He's been shot! Thom's been shot."

Tree's eyes seemed to have trouble focusing, his lips worked to get out a syllable that had no voice behind it.

Erik reached out and felt Tree's forehead. "You're sick, dream-boy." Remembering suddenly the mosquitoes, Tree's dreams about getting sick. He put his arms under Tree's legs and back, lifted. He was so light. Above him on the trail his father and his men had put Thom on the couch and seemed prepared to move on. Erik trudged up the slope slowly, out of breath.

"What's wrong with him?" Jean said when he'd reached the trail.

"He's sick, probably malaria. Something like that. My dad will know."

"I can't believe this, it's a nightmare, why did I come?"

Erik recognized more faces, guerillas he'd grown up with. They were all gray-haired and wrinkled now.

Erik's father, Jason, wrapped gauze around Thom to slow his bleeding. Blood was oozing from all over his body, soaking the couch. A fallen giant. There was no trace of a heartbeat, and they discussed whether they should bury him. Jean sobbed once and closed Thom's open eyes.

"We'll take him into the village," Jason said. "She'll know if he can be saved."

"Saved?" Erik said, trying to extract the outrage from the hope.

Jason shrugged.

What would there be to resuscitate? Erik looked down at the still body of Tree in his arms. A drop of sweat shimmered above Tree's eyelid, and Erik tried to hold himself together. They were supposed to get on a Greyhound, he remembered, go spend some time on the beaches of Mexico. He wanted to burn that couch.

The grizzly crew of guerillas in camouflage began digging a grave for the dead man. Erik studied the man. A normal man, a black canvas jacket with two bullet holes in it. This was his enemy. A man who would die for a couch.

Jason led those who weren't working on graves deeper into the valley.

"Everything is falling apart," Jean said. "The quest is over, isn't it?" She came to a stop on the trail.

"Why the hell are we walking this way? We've got to go back!"

"Your dad says there's some kind of village up here. But it's a long way. We'll be lucky to get there before nightfall."

"Then why are we going this way? We're not guerillas. We need a hospital." The group was already much farther down the trail. They were trotting, speeding the couch along.

"It's the right way," said a weak voice from Erik's arms. Tree cocked his eyes at an odd angle to try and focus on Jean, unable to hold his head up.

"Oh Tree, did you hear about Thom?"

Tree blinked, looked down the trail. The guerillas carrying the couch with Thom were fading into the distance.

Erik didn't want to follow, didn't want to be there when they unloaded the body off of the couch, the blood all emptied from it. Didn't want to be there when they scratched out a grave in the ground next to the trail with their rifle butts.

"What a crazy fuck, running into fire like that. Stupid fucker, fuck fuck fuck."

Jean shook her head, her eyes red. "I guess it was brave. But it was all useless. If he'd only been a couple minutes later, your father would have gotten there."

Erik shook Tree in his arms, filled with an angry frustration. "What are we going to do now, Tree?"

Tree came back to consciousness for a moment, then closed his eyes again.

They staggered along the trail, and the clouds descended and engulfed everything in fog. A lost land with only the barest hint of trail at their feet. The voices of the guerillas talking in Spanish seemed from another century. Erik carried Tree. He was aware only of the barely-alive body of one friend on his back and the dead body of his other friend somewhere ahead. And of the dead man they'd left behind, earth surrounding the body, mud filling his mouth. It all started with a waterbed. He was going to have a thing or two to say to that waterbed owner if he ever got back. And somewhere in front was a couch. It was just a couch. A couch that everyone wanted. Yes, the fucking quest was over—nothing was worth this much, was it?

Every once in a while, Tree mumbled in his sleep.

Erik's arms numbed with weight of Tree. They passed the valley, and to his right was what felt like a great drop-off. The fog obscured any bottom. The trail was thinly etched into a mountain. To his left the slope was steep and rocky enough to be considered a cliff. To his right a veiled vertigo. Erik nudged a rock off of the trail, and the fog enveloped it without a sound.

One of the guerillas offered to carry Tree, and Erik refused. Tree was his. His friend, his responsibility. He was dizzy and exhausted but sure-footed with an otherworldly determination.

The sun had been lost for some time, and the eerie light of the fog about them diminished. Jason passed a rope between them, looping them together in a line. If one falls, all fall, Erik thought. Could this possibly be smart? A bottle was passed around with increasing earnestness, and they could hear some soldier in front singing a drunken song. A hollow, frightening call of a giant bird sounded in the fog, like the call of some prehistoric creature spotting its prey.

"Where did they find booze?" Erik asked into the air so as to get the bottle directed toward him. The fog was so deep it now obscured the people in front and behind him on the trail.

"Patul," his father said from some meters ahead. "It's the pueblito we're headed toward. It's a smuggler's village, moonshiners. We arrived there last night. The best *trago* you'll ever find."

"How . . . how?"

"Well. That's a hell of a question. I don't really understand either. We came from Colombia. Took us a week. I was contacted by an old friend—I believe you know Per? We don't always see eye to eye, but in recent years we've had a bit more in common. He was wondering if I'd heard the rumors, and I had. We've known about the couch, or whatever it is, for a long time. The relic." Jason smiled. "I'm glad you're a part of it, proud of you."

Erik could feel a blush run through him, followed by the despair of having it all fall apart so miserably.

The trail on the cliff broadened and then turned into the opening of a tight valley, and they dipped underneath the fog. There was light coming from the valley, a tiny pueblo. Patul looked like a constellation that had fallen to the ground. Too far away from civilization for electricity or roads or the outside world to come nosing into what they did. Dark human forms that wove and slurred and carried on with drunken joviality began to materialize. The trail crossed a wooden bridge, and then they were in the center of the constellation.

A man named Angel, the soft *g* making the name *An-hell*, led them toward one of the lights—a mud shack with a blazing fire on the floor. The smoke coursing out the doors, the room blackened and shiny from years of fires, guinea pigs running underfoot. A crude wooden table listed in a corner. A giant, bored fat woman with a single lens in a pair of glasses watched them enter. They planted the blood-soaked couch with Thom on it near the fire. Erik set Tree on the ground, his back propped against a wall. He noticed for the first time that the couch had begun to fall apart. It had rips in the cushions, one arm seemed to be separating, and it was stained. Erik began to pull Thom's limp form off the couch, warning them the couch would make sure he was dead, but his father told him to stop. "Leave him on it. Rosita will move him if she thinks he should be moved. She knows."

"Yellow fever," Jason diagnosed after looking at Tree. "He hasn't been in the country long enough for anything else. He should be alright, most people his age pull through, but it won't be fun. Rosita might be able to do something"—he gestured toward the woman—"but he's too far in to stop it."

Rosita stood, dressed in multiple layers of colorful blankets dirty with soot and mud. When she walked, she angled her right hip heavily into the air, swept her foot out, as if a baby were clinging to one leg. She said something that Erik didn't understand.

"The couch can't stay here," Jason said. "She said it's got to leave before the full moon."

"*Si, Señora*," Erik answered when no one else volunteered.

She stared at him for a while, inspecting, and he tried an awkward smile.

Erik said, "Can you help Thom?"

She cleared her throat mightily, leaned over and spit a great mass of phlegm into the fire, where it hissed and crackled. She shrugged. "*Tal vez, tal vez.*"

Erik shuddered. Was it too late for helicopters, sirens, and the clean, waxy halls of hospitals?

She sent Angel out, and he returned a minute later with a plastic bottle of what looked like water. Angel took a draw off it, coughed, wiped his mouth sloppily, and handed it to Rosita.

Rosita took several giant swallows and poured the rest over Thom's body, shaking the bottle to get every last drop out. Then she took a burning log from the fire and lit the alcohol that she'd poured on him. It sprang to life, spreading quickly over him.

"Hey!" Erik yelled. "What in the fuck!?" They were cremating him right here, he realized.

Jean moved toward the woman, and Rosita held her hand up, snapped at Jason.

Jason put a hand on each of their shoulders, restraining them.

Thom's body was covered by a pure blue leaping flame. Rosita let it burn for only a few seconds, and then she pulled off one of her blankets and laid it over Thom, extinguishing it. She removed the blanket, then pulled half-a-dozen fist-sized rocks from the fire ring and put them on various parts of Thom's body. There was no movement from Thom. He's dead, Erik thought. This is ridiculous. Leave the poor fucker in peace.

"*Vayan.*" She waved them out of the room with the back of her hand. Erik and Jean backed slowly out the door. They left Tree asleep or unconscious. Angel closed the door behind them.

There was a quality to the darkness of Patul that Erik hadn't experienced anywhere else. Space and distance dissolved. The points of lights floated in their constellation unable to pierce the darkness. From over a hill came the sound of hoofbeats, the faint outlines of horsemen. There was a spookiness to it, an expectation of flaming arrows, a headless rider. A plethora of horror movies attempted to reinvent just this. This was what we were supposed to fear. There was no background hum, and that was what was simultaneously peaceful and unsettling. Hoofbeats retreated into utter stillness, the thinness of the twelve-thousand-foot atmosphere causing sound to fade into nothing. The mud and toil of the day dissolved into black-velvet canvas at night. This is what ancient villages must have looked like, he thought. I'm in the past.

Someone grabbed him under the arm, but he couldn't make out the face, only the fumes of a day's worth of drinking. He was led to an abandoned mud-brick house not in the constellation. A candle was lit. He was introduced to the townspeople, all of them a great leap of drunkenness ahead of him and waiting stonily in the darkness for his and Jean's arrival. Two more candles were lit, and then the party started. Angel, Edison, Galo, Julita, Maria, names he didn't catch. His father was there with a giant red accordion strapped around his neck, looking more like a bear in the circus than ever. Another guerilla mouthed a clarinet, her hair black and tangled and tied up with a knotted bungee cord. Angel took up Erik and Jean as a special project, passing them the *trago*, a clear liquid that smelled like turpentine, his arms around both of them, speaking in a slur achieved only under obscene amounts of the best liquors. Jean got up and danced a couple of tunes with Erik, both of them dancing the marvelous dance that only the drunk can dance, and then a giant, quiet villager broke into a dance beyond grace, his great form unrestricted by the pull of the earth. Erik and Jean watched him in wonder and drank steadily, drank with vigor, drank to forget, drank for their comrades, and the drinking was encouraged, the villagers each wanting to share a toast with them. Yelling each other's names before drinking.

"Galo!" Erik cried.

"Enrique!" Galo shouted.

"Julita!" Jean yelled.

"Djinn!" Julita answered, throwing the fire liquid down her throat.

And for each of those, Erik toasted for Thom or Tree, shouting their names into the night. And consciousness was like a phonograph with its power cut, a flywheel in its last rotations, a black hole. Gravity sucking dry the light of consciousness.

Erik woke up under a mass of blankets to see the remains of the slumber party. The guerillas, his father, and the Patulians were spread chaotically about the floor. He was wrapped around a girl from the village, both with their clothes on. How did that happen? He couldn't see Jean. He worked his way to his feet, amazed he wasn't hungover, took one step and realized he was still drunk. Sky leaked ultra-blue into every opening of the decrepit adobe.

He made his way outside, tripped about in the grass, took a leak. At one end of the valley, the way they'd come in, was a lake fed by three waterfalls charging down the steep cliffs. Beyond the cliffs were rugged mountains with peaks surrounded in clouds. The other end of the valley dipped down and slid into the fog again. Patul was between, a limbo of sunlight. Perhaps twenty adobe houses were scattered about the valley and up one hillside, but most were caved in and abandoned. Between him and Rosita's adobe where Thom lay was a painted hut with a cross on the door, a church of sorts which looked like it hadn't been attended since the Middle Ages.

Erik ambled back to Rosita's place, trying to figure out the path he'd walked in the night. The village felt empty. Sheep filed up a hillside, but the houses were quiet.

He found Jean and Rosita by the fire on Rosita's floor, which doubled as the town *tienda*. Tree was laid out against a wall, where someone had put some blankets down for him. A curious guinea pig had its front legs up on his forearm. A shifty smoke wallowed around at a height of four feet and above, encouraging everyone to sit on the floor. Thom lay on the couch, and to Erik's eyes was obviously dead. A statue of a man, a shocking paleness, eyes closed, hands crossed tomb-style over his chest. Heavy stones were scattered in patterns about his body. His clothes were riddled with holes and caked with dried blood and mud. Jean had one hand around a hot drink of some kind and the other resting on Thom's ankle.

"*Se . . . se murió?*" Erik whispered, fear in his stomach. *Isn't he dead?*

"*No. Le hace sangre,*" Rosita said. *He's making new blood.* "*Perdió mucho sangre.*"

"*Hay esperanza, entonces?*" *There's hope then?*

Rosita shrugged.

"*Y él?*" Erik pointed to Tree.

"*Fiebre. Solo hay que esperar.*"

"What'd she say?" Jean said.

"Tree's got a fever and it doesn't seem like she can do anything for him. Most people survive yellow fever but it's very painful."

"Thom's in a sort of coma," Jean said. "He's got a heartbeat. You should check out the bullet holes, they're really quite amazing."

"Ugh. I don't know, I never liked the sight of blood much. I used to faint when I was little, never went over very well at camp."

"There's no blood though. That's what's crazy. She's a . . . She's real, Erik. A witch doctor."

Erik gingerly put his finger on the fabric of a hole in Thom's shirt at his bicep and moved it around to see if he could see where the bullet entered the arm without touching Thom. He saw Thom's smallpox vaccination mark and kept moving the shirt, but couldn't find the bullet wound. He looked up at Jean. Maybe he'd found a rip that wasn't a bullet hole. There was a hole in Thom's shirt at his gut, just to the left of his belly button. Erik fingered that hole and saw another smallpox vaccination mark. "Uh . . ." he said.

"They're healed over. It's like he's been here for a month or something. Five months."

"Holy shit!" Erik shivered.

"It's amazing. I'm going to do an article on this for sure. It's just that . . . It's another thing that nobody is going to believe. And then the people who do believe it will all probably be parading into Patul. I'm not sure I'm ready for that."

"I've seen witch doctors before . . . but I didn't, I didn't think they could do this."

"It's because there's no road," said a voice from the door. Erik's father was there without his cap, in a black T-shirt, his eyes red. He took a step in, put his hand against the wall to steady himself. "A bit hungover this morning, how about you kids?"

"I'm still drunk." Erik smiled.

"Yeah," Jean said. "Same." She pressed fingers against her temple. "And the smoke isn't exactly helping."

"There are no roads, which means no civilization. Different rules govern Patul than most places. Once roads go in, the logic of science will come in, television will come in, a Western belief system, people will take painkillers and decongestants. They'll forget about Rosita with the allure of the new science, they'll believe less, they'll think she's the old way and Western science teaches us that new is always better than old. They'll tell themselves that the healing she did was just a fairy tale."

"Is a road coming in?" Jean's eyes were watering from the smoke.

"Supposedly, a couple years from now. That's what the government has been threatening, anyway."

"I don't understand what a road has to do with how she heals," Erik said crossly.

"The healing is a symbiotic process between the healer and the one being healed. If the one being healed believes in the treatment, then the healer will be far more successful. Even though your friend was passed out, the effectiveness of the healing is a testament to his willingness to trust outside the normal belief system." Erik's father shrugged. "I don't know. Seen it happen a hundred times though. She would have had generally better luck with him anyway because she was starting from scratch. He was basically dead. And I don't mean to imply the situation is otherwise yet. What I'm saying is that when the road comes in, her powers will become more or less useless to all but the most traditional people."

Rosita stirred the fire. She came to her feet with a groan and pulled a ball of yarn connected to a mass of wool from a shelf in a corner. Guinea pigs squealed before her footfalls, running into the shadows. She sat back down at the fire and began to spin the yarn, thumb and forefinger working the mass into a thick strand, her other hand holding the stick that wound up the spun yarn. With a nod in the style of someone who is accustomed to being obeyed, she gestured for Jason to sit next to her.

Jason moved gingerly, sat on a rock outside the fire ring. His beard was a collection of twigs and dirt and black hair.

A young woman entered with a blackened frying pan and a big stewpot and sat on the edge of the couch, her back to Thom. She put the pot of beans on the fire to heat and began to cook scrambled eggs.

Rosita waved her off the couch harshly and spoke to Jason in a language Erik couldn't understand. A language that sounded like a combination of Russian and TV static.

"What'd she say?"

"She said the couch can't stay. She said it belongs to the old peoples, and she doesn't want her people exposed to it. It's true. You've got to get it out of here soon. If nothing else, it's a lure for your pursuers, and she doesn't want them coming here."

"The old peoples? Does she know what it is?"

Jason conversed with Rosita. "She doesn't know. She just feels it."

"I was kind of hoping that we were bringing it here." Erik scratched at his head and mustache furiously. "I've had enough of being effking chased."

"This place seems like a perfect end to the article," Jean said. "To bring it to the most isolated place on Earth, a forgotten village."

"There are more isolated places, and more forgotten people," Jason said. "You've a ways to go yet. The closer you get, the harder it will be for your pursuers. Your destination will keep them away, keeps everybody away. The only reason you'll be able to go is because you are being allowed. That is, if the place really exists. If it hasn't turned to dust."

The cooking began to smell good, and the girl worked the food skillfully around the pan. Outside a rooster called out the sunrise, as it had done every fifteen minutes for the last three hours.

"I have a lot, *a lot*, of questions," Erik said. "Like for one who in the hell wants the couch so much that they want to kill us?"

"Ah." Jason blew air through puffed cheeks. "I can barely answer those questions. I know legends about the cloud city, and I know the council—"

"You know the council?"

"Yep. The council is as old as time. And so are their opposites. I think the council calls them the collectors. I mean old like thousands of years. I don't know for sure, and you're getting some of my politics here, but when I think of the collectors, I think U.S. politicians, I think television executives, the people who control North American society. I think of the rulers throughout time. Caesar. Any small group whose aim is to pacify a large group for the purpose of taking advantage of them. Organized religion. The same people who make nuclear bombs and repress technologies that would positively change the way people live. Collectors is a broad term. The people who make the world reliant on oil, because it makes them rich. Like Reagan. Or Nixon or Bush. But like I said, that fits in conveniently with my belief system."

"I liked Reagan," Erik said idly.

"You did not, you little shit!" Jason stood and feigned a backhand.

"Ha," Erik said.

Jason snorted, sat back down, pointed a comic, threatening finger at Erik. "You little skunk. But anyway, who knows. Those presidents may have been put there by the collectors, or they may just be subscribers to that belief system. Again, these are my politics. Maybe it runs a lot deeper than that. Maybe it goes down to human nature, religion, where we come from."

"I just still . . . goddamnit, I just don't know how I got mixed up in this. Why me?"

Jason laughed deeply, a bellowing sound. "You take after me!" Jason reached forward and grabbed a handful of the thick hair that jutted from Erik's head and shook it playfully, causing Erik's head to bob up and down and his teeth to clatter. "Damn good to see you, boy. It's been seven years or so, eh? But really, I don't have the faintest idea. You're one of the three. That's all I know. Something about the three that carry the seat. That's about as much of the legend as I know. We've lost all the legends, which weren't even legends in the first place. Anyway, you're in it because you've always been where there's trouble."

Jason pulled a gun out of his boot, went through its workings while they waited for food.

"This village is barely holding off the outside world," he said. "And to have the couch here much longer is going to endanger it. You've got to leave even if the other two are sick. Patul has ten percent of the population it used to have because the outside world has a terrific gravity. Most everyone here will want to talk about Ecuadorian soccer, which they only know about from watching TV in Cuenca. When there's a big game, they make a pilgrimage to the city, and then they become infected by the advertising, by the sights and sounds. There're very few young people left here. The allure of possessions and the fast life of cities is almost irresistible. This is no longer a pueblo. It's a corpse of a traditional pueblo, riddled with the worms of the modern world."

"Descriptive," Erik said. "What about Mom? How are the cooperatives doing?"

Jason glowed. "We're back together, you know. She's living with me. The cooperatives are same as always, same as here. Individualism, Darwinism, survival of the fittest. It's the same all over. Nobody wants to help everybody else for the common good. It seems impossible to work toward common goals without a hierarchy. They want to see what they can get for themselves. We've got a small army of believers, but there are just as many defections as recruits. Even Patulians have convinced themselves that they live in the middle of nowhere. Know what that does for one's self-concept? They do live in the middle of nowhere in respect to the current paradigm of civilization. But they live near the center of the world in the old ways. If you believe you live in the middle of nowhere, then you believe your life means nothing."

The eggs were nearly finished, and the smell called in the others. Hunger was aroused among the still-drunk and hungover.

My parents are back together, Erik thought. He realized the concept of having parents at all felt strange, exciting, comforting.

Tree stirred and moaned, and Erik went to talk with him.

"How you doing, dreamy?"

"Thirsty," he croaked.

Erik saw that there was blood on Tree's gums. The whites of his eyes had a yellowish hue. "Um, can somebody help me here? Tree is . . . uh . . . not looking good. Sorry to be blunt, Tree."

Jason came and looked at Tree and described the symptoms to Rosita. "He's got jaundice now. Common side effect of yellow fever."

Rosita ladled out a cupful of the same liquid Jean was drinking and directed that it should be handed to Tree.

"We need to carry on," Tree said. "Is Thom . . .?"

"I don't know." He looked at the room for some kind of answer, and Jason nodded. "He's in a coma?"

"We can put him on the couch and carry it." Tree mouthed the last words, voice failing him.

"I don't think so," Erik said. "You're not going to be carrying anything, bud. You look like shit. And I'm not going to risk doing any more damage to Thom."

They ate breakfast. The guerillas filed in, and the hut became crowded with burliness, beards, guns, excessive politeness. Erik listened to the excited banter about some kind of couch-carrying contraption the men and villagers were building. The news annoyed him, but he hoped it implied someone else might take over. He asked few questions—mostly because he didn't want to know the answers. He needed a respite and to look after his roommates.

They waited two days. Erik and Jean watched the fogs engulf Patul, drift out and leave sparkling rainbows in their place. The stars were so thick at night that the ground glowed. They played volleyball and soccer with the villagers, and the *trago* was passed around liberally. Erik fished in the mornings with his father, and a woman of the village repaired the holes in his clothes with not a few sideways glances at him at the state into which he'd gotten them. Independently of each other, Erik and Jean decided that Patul was the last real place on Earth, a place of magic. During the day, the villagers disappeared up hillsides with herds of sheep, calling singsong to each other across the valley.

The weather was erratic. With no warning, flower petals fell from the sky. One day a wind came up that threatened to unmake the place. It rushed from one valley end to the other, lodging saddles in trees and tree branches in rooftops.

Jean stayed up late each night with Thom and Rosita. She sat by the fire and communicated in hand signals with the village curandera. She learned to spin wool and talked to Thom in his coma, remembering their night together, speculating on the future, forming the foundations of a relationship by herself. She wondered what was happening inside him, where he was, if he thought of her. She spoke more honestly and hopefully than she ever would have dared had he been awake. She drew the wool out in her fingers, her palms aching from repetition. Thinking how handsome he looked, this great figure of a man, like a Greek statue, his arms crossed like a Viking on his funeral bier. In his helplessness and quiet, it was easy to talk herself into believing that she loved him. It was easy to love him.

It looked like a cross between a burn pile and a rickshaw, something that nature had grown or beavers built. A giant wooden thing that surely was incapable of moving, something out of the Stone Ages, with extensions and whirligigs springing from it. Jason was immensely proud of it and immediately began giving rides to everyone in the village. There was not a single wheel to be found in Patul, so the villagers had cut dozens of the strong, flexible switches that grew along the river and lashed them together in circles to form a wheel and spokes. The wooden axle went straight through the bed of the cart and powered a propeller out the back.

"That doesn't do anything," Erik said when he saw the propeller.

"What? We have a doubter," Jason said. "Mincho—explain our science to the boy, will you? My son, here is my resident inventor and contraption genius."

A short, stocky man with glasses that Eric recognized as one of his father's men came forward.

"It's a fog propeller. You'll be going through lots of fog."

Erik screwed up his eyes at his father. "A fog propeller?"

The crowd laughed.

"All this so we can lug that couch into the wilderness?"

"Yes, sir. And look at this baby here," Mincho said with a sly grin. "This winds up while you move and provides a levering effect on the ground." He began to move the cart, which wound a contraption underneath hooked into the axle. "When the tension is reached, well, you'll see, here." A number of sticks swept down violently along the underside of the cart, pushing the vehicle forward in a leap.

The cart was nearly overturned by the force, Erik saw.

"These switches could also be used as a brake," Mincho demonstrated. "Come on aboard."

Jean bravely climbed into the cargo area and motioned for Erik to take up the runners. He ran her around the grassy, sheep-cropped hill in the center of Patul. Since the whole thing, except the axle, was made of flexible switches, the shocks were amazingly smooth. A daddy-longlegs Cadillac.

"Rickshaw supercar!" Mincho yelled. He jumped into the cart next to Jean and leaned back like an emperor being taken to a ball. The bottom spring of switches built up enough tension and whipped under the cart, and Jean and Mincho bounced high into the air, coming down rattled.

"It'll work better when the couch is on here," Mincho said, realigning his eyeglasses.

Some kind of bird. Or a rat. The noise drifted in, had been active there in his body for a while, and brain, like a drunk telephone operator, only now began to sober up enough to patch through calls between the senses and memory. A scrabbling noise, small feet on dirt, and a chirp that scaled an octave, a reverse slide. A winged animal. Talking was heard, but in other languages, and the duration was too long for concentration. First things first. Brain going through the files, the sound was identifiable, it had been recorded before, it was in the memory banks. Match a visual image to the sound, or pull from the vocabulary a verbal identifier. Brain opted for visual, filing through hundreds of animal cards until it found one that seemed right, and presented it to consciousness. But consciousness felt uneasy. Some other memory there. It wasn't a bird, it was some kind of ground creature. Brain went back to work, presented another image. A 1970s-style rat, its hair long and ungainly, bangs obscuring the eyes, ruthlessly out of fashion. Shy. About the size of a shoe. Consciousness accepted the image. With two points, a visual and an auditory, a triangulation could be made into the abstract world of language: a guinea pig.

Why was he hearing a guinea pig? In a world filtered through one sense, what could be deduced?

Then sense number two came back in a rush of new data that brain worked feverishly to process: wood smoke. That was easy.

Dominating. What must be the smell of guinea pigs. Hay and dirt and wet dirt and wet hay. Cooking, the smell of burned corn. Oil gone acrid. Another animal smell: sheep? Human smell, the thick, iron-rich smell of menstrual blood, the salty diesel of sweat. But mostly wood smoke. Deduction: a barn. A campsite. A tent. A zoo.

Numb fingers. Numb everything. The memory of ache, a tingling of warning: *movement will be painful.* Coordinates? Position? On his back, arms crossed on his chest. Brain: *How they lay you in a coffin.* An uneven heat, the left cheek, down the shoulder, waist, thigh, a warmth like sunlight, like lightbulbs, the other side cool. Brain: *wood smoke = wood fire.* Deduction: he'd been here for a long while. He was sick. He was not dead. Certainly this couldn't be death. There was no mention of guinea pigs in the afterlife. Was there?

His brain called upon the memory functions and memory answered: _____.

For comic relief, brain presented the image of the Fonz jarring the jukebox with his elbow, the jukebox spinning to life. Memory? Calling out in the fog, calling out into spaces the size of which are unknown. Is this dark cave five yards wide, or five miles? There was no memory.

For a long time his body relaxed into the new information, until the strain of being conscious lessened. Brain suggested trying to tap into sight again. Which required movement. Which will bring pain. Send the signal, open the hatches. A great struggle to pull the earthy lids back. Input: blackness, but with the possibility of definition. A topography of black.

"Thom—Thom! Thom's eyes are open."

There was the sound of relief in this, and also panic.

"Thom? His eyes opened, did you see? Did he do that? Everybody come quick, the professor is awake."

Sound. In a recognizable language. The translator from sound to meaning cranking up. Oil splashed into the gears. A panic, a reply required. Was a reply required? It's all you brain. Your ball. Call it.

"Hey . . . Gilligan," Thom said. The lips chapped, the tongue a sloth in the mouth, fur having grown there thickly. "Think we'll . . . get off this island?" The words came like pencil scratchings in the air, the faintest of speech bubbles.

"Would we want to?"

A weight against him, the voice coming closely now. "Hell, this is paradise. But they're trying to kick us out. We brought evil to paradise."

Brain worked this. Biblical imagery. Utopian literature. A Joni Mitchell song. Travel brochures. Adam and Eve. Lost peoples. Lost empires. A couch.

"I'm on the apple?"

"Yep."

"Erik. What . . ."

"What do you remember?"

"You're hurting me," Thom said.

"Oh! Sorry!" Erik realized he'd been clapping Thom on the chest.

"Where's Jean?"

"She's with the villagers—long story. They've uh . . . they've been drinking since noon."

Relief: first blink. A re-wetting of the glassy surface. More definition, a series of tubes at right angles to another series of finer tubes. Coal black. Tar black. Beetle black. Eyes tracking along a tube to where the surface met with another plane. A wall. The black topography was a ceiling. Brain received a complaint. Systems failing. She can't hold together much longer at this speed, Captain. A submarine with a breached hull. The eyes failed to recover from a second blink. Sound melded to static. Red telephone to brain, wire cut.

Later. A fragment of consciousness returning. First: the memory of being shot. An opening up of the body, inside parts that should stay inside pouring from him. Then: an awareness of people around him. The fire crackling. His eyes closed, relieved at the anonymity of sightlessness, the effortlessness of it. Listening.

"It's a what?"

"A lost city."

"What do you mean, lost?" *A woman's voice. Jean.*

"That it can't be found. It—"

"Then how do you know it exists?"

Pause.

"We don't."

A fork being moved around a mostly empty plate. A plastic plate.

"Well . . . what makes you think it exists then? I'm just having a hell of a hard time believing that with satellites and airplanes and whatnot, a city can just be lost. And can't the people who live there find the outside world?"

"Maybe they don't want to be found. And they're still finding Incan and pre-Incan ruins here all the time."

"Yeah, but, yeah"—*Erik's voice*—"they're covered under hundreds of years of shit. Grass and trees and stuff. You guys are talking about a city with living . . . people. Right?"

"We think so. Living or something."

"I don't think you understand the scale here, Erik." *An unknown voice, a voice like cigars and turbine engines, like earthquakes and clay.* "We're in about sixteen thousand square miles of completely unpopulated terrain. Some of the rockiest, highest, cruelest terrain on Earth. Terrain that is mostly immersed in fog or cloud layer all year round. And beyond that area it is incredibly sparsely populated, and more or less the—"

"Which brings me right back to my original point. How in the fuck are we supposed to—"

"Same way you got this far, boyo."

"Uh, Dad, have you seen my . . . errr . . . fellow questers?"

"Thom will be fine. You've seen what she's done already. She'll get him ready." *That same voice, a growling bear. Dad?* "Tree's not going to be so hot. You will have to carry him on the couch."

"Listen, all I'm trying to say is, don't you think this would be a hell of a lot easier if there were a bunch of us and we all sort of spread out? I don't know, like what about walkie-talkies? This is the modern age. Certainly that makes a load more sense than sending three young city slickers and a couch into, as you're saying, twenty thousand square miles of hell."

Pause.

"And what the hell are we supposed to do when we get there? Drop off the couch and run? Shake hands? 'Hey! You old blokes been missing this?' And how do you expect us to get back, or is that in the plan?"

Pause.

"I'm sorry about this, Erik. I'd be scared stiff if I were in your shoes. The legend calls for three. We think that if more people go, you'll never find—"

"I could go in Tree's place." *This was Jean again, lovely Jean.*

"Any of us would love to go in Tree's stead, Jean, but we think only these three will be able to make contact."

"What legend? Or I should say, which legend? We've heard a million already."

"I know, I know." *Sigh.* "Nobody knows which is which. Or what is what. Just hazy ideas. But that's the way it works. You use the legend that suits you best at the time. The Cañari one you heard already. Three people will return the seat of power to the center of the world. Another one says it's a vessel protected by—*whatever*—and inside are the remains of the first humans. The *first* humans. Listen, nobody else has found this city. And we've looked for a long time. I think they are keeping us out. If we go with you—"

"But come on, let's be reasonable. Like, for example, why don't we rent a plane"—*Erik's sarcasm deepening to its sharpest value*—"and fly over the place so we know at least where *not* to look?"

"Can't. Do that." It was Tree! Good old Tree, sounding like he'd been run over by a semitruck. "The city . . . presents itself."

"I knew it, I knew it," the bear's voice said.

"Okay then, a moving city. A moving city." *Snort.* "How about we take a GPS thing so at least when we start to starve to death after a couple of days, you'll know where to find us?"

A new voice with an accent, like speaking from the bottom of a well: "The Lug-o-naut has room to—"

"The Lug-o-naut 147, you've got to call it what it is!" Erik said. "We agreed on the number."

The new voice, more slowly: "The . . . Lug-o-naut 147 . . . has room to carry fourteen days' worth of provisions."

"A real thrill machine."

Hurried steps and a new voice, out of breath.

"Jason, there's an encampment at the pass."

"Is it them?"

Pause.

"They didn't show any signs of packing up tonight. But there's a lot of them, maybe fifteen."

Rustling and movement. Then: "You have to leave tonight."

"What!? Look at these guys."

"I'm alright," Thom said, without having any idea he was going to say it. He opened one eyelid to 40 percent. "*Lo que sea mejor por el país.*"

"Thom!" Jean said.

And then he was being kissed.

Thom felt like he was made out of clay. His body still unidentifiable as his own. Frankenstein's monster. A golem. A poured cement statue someone had set free. He'd been full of bullet holes. What had the woman done to make him whole again? He stood where someone had helped him walk, the stars a Jackson Pollock painting above. He wove slightly, didn't dare take a step. Around him, the village had come alive to get the quest back on track. Tree was lying on the couch which had been loaded on some kind of wheeled structure. Thom shuffled to it, squeezed Tree's arm—the boy was asleep and breathing raggedly—and felt hopelessness bear down on him so heavily that he needed to lean on the cart.

Provisions were dug up from the villagers' private stores. Machetes and firewood and water and food. Blankets, a tent. Guns. Bottles of what they were calling *trago*, a clear liquid that set one on fire—someone had given him a swallow to get him out the door, and it had carried him this far. He'd need a hell of a lot more of it to get up the mountain they kept pointing at. Human figures ran around between the points of fire in the village, a village of wraiths. From somewhere in the dark came a stamping of hooves. A whinny of horses.

Gear for fourteen days. The number seemed so unbelievable to him he didn't dare contemplate it. He wanted a waterbed, a health spa, a massage. He'd been dead, hadn't he? *Come on*, people. Give a hero a break! He turned his head slowly to follow the passage of the wraiths, and Jean emerged from the blackness. She grabbed him about the middle.

"I wish I could go with you."

"You're crazy. I wish I could stay here with you." It felt like a long time passed between each phrase as he gathered energy for the next.

Jean put her face into his chest, and he felt something had happened to bring them closer. He did not know what it was, but was glad for it. He no longer detected the wary edge of people new to each other. There was an inexplicable comfort to the embrace.

"Come back," Jean said. "Let's spend some time together."

"Yes. We will. I will. In fact, I was thinking of slipping someone else in my place. My, uh, joints seem a bit Super Glued. How about that guy that's so excited about this couch carrier?"

In answer she squeezed him tighter, and he realized his fate was set. A number of people here would go in his place. But apparently they couldn't. Thom felt like he'd been underwater for a week. Like everyone had watched the same soap opera for the last year except him, and now he was expected to write a dissertation on it.

Rosita hobbled up and rested her hand on the arm of the couch and was quiet. Then she nodded and gave it a pat. She briefly felt Tree's forehead and smoothed back his hair.

She delivered a package she'd had under one arm to Thom and explained to Erik: one spoon of the brown liquid per day for Thom; one spoon per day of the gray for Tree.

After she'd finished she gave Thom's bicep a squeeze. "Suerte."

Then they were walking. There'd been a hurried round of hugs and well-wishing. The couch, Thom noticed, was disintegrating. The fabric worn, part of the wood structure falling apart. It was the weight a couch should be. They stopped frequently in the thin air to catch their breath.

Erik had the Lug-o-naut 147 strapped to him, pulling the contraption behind, Thom stumbling after him, trying to keep his distance from some propeller affixed to the back of the cart. Relearning the movements of walking. They looked like something from the ninth century, three boys on a crusade, traveling at night, bent and burdened, escaping the plague. Other groups of three villagers each were up in the hills as distractions and as watchers to make sure they got out safely. Thom watched the seven points of fire from the village move farther away, dim. They were on an old trail, headed deeper into the Andes. Erik in front of him swearing. Tree on the couch unconscious. Thom the sleepwalker bringing up the rear, vaguely aware of others above them, behind them, stealthy shadows, keeping the way safe, ensuring they took the evil object away.

They walked the trail all night. Watched the quarter moon rise behind them, set in front. Followed where the moon had landed. The trail was muddy and rocky, but the Lug-o-naut did well over the terrain. An organic mechanism with spidery reflexes that bounced and climbed well.

The villagers and guerillas had drifted off long ago, and he and Erik walked into a frightening silence at an altitude with few living animals and little plant life. The trail climbed out of the valley up a mountainside onto a higher rocky plain. A moonscape where little else grew but moss. A brook through the center of it.

Thom walked like a zombie. He'd step forward, and there was the memory of the bullets, there was his body opened up, his insides bared. Step forward again and the memory disappeared.

Only movement kept them warm.

Following through, Erik thought. What a pain in the ass. But here I am, look here, Erik following through.

"Tree," Erik called over his shoulder. "Tree!"

There was no sound from the couch.

"Thom, would you wake up Tree and ask him if this is the right direction?"

Thom caught up to the Lug-o-naut and shook Tree lightly. "Tree. Wake up." The kid was burning up. If he survived the trip it'd be a miracle, Thom thought.

"Where are we?" Tree said, his eyes not quite focusing.

"We're lost in the Andes," Erik hollered over his shoulder into the silent landscape. "Where the *effk* do you think we are? Can you give me an idea if I'm still hauling this thing in the right direction? It's going to kill me if I travel even one step out of my way."

"I . . . I don't know where to go," Tree said. "The dreams are gone."

"What!?" The cart came to a grinding halt. "What in the hell are we supposed to do?"

"Is it because of the fever?" Thom asked.

"I . . . don't know." Tree's voice faded back to unconsciousness.

"What are we supposed to do, Professor?"

"Camp. I'm exhausted. We'll see if he knows in the morning."

There was a sudden barrage of shooting stars. A buzz, a whir, and twenty stars went at once together across the sky. Meteors that traveled for the last five hundred thousand years to reach their destination: a fiery atmosphere, a bright death, the transformation to gas. They blazed over the sky like fireflies set free.

"Wow," Erik said. "I tell you."

They passed the night shivering in the small tent. Thom and Erik slept on the outsides. Tree was pinned between them, shaking alternately from fever and cold. When Tree woke for an instant through his delirium he displayed frighteningly yellow eyes, the pupils lone black dots.

A gray luminance made the walls of their tent glow dully in the morning. They'd gotten only a few hours of sleep, and the ground was too uncomfortable for more. Tree was even less lucid, answering questions that hadn't been asked and giving answers unrelated to the questions that were. He looked terrible, his skin an unnatural hue, lips cracked, his hair matted with sweat.

Erik pulled out Rosita's package and dutifully made Thom and

Tree take a spoon of their respective liquids.

They ate breakfast and packed, and then Erik and Thom stared at each other expectantly, not having the faintest idea where to go next.

"He's up there," Tree said.

"It's okay, buddy," Erik said. "We'll get you some help."

"On the shelf," Tree said.

"Mm-hmm."

"On the rock."

Erik nodded sharply, exhaled. Tree's eyes seemed to drift back out of whatever sort of consciousness that was, and Erik tried to remember if he'd given Tree medicine yet. Oh yes, just at breakfast. Was more in order?

They put the couch back on the Lug-o-naut 147 and gently hoisted Tree on top. The landscape was gray, desolate, heavy on boulders, with pepperings of mossy areas. Steep rocky juttings like skyscrapers climbed violently from the valley floor.

Thom and Erik were silenced by it.

With a loud *thwok!*, the cart shuddered and a thunderous rumbling erupted over the valley.

"Shots!" Thom cried and launched away from the cart, weaving wildly, his body high on adrenalin and the memory of previous gunfire.

Erik stared at the couch and saw a hole a mere two inches above Tree's head. He ducked and then heard a scream from somewhere far off. He saw Thom paused a hundred yards away, bent double out of breath and looking up at the hills around them. Whoever had screamed seemed gone—there had been a finality to the sound. The moonscape was quiet and still as if nothing had happened. Either the marksman had fallen off a cliff or something had befallen him. When Erik looked back at the couch, the hole had sealed itself. A flattened slug lay on a board of the cart, apparently spit out by the couch. He shuddered.

Thom picked his way back to the cart, ducking skittishly.

"Hey," Erik said.

"Shots."

"I know. One hit the couch, just above Tree's head. You heard the scream?"

"Let's get out of here. Let's get the fuck out of here *now*."

In all directions were sharp mountains, rocky slopes with low underbrush scaling up the sides.

"We've got to take it off the cart and see which way it wants to go," Thom said.

"I don't think that works anymore. Does that still work?"

"Only one way to find out."

"Dude, this isn't exactly the best of places. You noticed we're getting shot at?"

Thom shrugged. "You heard that guy's scream? We've got to go the right way."

They each took a side and lifted—the couch felt like a couch with a sleeping man on it ought to—it was heavy.

"Go that way first," Thom gestured with his chin toward the trail on the left. They took a few steps, backed up and tried the other trail.

"Same," Erik said. "Right? I didn't notice anything."

"Crap," Thom said. "Maybe it's broken. Maybe it doesn't work with Tree on it."

They set the couch back on the cart and debated direction in an anxious hush until, battered and frustrated by the other's faulty reasoning, they decided getting lost one way was just as useful as getting lost the next and moving was better than standing still.

"We've got to have faith," Thom said. "The city will show up, it has to, so the getting lost isn't really getting lost, it's letting go of direction so that it will appear before us."

"You, my friend, are talking out of your ass. I hope you realize that, Mr. Science."

"Yeah," Thom said. He scratched his head and sighed. "Yeah, I know. I'm new to this."

Erik shrugged. He pulled a coin out of his pocket. "That way"— he pointed to an uninviting stretch of mountains that seemed eventually to dip into a pass between two peaks—"is tails. That way"—he pointed to a comparably difficult stretch, the immediate trail rockier, wetter, the pass slightly lower—"is heads."

Tails was thrown. Thom took a turn pulling the cart. His body still worked even if it didn't feel like his own.

The couch was suffering, as if it were in league with Tree's illness, the two of them unraveling and disintegrating.

The landscape looked like an angry, roiling sea of lava that had suddenly frozen. Soon their ankles were bruised and bleeding from grazing against sharp rocks. They were constantly out of breath, tiptoeing along the outer outcroppings of the earth.

They paused at the edge of a great muddy basin too thick and deep for them or the cart to pass through. They were debating what to do when steam began to rise from the basin. It spread and developed into a choking, thick fog.

Thom called out in alarm. "Don't move, Erik! We'll be lost instantly." He breathed through his shirt to filter out the fog, worried some poison was spontaneously seeping from the ground. The fog continued to rise though, and under it was clear air. They crouched and could see each other under the roiling white ceiling.

"It's a—it's a cloud maker." Thom watched in amazement as a cloud floated high into the air to join several dozen others just like it.

"Yes, but look at the ground."

Where there had been a great muddy basin, the soil was cracked and dry like a desert. Erik tested it, and then they cautiously started across. Halfway across, the water rushed into the cracks from somewhere deep below. The ground became unstable, and then a bog of mud.

"Oh hell," Erik said. "Hell hell."

They made slow progress, each of them pulling on the cart, struggling to lift their shoes out of the mud. They heard a sound ahead of them like white noise, and the fog began to surge up about their feet, the mud boiling hotly in the process, and they cried out in pain.

Then they could feel the ground hardening and they struggled to keep on top of it, yanking the cart about to keep the wheels moving so they didn't become permanently mired. The fog rose to their waists. Thom could only see white. He heard a whir and looked down to see the Lug-o-naut 147's fog propeller spinning at full bore. It gave the cart a small extra push until the fog lifted, and then it went dead.

"So that's what that does," Erik said. "And here I thought it was going to be useful." When the mud dried again, Erik yelled "Run." They each grabbed a handle of the Lug-o-naut and ran as fast as they could, the mud cracking and crumbling off them. Tree bounced violently about on top of the couch. They saw the water begin to well up in the cracks just as they made it to the rocks. The ground they'd crossed turned into a mud bath again. Fog steamed from the ground, rose above them, and floated off as a cloud.

They crouched, catching their breath, watched another cloud birth.

"This is some place," Erik said. They continued across the rocks, and Thom began to feel more like himself except for a burning tingling where the bullets had entered. Alive, he thought. Where was my brain when I ran into the bullets? I'm not the hero after all. Azulman went with the Azulman suit. Perhaps it's not even my movie. I'm the confused sidekick, an extra with an identity problem. I'm not even in a movie, I'm just a guy who has made himself believe things he shouldn't. He felt simultaneously good and afraid. The air was the purest lung-cutting air he'd ever breathed. The size of the sky and the mountains, the size of everything, made his skin euphoric, his hair stand on end, his neck straighten. The place felt alive in a different way than plants and animals and birds. The very earth felt conscious.

They crossed a wide, shallow river, the river rocks were sharp against their shoes, and entered a valley with deep scars through it. Ravines twenty feet wide, crevasses with no discernible bottom, so that they traveled far out of their way to cross them at the narrow end.

Elusive, fickle trails wound everywhere. Paths would carry on for fifty feet and then stop dead without a trace, as if a spontaneous abduction had happened there. In this way they wove back and forth across the great valley toward the slope. Anxiously scanning the hillsides for anyone, friend or foe, looking for any niche that might conceal a live or dead city, inspecting each rock with a new eye: boulder or building block? Rock or ruin?

They broke for food, staring up at the gray cover across the sky. Thom pulled close the wool poncho that Rosita had given him to ward off the cold. A freezing rain started, and they piled the meager collection of their rain gear over Tree and put the hoods up on their ponchos. Huddled together next to the cart they took swallows of *trago* and split a hunk of bread while the ice accumulated over them.

"This is fucked." Erik sidearmed a rock into a nearby puddle, breaking the sheen of ice. "We don't have a clue where we're going. It's not like there's going to be a four-star hotel over the next ridge. Our food sucks. It's almost all rice and beans that we have to cook. Tree is the cooker. I hate cooking."

"Let's just make it up to that pass. We'll have a vantage point then."

Erik went to take a leak, and Thom packed up the food. The clouds opened up and let a terrifically bright beam of sunlight through, and the valley lit up with rainbows. Thom counted six.

"Do you see that!?"

"I see it," Erik said. "It's amazing, but the place spooks me. Let's keep moving. We're sitting ducks."

Thom reluctantly harnessed himself to the cart. He felt he could stay and watch the sky forever. The whole dome above them was painted with color, a localized aurora borealis, the rainbows no longer conforming to rainbow shapes. The arcs slowly twisted, stretched. Bands of color broke free and painted the sky. The rainbows and light carved a bright, narrow streak out of the valley. "If I didn't know better, I'd think the way was being painted for us," he said.

Erik looked up from cinching the food bag on the cart and nodded his assent.

I can follow omens, Thom thought. I'm carrying a magic couch, and now I'm allowed to search the landscape for what I think it's telling me. What else do we have but these signs, what clues can I steal from my surroundings? He felt ridiculous and happy and sick for allowing himself to trust their survival to a colored path in the sky.

The rain started to fall in earnest, and the sky turned to dark shades of gray again. Too tired to talk, they plodded until just before nightfall, deciding the territory was too dangerous to walk at night. Thom looked back to try to see where they'd originally come from. The terrain was foreign and unrecognizable, and the sky had gone back to being itself.

Erik struggled for an hour with the dry wood that the village had packed for them, finally getting the blaze strong enough to withstand the downpour. They fixed a cup of broth for Tree, who was barely conscious enough to get it down. Thom was soaked through and miserably wet. He hunched as close as he could to the fire while he cooked. After an hour, the rice was done but the beans hadn't budged from jawbreaker status. They salted the rice and ate it plain, swallowed it down with icy cold water, too tired to make anything else. Thom resolved to camp earlier tomorrow to get a head start on cooking the beans.

At first light Thom wriggled out of the tent to take a leak and stumbled onto a human skeleton bleached white. He yelped, and Erik came running. They stared at it for several moments without talking. There was no sign of anything else, no clothes, no tools, just the white skeleton lying on the rocks.

"Not an encouraging sign," Erik said.

"Hmm," Thom said. Brain calculated the rate of decay. "Funny that it's not buried."

"Funny?"

"Should we bury it? We should bury it," Thom said.

"I'm not touching it. You don't suppose it was some guy looking for a cloud city?"

Thom stared at the crags in the distance.

"Let's get out of here," Erik said. "Let's get you kids your dosages and pack up."

They walked along the jagged plain of rocks for several hours and eventually stumbled onto a ravine invisible until they were at its edge. It ran as far as they could see in either direction. Fifty feet deep and fifty feet wide with squat trees lining the bottom. A wide trail led into it.

"A trail," Thom said. He tried to spot footprints.

"As in, who made it?"

"Yeah. Animals?" Thom said.

"What animals?"

"I guess that's the question."

But at the bottom of the ravine the trail disappeared and their only option was to try to make their way across the mini-forest and hope that a trail led up the other side. The trees were only about fifteen feet tall, and their trunks were narrow, crooked, and bark-less, stretching up like serpents. Tree jostled around unconscious on the couch. They discovered an opening and made their way in, only to find it too dense to get the cart through. Thom swore. His wet clothes chafed and he was shaky with hunger. They retraced their steps and found another opening, struggled to get the cart through it.

Then the butterflies came. They appeared everywhere in the forest, the air filled with them, small white butterflies so thick in the air that Thom dared not inhale.

"Popcorn!" Tree was suddenly awake on the couch. "I dreamed this." His eyes were wild and yellow and bloodshot. He raised his head unsteadily.

"Great, great. Hi, Tree. Do you know which way to go?" Erik wiped sweat off of his forehead.

Tree stared in wonder at the butterflies. "Follow the butterflies?"

"Which one, wiseguy?" Erik cursed and looked up to see that all of the butterflies were moving in one direction, a butterfly funnel through the forest. They spun and spiraled around themselves like a twister on its side through the trees.

Thom trudged forward in a trance, pulling the cart behind. The forest opened up to allow a thin trail, wide enough for the cart if they walked in single file. The trees joined overhead so they could only see the sky in narrow holes through the canopy. The narrow tail of the butterfly twister was always just ahead, turning corners, winding through the forest. From the cliff above, the forest had seemed just a swatch of trees, but the path wove long enough for them to lose all sense of direction.

"Are they leading us, or fleeing us?" Erik said.

"They're so beautiful," Tree said.

The last of the butterflies whipped out of sight, scattering through the forest, a thousand feathers drifting away. They'd been led to a tiny clearing over which the trees hung down so steeply it was impossible to see the cliff walls above. The clearing had six identical paths leading out already. Thom couldn't remember which way they'd come.

Erik swore. "Hello? Hello! Maybe you meant to bring us a little farther? Fuck!" He pulled his hair, reared back and kicked the base of a tree half a dozen times. "Yoo-hoo! Cloud city! We're here with your . . . with your shit, hello? Payment C.O.D. Come and get it!"

The forest absorbed all sound.

Erik turned on Thom. "Really though, why can't we just leave it here? There might not even be a cloud city. Did you hear them talking about it? Nobody has an effking clue!"

"Per seemed to think there was one." Thom smiled. He felt fine. He was alive, there were butterflies, they were going to find Per's city. Who knew what was going to happen next? Maybe the trees would turn into people. Maybe they'd learn how to fly. Maybe they'd learn the origins of humans, all history made clear in a flash. The cloud city would know. Everything seemed magical. What was wrong with Erik?

Erik sat on the ground and scratched furiously at his head and face. "Tree, you've got to help us out here. I'm sorry you're sick, but buddy, you're the navigator. This is your job. We don't know fuckall where we're going."

There was no response from the couch. Tree's mouth was open slightly, his face red.

"Would you wake him up? Seriously, we can't just keep stumbling around in the wilderness expecting something to happen. Thom. You know what I mean?"

Thom smiled again. "Yeah. I suppose so." He wondered why he felt so good. It was usually his job to worry. He didn't feel like waking Tree, he felt like carrying on. Picking a path at random. Or maybe cooking some beans. That's what he wanted to do. He wanted to eat something. Thom removed the cart harness and went back to Tree, shook him lightly. "Hey, amigo, wake up. You want some beans?" Tree didn't feel as hot. Maybe the fever was receding. Thom shook him again, a little harder this time. There was no reaction. "He's pretty out, Erik. You sure you want me to wake him?"

"Yes! Am I the only one with any sense left? We absolutely must get an idea of where we're going. Remember the skeleton? Now picture three of them."

"But . . . he said he didn't know the way."

"That's his job. They said that we'll find the city the same way we made it as far as we had—and that's Tree's doing."

"But if he doesn't know the way? Come on, Erik. I don't think he's lying."

"He's going to know. Wake him up."

Thom sighed, regretted disturbing Tree. He shook Tree again, a bit harder. The kid was really out.

And then a terrible fear wracked Thom. He felt for Tree's pulse and couldn't find it. There was nothing. Not in the neck, not in the wrist. He put his head to Tree's chest and couldn't hear a heartbeat.

"Erik!" he screamed, and Erik jumped up ready to fight. "Erik!" Thom yelled again. He thumped Tree's chest with his fist.

"What? What!? What are you doing?"

Thom blew a huge breath into Tree's mouth and was deceived by the chest heave. "Tree!" he shouted. Then Erik was pushing him out of the way, yelling at him to calm down.

Thom sank to his knees, put his head into his hands, and cried. Erik was acting the skilled medical professional. The rhythm— blow blow blow—thump thump thump—blow blow blow—went on for a bit, and then there was silence. Thom looked up to see Erik fleeing into the forest.

Thom stayed where he was. Head back in his hands, not wanting to look up, not wanting to see anything. Hoping he'd look up and see Tree breathing. He had just had a fever, for fucksake, maybe he had pneumonia too? Could you have both at once? He couldn't be dead. He thought about looking for a pulse again, maybe they'd just missed it, but he couldn't bring himself to touch Tree again. Thom realized he didn't even know how old Tree was.

"I don't even know how old you are," Thom said without looking at the body. Thom thought of getting up and running into the forest as Erik had, running after Erik. They could just run and disappear from this. He didn't move. Kept his eyes covered. Heard no sound. Tree had dreamed the butterflies. No wonder the dreams had stopped after that; there was nothing more to dream, there was no future for the subconscious to ponder. He remembered Tree saying he didn't have much time. Why couldn't they have hurried? But for what? "For what!?" he yelled. Maybe Erik hadn't tried long enough, maybe there was still time. He could resuscitate him, yes, mouth-to-mouth.

Thom leapt up and put his mouth over Tree's, plugged his nose, blew air into him, watched the chest rise again. He did this four times, then beat over Tree's heart, two-handed blows, the cart and couch jerking from the shock, Tree's slim body buckling with each hit. Then four more breaths of air. Four more beats. Four more breaths. Four more beats. He tried past all hope. Nothing. There was just life here. He beat on Tree's chest. There was just life here! How could it go so easily? Like trying to pump life into a hundred and thirty pounds of soil.

Thom remembered the medicine from Rosita. His eyes stinging with tears, he dug through Erik's bag until he found the vials, and tried to distinguish one from the other. He uncapped one and poured the liquid into Tree's mouth until it ran down the sides of his face. Swallow, swallow it! He threw the empty bottle as high as he could into the canopy of trees.

The couch. The couch would bring him back—when Thom died they put him on the couch and he'd lived, right? But Tree had been on the couch, Thom realized, he died on the couch. He gripped

Tree's arm, ready to yank him from the couch, feeling the seconds
tick away. He felt for a pulse in Tree's wrist and found nothing.

He knelt back, sat on the ground beside the couch, jabbed his
palms into his eyes.

He didn't know how long he was there. When he looked up, it
was dark. The forest murky and frighteningly quiet. A weak moon
casting dim shadows in the clearing. There was no sign of Erik.
There were no signs.

He glanced at Tree's body. Still not moving.

Thom tried to think clearly. It was several day's journey back to
Patul. Tree had been dead for some hours. The boy was gone. Rosita
couldn't bring someone back three days after death, right? He pulled
a shovel out of their gear, avoided looking at Tree, and began digging
a hole. He dug with fervor. His sweat dripped onto the shovel, into
the soil. He'd seen a photo of Incan mummies; they buried their
dead in the fetal position. He worked at the hole for hours.

After the hole was dug, he built a fire and did his best to think
of some words to say. You said words over a person's body as it
went into the grave. That was how you did it. Certainly something
must be said about the navigator. About the wire sculptor. The
cook. The young hippie. The dreamer. The seer.

He put the beans on to cook. *Be practical*, brain instructed.
Preserve the life that is left. Feed the body. Hoping there would be
some change in the conditions. Some fact of life he might have
overlooked. "What's the hole for?" Tree might ask from the couch,
leaning up on one elbow. "Oh. Oh that. I was looking for treasure.
For lost cities. For the past. Silly me."

Thom put the tent up. Arranged two sleeping bags. Put Tree's
sleeping bag over him on the couch. This seemed to make sense.
Ate some beans. Brushed his teeth. Damn you, Erik. He couldn't
bury Tree without Erik there. Only one death per night, wasn't that
the rule?

There was a strange bug on the shovel handle. Black and shiny,
body the size and shape of a cigarette, but with three joints in it,
something that almost looked like pincers at its rear. Six crooked
beetle legs and a pair of long, telescoping antennae. It skittered up

the handle when Thom approached and seemed to look back at him over its shoulder. Its shiny black body reflected the orange of the fire. Thom shuddered, picked up the shovel, and walked to the edge of the trees and shook it until the bug dislodged. There were two more on the lid of the pot of beans. "Agh!" He picked up the pan lid and flipped it so that they followed the first one. There was one on his boot, in trying to kick it off he stepped on two others on the ground. Their exoskeletons made a sickening crunching noise with each step. The tent was speckled black with them. The ground crawled. They jumped into the fire, crackling and writhing. Thom yelled for all he was worth, picked up the shovel, and began to beat it against the ground. Shiny black insect parts trailed the arc of the shovel. A rancid, burnt-hair smell to the air.

Then he remembered the couch.

Tree's body couldn't be seen under the swarming insects, a festering shiny blackness. Thom screamed, flailing his arms around, flinging the insects from Tree's body, feeling himself being bit, each bite like a fiery poker stabbing. For every dozen he swiped from Tree's body, a dozen more replaced them, crawling over the back of the couch, up the sides of the couch, up his pant legs, on his arms, shoulders. Thom leapt back and shook his body, stamping and yelling. They were tangled in his hair. Biting his face. He moved toward the fire, throwing the insects into the coals. Then he ran for the tent, unzipped it, threw out the few bugs that had made it inside, zipped up the tent, and buried himself in his sleeping bag. All night long he heard them skittering across the top of the tent, saw the twitching black forms in the dying light of the fire, imagined Tree's body being devoured. His swollen hands ached hotly, the poison coursing up his veins.

In the morning, Thom huddled inside the tent. There were welts all over his hands and face and neck, but the swelling had gone down, and all he felt was a vague nausea. He finally risked unzipping the tent a crack. The ground was littered with giant black insect bodies, hacked to pieces. But nothing moved. He opened the tent all the way.

Erik sat on a stone in front of the dead fire, his head hanging down, his hands against his temples.

"Erik," Thom said.

Erik looked up, a strange, haunted look to his eyes, a great gash across his forehead.

Behind Erik, the hole Thom had dug was filled up.

"Did you . . .?"

Erik nodded.

Thom got out of the tent, put his boots on, slimed with insects. Pieces of the black shiny husks stuck to the soles.

"Did you, did you say some words for him?"

"I thought them." Erik's voice was hoarse and damaged.

"Did you sleep somewhere?"

Erik pointed to his forehead. "I woke up somewhere."

Thom walked to the edge of the trees and threw up the beans from the night before.

"That makes two of us," Erik said. He waited for Thom to stop retching. "I couldn't find my way. I ran and ran but couldn't get out. If you hadn't yelled, I'd still be lost. I started running back, and that's when. . . . I don't know what happened, but I woke up out there."

Thom nodded. "I had some trouble with insects." He showed Erik his hands. Then, after a long pause, "What about Tree's body?"

Erik grabbed two fistfuls of hair, shook his head. "I'm sorry I ran away. I'm so sorry. I don't want to talk about it. I don't want to talk about it."

Thom said, "We have to get out of here before the insects come back."

"Well." Erik swallowed. "What do you want to do?"

"How could the couch let Tree die?" Thom said. "I thought there were supposed to be three. He was the navigator."

"Maybe they want us lost. I don't know. Do we go back?"

Thom thought about what Tree would have done. He thought of Jean and Shin and Theo, of Rosita and the Patulians. He stared at the couch on the cart. It looked untouched by Tree's death—no insect limbs, nothing left of the feverish boy who'd inhabited it. In the dim forest light and with the memory of it swarming with insects, there was a genuine menace to it, Thom thought, as if it had called in its own army of cleaners. He didn't know to what degree it was responsible for Tree's death, but he didn't want to get too close to it.

Thom kicked the Lug-o-naut as hard as he could, and it shuddered. Through clenched teeth he said, "No. We go on, *amigo*. What else is there?"

"I'm afraid of that." He pointed at the couch. "I'm afraid of what might happen if we don't finish things. *I* want to finish things."

Erik scuffed at the fire ring with his feet. "Right. Right. I don't care what happens now. There's no way in hell I could find my way back anyway."

Thom covered the grave with stones, carved Tree's name in a piece of firewood with his knife. Set it carefully on top.

The grave was rough, but there weren't other options. He picked up a small, rough pebble from near the grave and pocketed it. An exchange. Leave Tree here, take the stone away.

"Erik . . . " he said.

"Don't think about it," Erik said, "just don't think about it."

They packed in a hurry and chose a path at random. Thom wondered if it was the path they'd come down. The forest looked the same everywhere. Their tracks were swallowed up by the resilient undergrowth as soon as they'd passed. The trail twisted about, and either side of the canyon was completely obscured.

They passed hours disoriented, trudging down one trail until it dead-ended, backtracking and taking another. Neither of them spoke except to communicate directions. It had seemed such a small canyon, a crevasse with a bit of forest at its bottom, but they were in an eternity of trees, a lifetime of darkness. Thom's brain tried and failed to keep direction, to map, tracing trails in his head, trying to overlay that on top of the view they'd seen from above. But it was impossible. Everything looked the same. Through the canopy above them, the sky was dark. They heard thunder in the distance. A heavy rain poured down on them.

The floor of the forest began to slope upward, and they took it as a good sign. Erik pulled the cart. Both of them feeling an intense hate for the couch. Their cross, their albatross.

After several hours of incline, the trees thinned and dwindled to nothing. The rain stopped. They could see the canyon walls again; everything above was immersed in fog. The floor of the canyon rose, and the walls lowered and finally they were out. They stopped, looked back, saw only a slim tree-filled crevasse. The ground continued to slope up, and they followed blindly until the sky became too dark and their hunger too intense. They camped, ate what they could find, and went silently to sleep.

Nightmares awoke Thom throughout the night until he woke finally and realized that a noise outside of the tent was not part of the dream. There was a deep grumbling, which at first sounded like a far-off boulder sliding down stone. But there was the sound of a pot clanking, a bag being rustled through. Someone was going through their gear! He shook Erik awake.

"What?"

"Shhhh," Thom whispered.

Erik's eyes went wide. "What is it?" he whispered back.

Thom quietly unzipped the tent a notch and looked out. The fog was thinner, and through it several stars twinkled faintly. A giant form on two legs was going through their cart. It had a great head and arms the size of tree limbs.

"Look," Thom mouthed. Frozen in fear.

Erik cautiously peeked out. "It's a bear," he whispered back. "Is it a bear? It's stealing our food."

"What do we do?"

"What can we do?"

"Where's the gun?"

"It's in the cart."

"Fuck. We've got to do something," Thom said. "We have to have food."

"We have to stay alive."

"I'm going out there."

"No, don't."

"Got to." Thom put on his boots as quietly as he could, unzipped the tent. He saw the bear's head turn toward him. "Hey!" he yelled.

"Get out of here!" His voice came out weak and scared. He tried again. "*Gitttaouttaherrrre!*"

The bear turned and walked away on two legs. It ambled slowly into the fog, and Thom saw there were dozens of forms at the edge of the fog. All around them, a perimeter of black shapes, impossible to distinguish in the fog and darkness. Animals? Humans? Creatures. They were being watched. Thom slowly moved to the cart, pulled the rifle out, trying to keep an eye on all sides at once. The visibility was strange, completely black in one direction, fog faintly lit in another. The shapes on the perimeter moving. Thom pulled the cart over next to the tent, snuck back inside.

"Do you see them?"

"Yes."

"What do we do?"

"I don't know. . . . Nothing. Let's just keep watch."

"Here." Thom handed Erik the gun. "You know how to use this better."

Erik propped the gun against his shoulder, sighted down the barrel. "It's tempting to take a shot."

"No, don't."

"Are we sure they're things? And not rocks?"

"I have no idea."

They watched for hours as the fog swirled in, made its own shapes, distorted those of the watchers. Thom's eyelids got heavier and heavier.

"I've got to sleep. Wake me up when you want to trade."

Thom woke up to Erik shaking him.

"I fell asleep. It's morning."

Thom looked through the tent door, could see it was morning only by the hue of the fog. It had thickened again so that they could only see a couple of meters out. There was a boxy shape half visible near where their fire ring had been.

"That's the couch," Erik said. "The couch is out there."

"Whoa."

The cart had been overturned and the couch dragged a few

meters toward the rocks. The couch looked the worse for wear. There were tears in the cushions. The right arm could be swung back and forth freely. Thom looked around for footprints, but the terrain was too rocky. He peered out into the fog, but couldn't discern any shapes. Were they still there?

"Is it okay?"

"It's beat up. Maybe they thought it was food."

"Maybe. The bear wreaked havoc with our supplies. It almost looks like he was doing it on purpose. The water jugs are all punctured, and the water has leaked out."

"What?"

"Almost all the food is gone. Little bits left. Crumbs."

"No." Thom inspected the overturned cart. He picked up stray grains of rice. No. He looked up at Erik, who was staring out into the fog. "What do we do now?"

"Let's keep moving. The sooner this is over, the better."

"We can't survive long without water."

"Maybe we'll find water." Erik tenderly touched the swollen gash on his forehead.

"I don't know if I'd trust the water out here. It should be drinkable, but everything else is so . . . rigged to fuck you up."

"Thom, we don't have a choice."

Thom nodded. "Alright."

They ate what they could. A handful of leftover beans that had been in the fire pit. Thom divvied up the rice he'd collected, and they put grains of it in their mouths to suck on. Thom fought nausea.

Erik dug in his bag and came up with the gray vial. "Do you have your medicine?" he said.

"Oh . . . ," Thom said. "No."

"Well. It's gone. There's one bottle left of Tree's, you want it?"

"No."

Erik unplugged the vial and drained the contents in a few gulps. "Which way?"

Thom stared at Erik but felt too tired to comment. He looked without hope into the various directions of whiteness. He walked around the camp and tried to figure out which way the ground sloped. Scouting was out of the question. They'd lose each other in the fog. "That way," he pointed. Suddenly feeling it. Knowing it. Like a weight in his forehead had tipped a certain way, put him off balance in one direction. "It's that way," he repeated, knowing desperately that he wanted it to be right and not something he'd made up.

They stumbled through the day, taking turns pulling the cart, sometimes going up, sometimes down. They crossed a small stream and each of them drank deeply, but there was nothing left to store water in. They walked through knee-high brush. Erik sampled the leaves to see if they were edible and violently threw up.

They carried weakly on until they could no longer see for the dark and the fog and then camped. But what was there to camping? Only sleep, a few grains of rice to suck on. They put the couch in front of the tent where they could keep an eye on it and slept.

The next day was the same, but colder. A foggy terrain. A lost world. Thom pulled the cart. Pulling up reserves of energy from somewhere, placing a grain of rice on his tongue. Drinking from a mud puddle. The way endless. Was he taking the couch to his death? Burying it in the wilderness with him? Bringing the couch back to some forgotten god?

Another night. Erik found a cigarette that he spent a half hour restoring to smokable condition. Another half hour of despair when matches couldn't be found. Discovering matches at the bottom of Thom's sleeping bag. They hovered around the cigarette like it was the last portal to their old lives. The dim cherry the only light in the universe.

In the morning Erik was feverish, the gash on his forehead deeply infected.

The wind blew fiercely, and the fog whipped about them, eddying and swirling. They put the couch back on the cart.

A great wind leapt up, and before they could react, their tent and sleeping bags were swept into the air like feathers on the wind. Thom stared after them, watched them dim and disappear into the whiteness. The hope within him whittled to a twig.

And then, fifteen minutes after they'd started, the cart spontaneously fell apart.

Thom continued to walk, oblivious. The harness lighter, he stumbled on until he heard Erik yelling from behind. He turned to see he pulled nothing. The cart was crushed under the weight of the couch. All that was left of the Lug-o-naut 147 was a heap of splinters.

"Oh," Thom said.

Erik was too tired to speak.

Thom saw that Erik's clothes were disintegrating, his pants beginning to resemble something the Hulk would wear. The clothes that Per had given them. Had Per searched for this city? His brain turned on him in his exhaustion, saying what he ought to know. Going deeper into the wilderness against all logic, against all instinct for survival. Brain: *There is no city. You have been misled. You will die.*

He felt a wave of nausea come over him, leaned over and had a violent bout of dry heaves. He stood up, wiped a few flecks of spittle from his mouth. His muscles and joints and bones ached. He couldn't trust his eyesight, it blinked in and out of whiteness. Staring at the couch and seeing it suddenly as white and without shape. The bites on his hands and face itched. He couldn't remember the last time he'd been dry. Erik swayed back and forth, stared at him blankly, waited for Thom to make a decision.

If only they could see. Sight would allow them an understanding of the land. Logic would help with the finding. *Where would you build a city that wasn't meant to be found?*

I will find it, brain. He dug his last two remaining grains of rice from his pocket, put them in his mouth to rid himself of the taste of bile. Resisted the temptation to hungrily chew and swallow.

"How's it going?" Erik croaked with the careless recklessness of a man who knows all is lost.

"Fine." He tried to smile back. Muscles wouldn't work. "Fine."

The burning red under the skin near Erik's gash had grown. The swelling was obscene. "Okay," Erik said. "Okay." He tried to raise his fist in a gesture of carry-on! but it only went halfway. The wind surged up, and Erik lost his balance, tipping sideways, recovered five feet away.

Thom understood what the options were. He leaned down, grabbed the back and underside of the couch in his big, itching hands, and lifted it in a single, weight-lifter's motion to his shoulder. Energy welling up somewhere in his belly, up through his chest, a blooming into his throat. He roared as best he could.

"Yeah," said Erik. "Yeah!" A dizzy smile. He hugged himself, and his teeth chattered.

They left the rest of their worthless gear. Pots and pans. Cooking utensils. Gun and knife and matches. There was no energy for anything except carrying the couch.

Erik fell. Thom turned and, seeing nothing, slowly traced his way back to pull him to his feet again. After that, he kept Erik in front. Watched the fur of Erik's head dip, lurch back up. Falling asleep as he walked. Hypothermia, Thom thought. Pneumonia.

The ground sloped upward. The fog stifled their breathing. Thom sucked a condensated drop of water off his sleeve, and then another, but the drops evaporated into the desert of his tongue, inspiring thirst more than quenching it. Somewhere beyond the atmospheric shell about them the sun was going down, and light was wisping away, dissipating into space. Erik stumbled again, fell onto his face, didn't move.

"Erik," Thom said, wanting nothing more than to lie down next to him on the ground. "Erik, get up." He nudged Erik with his toe. "Get up." The weight of the couch carved into his shoulder.

Nothing. No sign of consciousness.

"Come on, Erik." He tried to flip him over with his foot. Thom stood over him, his eyes losing focus. Brain fashioning an endless loop for him. An eternity of a woozy, half-conscious split second of hovering drunkenly over Erik.

Thom knelt, balancing the weight of the couch on his shoulders. He grabbed Erik's shoulder and pulled him over. There was gravel and sand in his wound, and his eyes were closed. A belabored breathing. The body wracked with fever.

"Erik," he said. Erik's shivering had stopped. It wouldn't be long out here before he died. Could he leave him? Thom tried to imagine going on, knowing that his own fate was just a short ways off, that bringing Erik along would only speed that fate.

Thom steadied one end of the couch against the ground, rolled Erik onto his stomach. With his left hand anchored to the ground, the couch on the left shoulder, Thom jabbed his right hand under Erik's middle, paused, exhaled, too exhausted for any kind of frustrated tears. He flexed, lifted Erik at his center, his head and legs drooping to the ground, dragging. He heaved, straining, managed to drape Erik limply over his other shoulder. Now to stand. His knees felt embedded in the ground, bloodied. He tipped his center of gravity back, rolled onto the balls of his feet and thrust upward. The couch on one shoulder, Erik on the other.

He took one slow step. His mouth felt like he'd been sucking on a vacuum. His equilibrium was broken, his inner ear stuck on a carnival ride. He took another step, steadying himself, knowing he'd never get either weight back on his shoulders were he to fall. Brain had gone silent long ago. His only thought: take one more step. A faint nerve signal from the left arm: ache. Another step. The hill was steep. Another step. Hours of night. Another step.

Thom came to consciousness on his knees, the couch and Erik pressing him into the ground. Had he just fallen, or had he been here for a long time? He wanted to fall the rest of the way. He pleaded with himself to give up, to lay down there. With his hand he tried to feel a pulse in Erik, some sign of life, and then stopped before ascertaining for sure, not wanting to know, not wanting the choice. He thrust his legs under him and stood. Took a step.

Woke on his knees again. Had he come one foot or forty? Thrust up. He had to point toward that off balance weight in his forehead. The drunk falling asleep at the wheel, dreaming the road, dreaming he drove. Another step. On his knees again. Up. On.

And then a violent awakening, his middle splayed over the edge of the couch, Erik lying with his head against rock. Thom's left hand was trapped underneath the couch, crushed. He forced himself to move, with immense effort righted himself and his burdens. Something possibly wrong with his hand. On his feet. Another step. The memory of his face against gravel.

Was he dreaming? Another step. The wind cycling about, the fog gray-black. And then a shape began to emerge in the nothingness, Thom still unsure if his eyes were open or closed.

The shape widened, opened. A black form in the blur of gray that Thom stumbled toward. By the time he was upon it, it dominated the landscape. For a merest moment Thom saw pillars and stone and temples and everything he'd hoped for. A great city lost here in the fog. But it was not a city, it was never a city, it was a hole. Thom let out a dispirited sob. The density of the fog made it impossible to see what it was—the opening of a volcano? A great crevasse? It stretched, blocking his way to the left and right. He eased alongside it, trying to get an idea of how large it was, the weight of his burdens cutting deeply into his shoulders. He felt as if his organs were compressing, his knees fusing, his hips grinding to dust. In a quick instant there was a gap in the fog and he saw the enormity of what was before him. An opening into the earth with no discernible bottom that spanned what seemed miles in either direction. Mist had begun to bead and freeze on Thom's eyelashes. The temperature was dropping. He stared at the opening, trying to discern any kind of ledge or shelf or bottom. The fog seemed pulled into it, as if the hole drank from the atmosphere. The rim was rock and dirt.

A hole to throw yourself into, brain quipped, awakened by a new challenge. Thom stumbled closer. He tried to find resources within himself to walk around this new obstacle. He edged closer to the hole, tried to see if he could walk down, but all he saw inside it was blackness. Could he climb down one side and up the other? He kicked at a stone on the lip. It glided silently and eerily into the blackness. Then the edge collapsed beneath him.

Thom bounced heavily against the rim, the deadweights of the couch and Erik landing on top of him. All three of them slipped over the edge and into freefall. He felt himself spinning, felt the depth of the hole underneath him, an echoing soundlessness of infinite space, a black hole of a hole that would suck him into another dimension.

He took a deep, frightened breath and noted how easy it was to breathe without the weight of his body and burdens. He felt an immediate release from responsibility, a release from life. He was falling fast, and he wasn't entirely sure he minded.

He braced himself, knowing that any second he would land on something hard, something permanent and immortal that his feeble mortality would be no match for. He looked back and could see the mouth of the hole above, the only visible light, a gray opening that receded and closed above him like a great gray eye winking.

So this is how the story ends, my story. He tried to relax into it and remembered that relaxed car-accident victims fared better than tensed ones. He tentatively tried a holler, but the sound traveled down and ahead without echoing back.

He became aware of his body, his frigid fingers, the bruises on his shoulders, his battered legs, his deflated stomach. He idly pondered each joint, and waited for his life to begin flashing before his eyes. Did one will this to happen, this pre-death flashback, and was there any way to prevent it? He braced himself for the relentless stream of computer screens, his timidness in his colossus self, the emotionally crowded space of growing up fatherless, and the rest of his life screened pitifully through his mind.

How deep could a hole be?

He tried to look in the direction he was falling but couldn't tell which direction was which. There was no sign of the couch or Erik. Only a vague feeling of vertigo and being unable to touch anything solid reinforced the notion that he was falling.

This last month was different, he thought. Perhaps life wasn't an endless loop of uncomfortable drudgery after all. Or rather, perhaps heaven was an endless loop of one's choosing. But the problem was, he hadn't created the time from which to pluck a perfect endless loop.

At least the couch was forever lost from whoever else had wanted it. Certainly no rescue team could plumb a crevasse this deep.

Two hundred kilometers per hour, brain dug up from some lost corner: *the terminal velocity of a human falling through the atmosphere.* So how many kilometers underground was he now?

He thought of Erik out there in the dark with him. Unconscious and falling. Lifelessly bound for lifelessness.

His mother would be heartbroken. It struck him that this was exactly the sort of fate that mothers feared for their only sons. His father had abandoned his mother by returning home from Vietnam in a bag, and now her son was mangled at the bottom of a hole south of the equator. She would turn to painkillers and depression drugs, or just turn, like a pear in the sun.

"Mom," he said in the dark, and tried to send her a psychic message of apology. "I was foolish, I went looking for that which cannot be found."

I've done it then, he thought. Was I returning it or destroying it? Is there a difference?

He felt calm and almost giddy. A hazy warm pleasantness spread through his limbs like hot chocolate.

Hypothermia, brain observed, coming to him as if from the end of a long tunnel. But what did it matter? He was a speeding icy comet, center-of-the-earth bound.

Even so, he folded himself up, collapsed his limbs into a tight ball. Yes, now a meteor. I want it, he thought. I don't want a delirious, hypothermic death. I only get one last sensation. This is it. The cannonball. The only dive I ever learned. All the kids at the public pool laughing, shouting, "Thom! Thom! Cannonball!" The big kid makes the big splash.

He would accelerate to a new terminal velocity, pass Erik. I'm conscious, I'm the one who made it, I finished this affair. I deserve to be first.

The most exquisite endless loop could have been fashioned from his time with Jean. In a pinch, in the absence of twenty, forty, sixty years together, he could take their one Cuenca night even with its awkwardness and drama, its distrust and pleasure, and try to forge an eternal existence with that. With Jean, for the first time in his life, he'd realized that leaving that caravan of raucous insecurities wouldn't have been too bad.

The wind was not what he would have expected for such a fall. Or he was getting used to it. Or there was no air to speak of.

And maybe that caravan hadn't yet caught him up, maybe he was Azulman, diving gloriously to his death, mission accomplished. Maybe he had indeed made that transition from overturned cockroach to human, pupa to butterfly, egg to eagle. He was soaring.

He spread his limbs wing-wide. "I am Thom!" he yelled down the hole. "I am a kamikaze, I am a suicide bomber, I claim victory in my Jihad against the cancer blighting the American soul. A piece of furniture. A couch."

Dramatic, brain quipped.

"Yes," said Thom. "Yes! I know! And I know you too, dear brain. Now is your chance, speak all you want."

Oh, brain said, and was silent.

He expected death at any instant, though a suspicion began to creep in. Perhaps this was his fate, to fall through the earth, to yo-yo through the center from one end to the other. This was hell, then, this was his interpretation of Sisyphus, to get ever closer to the surface only to yo back the other direction. Or perhaps this was only the routine descent to hell. Perhaps he was just another passenger on that somber train.

But I don't believe in any of that, Thom protested mildly, and then remembered he was open to whatever strange ace the universe had up its sleeve.

But Jean.

Hadn't he been close there, hadn't there been something? Hadn't his *Titanic* suddenly skirted the iceberg his life might have been? And Erik still hurtling above him. This was no end. This was some joke, this was a perversity, a meaningless fable. Had he or had he not eradicated the dread couch? I deserve my just rewards. Half the kingdom and the princess too.

This was an outrage, and nasty letters would be written, I can tell you. Letters to the editor, for one, to the publisher. "I expect every one of you to write your congressman," he said into the dark.

Who has voted me off this island? After the work I've done for humanity.

I've got to climb back up, I've got to get out, Thom realized. I've finished my quest. Patul is the fucking cloud city, you deluded fuck. Our past is in ruins—it's time to find Future City, time to make it. There's still time not to repeat ourselves. He thrashed against the air, seeking a wall. "I'm not through yet," he shouted in the direction he believed was down. He set every muscle to work fighting gravity, clawed against the air and tried to climb his way molecule by molecule out of the hole. Swinging his big arms with all the force that was left in him, pushing at the air, trying to put anything between him and his descent.

And then, amidst his thrashing, above him, like a gauzy curtain slowly opening, appeared the most delicate thumbnail clipping of moonlight.

He stared at it in disbelief. His brain was immersed in the depths of a sea. As if he'd just discovered the direction he'd been swimming was away from the surface. A heavy, overpowering exhaustion poured over him as his vertigo subsided. He was lying on the ground.

A hooded face eclipsed the moon and said, "It always feels like falling." The voice had a strong accent and sounded apologetic. Thom's brain repeated this phrase dully before he understood that he'd heard it. That a voice had spoken that was not Erik's and not his own. The moon reappeared as the figure retreated.

"What?" Thom said.

"The axis mundi. It feels like falling," the voice said, and then was gone.

Thom rolled the words around in his mind trying to remember what an axis mundi was. Some kind of connection between sky and land.

With an effort he lifted his head and saw Erik lying facedown across his legs. He spotted the tail end of the couch being dragged away by a group of hooded figures. Then they stopped and surrounded it. There were half a dozen or so of them, but whether it was the cloaks or the moonlight, he couldn't quite get the number, like trying to count fish in a school of fish. They spoke quietly. The couch was a wreck. What appeared to be its left armrest sat detached not three feet from him, its invincibility apparently worn off. One of the hooded figures reached toward the center cushion and then shied back, as if afraid of getting bitten. Another stepped up, her hood down and long stringy hair showing. She pulled the center cushion off and reached deep into the couch with both hands and withdrew an object the size of a shoebox. It was a box, Thom saw, and the woman—was it a woman?—removed the lid and they peered inside.

"Hey!" Thom said. He wanted to get up but his body felt as if it were made of sand bags and clay. "Hey," he said.

They looked up from where they'd been sifting through the box and then returned their attention to it.

Goddammit, Thom thought. Hello brain? Engine room? "Listen, can I get some kind of explanation here?" he called again.

One separated from the group and approached him. "This is for you," she said.

He could see a tiny reflection of light in her eyes. She held out what looked like a small stone.

"Well hi," Thom said. "Can you help get Erik off of me?"

"Erik will be fine. Please take this."

Thom held his hand out and she dropped the stone into it.

"You understand I'm a little bit confused?" he said.

"Yes," she said. "It's a long way back. Good luck."

"Who are you guys? I mean. What is this?" He held the stone up toward the moon to try to discern its color.

"A seed. The couch, it was protecting the seeds."

"What?"

"It was like a shield, a shell, around the library."

"The library?" Thom said and he felt the hair stand up on the back of his neck. "A library. Not books?"

"No. From the first garden, seeds to all of the trees. Seeds to the plants and ideas that have been lost. The Tree of Knowledge is in there, the Tree of Life, the Tree of Forgiveness, the Tree of Clarity, and lots of other trees, trees you wouldn't have names for."

"Oh," Thom said. "Whoa."

"Plant the seed I gave you, Thom," she said and turned away.

"Wait," he said, but the entourage receded into the mist and dark and cold, towing the couch after them.

Understanding rushed in at Thom then, through vessels cleared of their plaque. They'd come bearing seeds from Eden, and from every garden since. They had carried two things, balanced in opposition, a shell and a nut, the couch and its cache, the power to destroy and the remnants of what it had destroyed. All of the gifts that humans, in their industry and genius, had destroyed.

There were figures there and not there, apparitions shimmering in the foglight. One seemed to linger and for a moment Thom almost thought it was the thin, stooped figure of Tree.

"Hello?" Thom called out into the dark but his voice was weak. He struggled to catch another glimpse. "Tree!" he yelled and felt sure he saw the figure wave. And then Tree turned to follow the rest of the cloaked figures into the fog. *Trees*, brain said. *Tree*.

Then Thom and Erik were alone. He lay there under the sky until he found it within himself to move.

After a while Erik stirred and groaned.

"Erik," Thom said gently, "let's get up. Let's go home."

Two satchels had been left behind for them. In the open neck of the closest one Thom could see the moonlit sheen of an apple.